PRAISE FOR ALAN CARTER

Ladies and gentlemen, we have a new entrant into the higher echelons of Australian crime fiction writing. — *Sun Herald*

... a gritty and engrossing look at crime and racism in a small Western Australian town ... a promising new talent in the field of Australian crime fiction — *Australian Book Review*

... there are many layers to this story, genuine 'aha' moments and a very strong cast of main and supporting characters — *Australian Bookseller+Publisher*

Plenty of dismembered corpses and a dark sense of humour set the scene for an enjoyable debut. — *Sydney Morning Herald*

... riveting reading — *The Examiner*

[The characters] all speak with that authentic voice which you only find in the best crime novels. — *Courier Mail*

... a home run from the first chapter — *Daily Telegraph*

... this debut captures the desolate coastal essence with just a touch of the Wintons — *Qantas The Australian Way*

... a novel that grips from the first page to the last — *An Adventure in Reading blog*

... enough action and intrigue to keep any reader up late at night — *suite101.com blog*

To my mum and dad, Nancy and Billy

ALAN CARTER

GETTING WARMER

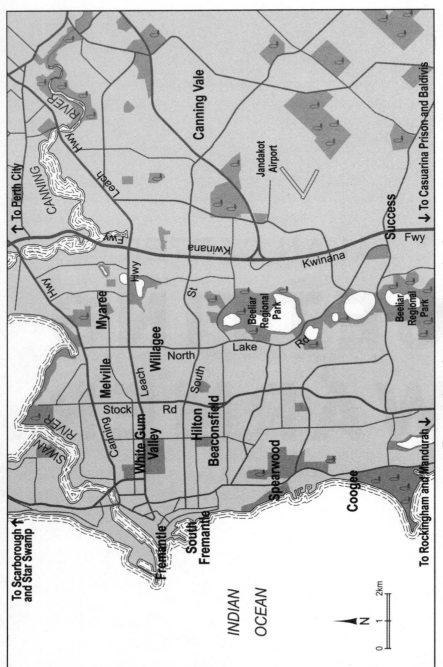

Fremantle and surrounding suburbs

Nec prece nec pretio ... a recta via deduci.

Neither by entreaty nor by bribery ... be drawn from the right path.

Fremantle City motto

PROLOGUE

'Do you hate them?'

'Why would I?'

'What's going through your mind at the time?'

They've sent me a Psych graduate from Edith Cowan. Can you believe it? She's told me more about herself in the first five minutes than she'll get out of me in the next five years. Fresh out of uni and she reckons she can just enter a mind like mine and have a look round. Don't go in there, darling, you might never get out again.

'Nothing.'

'Nothing?'

'That's right. Nothing's going through my mind at the time. Empty. I don't hate them. I don't get a blood lust every full moon. Here today, gone tomorrow. Nothing personal.'

She's talking about the ones who survived. I'm not. She finishes writing her notes and gives me a pretty little frown.

'I find that hard to believe. I mean, their injuries. You seem to have so much anger inside you.'

'Are you calling me a liar, Marissa?'

I can see up her skirt, the smooth inside of her thighs. She knows it. She shifts, moves the notepad to block the view.

Too late, it's in my head now and it's in yours too.

Isn't it, Marissa?

She feels my eyes on her, hears my voice inside her. Wishes she hadn't taken me on. Now she is all alone with me, I remind her of all the bad things in her sorry life. She feels me under her skin. She feels me in all her private places.

I know I've won. Again.

1

The cadaver dog lay in the meagre shade of a paperbark, panting for dear life. It was heading for another forty-degree day, the sixth in a row. There was smoke in the air; a few kilometres away a grey column billowed into the sky: one of a handful of maliciously lit bushfires ringing the city. Detective Senior Constable Philip 'Cato' Kwong checked the time on his mobile: 9.36 a.m.

A handler gave Mintie some water. As dogs went, Mintie was not half-bad. She was generally quiet, good-natured, and served a useful social purpose. Cato, no big fan of dogs, had come across plenty of humans who couldn't tick those three boxes. Minties: the police PR department thought it was a good idea to hand out the lollies to teenagers maddened by grog on Australia Day. Maybe it would help them stop and think before throwing a punch or glassing a stranger. All would be revealed next Tuesday, January 26th. The dog stirred herself, lapped gratefully at the bowl and reluctantly followed her handler back into the glare.

The search grid was approximately ten by twenty metres. It was in a patch of bush reserve known as Thompsons Lake, at the southern end of the freeway. The lake itself had gone down the gurgler with a succession of dry winters followed by the summer heat. All that remained was a crust of cracked mud and desiccated waist-high grass. To keep the native animals in and the feral cats and dirt bikers out, the whole area was ringed by a high fence. That posed the first problem. How do you get a body in? They'd all just trooped through a turnstile gate on Russell Road like they were headed for a day at the Royal Show. There were vehicle access tracks into the park but none near here. Cato could think of plenty of places to bury a corpse but this wasn't top of his list.

White-tailed black cockatoos screeched tetchily from the treetops. The handler whispered to Mintie, patted her and set her free to follow her nose. A line of uniforms and emergency service volunteers started another grid sweep.

'I'm pretty sure I left her over there.'

Cato looked at the man who spoke. Gordon Francis Wellard: nudging late-forties, goatee, jaded bohemian look. Shorter than Cato had imagined but there was the hint of muscle to deter those who might want to take him for granted. Laugh lines spidered out from crafty eyes. You could imagine him sitting outside Gino's midmorning, stretching out his macchiato and pontificating on the dearth of arts funding in a so-called boom state.

Wellard was sitting handcuffed in a fold-out picnic chair between two corrective services officers, all of them sharing a smoke and a joke. It was a big day out for him. Wellard was already serving life for one murder. Now they were searching for another earlier victim, Briony Susan Petkovic. Bree, as her mother called her, had been missing for over five years. This was unfinished business for the missing girl's mother, Wellard's ex-wife. That was her, standing a few metres away in a sun hat, singlet and cargoes holding a metal T-probe.

Shellie Petkovic had known Wellard had something to do with it from the moment her daughter went missing. According to the files, she had endured Wellard's taunting for the last five years. She had pleaded with him to give Bree up. Countless prison visits, some at her request, many at his invitation, some lasting the full hour, others just thirty seconds. All to no avail. He made it up as he went along, according to how he might be feeling that day.

But now that he was locked up and thought he had something to gain, he'd finally reconsidered his position. The police had been nervous about putting his bizarre conditions to the mother but she'd consented without hesitation – anything was better than not knowing. So here she was with the T-probe, prodding the earth for her daughter's body under the direction of the murderer. In spite of the heat, the idea made Cato's skin goosebump.

'Or maybe over there?' Wellard said, a pensive finger to his lips, like he was deciding where to put the new furniture. 'Yes, getting warmer, definitely.'

Funny as.

DI Mick Hutchens stepped between man and ex-wife, obscuring their views of each other and trying to keep the whole thing from unravelling. This was his idea. DI Hutchens obviously scented a result. All Cato could smell was sweat, smoke and something sour.

Mintie barked once, wagged her tail and pawed at a patch of sandy ground.

They surrounded the dog as she sat waiting for her treat. The handler patted Mintie and gave her a dog lolly. Hutchens had a glint in his eye. He nodded at a minion and a T-probe went into the parched soil. There was a soft scrape, like a hiss, as if the earth was exhaling a long-held breath.

The probe hit something. The underling pulled it out, marked the spot, and tried again a few centimetres away. It hit something again. A few centimetres further away, another strike. A sob escaped from the mother. Wellard had gone dead quiet. On the outer fringe of the circle he tried to stand to get a closer look but the corrections officers pressed him back into his seat.

Cato stepped back with the rest as the shovels came out and two men began to dig.

A stench rose. The body was crawling with maggots and other insects. Flies descended on the uncovered feast. It was about a metre and a half long and it had four legs.

'It's a fucking pig,' observed Hutchens.

Wellard giggled from the comfort of his picnic chair. The mother screamed and swung her metal T-probe at his head. Cato instinctively stepped in to protect him and that was the last thing he remembered.

2

Friday, January 22nd. Midmorning.
Fremantle, Western Australia.

The place stank of stale beer and alcopops and the floor stuck to her shoes. Lara Sumich shoved her ID into the bar manager's face. He looked like he hadn't slept much, nor had he brushed his teeth recently.

'What can I do for you Detective. Senior. Constable?'

His name was Luke and he'd addressed his question to her chest.

'The security video footage from last night. I'd like to see it.'

Luke looked puzzled. 'I don't remember any trouble?'

'A bloke got a bottle shoved in his face outside on the street. He reckons he had a bit of push and shove earlier on in here with the guy that did it.'

'First I've heard of it.'

'Maybe you need to streamline your internal communication processes.'

'What?'

'Talk to your staff a bit more.' Lara was losing patience. 'The footage?'

'Magic word?'

'How about Liquor Licensing? Can we get a move on?'

They went behind the bar, down a cluttered corridor and into an office. It was standard-issue grubby: desk, chair, paperwork, ashtray, computer, and a poster of a naked young woman body-painted in Dockers colours and holding a Sherrin footy. The two video monitors were on a separate table: one full screen and the other split into four, feeding from cameras on the dance floor, behind the bar, in the foyer, and covering the entrance. On one of the screens a cleaner crossed the dance floor, mop and bucket in hand, and on another pedestrians hugged the shade outside as the heat built.

'Disk or thumb drive?' said Lara.

'We can do both, which do you prefer?'

'Disk. Everything from about eight until closing.'

'No worries.' Luke clicked and tapped for a while, then handed her two disks. 'Happy viewing.'

There was a muffled yelp and on the monitor Lara saw the cleaner run back onto the dance floor waving her arms. Lara followed Luke back down the hallway.

'Mister Luke, Mister Luke!'

'What now for fuck's sake?'

'Mister Luke in the toilet.'

'What are you on about?' He turned to Lara. 'They're cheap as chips but you can't get any sense out of these people.'

Charming. Lara didn't bother replying.

'Go now, Mister, look in the toilet. Men's.'

This time Lara led the way, gesturing for the pair to wait as she nudged open the door. Nightclub toilets tend to be a bit whiffy but this one smelled like an abattoir. All of the cubicle doors were open, except one. Blood was coming from in there, a dark and sticky puddle on the scuffed blue tiles. Lara looked under the door gap and saw feet in a pair of skanky trainers. Not wanting to contaminate the immediate scene, she went into the adjoining cubicle, stood on the bowl and looked over.

Cato Kwong felt the lump on his head. It was just above the hairline to the left of the temple. It had gone down a little but was still tender. The wound hadn't needed stitches, just the medical equivalent of glue and sticky tape. He'd been out cold for five minutes before waking with the migraine from hell and blood gumming his left eye. He dimly recalled the mother sobbing 'Sorry, sorry', Wellard being led away cackling, and DI Hutchens swimming into vision.

'Cato, mate, you okay? Thatsaboy.'

He'd been released from Fremantle Hospital after scans and tests confirmed no skull fractures or apparent brain damage. Cato spent the evening at home nursing a headache and evil thoughts about DI Hutchens and Gordon Wellard. After swallowing a couple of

Panadol, he'd opted for an early night. No Jake until Tuesday, they were going to the Australia Day Cracker Night down at the harbour and then the boy would be staying the rest of the week before going back to mum and her new boyfriend.

Cato took a sip of coffee and looked out the window across the low roofs of Fremantle and the shimmer of Indian Ocean beyond the Norfolk pines. Another forty-degree day, but this time he was in an air-conditioned open-plan office. Now there was the paperwork and the post-mortem on Wellard's big day out.

Gordon Francis Wellard was a sadistic, controlling, attention-seeking psycho – they were ten a penny in Casuarina, Western Australia's maximum-security chook house. But he was reputedly DI Hutchens' psycho, an informant groomed since the early days of the DI's career. Both men had prospered along the way: Hutchens with his career trajectory and Wellard with his seeming untouchability in whatever he was accused of doing over the years. Now he'd embarrassed Hutchens by being sent down for murder. Wellard needed to redeem himself. He should at least tell them where the bodies were buried.

Hutchens really believed he'd got through to the man. 'Look Cato, I know he's a prick but he's staunch. He'll do the right thing. He owes me.'

According to the file, Shellie Petkovic had endured three years of wedded hell with Wellard. The first thing she did when she was free of him was to revert to her maiden name. The charismatic man she thought she married revealed his true colours on their honeymoon at Kalbarri Beach Resort. A trivial argument ended with her needing two dozen stitches at the local hospital. Over the next two years Wellard bullied her, bashed and abused her, raped her, stole from her, and stalked her. Every time Shellie tried to leave she was menaced and manipulated into compliance. Bree, her daughter by a previous relationship, bore witness to the unfolding nightmare and, like Shellie, fell under his control. At thirteen Bree was skipping school, by fourteen she was drinking and doing drugs supplied by Wellard, and by fifteen she was a missing persons statistic.

During one of those rare periods when Shellie had found the

nerve to seek refuge with a friend, she received a phone call from her daughter. Bree said she was with Wellard. That was the last time they spoke. Two days later, when asked where Bree was, Wellard said he didn't know. Neighbours reported hearing a row there that night of Bree's call but they'd reported lots of rows and nothing ever came of it. No trace of Bree was found and no matter how hard they tried, police could not pin her disappearance on Wellard. Briony was a wayward child, they concluded, she could be anywhere. After her daughter went missing, Shellie Petkovic found the courage to leave Wellard for good. The case remained open but the file gathered the computer equivalent of dust. Shellie kept bothering the police, reporting cryptic, taunting phone calls and comments from Wellard, but all they could advise was a restraining order to add to the bundle she already had on him. Two and a half years later, Wellard was arrested for the murder of his new de facto, Caroline Penny. He was found guilty at trial and locked away.

Facing life inside, Wellard had made contact with his old mate DI Hutchens and offered up Bree's whereabouts. Maybe he was angling for favoured status and early parole for his cooperation. Maybe he just wanted to remain the centre of attention and have a bit of fun. Cato could only go off the official reports and they didn't have a space on the forms to record any individual psycho's twisted raison d'etre.

Cato's head had started to pound again. He had no idea what his boss was expecting from this paperwork. A whitewash? A delicately underplayed mea culpa? A flick pass to a scapegoat? Cato had been down this path before and vowed, if only to himself, never to cover Hutchens' padded arse again. Yet here he was, in from the Stock Squad cold and granted a second chance in Hutchens' hand-picked Fremantle Detectives squad. Maybe this was the price he was destined to pay for his sins, trailing behind his boss with a yellow plackie bag and a pooper-scooper. Cato steeled himself for a face-to-face with Hutchens. He was about to knock on the DI's door when it opened.

'Just the man I wanted to see,' said Hutchens. 'A Stock Squad expert.'

'Sir?'

'That pig we found yesterday. Some sick bastard murdered it with a fucking nail gun. Can you believe these people?'

'That's probably a job for the RSPCA, boss.'

Hutchens patted his grey forward-comb. 'I know, it's just sick, that's all. Poor bugger, never did anyone any harm.'

Cato had never imagined the DI would have a soft spot for all creatures great and small.

According to Hutchens, the preliminary forensics on the scene had found no trace of the missing girl but had revealed the horrors of the pig's last moments at the hands of a sicko with a nail gun. Whoever did this would show up on their books sooner or later; sickos tended to switch species at will. In the meantime they had to deal with the wash-up from the Wellard fiasco.

'I'm going to see the fucker tomorrow, wring the bastard's neck,' said Hutchens grimly. 'If he thinks this is the way to get what he wants, he's dreaming.'

'What *does* he want?' said Cato.

'Twenty minutes in the showers with a big rough boyfriend to focus his mind, that's what.'

'What do you want me to do with the report? I haven't got much room to move. Too many witnesses.' Excuses excuses; so much for Cato's solemn vow of truth, integrity and no more pooper-scoopers.

'Fuck the report. What's wrong with the truth? Shellie consented to the terms of the search because she'll do anything to find her daughter. Not my fault Wellard's a prick. Write that, write whatever you like.' Hutchens gave him a funny look. 'You worry about the paperwork too much, Cato, you're turning into a bureaucrat. I hired you to be a copper.'

'Sorry sir, I do my best.'

'Instinct, mate, that's what it's all about.'

'I'll remember that. Thanks, sir.'

'What's all this "sir" shit? We're not on parade. You taking the piss?'

'Never.'

'Good. Go and see Shellie. Get her squared away.'

The phone went and Hutchens grabbed it. A moment of murmuring and his frown dissolved. 'Fucking beauty. See you in ten, Lara.'

'Good news?' said Cato.

'Too right.' Hutchens beamed. 'Body in the dunny at the Birdcage, blood all over the place.'

3

'So let's get this straight. Johnny-boy's doing his number twos, door locked, and somebody slits his throat. That right?' DI Hutchens was staring at Lara, waiting for a response.

'The pants were undone, sir, but not pulled down. He hadn't got as far as that.'

A cordon tape had been strung around the outside of the nightclub. The lanky funereal Duncan Goldflam and his forensics team were already at work. Metal stepping plates led to the locus and some bloody footprints and other items of interest had been isolated, photographed and numbered. The place was lit up like a film set, distorted shadows played across the wall.

'So where does our assassin come from? The gap under the door? Over the top of the partition? Up through the bowl?'

'Too early to speculate, sir.'

'Come on, Lara, that's what we're paid for. I was just telling Cato here, we're forgetting how to be coppers.'

Cato Kwong had sidled up to within earshot. Lara gave him a friendly nod and a smile. It was all part of the unspoken and uneasy truce. He had unravelled her work on the Jim Buckley case in Hopetoun and taken what should have been a first homicide scalp away from her. Lara had used all the tricks in the book: planting evidence, manipulating witnesses, burying any contradictions. None of it had fooled Cato bloody Kwong.

'Once forensic's finished the preliminaries we'll be able to speculate more freely, sir.'

'Hmmm. And no name yet, that right?'

'Not yet.' It was a lie. She'd recognised him the moment she peered over the toilet partition. She still hadn't worked out the possible implications of her previous dealings with him: until she did she was keeping quiet.

Hutchens turned to Cato. 'What do you reckon, then?'

Cato acknowledged Lara's presence with a wink. 'All very interesting, boss.'

Lara studied his expression but it was inscrutable.

There was nothing so tawdry as a nightclub in daytime, mused Cato as he drove away from the Birdcage. An inquisitive throng of onlookers had gathered at the crime-tape perimeter: licking ice-creams, sipping cold drinks and coffees, taking pictures with their phones. Murder: the latest Freo tourist attraction. Supposedly it was Cato's job to collate witness statements. God knows how many people passed through the place last night. He'd get on with tracking them down as soon as he'd run this little errand for DI Hutchens.

Shellie Petkovic lived in a Homeswest state housing duplex just off Lefroy Road, near the high school. There were stained mattresses and rusty half-bikes out on the verge but council collection day was still a few months off. Hers was a corner unit, distinguished from the others by a homemade mosaic number on the wall, wind chimes, and a crystal rainbow-catcher dangling in the window. Music, of sorts, doofed from the neighbour's place. Cato rapped on the security flywire. The air was still and there was no shade in the midday street. Shellie unsnicked the latch and, without a word, disappeared to the shadows inside. Cato followed. The house smelled of cat: there was a plump tabby curled up on an armchair. Shellie had retreated to the couch. Despite the heat she was beneath a doona, watching him.

'I'm meant to ask how you're going but I can see for myself,' said Cato.

'Yeah? What do you see?'

'Somebody who's had a gutful.'

'And?'

'I'm sorry.'

'Thanks. Can you see yourself out?'

He was dismissed but her gaze never left him. Shellie's eyes were a striking blue-grey; in this context they were intense and unforgiving. Her dark hair was spiked, matted and craving attention.

On the mantelpiece was a framed photo of a younger smiling Shellie and a little girl wearing a pink tutu and fairy wings.

'My boss needs to know where you sit with all this ... business.'

'What do you mean?'

'Are you going to take it any further?'

'Tell your boss it's none of *his* bloody business.'

'Okay.' Cato wrote his mobile number on a card and left it on the table. 'Anything I can do, just call.'

'How's your head?'

He fingered the lump and smiled. 'A mere flesh wound.'

'Pity you got in the way. I could have finished the bastard off.'

'How are you going with the witnesses?'

Lara Sumich had perched herself on the corner of Cato's desk. She sipped a glass of water and held the coolness of it against her neck where her shirt buttons began. Over the course of the day her brown ponytail had wilted in the heat.

Cato studied his computer screen. 'The cleaner and bar staff are in hand. The doormen are being chased up. The punters? Upwards of two hundred of them. Thursday night is Retro '80s night apparently.'

'The 80s? What music did they have then?'

'Men at Work, Spandau Ballet, Madonna, that kind of stuff.'

'I was probably a bit busy with my Barbie dolls.'

He'd walked into that one. There was, at most, a ten-year age gap between them but Cato felt like a Neolithic relic.

'A lot of the punters are students from Notre Dame, Murdoch, plus some backpackers and Thursday-night regulars. So between the club membership list, the unis, the hostels and the CCTV, we should be able to round most of them up, eventually.' He sat back in his chair and folded his arms. 'You've got the CCTV, is that right?'

'Yeah, I'm just checking something out, I'll chuck it your way later this arvo.'

'Thanks.' Cato returned his attention to the computer. 'Lucky you were on the scene so quickly.'

'There'd been an assault complaint. I was following it up.'

'Any connection?'

'No, not as far as I can tell.'

'Any ID on the victim?'

'Not yet, no.' Lara finished her water and stood. Cato caught a waft of that expensive scent she used. 'Squad meeting at five,' she said. 'See you there.'

'His name is Santo Rosetti. Thirty-two. Current address: his parents' place in Spearwood. Previous for drug possession and dealing: mull, eckies, methamphetamines, special K, the usual.' Lara surveyed the crowded room; all attention was on her. DI Hutchens had made it clear he was in charge but that she could run the day-to-day. She updated them on developments. Santo's bloody wallet had been fished out of a builder's skip that afternoon. Any cash was gone but various cards remained, Medicare and driver's licence included. Now there was official identification through proper investigative channels, it made life a bit easier for Lara. She didn't need to own up to knowing him. 'Known associates, linked in with the Apaches but also flirts with the Tran brothers out of Baldivis.'

'Sounds like a dickhead sandwich,' muttered Hutchens.

'Certainly living dangerously,' Lara said. 'I assume Gangs and Major Crime will want to be in on this one, boss?'

'Over my dead body,' said Hutchens. There was a murmur of approval from the assembled throng. They wanted first crack at it. Hutchens gifted them a smile, the benign dictator. 'I'll work out the parameters with Major Crime. Cato, you go liaison on Gangs. They know you. Keep them sweet, keep them ignorant, keep them away.'

Lara kept her murderous thoughts to herself. Kwong was the last person she needed in that position. Hutchens looked at her like he could read her mind.

'Are we any closer to working out how they got to him behind closed doors?'

'Preliminary blood spatter suggests he most likely died in the cubicle.' Lara glanced over at Duncan Goldflam and he nodded assent. 'So the killer must have been in there with him, invited or uninvited, and then left over the top of the partition.'

'Why the pantomime? Why not just do him and leave the easy way?'

'Deliberately trying to confuse us, sir, bit of a distraction?'

'Good girl.'

Lara gave a neutral nod instead of sticking her fingers down her throat. 'So, we're focusing on witnesses and the CCTV and we'll be looking for any solid connections to the Apaches or the Trans among those who were there. And we're still looking for a murder weapon.'

'I think you'll find it's a fucking big sharp knife,' said DI Hutchens. 'Weekend leave cancelled, the overtime's on me; see you in the morning, folks.'

Cato had grabbed a pad thai at the food markets along the street from the office. It was still early enough in the evening to get a table outside. He was doodling over a cryptic crossword from a *West* that had been abandoned in the police canteen. The front-page headline gave a running total of how many asylum-seekers and how many boats had showed up in the last twelve months. That was the state of play these days: the refugee convention distilled down to its pure mathematical essence.

Cato was getting nowhere with the cryptic. *Nautical practice for figuring out the fatalities.* Four and nine. There was an 'a' three letters in. *Boat* something? The sea breeze had finally arrived and mingled with the sweat and suncream, hot concrete, car fumes, and spicy aromas from the food hall. Cato had fixed up a meeting with a DS from Gangs later that evening. The trawl on Birdcage punters was beginning to show results and a team had been established to interview them and follow up more names as they emerged. Mobile phones would be temporarily sequestered from the clubbers in case they held any helpful pictures from the big night out. Lara hadn't passed over the CCTV yet, he'd remind her when he got back to the office.

His TO DO list was taking on a life of its own: witnesses, footage, Gangs liaison, keeping tabs on Shellie Petkovic. He could still feel those eyes on him. He wondered how she made it from one day to the next; joining your fate with a man like Gordon Wellard and seeing your own daughter infected by his poison. Knowing he's the one who has taken her and won't give her back. Knowing it's nothing more than a joke to him. And knowing there's nothing you can do about it. Cato couldn't fathom how he might feel if somebody had done that to his son. The charade in the bush had disgusted him. Cato studied the faces of his fellow diners and tried to recall what it was like to live a day without thoughts of shallow bush graves or blood-drenched toilet cubicles. Blank. He looked down at the crossword again and this time he saw it. *Nautical practice for figuring out the fatalities.* He clicked his biro: Dead Reckoning.

Cato clamped the remaining noodles onto his chopsticks, swallowed, and headed back to the office.

4

Cato had been through the CCTV footage twice and seen nothing that pricked his attention apart from a blurry scuffle on the edge of the dance floor that fizzled out in thirty seconds. Santo Rosetti appeared at various points, talking to people, drinking, dancing – badly. No menacing Apache bikers or Vietnamese gangsters joined him for a bop to 'Land Down Under'. Cato handed the disks over to a dogsbody for more concentrated scrutiny and to organise photo printouts on any punters not yet identified and rounded up.

'Cato. Return of the Jedi. How was Stock Squad?'

'No great chop,' said Cato. They shook hands. 'Dirty Harry: long time no see.'

It was Detective Sergeant Colin Graham: Gangs, or 'Organised Crime' as it said under his name on the TV news. Regular media exposure agreed with him. He'd lost about ten kilos in the eight years since he and Cato had worked together. The hair was carefully groomed to appear unkempt and he looked nearer to thirty-five than the forty-five he really was. They wandered over to the kitchen where Cato clicked on the kettle and spooned some Colombian into a plunger. 'Milk and one?'

'Black and none.' Graham patted his flat stomach. 'Need to keep the gut down. New wife, Tania, doesn't take any nonsense.'

'Congratulations. It suits you.'

'I know, I'm a lucky man. How about you? I heard you and Jane split.'

Cato shrugged. 'The statistics were against us.'

'Shame, I liked her.'

'Yeah, me too.' Cato changed the subject. 'Still in Como?'

'Floreat. Tan wanted to be near her folks.'

'Expensive?' A nod. 'Nice bowling club I hear.'

'You should check out the library sometime. Awesome.' Graham looked at his watch. 'So, Santo Rosetti, what happened?'

'Somebody slit his throat last night.'

'Leads?'

Cato studied his former colleague: did Graham, as usual, already know the answers to the questions he was choosing to ask? 'We're looking at the Apaches or the Trans. Apparently he was playing for both sides and not the sharpest knife in the drawer.'

'One way of putting it.'

'How much do you know about him? Any helpful hints?'

Graham poked his head out the door of the kitchen, checking who might be in earshot. 'Between you and me, you might want to tread carefully on this one.'

'Always do. Why this time?'

'Santo's one of ours.'

'How do you mean? Informer?'

'He was a UC, Cato. One of *ours*.'

Cato got home just before midnight. On the corner, the South Beach Hotel – which everyone still called the Davilak despite the makeover – was closing up. Cato lived in what the real estate agents cheerfully called a 'cosy worker's cottage' at the park end of the street, five minutes walk from South Beach. It was a poky little one-and-a-half bedroom place he'd bought for sixty grand long before he met Jane. He'd kept it and rented it out during their marriage. Had he already, even in those early days, seen it as a potential bolthole? He'd moved back in after the split. He knew he'd be battling to find something like that within cooee of Freo for less than half a million these days.

Cosy it might be, but with the neighbours only a metre away through fibro walls he knew they wouldn't appreciate any music, even classical, at this time of night. He could use the headphones but he was feeling too irritable and claustrophobic. Another stinking night: he really should bite the bullet and invest in air conditioning but every year he managed not to. The Fremantle Doctor, the revitalising sea breeze, was often in by midday. These heatwaves usually didn't last, he reasoned, and he couldn't bring himself to shell out wads of cash for something he might only use ten, maybe fifteen, days a year. How else to relax and try to sleep? Crossword? He'd left it in the office.

Dead reckoning. According to DS Colin Graham, only a handful of people knew Santo Rosetti was an undercover cop. Cato shed his clothes, doused himself under a cold shower, flicked the fan to number three, and lay on the bed. Had Rosetti's cover been blown? A nightclub toilet is a fairly public place for an underworld-style hit but the pantomime with the locked cubicle door didn't add up. As DI Hutchens had noted, the usual gangland MO would be to just leave the victim on display and send a clear message or, even better, take him out bush and make him disappear. Cato also couldn't shake the feeling that Lara Sumich knew more than she was letting on. Her presence at the club on another, seemingly trivial, matter was one hell of a coincidence.

He could feel himself nodding off. Great. Finally. That's when Madge, next door's Jack Russell, started up. She had a high-pitched demanding yap – she was used to getting her way. Whenever Cato brought up the subject of Madge's night-time barking with her owners they looked at him like maybe they should be wearing a necklace of garlic and waving a crucifix at him. A non-believer: somebody who, gasp, wasn't really that into dogs. Cato pulled his pillow over his head and fantasised about meatballs laced with Ratsak. He was an ace detective after all: if he couldn't dream up the perfect murder, who could? The thought calmed him to sleep.

Cato's mobile buzzed on the bedside table. Caller ID: unknown. He squinted at the time on the screen. Six ten.

'Yes?'

'It's me, Shellie.'

Cato sat up. 'Shellie? Everything okay?'

'No.'

'What's going on?'

Her voice cracked. 'Why can't he just leave me alone?'

5

Saturday, January 23rd. Early morning.

Ten minutes later Cato was at Shellie's place. The sun was up and the easterly was still cool. Some dawn strollers headed down Lefroy hill to the beach with their dogs and babies. Shellie was standing at the door when he rolled up: she was wrapped in a dressing gown, her eyes red and puffy. When he walked over she leaned into him and started crying. Her hand uncurled to reveal a small heart, moulded silvery alloy, on a cheap silver chain.

'It's her locket. She wore it all the time.'

Cato held out a pen for her to hook it over. Her prints and DNA would already be on it but he aimed to keep his off.

'How do you know this is Bree's? You can probably buy these anywhere.'

She shrugged. 'I just do.'

They went inside the unit and he made her start at the beginning.

'I woke up early; I don't sleep well these days. I opened the front door to let the cat out and it was there on the doorstep. A letter.'

'Show me.'

They walked over to the kitchen table. There was a standard A5 envelope, yellow, her name and address handwritten in block capitals in black ink. No postmark or stamp. 'There's something inside, a note, I couldn't bear to read it.'

This time Cato went to the bother of retrieving a pair of forensic rubber gloves from the car. He snapped them on and fished out the note: plain white paper, A4, folded once. Two words in handwritten block capitals in black ink: *FINDERS KEEPERS*.

A low groan seeped from Shellie; she slumped onto a chair, head in hands. Cato spoke softly. 'Wellard's inside. Obviously he couldn't have done this himself. You've no idea who this could be from?'

She didn't look up. 'No.'

'Would Wellard know your address?'

'Not from me.'

'How many people know you live here?'

'Apart from official places like the welfare or the bank or the power company, nobody.'

'Nobody?'

She summoned up a bleak, tear-filled smile. 'Nobody. You, the police. That's my life.'

He crouched and put a tentative arm around her shoulder and wondered how much torment one person could be put through.

Shellie shook her head. 'I just want him to stop.'

Cato flipped out his mobile and woke up his boss.

It was just after nine by the time they got access to Gordon Wellard. They were on the freeway and passing Jandakot aerodrome as a Cessna lifted lazily into the cloudless sky. Cato wouldn't have minded being on it. On Thomas Road there was a garden centre with two shiny fibreglass elephants, one red and one yellow. Hutchens was playing with his new smartphone; he'd discovered the GPS app and couldn't get enough of it.

'Right, just after the elephants,' Hutchens murmured.

'Cheers.'

Cato had stopped pointing out to his boss that he already knew the way to Casuarina. He'd had this all the way down: left onto South Street, right onto the freeway, left onto Thomas. Right, just after the elephants.

The walls, wire and buildings that comprised WA's maximum-security corrections facility came into view through the straggly she-oaks after which it was named. They were met at reception by a tall, balding man with glasses. He looked like a chemistry teacher but his badge said *Geoffrey Scott, Superintendent*. According to Scott, a cell and full body search on Wellard had already been done. Nothing of note.

'This is turning into a bit of a circus isn't it?' Scott pushed his wire-rimmed specs back up to the bridge of his nose. 'Maybe it's about time Mr Wellard stopped getting all this attention and we left him to rot in anonymity.'

'Thanks, Geoff,' said Hutchens. 'We all appreciate the great job you guys do here.'

Scott snorted and ushered them into an interview room. 'We'll bring him up.'

'Any chance of a coffee?' said Hutchens.

'No,' said Scott.

Wellard was brought forth in his grey visits overalls. They emphasised his gnomic qualities. What had Shellie Petkovic seen in this man to hook up with him in the first place?

Hutchens led the charge while Cato pretended to study some paperwork. 'You've been bothering Shellie again. What's going on?'

Wellard ignored Hutchens and looked at Cato. 'What are you reading?'

'None of your business,' said Hutchens. 'Why are you giving Shellie all this grief?'

'Don't know what you're talking about. My radio got smashed this morning. Who's going to replace it?'

'Boo-hoo,' said Hutchens. 'I don't care about your radio. You've done this before, Gordo. Just over a year ago you got one of your weird little friends to do the same thing. Same type of envelopes, same silly word games. We got him and you got nine months extra on your sentence.'

'Concurrent. How is Billy by the way?'

'Billy overdosed last October. Very sad. You're a sadistic little prick and you've been giving everybody the run-around. We're getting sick of it, mate.'

Wellard studied his fingernails. They were in need of clipping and they had an unhealthy yellow tinge. 'Are we? Mick?' He twisted his head back to Cato. 'The radio. Can you write that down in your file, son?'

'Who've you been talking to lately, Gordon? Who did you set on Shellie this time?' said Hutchens.

'How is Shellie? Keeping well?'

'Suit yourself,' said Hutchens. 'We'll check your phone records and visitor's log. Look at people who've come out of here recently. You're not helping yourself with this crap, mate.'

'She's been through a lot, that woman.' Wellard shook his head sadly.

Cato showed him a photocopy of the note. 'What does this mean: *FINDERS KEEPERS*?'

'Dunno. Losers weepers maybe? Are you sniffing around my Shellie?'

Cato felt heat rising in his face. 'Where is Briony Petkovic?'

'Shellie likes you. I can tell by the way she looks at you. Like lovers in the park you were, down at Beeliar.'

'That's a vivid imagination you have. Where's Briony Petkovic?'

'None of your business. Just like my Shellie. She's not for sharesies. She should know that by now.'

Cato closed the file and stood up. 'Some things you can't control, buddy.'

Wellard chewed briefly on one of those yellow nails. 'Leaving already? No offence meant, mate. Nothing personal.'

Hutchens addressed the guard. 'He's all yours.' He and Cato walked out; Cato taking some comfort in the knowledge that, on the way back to his cell, Wellard faced a probing strip search before getting back into his uniform greens.

The heat bounced off the prison car park. The sky was painfully blue. Cato zapped the locks of the Commodore and they drove off with the air con up to full. The fires were on again: two columns of smoke over the southern hills of the Darling Scarp out Karagullen way, and one close by in bushland near Success. Whoever chose that name for a suburb needed to be strung upside down from a lamppost. Vivid orange Christmas Bush splashed the freeway verges as they sped north. The oncoming lanes were already clogged with the exodus south for what many were planning as an extra long, long weekend because the public holiday fell on Tuesday. Stuck in a forty-degree traffic jam: some holiday.

Cato blew out a breath and ran a finger around his sweaty collar. 'I feel like taking a shower after a few minutes in the same room with him.' Hutchens was uncharacteristically quiet; it made Cato nervous. 'What do you reckon?'

'What? You and Shellie? Best wait until this is all over, mate. Protocols and that.'

'Very funny.'

'Wellard's a sick fuck.' A sideways glance. 'You don't fancy her do you?'

'No!'

'Touchy.'

Cato flicked on the radio. Whoever last used the car had it pre-set to a frantic babbling pop station. He found Classic FM and some flute music he couldn't put a name to.

Hutchens stabbed it back into silence. 'Sounds like fucking *Play School*. What's going on here, Cato?'

'You tell me.'

'Meaning?' Less a question, more a warning.

'Wellard seems to think he's in charge.'

'And?'

'You and him go back a long way. Aren't you meant to be the one in charge?'

'You saying I'm not?'

'Again, you tell me.'

'I'll keep you posted, Detective Senior Constable.' Hutchens mobile beeped. 'Shit. Another budget meeting at HQ.'

At that point Cato remembered the news he'd forgotten to pass on to Hutchens from DS Colin Graham. 'Did you hear about Santo Rosetti?'

'Birdcage Boy? What about him?'

'He's one of ours. Intelligence undercover.'

Hutchens did a slow chin-tilt to click a vertebra. 'Santo's a dog and you're only telling me now?'

'I learned late last night. I slept, woke up, talked to Shellie, came out here with you. Got distracted.'

'Does Lara know this?'

Cato coughed. 'Thought it best that you hear it first. Protocols and that.'

'Good boy. Now call her, she might appreciate an update.'
Hutchens glanced at the clock on the dash. It was still only midmorning. 'Group hug. Noon. Pass it on.'

Lara Sumich sat outside the Spearwood home of Giuseppe and Sara
Rosetti. It was a fairly typical paved Italian palace with European
flowers in the front yard, plenty of brick and tile, some columns, and
a spotless driveway regularly swept and hosed. Lara hadn't been
able to make any sense of what the Rosettis were on about. It wasn't
just their shocked bereavement, or their age, or their limited grasp
of English even after nearly forty years in the country. It was like
they were talking about a different Santo.

Lara started the car and headed towards Coogee and the coast.
There was a whisper of a sea breeze so she left the air con off
and opened the windows. She had known Santo. He was a junkie
sleazebag. A parasite. He would sell his mother for the price of a fix.
A pathetic low-life loser. Quite a fall from grace then from the Santo
described by Mr and Mrs Rosetti, and only barely recognisable
from the photo they proudly showed her of a young and clean-cut
Santo graduating from the WA Police Academy several years before.
So had he gone badly wrong somewhere along the line and dropped
out? No, they said, he was still a policeman. They'd already had a
visit from some brass from HQ. Apparently they would keep them
informed. Lara would have appreciated being in the fucking loop
too.

Her phone buzzed – caller ID: Kwong. She let it go through
to message bank. Once it beeped she checked to make sure there
would be no surprises when they did catch up.

*Hi Lara, Cato here. The boss has called a meet for noon. Some news
from Gangs about your man Santo: turns out he was one of ours, a UC.
Interesting times huh?*

The message ended with a self-deprecating chuckle. How long
had he known? She chucked her mobile onto the passenger seat and
shifted gear.

'You bastard,' she hissed.

6

Cato and Lara sat in the visitors chairs, knees nearly touching.

'You two playing nicely?' said DI Hutchens from the other side of the desk.

'Yes sir,' they said in unison.

'Too busy for silly buggers around here. Got that?'

'Absolutely,' said Lara.

Cato was still out of sorts after his hot, short night's sleep and his early morning dramas. He was wondering how he could administer a tainted meatball to Madge without suspicion immediately falling on him. Perhaps he could manoeuvre another neighbour into prime-suspect status. Maybe he should spend some time grooming the dog, pretending to be friends to divert attention. He wondered if he had it in him to be so dastardly.

Hutchens glanced at an incoming text message. 'You with us, Cato?'

'Anything specific you're getting at, sir?' said Cato.

'Santo. Major Crime is getting antsy. If we're not careful they'll move from "strategic overview" to complete takeover.'

Lara crossed her legs and folded her arms. 'He's not in the personnel database anywhere, sir. If we'd known this yesterday ...'

Hutchens raised a hand. 'Nobody's blaming anybody here, Lara. Santo's been wiped from our files for obvious reasons. These days you can find CIA agents on friggin' Facebook. We didn't know about Santo because we weren't meant to know.'

Cato watched Lara's defensiveness evaporate.

'Look, we really don't want the Armani brigade up our arses so I'm drafting in extra bodies. Our bodies,' said Hutchens. 'Overall I'm in charge but at daily case-management level I think we need at least a DS on this.'

'Who did you have in mind?' said Lara.

Hutchens cleared his throat and waved his hand at a list on the desk. 'Nothing concrete yet. Any preferences, Lara?'

Cato liked Hutchens' new management style – Choose Your Superior.

'Meldrum is due back on Monday, sir. He's very experienced.'

Lara had Meldrum twisted around her little finger. Surely Hutchens wouldn't let that clock-watcher run a case like this?

'Back from where? I didn't realise he'd gone.'

Precisely, thought Cato.

'Holiday. Down south, I think,' said Lara.

'Beautiful.' Hutchens nodded. 'Meldrum. Good idea, my thinking exactly. Run it for the rest of the weekend then brief him first thing Monday.' Lara scribbled a note. 'I've also been offered DS Graham on full-time secondment from Gangs to consult and advise on specialist matters.'

'I understand, sir,' said Lara.

'Where do you want me, boss?' said Cato.

'Gangs will be well and truly inside Rosetti now so you won't need to go liaison anymore. Stay working with Lara on the witness stuff.'

'So I answer to Lara for the rest of the weekend and then Meldrum from Monday?'

'Got it. Spot on, mate.'

Cato cleared his throat and avoided eye contact with either of them. Lara's ponytail bobbed as she made for the door. Cato hadn't worked out how she was still in the squad after the stunt she pulled in Hopetoun. He said as much to Hutchens once Lara had gone.

'We all deserve a second chance, mate. You of all people should know that.' Cato stood to leave but was waved back by Hutchens. 'I'm also keeping you on the Wellard thing. He's taken a dislike to you. That could work in our favour.'

Santo Rosetti's innards rested in bags and bowls on a steel counter. His body lay pale and deflated on a trolley. The pathologist, a Glaswegian with rosy cheeks and a shiv in her voice, was summing up.

'Mr Rosetti died of blood loss from the slit throat, one strong and efficient movement by a right-hander with a very sharp knife. He had alcohol, heroin and ecstasy in his system, meat and salad in his tummy, and traces of semen in his mouth and throat.'

Lara looked up. 'Recent?'

'I'd say so. He didn't get a chance to swill or clean his teeth between that and dying. I don't know about you, petal, but I prefer a good gargle as soon as possible after the event.'

Colin Graham coughed.

'So he could have known the killer,' said Lara, almost to herself.

Professor Mackenzie instructed her assistant to set about putting Humpty Dumpty back together again. She peeled off her rubber gloves. 'He knew somebody well enough to be giving him a wee blowjob. Was this same person the murderer? That's your department.'

'Fancy a beer, Lara?' said DS Graham.

They were upstairs at a balcony table at the Sail and Anchor. It was midafternoon and a weak sea breeze floated through scented with gum, salt and cigarettes. Lara's mind was half on Santo Rosetti and half on DS Colin Graham. Down below, a sword-eating pirate busked the Saturday crowd, and souped-up cars dawdled and doofed on the Cappuccino Strip. It was hot and there was plenty of flesh on display, some of it more appealing than others. Lara noticed Graham's shiny new wedding ring. Didn't mean much in this job.

'Gangs keep you busy?' she said after a mouthful of pilsener.

'Plenty of dickheads out there trying to kill each other. I'm happy to let them get on with it as long as there's no collateral damage. It's the free market at work.'

'I thought they were more sophisticated these days?'

'Oh sure, high-tech, market-savvy, good lawyers and financial advisors, but if you put lipstick on a pig, it's still a pig.'

'The firebomb in the bikie tattoo parlour last weekend?'

'Exactly. The Trans again. Subtle as. God knows what that was about.'

'Maybe they spelt someone's name wrong.' Lara swivelled her glass absent-mindedly. 'What was Santo's job?'

'Staying in the thick of things. Doing little favours for as many people as he could. Hearing the whispers. Names to faces. Bit of stirring here and there.'

'Stirring?'

'Whenever things look like getting a bit too calm and cosy we like to give them something to fret about. Preferably each other.'

'Divide and rule,' said Lara. 'Was that what got him killed?'

Graham leaned forward, resting his elbows on the table. 'Haven't a clue. Any thoughts?'

Lara could tell she was being toyed with. Graham wanted to find out how much she knew. Were he and Kwong some kind of tag team? Did they know she and Santo had a history? Fuck him: two could play at that.

'It's a logical conclusion.' She took another sip from her drink. 'Either his stirring got him into trouble, or his cover was blown. Or both. He was playing all sides. Bound to piss somebody off sooner or later.'

'He kept dangerous company,' Graham conceded. 'In some ways I'm surprised he lasted this long. It's a dangerous game, very high stakes. The meth market in WA is the most lucrative in the country. Cashed-up miners wanting to party during their time off and happy to pay up to fifty percent more than anybody else because it's only money. No wonder the Eastern State outfits want to muscle in. Everybody wants a piece of the action and they don't mind spilling blood for it.'

Lara nodded. 'Care to speculate on the blowjob?'

'I wasn't aware Santo played for the other team but it takes all sorts.'

'Sex crime? Crime of passion?'

'Well there was sex and there was a crime but I'd be keeping an open mind. Passion? You'd expect a bit more frenzy usually. There was plenty of blood but just the single wound, albeit a very big one.'

Lara grimaced. 'What a seedy way to go: a toilet cubicle in the bloody Birdcage.'

'My nanna used to always say you should choose your friends wisely.' Graham shook his empty glass at Lara. 'Your shout.'

Cato spent the afternoon chasing down witnesses from the Birdcage, arguing with whoever was manning the phones at the Student Guild about matters of privacy versus law enforcement, cross-referencing new names against the offender database, and adding all new information into the emerging timeline. It was solid coppering but he felt like a cog in the machine and resented the fact that he was answerable to the less experienced and, in his view, decidedly dodgy Lara Sumich.

Cato's mind returned to Gordon Francis Wellard. The man had got under his skin. Every day you came up against hard cases, sociopaths and predators. Unsurprisingly, nearly all had tickets on themselves, an arrogance and sense of entitlement way beyond their real worth. Wellard was no exception: he attributed no value to anyone or anything except himself and, in Cato's view, Boom Town was breeding a whole lot more like him. Depending on which school they went to, some of the psychos would end up in Casuarina, others in the high corporate towers of St Georges Terrace.

FINDERS KEEPERS. What game was Wellard playing with Shellie now? Over a year had passed since the last incident of this nature, menacing letters posted by one of Wellard's saddo acolytes. Why was it happening again and who was helping him out this time? It could be a threat; a claim over what Wellard considered to be his property. The apparent antipathy towards Cato might be real or just another game. Wellard had been eyeing everyone keenly out in the bush that day. Whatever he thought he saw, it was certainly high on his agenda now, if only as a tactic. And he'd added Cato to his list of playmates.

The pendant, the note and the envelope had all been sent off for forensic tests. Cato wasn't going to try to second-guess the outcome. The previous batch delivered a year ago by Weird Billy left enough traces to lead right to his door. Had Wellard and his outside associate, whoever that was, learned their lessons since then? On the matter of the accomplice, there had been no phone calls or prison visits or recent releases that linked to Wellard. Was Shellie in danger from this person? Short of organising a round-the-clock guard, which was unfeasible and unlikely from a bean-counting perspective, the best they could do was cross their fingers and make sure she locked her doors. Cato was tempted to log back into the system and look up everything he could find on Wellard. He resisted: it would be easy to get obsessive and the bastard was already commanding more attention than he deserved.

'Fuck, that was nice.'

They were in Lara's apartment overlooking the Round House at the West End: old Fremantle, new money. It hadn't taken much longer to get Colin into bed. Another couple of beers at the Sail and Anchor, a loosened button, some eye contact. Graham enjoyed his sex and was upfront about it, even skilful here and there. There was something else about him that was less tangible yet still tantalising, a quiet self-confidence and a sense that anything was possible, no limits. Maybe he could take her places she'd never been before. Like a job in Gangs or Major Crime.

She rolled off and lay beside him, head propped on her hand. 'I like your idea of inter-departmental liaison, Detective Sergeant.'

'My pleasure ma'am. Are you always this diligent?'

'Consummate professional.'

Graham reached over to the bedside table and checked the time on his mobile. He seemed to be satisfied with what he saw.

Lara let her fingers wander. 'How long are you going to be around for?'

'As long as it takes.'

As he rolled towards her again she saw something in his eyes. Was it just intense concentration on the job at hand, or was there an element of calculation? Not for the first time that day she wondered: did the DI really call you over to help us out, or did you invite yourself? She clawed at his buttocks and drew him in.

7

Sunday, January 24th. Morning.

To some ears it sounded repetitive and to others restful, even meditative. For Cato, the Bach Prelude offered a promise of resolution, of homecoming. He went to the outer reaches of the keys and, just as it seemed the pattern would collapse into chaos, he returned to the fold. In some moods that same piece could induce vertigo, a sense of teetering on the edge of the unknown. The upright Kawai had recently been tuned by an old Hungarian from out Willeton way and, in playing it, Cato felt like a dear friend had returned to him. He wound down from the piece and sat back, Sunday-morning relaxed.

For the second night running, Cato hadn't slept well. Madge had barked for a full hour after he got home. The owners were either out, deaf, or oblivious. Cato had gone into the backyard, grabbed the hosepipe and squirted it over the fence. It didn't work, Madge just yapped all the more. In bed, Cato had been too hot and all the fan did was move around the dead, warm air. As far as he was concerned, the lie-in today was well deserved. It was eight-thirty and he had made up his mind to do big fat nothing.

There was a rap at the front flywire. It was Madge's master, Felix something or other. Cato dug deep for his neighbourly face.

'How you goin'?'

'Great. Yeah. Cool.' Felix tugged at the grey soul patch under his lip and gestured towards the piano. 'Um, any chance of keeping it down a bit, dude?' He nodded back towards his own house. 'We're in the middle of a yoga session. Bit distracting.'

Cato knew it was more than his job's worth to headbutt Felix. Just then Madge waddled up the path behind her master, wagged her tail and squatted against Cato's geraniums.

'How about we make a deal? You keep your dog quiet at night and

I'll play the piano at a more convenient time?'

Felix picked Madge up and hugged her to his bosom. 'I only asked. Sorry to have disturbed you.' He retreated huffily down the path with his striped Bali pants flapping in the strengthening easterly.

Cato couldn't help himself. 'Dog Act, 1976: read it.'

So much for making friends and diverting suspicion, thought Cato. Madge panted over Felix's shoulder. It looked like a smile.

Lara Sumich frowned down from her balcony. Fremantle on summer Sundays was the pits. All those tourists, and the bogans from the burbs, clogging the streets. She hated it. She'd woken early, gone for a run, done the grocery shopping and cleaned her apartment. Colin Graham didn't stay over. He would have been back in the arms of his new wife by midnight. Lara had felt strangely abandoned after he left. It wasn't how she'd planned to feel.

For the last couple of hours she'd been wading through the cesspit of Detective Constable Santo Rosetti's double life. He'd put on a very good performance as a low-life junkie loser for the last two years. All that his parents knew about his unkempt appearance and weight loss was that he was doing some special plain-clothes work and they were not to worry about it. His comings and goings at home had been increasingly erratic. Sometimes they went weeks without seeing him. Santo had not only kept his parents in the dark, he'd fooled Lara too and that really pissed her off.

She remembered her first encounter with him over a year ago. It was not long after the transfer from Albany to Fremantle and she was keen to get some early runs on the board after the Jim Buckley murder case had collapsed. Santo had been picked up for selling mull to some kids in Timezone. If losers have a certain sour smell, then he reeked of it. Lara was onto him immediately; cajoling names out of him, worming into his mind the painful price he would pay for dobbing in those same names, and then drawing him back in with her offer of protection.

'I'm the best friend you've got, Santo. Those guys'll put a blowtorch to your nuts as soon as look at you.'

'You're not doing so bad yourself, Detective.'

She'd played him beautifully, or so she thought. Santo had fed her regular titbits ever since: who the players were, who was working for whom, who was ripping so and so off, who was taking deliveries and when. She'd made a few worthwhile busts and helped him out with a few nods and winks to uniform colleagues whenever he got arrested for doing something stupid – which was quite often. He was always pathetically grateful and eager to please. And she had been sucked in, big-time.

Had those dobbings been strategic, or just expendable crumbs from Santo's table? What kind of undercover hotshot, as Colin Graham hinted Santo was, allowed himself to keep on getting arrested for blatant stupidity? That was no way to win the trust of the big players in the drug league and work your way into a useful position with them. Something clenched at her gut. Maybe *they* weren't the target. Maybe *she* had been, all along. And if Santo had been targetting her then who, of his colleagues, was also taking an interest? Colin Graham? He certainly acted like he knew everyone's secrets. No, it couldn't be her. There were other cops out there a lot worse than Lara. She was getting paranoid; time for some fresh air, sunshine, and the great outdoors. Late afternoon. The bogans should be heading home to the burbs soon.

Cato nursed a flat white at an outside table at X-Wray Cafe. He was surly and sleep-deprived. He checked the time on his mobile and made up his mind to have an early dinner followed by an early night. After several false starts he finally caught the eye of one of the uber-confident waiters, ordered a pasta thing and another coffee, and returned to his cryptic. Six down – *Colourful catch leads nowhere*. Easy. Red Herring. After Felix the dog man had left, Cato had phoned Shellie Petkovic to update her on the investigation into the mystery package and the prison conversation with Wellard. He wasn't obliged to be so attentive, it wasn't in his job description, but Shellie's desolation was hard to ignore. He'd recommended she keep her doors locked, just in case.

'Why?'

'Wellard's accomplice knows where you live and is trying to scare you.'

'I'm not scared.'

'Why not?'

A pause. 'Keeping the game going, that's what Gordo's about. Harming me physically would bring it to an end.'

Cato hoped she was right. 'All the same,' he said. 'Look after yourself.'

She'd thanked him, her voice a thousand miles away.

The sun was dimming and the breeze had picked up. The Sunday afternoon coffee and cake crowd was being replaced by dreadlocked groovers waiting for the evening live-music session. The poster showed an angelic young woman with a nose stud and an acoustic guitar. Her name was Ocean Mantra. Cato feared the worst and hoped his pasta would hurry up. Twelve across – *Agent of fate seems in trouble.*

'This seat taken?'

Cato looked up. It was Lara Sumich. Fremantle was like that, for all the crowds and hubbub it was hard not to come across a familiar face. Hopetoun on steroids. He folded his paper. 'Help yourself. I didn't think Sunday evening acoustics would be your scene.'

She sat down and a waiter instantly appeared. Funny that. She gave her order. 'What do you think my scene is?'

Cato pondered the matter for a moment. 'You've got me.' He waved his hand at the assembled braids and face-piercings. 'But this didn't figure.'

Lara drank some water. 'You were wrong, Mr Kwong.'

They sat in uncompanionable silence for a few minutes, then Cato's pasta arrived. Lara told him not to wait so he dug in. 'How's it going with our Birdcage Slasher? You and DS Graham getting along?' he said.

'Like a house on fire,' said Lara.

'Any progress?'

'Of sorts.'

'Not into shop talk, are you.'

'Au contraire, tell me about your old friend Colin.'

Cato took another mouthful of linguine. An agenda was a given with Lara Sumich: checking out the background of her new colleague was to be expected. What was in it for Cato to help out? Nothing. 'Good bloke,' he said.

'Ambitious?'

'No more than the rest of us.'

'I hear he's in line for DI soon.'

Cato wiped some pesto from the corner of his mouth. 'Then you know more than me.'

Lara's fruit juice arrived. She gifted the waiter a smile and he retreated with a swagger. She closed her lips over the straw and sucked briefly. 'Hutchens was forced to have him. Part of the deal to keep Major Crime and Gangs from taking over the case.'

Cato shrugged. 'It happens. Hutchens is big enough to take care of himself.'

'So you don't think Graham's got any other agenda then?'

'I think Col's got bigger fish than us to fry. Either way it'll keep our DI occupied and that's no bad thing.'

'I'm sorry if you're pissed off about the Rosetti line-of-command issue. That was Hutchens' idea, not mine.'

'Yeah?' Cato peered at his pasta.

'And we are on the same side after all,' she reminded him.

'Right.'

'So how's it going with your missing body case?'

'Nowhere fast. He's wasting our time and doing the mum's head in.'

'She's the ex-wife, that right?'

'Right.'

Lara sniffed. 'Sounds like the mum needs to choose her friends more carefully. Some people are born victims.'

'Thanks. I'll tell her next time I see her.'

There was a commotion at the far end of the cafe. Raised voices, scraping chairs. 'Sounds like somebody's *Green Left* subscriptions are overdue,' said Cato, looking to extricate himself from an uncomfortable conversation.

Lara reached inside her shoulder bag and fished out a taser. 'Must be well overdue, one of them has pulled a knife.'

Cato had neglected to bring his taser or gun with him. Sunday afternoon. Off-duty. X-Wray Cafe. Silly really. The only useful looking weapon close to hand was Lara's table order number – made out of metal and about a foot long with a bit of weight to the base. It would have to do – at least it was Number Seven, lucky in Chinese numerology, symbolising togetherness. Cato took a last scoop of pasta and they both headed over to do their duty.

'Police. Drop the knife and lie down or I will use the taser.'

Tables and chairs scraped and a space opened up around them. The guy with the knife was young, African background, he had a wiry muscularity and a calm, determined expression. The others were three white kids with that dressed-down affluent student look: the tongue studs would disappear soon after their graduation and a good job beckoned. They were terrified, scrambling across each other to get out of the way. Lara produced some ID from her pocket. 'Police. Drop the knife now.' She levelled the stun gun at the young man's chest.

His eyes seemed to welcome this new challenge. Cato edged around to try to get behind him. That's when it kicked off. Cato had never seen anybody move so fast. The African held up a chair to shield himself from the taser and lunged at Lara with the knife. The taser darts missed their target, one sticking in the bottom of the chair, the other ricocheting off and hitting one of the students. The blade connected with Lara's arm and she yelped as a gash opened up. She lost her balance and fell. Cato swung his Number Seven hard and low and connected with a kneecap. The African grunted and smacked the chair into Cato's face, stamped on Lara's head as he skipped past, vaulting the railings into the street. Disoriented by the blow, Cato scrabbled for his mobile and called in a description and direction to the police hotline. No way was he going to catch him; the horse had bolted.

Cato helped Lara to her feet. The stomp had produced a cut lip and the beginnings of a black eye. Her arm would need stitches. Cato had received a hefty whack to the side of the face with a chair leg but it hadn't broken the skin. The waiter appeared from the kitchen, confused by the scene of disarray during his absence: upturned tables and chairs, customers cowering in corners. He spotted the number in Cato's hand.

'Number Seven? Your lentil burger.'

Lara announced that her taser was missing.

Meanwhile, Cato had just worked out that last crossword clue. *Agent of fate seems in trouble*. Seems in – an anagram. Nemesis.

8

Monday, January 25th. Midmorning.

There was an alert out on the African and the missing taser. According to the students, none of whom claimed to have met him before, one moment it was laughs and jokes and all cool together – the next it was like, *Saw III* or *IV*, or whatever, dude. Other witnesses from the cafe had overheard a racial insult and an accusation of theft. The students hotly denied it but maybe they weren't as laid-back as they claimed to be. Lara Sumich had six stitches in her arm, a black eye and a puffy lip. She was ensconced with the returned DS David 'Molly' Meldrum, doing a handover on the Rosetti case. DS Colin Graham was over by the water dispenser taking everything in and acting bored. Cato had a bruise and scrape on the left cheek.

'What's going on around here, Cato?'

'Boss?'

Hutchens waved vaguely at Lara, at Cato, at everything. 'The stuff with Lara; bloody Col Graham hanging around like a bad smell, Wellard, Rosetti, mad Africans. The lot.'

'Monday morning blues?'

Hutchens didn't seem amused. He shepherded Cato into his office. 'Take a squiz at that.' He slung a thin, glossy A4 booklet across the desk. The front cover had a photo of a smiling Anglo nuclear family on the lawn in front of their modest McMansion. It was titled *Safer Streets Initiative*.

Cato didn't like the look of this at all.

'The Premier is concerned, Cato. Baffled. He can't work out why we're not all happy little vegemites, if we're all so rich from the mining boom and riding the storm of the global recession, blah blah blah. Instead there's all this rage, unkindness and thuggishness on *his* streets. That ...' Hutchens poked the report with his stubby forefinger, 'keeps the poor bloke awake at night.'

Fair point. Cato sometimes succumbed to the same thoughts himself. Every weekend there was a catalogue of glassings, stabbings, road rage, out of control suburban parties. The preceding weekend was no exception. Your average West Australian was statistically far more likely than most other true blue Aussies to end their night on the town in an induced coma from a king-hit. Welcome to Boom Town.

'Thoughts?' said Hutchens.

'Money can't buy me love?' said Cato.

'That's why you're on the team, Cato mate.' He tapped his forehead. 'Deep thinker.'

Hutchens closed the door, sat Cato down and proceeded to tell him what he had in mind.

Lara finished briefing DS Meldrum and began to review some of the footage from mobile phones confiscated from Birdcage patrons. Based on the CCTV and cash till receipts on the door, she estimated there were at least twenty to thirty patrons still unaccounted for. They were working through the list of those they did have but so far nothing of consequence had materialised. Nobody had seen or heard anything. The hard word had been put on the club and the local unis and hostels to rustle up a few more names. In the meantime the mobiles still needed to be checked. DS Graham was standing beside Lara's chair.

'Can I help you?' she said.

'I was about to say the same.' He crouched down and helped her unpack the jiffy bags holding the phones. They spread them out on the desk, each in their own labelled Ziploc. Some looked decidedly grubby, many smelled of beer and cigarettes. 'By my count that's about forty each,' he said.

They snapped on rubber gloves and started scrolling through the photo folders. Mostly it was hugs, kisses, pouts, silly faces, and lots of sculling.

'Ever feel you're missing out on something?' murmured Graham.

'No,' said Lara.

Santo turned up in one of the shots, in the background. Lara checked the time recorded on the phone. So he was still alive at 11.43 p.m. More phones, more poses. No familiar faces, no more Santo. An hour or so later they finished ticking off the list between them and put the phones back in the bag.

'Fancy a coffee?' said Graham.

'Not feeling too sociable today, thanks.'

'Could be worth your while.' That look of his, somewhere between a tease and a threat.

'Santo had pissed off the Trans. It was only a matter of time. Those boys don't forgive or forget and they don't take prisoners.' DS Graham looked around the coffee shop conspiratorially.

Lara licked froth from her swollen top lip. It stung. The faux leather armchair stuck to her back and a fly strolled over an abandoned blueberry muffin on the uncleared table in front of her. 'Could just as easily have been the bikies, he was supposedly playing them both. Why specifically the Trans?'

Graham looked away, playing enigmatic.

'Stop pissing about, Colin, you're either part of this or you're not. I'm in no mood for games.'

'No, you're right. Sorry, Lara.'

His hand closed over hers. She withdrew it. 'Tell me what makes you think it's the Trans.'

'We have a high-level informant. He told us Jimmy Tran planned to do Santo himself, sooner rather than later. They believe Santo was passing on valuable information to the Apaches. Some deliveries had gone missing.'

'Who's the informant?'

'Classified. Sorry.'

Lara shook her head, unconvinced. 'I don't blame them for not trusting Santo. He was a liability. He couldn't sell weed to a bunch of teens in Timezone without getting busted. But passing on valuable information? Bullshit.'

'Bit harsh. You don't have the inside run on what he was doing.'

'No, but you seem to. All I'm going on is available proof, like his arrest record and ...'

Graham's eyes narrowed. 'And what?'

Personal knowledge.

Instead she said, 'Gut feeling. So, apart from scuttlebutt, what hard evidence do you have for looking at the Trans?'

'This has got the Trans written all over it, lashings of blood. They have no rules, no boundaries. We need to start playing the game their way or they'll walk all over us. Since when do we need "hard evidence" to kick down the doors on people like that?'

'Since they could afford good lawyers. I don't know how you do things in Gangs, but I can assure you DI Hutchens will want more before making a move.' She drained her coffee. 'He's been burnt once too often.'

Graham smiled. 'You're a hard case. Loosen up a bit and you'd go down well in Gangs, Lara.' He fished a mobile out of his pocket and scrolled through until he found what he wanted. 'Recognise anybody?'

It was Santo at the Birdcage, in the background of another backpacker-sculling competition. He had a beer in one hand; the other hand was around the shoulders of a blurry long-haired guy. 'Where did you get this?' asked Lara.

'It was in my pile.'

'So why didn't you raise this back in the office?'

'Walls have ears.'

'What are you on about? We're all on the same team aren't we?'

'I'd like to think so.' Graham cocked his head. 'Lara, we have to be able to trust each other.'

Since when, she wondered? 'He looks familiar. Who's the boyfriend?' she pointed at Santo's companion, already knowing the answer.

Graham winked. 'Jimmy Tran.'

'That shirt of his, white T with black trim, was involved in a scuffle earlier in the evening and may have been responsible for a glassing outside later.'

'Perfect,' said Graham.

Cato now knew, on one level at least, why he'd been sidelined from the Rosetti case. Hutchens had plans for him. It must have emerged at the management meeting at HQ yesterday. Cato was, as of half an hour ago, the Fremantle representative on the Safer Streets Task Force, or SSTF; already sniggeringly referred to as the 'Stiffies' by his colleagues. Fremantle, Northbridge, Hillarys, Claremont and Leederville were all recent street-violence hotspots garnering unpleasant media scrutiny and *something has to be seen to be done*. A combination of intelligence, high-profile policing and zero tolerance would apparently send a strong message to the thugs of Boom Town – *Stop it or the Stiffies will get you*.

Cato smelled a rat. They had a cop-murderer out there, a very public throat-slashing with hundreds of potential witnesses to process and the possibility of organised crime involvement. The case was being run first of all by Lara Sumich, a junior officer with a limited and discredited track record, and now by DS Meldrum, a man nobody had missed while he was on leave. Meanwhile DSC Cato Kwong, a star at least in his own mind, was relegated to the Constable Care Committee. It was a criminal misuse of his talents. But what was behind all this bullcrap? DI Hutchens was obviously the key. Cato knew he'd pissed off his boss by suggesting that Gordon Wellard seemed to be in control of the old cop–informer relationship with Hutchens. Was the DI that petty-minded and vengeful? You betcha. Maybe a nerve had been struck or maybe it was plain old hubris. Either way this was as good a way as any of telling Cato to pull his head in. His mobile pinged. A text from Jane.

Don't forget Jake, tomorrow 5.30

The Stiffies task force assignment did at least have one upside: it was a low-impact, nine-to-five desk job. It meant nothing could stop him from getting to Cracker Night with his son.

The Tactical Response Group love themselves, thought Lara. The heavily armed men-in-black had done their ninja thing with the armoured car and battering rams on the Tran compound in Baldivis, a semi-rural enclave south-east of Fremantle. The property was a rundown treeless five-acre block, bordered on one side by a freight railway line littered with cans and broken bottles and on the other by a neglected potholed road scarred with burnout marks. 'Compound' was the only way to describe it: the place certainly didn't look homely. A squat characterless prefabricated house with all sources of light and fresh air blocked by bars and reinforced mesh screens. A slab of concrete with a cheap plastic table and four chairs: the entertainment area perhaps? Two outlying sheds, equally ugly. The gates to the property were high, fortified, and electronically operated from inside. *Chez Tran* bristled with high-tech security and surveillance equipment and, just to make sure, three pit bull attack-dogs – now dead, courtesy of the TRG.

'This place needs a woman's touch,' Lara said, as she strolled past the canine corpses to inspect the prisoners.

They were facedown and handcuffed, each with his own personal ninja standing guard. The two Tran brothers, Jimmy and Vincent, were there plus three of their friends. DS Colin Graham was in a crouch over Jimmy. A safe distance away, DI Hutchens fielded a media doorstop flanked by two of the black-clad TRG for sex appeal. That would keep him occupied for a while. There was a bushfire less than three kilometres away, lit just that morning. It was fanned by hot strong winds from the east. If the south-westerly Freo Doctor didn't show up soon, that fire would keep on coming right over this part of Baldivis. As Lara neared, Graham finished his chat with Jimmy Tran and stood up to acknowledge her.

'Not much of turnout,' Lara said, nodding at the prostrate gangsters. 'Five weedy blokes. I was expecting a cast of thousands. All scary. This all there is?'

'These are what you might call the core management team. They tend to subcontract out. Or maybe franchise is a better way of putting it.'

'Franchise?'

'They run a very successful loyalty program. The last bloke who crossed them got his hands and feet chopped off with a machete. It was on YouTube for a couple of days. Got over two thousand views before they took it down.'

Lara grimaced and nodded down at Jimmy Tran. 'He confessed yet?'

'Thinking it over.' Graham led her out of earshot. 'The place is clean, metaphorically speaking anyway: a shame but not unexpected.' He looked around and sniffed the burnt air. 'They must keep the drugs and guns elsewhere. Fiendishly clever, the Trans.'

'Dastardly,' agreed Lara. 'But it would be nice to give something to DI Hutchens for agreeing to put on this circus.'

'Happy snaps on the mobile not enough you reckon?'

Lara looked thoughtful: the media doorstop was heading for a lacklustre wind-up. She went around to behind one of the prone Tran underlings and stamped hard on his ankle. He yelped and cursed and struggled to his knees. Lara positioned herself between the TRG man and his newly wounded charge, enabling the underling time to get fully upright. Game on. All media were now running and pointing in her direction. The man limped towards Lara.

'That hurt, you bitch.'

Lara took out her gun and ordered him to the ground. DS Graham covered his smile with a hand cupped thoughtfully over his chin. The TRG were circling and shouting orders. The news cameras rolled. The limping man was already handcuffed, he'd be mad to push it any further. Lara levelled her gun at his chest.

'Do it. Lie down.'

He didn't. The ninjas were closing in but he seemed oblivious to the heavy weaponry levelled at him. They wouldn't shoot a handcuffed and unarmed man in front of the TV cameras, would they? Only a few seconds had elapsed since the stamping but it felt longer.

'Final warning.'

He took another painful step towards Lara. She wondered if she'd miscalculated.

There was a string of Vietnamese from Jimmy Tran and the man did as he was told. Lara found she was kind of disappointed but DI Hutchens was beaming. This guaranteed him some airtime tonight.

The TRG reassumed control, one of them whispering out from under his black helmet like Darth Vader. 'You made me look like a dickhead there, love. That wasn't very nice.'

9

Jimmy Tran was flanked by his lawyer: an expensive-looking young man from St Georges Terrace. Damien was his name. It must have been a toss-up: boy band or law school? He fancied himself, big-time. Lara didn't. She preferred a touch more testosterone and a touch less pout.

'Why is my client here?' It was a private school drawl – Christ Church Grammar, Scotch or some such place; house as big as a suburb and Daddy never there. It pushed all the wrong buttons for Lara because it was her world too.

'Your client is here to assist us with a murder inquiry.'

'You could have phoned or knocked on the door and asked nicely. A raid by your "paramilitaries" is all a bit ...' he stifled a yawn, 'melodramatic.'

DS Colin Graham cleared his throat. 'Your client has a violent criminal history including the use of firearms and he lives in a fortified compound protected by attack dogs. It was a necessary precaution. Now to business.' Graham shifted his attention. 'Jimmy, where were you between eight p.m. last Thursday and six a.m. the following morning?'

Jimmy Tran had his long hair tied back in a ponytail. His face was thin, features sharp, complexion fucking awful. He was pushing thirty-five and probably worth a few million but still wore grimy, scabby trackies and a threadbare T-shirt like a teenage street hood in a ghetto. Tran looked at his lawyer as if he didn't understand the question and perhaps needed a translator.

'Sorry?' he said, piling on the accent.

DS Graham grinned. 'Jimmy, you've been here for at least twenty years, you're as fluent as a Freo wharfie. Let's stop buggering about and get on with this, eh?'

Jimmy addressed his lawyer again, maintaining the accent.

'Why they kill my dog?'

'We kill your dog cause he ugly, like you,' Graham mimicked nastily. 'Grow up, mate, the sooner you cooperate the better.'

'What's your role on this investigation, DS Graham?' asked Damien the Lawyer. 'You're normally based in Central aren't you?'

'None of your business, son.' Graham switched his steely blues from the lawyer back to the gangster. 'Jimmy? Where were you?'

'I was out drinking with some friends during the evening and then went home to bed.'

'Where were you drinking and who with?' said Lara.

'Fremantle, from about eight til midnight: I was with Vincent and Mickey.' The brother and the underling with the sore ankle.

'Name the venues.'

'Newport. Norfolk. Sail and Anchor. And we finished off at the Birdcage.'

'Anybody there that you knew?' asked Graham.

'Your Constable Rosetti.'

'Constable?' said Graham.

Tran broke into a chuckle. 'Nice try, mate.'

Cato finished early and called in to see Shellie Petkovic on the way home. He had nothing new to report, he just wanted to check how she was going. He rapped on the flywire and braced himself for another tense exchange in the gloom of the Homeswest duplex.

'Hi, how you going? Come in.' Shellie opened the door and stood smiling in a pair of denim cut-offs and a T-shirt. 'Coffee?' she said over her shoulder as Cato followed her inside.

The dark pit of despair was now bright and homely with curtains flung back, flowers on the coffee table, and a freshly vacuumed lemony smell. A CD on low: Dusty Springfield was *Wishin' and Hopin'*.

'Sure. White and none thanks.'

Her bare feet padded behind the kitchen counter and she reached into a cupboard for a jar of instant. Cato held his usual coffee-snobbery in check; this wasn't the time or place. Shellie's eyes shone, her black hair loosely tied off in bunches, her skin glowing.

Cato uncomfortably realised he couldn't take his eyes off her.

'Feeling better?' he asked dumbly.

'Much. I've decided that arsehole isn't going to run my life any more.'

'Right. Good.'

'I know he'll never give Bree back. I've stopped hoping he will.' She handed a coffee to Cato, looking straight into his eyes. 'If he was dead it would make it all easier, no more of his stupid cruel games.' She stirred her cup. 'But fantasising isn't going to get me through this, is it?'

They sat facing each other across the coffee table. Shellie on the couch, legs curled up under her and hands cradling the hot mug. Cato took the cat's chair while puss-puss glared at him from the windowsill.

'Her name is Miranda. Had her for eight years. Bree named her.'

'Miranda the Cat. Got it,' said Cato.

'Your business card says "Philip" but I heard Mr Hutchens call you "Cato". Where's that from?'

'A nickname from Academy days. *The Pink Panther*. Cato was Inspector Clouseau's Chinese manservant.'

'Do you mind being called that?'

'I got used to it. Been called worse.'

Shellie touched her temple. 'Your head looks a lot better. But I don't recall giving you that bruise on the other side.'

'Been fighting again. Perils of the job,' he smiled.

'So what happens next?'

'We keep on digging. If nothing else we'll aim to take his sick friend off the streets so you don't get any more packages.'

'Gordon denied it, then?'

'For what it's worth.' Cato wasn't sure if he should ask the next question but he did anyway. 'What did you see in him?'

'God knows.' She thought about it for a moment. 'Love is blind. And stupid.'

'He was hurting you as early as the honeymoon.' Cato meant to sound supportive and understanding but it emerged more as an accusation.

She shrugged. 'He said he was sorry. Every time.'

Cato drank some coffee.

Shellie seemed to read his mind. 'I don't know how you do your job. Dealing with all this crap day after day.' A rueful twist of the mouth. 'Dealing with fuck-ups like me.'

'I was meant to be a famous concert pianist but I failed the audition.'

'You're only half-joking aren't you?'

'Half-jokes are my speciality.'

'They're a good way of keeping people guessing.'

The scrutiny was unsettling. Cato drained his coffee and stood to leave. 'We'll keep you informed of developments.' He handed her the cup. 'And we'll keep looking for Bree.'

She had a strange look on her face. 'Thanks. Philip.'

'Jimmy Tran is taking the piss.'

The interview had run out of steam so they'd adjourned for a while. Lara and Colin had reconvened in the canteen. It was early evening and they shared some sushi from a nearby takeaway. Jimmy didn't deny he was in the Birdcage that night, didn't deny being involved in the brief scuffle earlier by the dance floor, didn't deny that was him pictured on the mobile with Santo. Nor did Jimmy deny that his penis had been in Santo's mouth. 'He love me long time,' he'd pouted in his mock ladyboy persona, the sing-song humour never reaching his eyes. But Tran did deny murdering Santo and shoving a bottle in a stranger's face later on.

'Cocky for sure,' said Graham. 'He knew Santo was a cop and doesn't mind letting us know that he knew.' Graham squeezed a little plastic fish full of soy sauce onto his sushi. 'Somebody invented these soy fishes and a factory somewhere makes them, China probably. Keeps all these people in a job. How good is that?' He lobbed it into a bin. 'We're still a long way from pinning this on Jimmy. Any ideas?'

Lara ran her hand along his thigh. 'Maybe we can conjure up some magic from somewhere.'

'Abracadabra,' he said.

Cato was at home playing some Schubert on the Kawai but his fingers felt like they belonged to someone else: maybe a tone-deaf brickie with arthritis. He rested his left hand on the bass keys, noticing again the naked space where his wedding ring used to be. It had taken nine years for Jane to give up on his working hours, his obsessions and emotional distance. He hadn't even seen it coming, too busy feeling sorry for himself when the bosses scapegoated him for a murder case frame-up. Bygones were bygones. Now he was back in the job and he had access to his son. Jane wasn't coming back but he knew there was someone out there somewhere waiting for him to come into her life. Must be. And next time Cato would be different.

So what had brought about Shellie's transformation? One day the mystery package – cruel and taunting, Shellie the despairing victim. The next, a new-improved walking-on-sunshine Shellie. Medication or meditation? Whatever, the effect was electrifying.

Are you sniffing around my Shellie?

Wellard, not your average raging sociopath it seemed. No, he was apparently gifted with prescience and telepathy.

She likes you. I can tell by the way she looks at you.

Maybe Wellard really could read the dark souls of men and women. Cato doubted it though. Sexual attraction would have been the last thing on Shellie's mind that day as she prodded the ground searching for the corpse of her daughter. But what about since then? Shellie's eyes across the rim of a coffee cup. Was the new-found chemistry real or was it a poisoned seed planted by Wellard? Either way it was wrong, Cato needed to watch his step and his hormones or risk a shipload of professional grief. He also needed to get some sleep.

Madge started barking. Cato was in a mood to kill that bloody dog. That's what happened when you daydreamed about psychos. He closed the piano lid and went out into the street: the moon was three-quarters full and a breeze tickled the leaves in the trees. The lights were off next door. Mr and Mrs Madge must be out again. Cato picked some fist-sized bits of plaster out of the builder's skip across the road and opened the side gate leading to Madge's backyard. The terrier's barking was at fever pitch as the intruder ventured further into enemy territory. Cato threw a lump of plaster at the dog but missed. Madge scampered away, yelping and barking furiously. Cato threw and missed again. He steadied his aim for one last try. The backyard light suddenly blazed and a naked, semi-erect Felix stepped out onto the patio with a hockey stick held high.

'What the hell do you think you're doing?' said Felix.

10

Tuesday, January 26th.

Cato woke up sweating. No, it hadn't been a dream: he really did have a naked encounter with his neighbour last night. Cato had looked Felix straight in the eye – he didn't want to look anywhere else – as he concocted a story about seeing off a prowler. Mrs Madge also made an appearance in a rumpled negligee, black with a scarlet bow. From the recesses of his mind Cato remembered her name, Janice. Felix seemed sceptical about the prowler tale but he was not going to call the police, this time, because he'd never really trusted 'The Pigs' and besides, with Cato being kind of 'Asiatic', there was no way they'd give him a fair go. Cato had thanked him and they all went to bed – their own.

Cato and Jake were going to the fireworks on the Esplanade tonight, come hell, high water, or even a Safer Streets Task Force meeting. Jake would be dropped off by his mum at 5.30. Cato needed to clear the decks at work and be firm with his boss, his colleagues, and particularly himself about keeping to the arrangement. This was the new Cato: promises made were promises kept. Family first, work second. Got it? The best way to keep things simple for the next few hours was to nod and smile and say yes to whatever Hutchens wanted, within reason. Cato swilled the remains of his coffee and headed for the door.

At the police station he nodded good morning to Lara Sumich and Colin Graham, hunched together in a low murmur. DI Hutchens was in his office on the phone. Around the cop shop there was always an air of anticipation on Australia Day: a semi-war footing in anticipation of a busy night locking up drongos. Cato logged on to see what was new. There was nothing on the forensics on Shellie's pendant and package: it wouldn't be high on their priority list. Through the partition window, Cato could see Hutchens pacing back and forth, deep in thought. That usually didn't bode well. Cato tried his best not to catch Hutchens' eye.

'Detective Senior Constable Kwong.'

Too late. 'Boss?'

'In here.'

Cato wandered in and put on his helpful and obedient face.

Hutchens waved in the general direction of his phone and computer. 'Another night of stabbings, glassings, and general mayhem. What's happening with Safer Streets?'

'I'm onto it, boss. Just collating some local intelligence stats with a view to having a comprehensive status update ready for the first meeting.'

Hutchens seemed taken aback. 'Good man.' He reminded Cato of an old half-blind dog that knows you've got a ball behind your back. A bit weary, suspicious, yet interested in possible developments. 'Any forensics on Shellie's mystery package?'

'Nothing yet but I'm chasing it. Anything else?'

'No, but we should have a look at Wellard's known associates. See who the postman could be.'

'I'll get onto it, boss.'

'You feeling okay? Not crook or anything?'

'Never better.'

'You're not fooling anyone, you know.'

'Sir?'

'All this polite, helpful, obedience shit.'

'Right, boss.'

Cato retreated. Hutchens had obviously given up on chasing the ball, decided to nip an ankle instead.

'How's your ankle, Mickey?' said Lara.

'Gofuckyerself,' said Mickey.

'That's not very nice, I only asked.'

Mickey Nguyen had a legal aid lawyer, not the smart expensive young man his boss used. The lawyer's name was Rebecca, she had lots of blonde frizzy hair and tired eyes. 'Is Mr Nguyen going to be charged with anything, Detective Sumich?'

'At this stage he's assisting us with our inquiries.'

'You brought in the TRG, handcuffed him, assaulted him,' a frown in Lara's direction, 'held him overnight, and he was only "assisting you with inquiries"? What do you do to people you really don't like?'

'Sorry,' said Lara. 'I didn't see his foot. Just stumbled, you know?'

'So he is free to leave at any time?'

'Of course.'

Mickey started limping towards the door.

'How's your old man?' said DS Colin Graham.

Mickey turned. 'Fuck you, too.'

Graham opened a file in front of him. 'Your dad's very sick but he's not due for release for eighteen months.'

'Is there a point to this, Detective?' said Rebecca. 'If not then it appears my client would like to go home.'

'Cancer isn't it? Days are numbered I hear. Your mum must be heartbroken, Mickey.'

'Detective?' An icy warning from the lawyer.

'If I had my way he'd be released on humanitarian grounds,' said Graham.

'This could be viewed as unfair pressure or inducement.' Rebecca tapped her pen lightly on her legal pad. 'If the situation is as you describe, then Mr Nguyen's father is likely to be released on humanitarian grounds anyway.'

Graham shook his head. 'Minister's discretion. Organised Crime's advice has been that he is a serious risk to public safety. Who knows what or who's on his bucket list.'

Mickey hadn't taken his eyes off Graham. 'What are you offering?'

'I'm not at liberty to offer anything Mickey, that would be unfair pressure or inducement, but circumstances and priorities change. It's a very fluid situation.'

Mickey sat down again. 'What do you want?'

Willagee must have been one of the suburbs the Boom forgot. Cato drove past houses scarred with graffiti, the rusted hulks of abandoned cars moored in litter-strewn driveways. He'd come along North Lake Road past Moorhouse Street, once home to WA's very own infamous husband and wife murder team. According to DS Meldrum, whose kids went to the local school, the address of Mr and Mrs Birnie's house of horrors had become a tiebreaker question at community quiz nights.

To be fair, even Willagee was being kissed here and there by the side winds of prosperity. Some houses had been renovated, some driveways hosted the obligatory turbo ute or Prado. And given the proximity to Fremantle, it was only a matter of time before the real estate prospectors turned a sparkle in the seam into a fully-fledged gold rush. Until then, Cato would curb his enthusiasm.

The police database reckoned that Gordon Francis Wellard was Johnny-Few-Mates. His known associates could be counted on the fingers of a clumsy chef's hand. Two were dead, from an overdose and car crash respectively, and another was in Karnet Prison Farm, no doubt abusing the chooks. That left an old girlfriend and meth partner, Karina Ford. Cato wondered if she'd changed her name by deed poll, some people were like that about their cars. Her driving licence record, suspended as it was, gave an address in Greig Street, Willagee.

Cato pulled up outside the house where Ms Ford lived. It looked respectable enough, the grass was mown and the windows were intact. Willagee was like that: your neighbours could be honest aspirant battlers on one side and drug-fucked dropkicks on the other, with serial killers over the road.

A heavily pregnant teenager left the house pushing a stroller with a sleeping toddler. Her rat-tailed boyfriend was doing his best to wake the kid up by constantly bouncing his basketball. He was twitchy and hyper and possibly on something.

'Fuck you looking at?' they both said to Cato in passing.

He ignored them and knocked on the locked security screen.

'Don't need any,' said the smoky voice from inside.

'Not selling any,' said Cato flashing his ID. 'Police.'

'Done nuthin',' said Karina from the forbidden gloom.

'Good,' said Cato. 'Open up and talk to me or I'll stand here all day looking Chinese.'

'I'm not prejudiced, I'll ignore any bastard.'

Sometimes Cato missed Hopetoun, the pleasant everyday exchanges of simple country folk. 'Karina, you heard from Gordon Wellard lately?'

The screen door unlatched and Karina blinked at the daylight. She was wearing tight denim shorts and a singlet that might have looked good on her twenty years ago. 'Why?' she said through a curl of cigarette smoke.

'Let me in and I'll tell you.'

'Suit yourself.' She walked back inside and Cato joined her in the fug of cigarettes, old mull, and something chemical. Jerry Springer was on TV: two reasonably presentable middle-aged women were locked in mortal combat over the affections of an obese smirking twenty-year old in a turned-back baseball cap. Karina muted them. 'Freaks.'

'Thanks,' said Cato. He nodded his head back in the direction of the departing teenage parents. 'Yours?'

'She is, he isn't. What's it to you?'

'Just being chatty. Going to be a nanna again soon then?'

'Yeah. Can't wait. Waddyawant?'

'Do you hear much from Wellard these days?'

'Why would I? He's locked away. Good riddance.'

'Not friends any more then?'

'I was his last shag before he got arrested. We made soulful love and did drugs for three weeks. No big deal. We all move on.'

'Was he ever violent with you?'

Karina's tongue probed something in her teeth. 'That any of your business?'

'No. But was he?'

'Nah. Wouldn't dare.'

'Why?'

'Even scabby street mongrels know when to snap and snarl and when to just sniff your bum and keep things friendly.'

A mind-boggling image: Cato shook himself free of it. 'So you don't keep in touch?'

'Already said that. What's he done now?'

'His ex-wife, Shellie, got a package in her letterbox. Stuff to do with her missing daughter.'

Karina stubbed her cigarette into an ashtray and dug out another. 'Poor cow. You reckon I helped him with that sick shit do you?'

'What sick shit's that then?' said Cato.

She squinted at him. 'He thought it was funny, taking the piss about her missing kid. I told him to get a life.' She laughed humourlessly. 'Now he's got one, he's serving it.'

'Do you remember the words he used?'

'Sure mate, I even wrote them down in case they'd be needed in the future. I'll just go and check my filing cabinet.' She dragged on her new cigarette and blew the smoke upwards like she was concerned about the effects of passive smoking. 'Look, he's a sick prick, she needs to ignore him and get on with her life.'

'Anything else?'

'Nah.'

'So you didn't help him out with his latest stunt, Karina?'

'Piss off, mate.'

'Just asking.'

'The answer's no.'

'Can you think of anyone else that might help him?'

'Plenty freaks out there. Take your pick.'

Cato gave her a business card. 'Call me if you think of anything.'

'Sure, honey.'

He left. She de-muted Jerry Springer.

'So, Jimmy, tell us about you and Santo Rosetti at the Birdcage.'

Damien the Expensive One sighed. 'My client has already answered your questions as to his whereabouts that night. If you're not going to charge him with anything then you must release him. He's been in custody for over twenty-four hours now. This is ridiculous. It has to stop.'

'He's told us he was there but we still don't have the detail of what transpired,' said Lara.

'I already told you. I had a few drinks with Mickey and Vincent and Constable Rosetti, and left.' Jimmy Tran clicked his neck a couple of times.

'What time?'

'About 11.45 maybe.'

Lara checked the file. 'There's no CCTV showing you leaving at that, or any other time.' In fact there was none showing him going in either.

Jimmy shrugged.

'Is there another door you use to go in and out of the Birdcage?'

'Maybe the camera's on the blink?'

'Or maybe you went out over the roof. There's a door leads up there and any number of ways down to the street then.'

'That right?' said Jimmy, wheels turning behind the furrowed brow.

'And then you went and put a bottle in Samuel Ho's face?'

'Who?'

'The guy you had the push and shove with earlier. It's on CCTV.'

'Does he say it was me?'

'Yes.' Lara had called the battle-scarred accountancy student out from his summer job to look at some photos of Jimmy, Vincent, and Mickey. Ho had picked Jimmy.

'Mistaken identity. I'm sure once he's had time to reflect.'

And time for a visit from some of Tran's comrades.

DS Graham fidgeted impatiently; the issue of glassing an innocent bystander clearly wasn't his main game. 'When and how did you find out Santo Rosetti was a police officer?'

Tran gave him a sly grin. 'A little bird told me. Can't remember who, or when.'

'How did you feel when you learned about Rosetti?' said Lara.

'Somewhat surprised to tell the truth,' said Jimmy, mimicking her private school accent. 'I felt badly let down not to have been admitted into his confidence.' His eyes danced. 'I thought I knew all his secrets.'

'Betrayed? Angry?'

'Why? His career choice is up to him. I'm the last to judge.'

'We hear otherwise,' said Lara.

'Yeah? Who from?'

'Where did you dispose of the knife, Jimmy?' said DS Graham.

'What knife? Are you accusing me of something?'

Graham slid a printout of the mobile photo of Tran and Santo across the table. 'You heard Rosetti was an undercover police officer, he had been working for you as a courier and dealer, you believed your operations to be under threat, you went to the Birdcage with the express intent of killing him.'

'I don't know what you're talking about, Detective. I'd like to go home now.' Jimmy and his lawyer rose to leave.

Lara stood too. 'James Tran, I am arresting you for the assault of Samuel Ho, and on suspicion of the murder of Santo Rosetti.'

Damien the Lawyer shook his head. 'I hope you have evidence to back these charges, Detective, or I'm going to be kicking up quite a fuss.'

'We wouldn't be doing this if we didn't, would we?' said Lara.

DI Hutchens should have been pleased at the news from the Rosetti camp but Cato detected more than a hint of concern as his boss scowled out across the open-plan office. DS Meldrum, ostensibly the Rosetti senior case officer, wore an expression of bewildered triumph. Cato was reminded of the Winter Olympics a few years ago when the Aussie speed skater won gold because everybody in front of him fell over.

Lara and Colin looked fired up. Now they had Jimmy Tran formally arrested and locked up for a few more days, they would have to work fast to build the case for a murder charge. Witness statements, forensics, CCTV, motive, method, and opportunity would all be viewed through the lens of 'Jimmy Tran dunnit'. Knowing Lara's track record for manufacturing evidence, Cato didn't fancy Jimmy's chances and he could understand Hutchens' worried frown.

It was midafternoon and Cato still had about two more hours of dodging any task that might come between him, Jake, and Fremantle Cracker Night. He logged on and acted like he was doing something important. Hutchens' shadow fell across his desk.

'Busy?'

Cato held up a hand while he concentrated on his computer screen. 'Just digesting some fascinating statistics that I need to present to the Safer Streets Task Force on Friday. Did you know somebody in WA gets assaulted every six minutes?'

'And he's getting sick of it, right?' Hutchens was out of sorts. 'Your old mate Colin. What's he up to?'

'Up to?'

'Getting cosy with Lara. Hanging around like he owns the place. Being smug.'

'Didn't you invite him in?'

'After a fashion.'

'What's that mean?'

'I accepted Gangs' strong advice that I should ask for a loan of somebody. He volunteered.'

'Very commendable,' said Cato. 'He's experienced, knows the territory, should be an asset.'

'I wanted a yes man, not a conniving tosspot.'

'Bit early to write him off?'

'Never too early to take a dislike to somebody.'

'He gets results.'

'Yeah? So how come those gangsters keep turning up on *The West* social pages with a glass of Moet and a WAG in a posh frock? How come they're not eating gruel in chokey?'

'I doubt that's down to him.'

'Probably not but I still don't like the prick.'

'Well you could always send him packing and give me some proper work to do instead of this ... stuff.'

Hutchens smiled grimly. 'Teamwork, Cato, that's the thing.'

Cato copied and pasted another statistical tract and clicked the print button. 'Did you know that as many as two out of three burglaries and bag-snatchings in the Fremantle area in the last six months are attributable to that gang of street kids that hang out at the car park in Cantonment?'

'That's the spirit, Cato. Round 'em up, beat the crap out of them and shoot the ringleaders. It'll look good at the next committee meeting. Big tick from the Premier.'

'Love to, but it'll have to wait until tomorrow.' Cato made a show of checking the time. 'Cracker Night with my son. Non-negotiable.'

'How was your kebab?' said Cato.

Jake shrugged and nodded and took a swig of Coke. They were sitting in the window of Ali Baba's on South Terrace: the light fading and the crowds building. Jake seemed to find everything mildly interesting, except his dad. Year 6 and the boy was already tall, inherited both from Cato and Jane, and his face wore an aloof, self-contained expression. They disposed of their wrappers and crossed the road down Essex Street towards Esplanade Park, following the throng. The park, as expected, was chockers with families, rugs, picnic chairs, Aussie flags, glow-sticks, kids running amok. Cato found a space under a Norfolk pine, unpacked two camp chairs from their sausage bags, and parked himself. Half an hour to blast off, he wondered how this spot was still free so late in the day. He felt a splatter on his ear and shoulder and realised why. Above them a pink and grey galah shook its tail and resettled. Jake was smiling, at last.

'Bird shit is meant to be good luck,' said Cato wiping himself down.

'Looks like you'll be having lots of it,' said Jake.

'So how's the piano going?'

'Gave it up, it's boring.'

Cato held onto his open, non-confrontational face. 'Really? When? Mum never mentioned it.'

'Why should she?'

'No reason,' said Cato airily. 'Taking up anything else?'

'Electric guitar. Simon's in a band, he's teaching me some cool stuff.'

Simon. Jane's new boyfriend. 'That's great,' said Cato.

'He's got a Gibson.'

'Wow.'

Night had fallen. Anticipation crackled in the air. Wasamba moved through the crowd, drumming, whistling and generally adding to the racket. Seagulls squawked and Aussies Oi, Oi, Oied. Jake, in spite of his pre-teen coolness, allowed his elbow to touch Cato's. They sat in companionable silence and took it all in. The radio-host MC announced that it was just two minutes to Cracker Night ignition.

There was movement a few metres to the right, pushing and shoving and raised voices. Cato could see a gang of youths in Bintang singlets and one with an Aussie flag on his T-shirt and the words 'Born and Bred'. They'd formed a circle: somebody in the middle of them, the target of their aggression. Cato heard the words 'Fuck off, we're full'. Not now, not near me, thought Cato. He knew there were security guards and uniformed police doing their rounds, they could deal with it.

The commotion built and suddenly a yell.

'He's got a knife!'

A figure raced past.

'Jake, stay here and don't move. I'll be back.'

Cato turned to his picnic neighbours, a couple with a toddler, and asked them to keep an eye on Jake. Then he gave chase.

Even in the dimness and the chaos he could have sworn that it was the same African bloke he'd encountered at X-Wray Cafe on Sunday. If so, then the Aussie Born and Bred gang had picked on the wrong man. He was heading towards Marine Terrace and the Esplanade Hotel and from there he could disappear into the warren of Fremantle back streets. He was about twenty metres ahead of Cato and the gap was widening. Cato cursed the crowds, the dark, and his lack of recent exercise. The playground loomed, parents still pushing their kids on the swings in the half-light. The fireworks countdown had started, everybody in unison – ten, nine, eight ... Cato dodged the swinging kids and narrowly avoided a pram. Seven, six, five ... Up ahead the African lunged at someone who'd tried to grab him and lost precious seconds. Three, two, one ... the world exploded.

The crowd oohed and aahed and looked skywards. Cato followed his man across Marine Terrace into the West End, colours bursting above. The buildings were grand and ornate, mainly three-storey, dating back to the early days of the prospering port, and now mostly occupied by Notre Dame University. Here and there an opening into a backyard, an alley blocked by a barred gate, a burst of light from a secured keycard entry into luxury apartments. Cato was aware he was running out of puff, worried about leaving Jake on his own, and now he'd lost sight of his target. He stopped and tried to listen.

There it was, a scrape and the sound of laboured breathing. Not his own.

The sky popped and cascaded in orange and green. Three hundred metres away he could hear the hubbub of music and a large crowd enjoying itself on the Esplanade. Here there was the beginnings of a breeze, muffled rattlings, and two men gasping for air. The street was deserted, cars filled every available space either side, an empty can rolled along the gutter. Cato found himself at the opening to a small courtyard leading to a row of mews-style cottages. Old stone, plenty of greenery, and too many doors to choose from.

'Another minute or so and this place will be crawling with police.'

Nothing. Even the breathing had stopped.

'You stabbed one of our colleagues the other day. I don't fancy your chances when we haul you out of there.'

A massive white globe burst and fizzed overhead followed by the boom. Cracker night was heading for its climax.

'Let me take you in. Keep it simple, keep it easy. Nobody gets hurt.'

Cato didn't believe it himself. Even if they got as far as the lock-up without any trouble, Cato knew that once he signed off and left, the tasers and the batons would come out and it would be party time.

A rustle amongst the foliage and there he was. Slightly shorter than Cato remembered: incredibly thin and his skin shiny with perspiration, reflecting the colours of the night as it flashed and exploded all around them. He stood, Reebok'd feet slightly apart, face expressionless, a knife in his right hand. He had already noted that Cato was unarmed and he stepped forward casually. Cato felt the knife slide into him, dimly aware of how stupidly easy and quick it had been. No drawn-out danse macabre, no ducking and weaving. Just a swift and casual delivery of death.

Both men had their hands locked on the knife handle: one to push it in deeper, the other trying to prevent it. Warm liquid splashed on his fingers and Cato knew it was his own blood. He smelled the breath of his assailant and noticed the flash of his teeth.

'Do not struggle, my friend. Accept it.' A soft voice, almost apologetic.

The knife was tearing upwards and twisting. Cato headbutted his attacker: hearing the crunch of gristle and, beyond that, the sound of approaching steps and voices. Cato shed a tear for his abandoned son and slipped to the ground as the last of the rockets shattered the sky and the blasts faded to silence.

11

Wednesday, January 27th.

Lara Sumich was on her early morning run when she saw the crime-scene tape a block away from her home. A grog-fuelled Australia Day bashing, no doubt. She kept her head down, hoping not to be recognised by the duty crew, and kept on running.

She followed her usual route along the bike path past the multi-storey boat parks and repair yards, the sailing club, and down to the old Coogee power station. The tall waterfront apartment blocks at South Beach cast a welcome shadow over the running track. The ocean was once again blue and flat, the surface showing faint ripple traces of a strengthening easterly. A pod of dolphins broke through about a hundred metres out and two horses and their riders cooled in the shallows after a beach canter. A dog chased a tennis ball into the water. Another perfect day. So why was it she felt like punching somebody?

She was no nearer to finding out what was really behind Santo Rosetti's undercover job yet here she was on the verge of wrapping up his murder and putting away Jimmy Tran, a major player in the local drug scene: a value-added scalp, all courtesy of DS Colin Graham. Her blood pounded at the memory of him from last night as the fireworks flared outside her window and he buried himself inside her. She knew he was manipulating her in some way, leading her along, but she still didn't know why. In the meantime, she could handle him and she could think of worse ways of being used. So why the urge to punch somebody?

Whatever it was that was boiling inside fuelled a sprint to the power station gates. They needed more to stitch up Jimmy Tran over the next few days: some forensics, a DNA match on the sperm found in Rosetti's mouth: blood, fibres, witnesses, et cetera. She looked forward to working closely with DS Colin Graham to find it all, as they surely would. Was he really her ticket into a specialist squad like Gangs? Maybe. Manipulation could be a two-way street. On the way back she sprinted the last hundred metres along the bike path to the Round House, the colony's first public building – a prison of course. Bending hands on knees to steady her breath, she noticed the crime-scene tape again and wandered across to check it out. That's when she heard the news about Cato.

By the end of the day they had a DNA match on the semen: it was indeed Jimmy Tran who had been Santo Rosetti's special friend. The obvious proximity of the blowjob had also put mutual traces of skin, fluids and fibres on both men. But there was no indication of any blood on any of Tran's clothing and, given the mess and arterial blood spray, there should have been. They'd recovered what seemed to be the same white T-shirt with black trim he'd been wearing that night and had tested all his other clothing, footwear and his washing machine filter. Nothing. No murder weapon either.

Mickey Nguyen, Jimmy's henchman who had provided them with the tip about the rooftop entrance to the club, had been put under intense pressure by DS Graham to go further and comprehensively dob in his boss. It wasn't working. Even the leverage of Mickey's incarcerated dad wasn't enough: maybe the consequences of transgressing would be too great for all of the family. Fair enough. Who wanted to end up on YouTube Tran-style? So, they could provide means, motive and opportunity with Jimmy Tran and they had some objective forensic backup, but a good lawyer could still show it all to be circumstantial and not beyond reasonable doubt.

'A Chupa Chup in a toilet cubicle does not a murderer make,' said DI Hutchens rather poetically and Lara nodded glumly.

'With his record it should be enough. The jury just needs to take one look at him.' Colin Graham leaned against the wall, relaxed, arms folded.

'Meaning?' said Hutchens.

'The tide is turning. People are sick of ethnic gangs terrorising society. They want us to put a stop to it.'

'Thinking of going into politics, Colin?'

'Not yet. Unfinished business.'

Hutchens shook his head. 'It might suit you to put all this down to ethnic gangs, mate, but the stats show that for every dickhead Tran there's ten drongo Smiths. And most of the scumbag Apaches are dinky-di. Has Gangs got lazy and racist, or is it just you?'

'Didn't quite figure you for a bleeding heart, sir.' A smile to disarm any charge of insubordination.

'Yeah? Well you're meeting all my expectations, Col.'

Graham held Hutchens' gaze. Lara pictured proud elks locking antlers on the high plains, or was it more like two feral old goats banging heads in the bush?

'Okay, charge him then,' said Hutchens, stalking back to his office. 'And make sure your name is all over the paperwork, DS Graham. Credit where credit's due.'

'What did you think you were doing?'

'What?'

Cato had lost track of time. Outside his hospital window it was dark. Early dark or late dark he couldn't tell, he kept falling asleep at odd times. The pain and the painkillers were fogging his senses. DI Hutchens had an end-of-day look about him so it must be evening. As to what day, that was anybody's guess.

'Tackling an armed man, alone and unarmed. Think you're Batman or something?'

'I recognised him from the stoush at the X-Wray. Couldn't resist.' Cato tried to find a more comfortable position. There wasn't one.

Hutchens held thumb and forefinger slightly apart. 'Missed your vital organs by that much, dickhead.'

Cato realised this was Hutchens' way of showing he cared. He didn't want things to get too emotional. 'What's happening with Wellard? Any developments?'

'Pressed the pause button. No urgency, Shellie's not jumping up and down about the package and Wellard isn't going anywhere.'

'Safer Streets?'

Hutchens waved in the direction of Cato's wound. 'You didn't need to go that far to get out of it. I've delegated it away until you're better.'

Silver linings. 'Who to?'

'The new boy, Thornton.'

A recent Eastern States blow-in whose ambition outweighed his intellect: a perfect fit for the task at hand. 'Is he up to the responsibility?'

'He's from Sydney. Got a degree.'

'True.'

Hutchens' Hawaii-5-0 mobile chirped to life. Smartphones might come and go but Hutchens' ring tone had remained a constant. Cato took a sip of water and wondered how Jake was dealing with his father's near-death experience.

'Fuck me,' said Hutchens, a half-smile curling his lips as he wrapped up the call.

'Good news?'

'Could be. That knife they found sticking in you. We've got fingerprints and a blood match.'

Cato winced. 'I could have probably figured out the blood part myself.'

'Not so fast, Cato-san, our knife man has been busy. It's also got traces of Santo Rosetti's blood and DNA on it. You'd think the killer would at least wash his knife properly between stabbings.'

Cato paled. 'But that means ...'

Hutchens nodded. 'Two things, mate: DS Colin Graham is fucked, and you better gets some tests done. Rosetti wasn't the most hygienic of chaps. Turns out he had hep C.'

12

Thursday, January 28th. Late morning.

'His name's Dieudonne,' said Hutchens, beaming.

'Dieudonne What?' said DS Graham, sulking.

'Just that. One word. Pronounced "Dee-ur-donnay", according to the lady at Freo Migrant Resource Centre. It means given by God, or God's gift, something like that. Very popular name in certain parts of Africa, she says.'

'Hmmm,' came the reply. Graham checked his watch like he had an urgent appointment elsewhere.

'Age nineteen, arrived as a refugee from the Congo about four years ago.' Lara was reading from the computer screen. Fingerprints on the knife, and Dieudonne's blood on Cato's face after the headbutt had been matched and pinged in the system. He had previous records for low-level, gang-related violence. 'Last known address Mirrabooka but our colleagues north of the river reckon he hasn't been there in at least six months.'

'Child soldier apparently,' said Hutchens. 'No family, all slaughtered in the jungle somewhere. Save the Children saved him and now he's ours.'

'Thanks a bunch,' said Colin.

Lara scrolled her screen. 'According to his juvey report, the social worker reckons he's bright as. Missed out on his schooling back home, so since he got here he's been making up for lost time. Until late last year he was studying WACE-level Literature and History at Tuart Community College.'

'Fucking hell, a poet warrior,' said Hutchens. 'Is this a dagger I see before me?'

'He could have found the knife after Jimmy Tran finished killing Santo with it.' Colin Graham said.

'Good thinking, Col, we shouldn't jump to any hasty conclusions should we?' Hutchens was enjoying himself. 'Either way, introduces a bit of reasonable doubt, do you reckon?'

Lara kept her eyes on the computer. 'Assaults, criminal damage, affray, possession of weapons, gang fights.' And slicing my arm open, she might have added. She would also need to get some blood tests done.

Graham was peering at the photo on the screen and nodding now. 'He looks familiar. The street gang he ran with was on our radar for a while last year. We'd heard they were thinking of stepping up to the big time.'

'And?' said Hutchens.

'Turned out to be bullshit: a Facebook rumour. They're wannabes but don't have the nous or the discipline.'

'So did your radar pick up anything about him, specifically?' said Lara.

'Nothing. A dumb thug like the rest of them.'

Hutchens tutted. 'Another one of your troublesome ethnics, Col. By the way, did you formally charge Jimmy Tran yet?'

'Last night.'

'Oops,' said Hutchens. 'Better go and untangle that little mess, eh? Don't need a lawsuit at this stage in your career.' A tap on the shoulder. 'Lara, could you put an alert out for God's gift please, love?'

The days passed into the weekend. Under orders from Hutchens, Jimmy Tran was released with a stern warning from DS Colin Graham.

'We're watching you.'

Tran twisted his lips. 'It's mutual, mate.'

Dieudonne had gone to ground. A number of young African men received some unwelcome attention from the police but none of them were him.

Cato's strength slowly returned. He was visited twice by Jane and Jake: the former harbouring a grudge about him abandoning their son to give chase, the latter eager for details on what had happened.

'Why didn't you just shoot him?' said Jake.

'Forgot my gun.'

By Sunday the hospital was ready to send Cato home with some industrial-strength painkillers, spare dressings and instructions on how to change them, and strict orders to rest for the coming week. Fine by him, he'd been going stir-crazy: he'd read every page of every available newspaper or magazine and completed all the crosswords and other brainteasers. He was even getting the hang of Sudoku, his father's metier, and gaining an understanding of what the old man had meant by the patient elimination of the impossible. Cato looked out of his fifth floor window at the port city spread below him: the sandstone buildings, the Norfolk pines, the ocean beyond. Sunday, the town would be throbbing with tourists: most blissfully ignorant of any bloody undercurrents as they strolled in the sunshine. According to that morning's *Sunday Times*, a random traffic stop in Rivervale had netted just over half a kilo of ice, and a couple in Willagee had been hospitalised after a violent home invasion related to a drug debt. Oh, and there'd been another weekend party riot.

At least the hospital was air-conditioned. The heatwave was still in full swing and breaking all sorts of records. Maybe he should have gone home to his sister's place but she had their father living with them now along with his Parkinson's disease. One cranky invalid was enough.

It was early afternoon by the time the hospital paperwork was completed and the taxi dropped Cato home. The heat and the pain from his wound made him dizzy. He took an age getting out of the cab and the driver tutted and wanted to take him straight back to the hospital. Inside the house it was cooler, just. Next door, Madge barked and Cato recalled something useful he'd read during his idle hours on the ward. He chucked five days worth of junk mail onto the kitchen table, shuffled through to the bedroom and passed out.

Madge barked. It was night, a full moon visible through the open curtains. Cato reached for his mobile and inhaled sharply as the movement reminded him of the stab wound. According to his phone, it was just after nine and he'd missed two calls from numbers he didn't recognise.

Madge barked again. There was a scraping noise down the side path outside the bedroom window. Somebody had just gone through the gate.

Madge growled. The lights were off in Cato's house, yet someone had seen that as an invitation to venture further onto his property. The footsteps were moving again, heading towards his backyard. The grapevine spanning the fence between the two properties rustled. Cato pictured the route from his bed through the kitchen to the laundry door that led out back. He tried to picture weapons along the way. His gun was in a locker at work. He didn't keep any personal spares at home like some of his colleagues did. Kitchen knives? His stomach clenched at the thought. A cricket or baseball bat? No joy, Jake was into soccer and basketball. And as for tools, they were outside in the shed.

A footscrape on the back path leading to the laundry door. Cato still hadn't moved from the bed. His pulse raced, his mouth was dry. He realised he was afraid. A rattle: the flywire on the laundry door. A creak: they were trying the handle. He couldn't remember if he'd bolted it when he left the house all those days ago: he often forgot.

A step on the tiles inside the laundry: no, he hadn't bolted it.

A click and a shaft of light in the hallway. More confident footsteps now, illuminated, purposeful. Cato lay paralysed on the bed: breath shuddering. A shadow fanned across his bedroom door.

'Who is it, who's there?' His voice came out at too high a pitch; the faltering tone of somebody who has already lost.

'Philip?'

And there now in the doorway stood Shellie Petkovic.

'You're bleeding,' she said.

'Why didn't you knock?'

Cato popped a couple of painkillers while Shellie Petkovic finished changing his dressing.

'I did but nobody answered. The neighbour said you were home. I thought you might not be able to get up. Thought you might need help.'

'Fair enough but it's kind of late, Shellie.' Stabbing pains aside, the feel of her fingertips on his skin was not unpleasant. 'What are you doing here?' he asked.

'Tending to you.' She scrunched up the dressing wrappers and placed them on the bedside table.

'How did you know where I live?'

'You're famous. You were in the community newspaper – "Freo Hero Cop Stabbed".' Shellie placed her small warm hand over his. 'There were a couple of old dears in the IGA talking about you, Noelle and Norma, they were very proud because you live in their street. I accompanied them home, helped them with their shopping bags, and we got talking. I asked them to point your place out.'

'You'd either make a great cop or a very scary stalker.' Cato's smile slipped away. 'So why are you really here?'

Her eyes dropped. 'I got another package. It came on Friday in the mail. I wanted to show you.' She dug around in her canvas shoulder bag and produced an A5 jiffy bag. She emptied the contents onto the bed, a folded sheet of paper and a black plastic bangle with a silver star pattern. 'Bree's,' she said.

The paper had two words written in block capitals: *LOSERS WEEPERS*.

'How would someone else have access to her possessions? You really can't think who this might be?'

'Gordon's behind it, he has to be.' Her eyes brimmed. 'It's got to stop.'

'Why didn't you take it to the police station?' said Cato.

'I don't trust anyone there anymore.' Her eyes crept back to his. 'Only you.'

This was getting weird. 'It couldn't wait until daylight?'

'Sorry. I just needed to talk to someone.' A sigh and a trembling lower lip. 'I've been climbing the walls.' Shellie was absent-mindedly stroking his stomach even though the dressing was already stuck down. It wasn't easy to concentrate.

The envelope was postmarked Perth, three days ago. It could be tested for the usual traces. 'You definitely have no idea who's doing this?'

'No.'

'The timing is interesting.'

'What do you mean?' Her voice had risen, a defensive edge, the stomach-stroking had stopped. Pity.

'Nobody's been paying any attention to Wellard for over a week now.'

'And?'

The stomach-stroking resumed and his concentration evaporated. 'I don't know, he likes the limelight, doesn't he?'

At that point Shellie leaned over and kissed him on the mouth.

13

Monday, February 1st. Midmorning.

Lara Sumich had reviewed the nightclub CCTV footage and the mobile phones confiscated from the patrons and could still find no trace of the African, Dieudonne. Did he kill Santo Rosetti or had he just picked up the murder weapon after it was discarded and used it on Cato? She remained convinced that Jimmy Tran was still their man and that this was a red herring. DI Hutchens' insistence on releasing Tran could be a recognition of the weakness of their case, or maybe just a way of protecting his turf and striking back at Colin Graham. But surely even Hutchens wouldn't let a murderer go free just to score a point?

Graham sat a few desks away, leaning back, right foot resting on left knee, talking quietly into his mobile. His head and shoulders were silhouetted in the glare from the window: a blurry shadow and a low insistent voice. He seemed like a stranger today. He'd spent the weekend playing Floreat family man so she hadn't seen him since Friday.

He ended his call. 'How was your weekend?'

'Good,' she said. 'Yours?'

'Good.'

She tapped the disks in front of her. 'No sign of Dieudonne at the club.'

Graham strolled over and sat on the edge of her desk. She caught his smell of soap and deodorant.

'Jimmy's our man. We need to focus on him. The African is a sideshow and I don't know why the DI's got such a hard-on for him.'

'Don't you?'

'No. Jimmy has form, he had means, motive and opportunity, and it was his semen in Santo's mouth. Good enough for a jury under most circumstances.'

'But Dieudonne's the one linked to the murder weapon.'

'He's a street thug, no way could he pull this off. He'll have found the knife in a gutter and claimed it. Look, the Trans have been doing bad things for too long with nobody laying a finger on them. They kill, they maim, they extort, they sell drugs to our children. I've come close before but they always skate. I'm not going to let that happen this time.'

Lara had received an email that morning from Samuel Ho's family lawyer. Her client now believed he may have been mistaken in his identification of Jimmy Tran as the man who twisted a bottle in his face. Ho wished to drop the matter and get on with his life. No witnesses, Jimmy Tran walks again. Lara could see Graham's point.

'And proving the DI wrong would just be a bonus?' she said.

'Got it in one.'

'So what next?'

'Let's go and find some proof to lock Jimmy up with.'

'Starting with?'

He mimicked DI Hutchens' low rumble. 'Facts and evidence, Lara, facts and evidence.'

When Cato woke, Shellie was gone. Had he dreamed it all? The kiss seemed real enough. He hadn't recoiled or protested that it was wrong; though he knew it was. He had received her mouth, hungrily. Only then, after the fact, did he remember to do the right thing.

'I can't do this, Shellie. Much as I might want to.'

Her eyes searching his face, 'What?'

He held her gently away from him. 'This.'

'Why not?'

Cato knew that what he was about to say sounded silly, wooden, old-fashioned even. 'Regulations. You're a victim of crime and I'm a cop.'

She looked puzzled. 'You gay or something?'

'No, but I have had a bad week.' The attempt at levity didn't translate. Cato saw the hurt and rejection in her eyes. 'The way we've got to know each other, it's not normal. If it wasn't for Bree and Wellard we wouldn't be here. This – us – it isn't real.'

Shellie nodded and rose to leave. He'd tried to think of something good and meaningful to say. 'Sorry.'

'Yeah.' Shellie closed the door behind her.

Why had Shellie brought the second package to him and not taken it directly to the police station? Was it really about who she could and couldn't trust? Cato recalled the night before, her hands on his stomach, the kiss. He'd led a lonely monastic life the past year or so and the attention was flattering for all that it was wrong. There was a pang of sadness and regret; he still wasn't sure whether doing the right thing was really the right thing to do.

Cato rolled out of bed and headed for the bathroom. He stood naked before the mirror, a patch of white gauze just above and to the left of his pubis. He had at least a week before there was even the thought of returning to work and that would be dependent on a medical check-up on Friday. It was time he could use to recuperate, to straighten out his thoughts. Without Hutchens looking over his shoulder, Cato could investigate the matter that seemed to have troubled his boss and triggered the diversion off to bullshit tasks like Safer Streets: the backstory on Wellard. And if unlocking some of Wellard's and Hutchens' past brought him a step closer to finding Shellie's daughter then that had to be a good thing. Cato would certainly feel better anyway. He stepped under the shower, keeping it cold and at half power.

Lara watched Colin Graham do what he did best: well, second best. They were doing the rounds of the cafes, bars, and pool halls of Northbridge: shaking hands, shooting the breeze, whispering in ears, slapping shoulders. She could picture him at the top end of town, working a room and doing the big deals. He was a natural, everybody's friend. Lara felt a twinge of jealousy: she knew that she would never be able to do exactly what he did, that male cop–crook brotherhood thing. She was the wrong class and the wrong sex. And he could turn his performance on and off like a tap.

The Trans might have based themselves in Baldivis but they were a statewide enterprise with national and international connections. For all that, Northbridge remained a favourite haunt of many of their 'franchisees'.

Graham caught her eye. 'Got another whisper on Jimmy Tran. Let's go.' He took her elbow and guided her to the door.

She shook him free, surprised by her own ferocity. 'Where?'

'Fancy Greek for lunch?'

Zorba's was Greek on a stick: the Parthenon painted on the walls along with lots of blue sky, sea, and little white churches. Plate-smashing music piped out of the ceiling. A Greek *yia yia* ran the till and an old man in a fishing sweater and cap stood around waiting for somebody to hand him an octopus to slap. Lara and Colin took their table and ordered metzes and souvlaki. Colin checked his watch as the doorbell chimed.

'Right on time,' he grinned.

A Vietnamese youth in his late teens, swathed in Adidas gear, marched up to the till and started issuing orders to the Greek nanna. Whatever she was thinking, she kept her face neutral as she handed him an envelope. By the look on the old man's face, he was ready to start the slapping now – octopus or no. The youth stood directly in front of him and stared him out. The old man was meant to fold but he didn't. The boy had had enough fun; he left with his envelope and a smirk.

'Jimmy Tran's mob runs a Greek restaurant?' said Lara.

'Let's say he's a silent partner.' Graham lifted his chin towards the old man and invited him over for a retsina. He joined them, still glowering. 'Christos, how's business?' said Graham.

'Shit.'

Graham looked around the room, three-quarters full. 'Not bad for a weekday lunch, though.'

Christos thumbed over his shoulder. 'That greedy little prick just took thirty percent.'

Graham shook his head in sympathy. 'You should report him, mate, get them off your back.'

'Sure and this place gets burned down, my wife, my children, my grandchildren get threatened, I get a knife in the gut. You lot going to help me then? Too late.' He cleared his throat in disgust, looking for a non-existent spittoon.

Graham took a sip of retsina and grimaced. 'How do you lot drink this stuff? Fucking Pine O Cleen.' Christos didn't bite. 'I think I can see a way out of your problem, mate.'

The old man took his cap off and slapped it on the table. 'I'm listening.'

Cato had retreated to the lounge room, the coolest in the house, and was surfing the internet reports on the arrest and trial of Gordon Francis Wellard for the murder of his de facto, Caroline Penny. She was fifteen years younger than him. The photos showed a youthful blonde with a happy, pretty face. Caroline was a Welsh backpacker who'd stayed on and fallen in love with Perth and, it seemed, Gordon Wellard.

Wellard had met Caroline Penny approximately fourteen months after Shellie's daughter was reported missing. As with his relationship with Shellie, here too there had been a number of domestic violence callouts but no charges were ever pursued. Wellard had a patchy work history and was known to use mull and crystal meth, probably paid for by Caroline's wages from the local TAB. At some point Caroline's mother, who lived in Aberystwyth, had raised the alarm about lack of contact from her daughter. Wellard had taken to answering Caroline's mobile and either denying all knowledge of her whereabouts or making cryptic teasing references to her fate. Wellard really was a twisted piece of work, thought Cato. He stood and tried to stretch the kinks out of his back but his stitches complained loudly.

Caroline Penny was found in a grave in Star Swamp just north of Scarborough. She'd been beaten to death. Gordon Wellard was picked up at a caravan park in Dongara a few hundred kilometres up the coast. At trial he denied everything but he'd left his DNA all over the body, stomp marks matched his boots and a ring imprint on her cheek matched the one on his right pinkie. Forensic awareness clearly hadn't been his strong point back then. Wellard had been led away from the dock with the victim's mother screaming, 'Good riddance to bad rubbish.' Quite.

Cato needed to be online at the cop shop to dig deeper but he was officially on sick leave. Any attempts to access such information by remote or by proxy would trigger alarms in the system and maybe some probing questions from DI Hutchens. Through the window Cato could see the kalamata tree moving in the breeze. He popped some painkillers and went round the house opening windows and doors to let the Doctor sweep through. His mobile sounded, he checked the screen; the number was vaguely familiar.

'That you, Kwong?'

It took a moment to place the voice. 'Karina?'

'Did you set those animals on us?'

Karina Ford's Willagee home hadn't been particularly inviting last time Cato visited. Now it was utterly trashed with crime-scene tape still fluttering on the perimeter. The security door hung on one hinge, the wire mesh buckled and split. The flat screen TV that once graced her lounge with adventures in Springer-land lay smashed on the floor. There was glass everywhere. And splashes of blood. Cato found a seat and lowered himself into it with a grimace. He'd taken a taxi, not yet ready to drive or even move, but Karina's pleas couldn't be ignored. It was hers and Shellie's that had been the missed calls on his mobile over the weekend.

'You left me your card, you gonna help us or what?'

'The police who attended, what did they say?'

'Two smart-arses from Murdoch. Pommie blow-ins. Looked at me like I was the shit on their shoes. They said they'd get back to me. Keep me informed.'

'So what happened?'

'Friday night. I was out at a mate's, getting pissed. Crystal and Tyson were home with little Brandon.' The teenage parents and the toddler. Cato measured his breathing as a spasm passed through his gut. 'What's up with you?' she said.

'Been stabbed.'

'Sorry to hear it. Appreciate you coming out, mate.' It seemed genuine. Cato nodded for her to go on. 'I got the story from Tyson before they took him away. Three big blokes with balaclavas, baseball bats and hammers. They took to Tyson first. Smashed his hands, ankles and knees. Busted his teeth. He doesn't talk real good at the best of times.'

The throwaway story in yesterday's paper: a couple assaulted in a home invasion. 'The report mentioned a drug debt?'

Karina dragged on her ciggie. 'Tyson's a dealer and a dickhead but he's not suicidal. He should know better than to owe money to those bastards.'

'Which bastards? Do you know who he was working for?'

'Some pricks up in Northbridge. If they'd left it at just him I probably would have thanked them. Never liked the little tosser anyway.' Her face crumpled and her eyes filled. 'They started on Crystal next. Hitting her on her pregnant belly over and over and making him watch.'

'Christ.' Then Cato remembered the toddler in the stroller. 'Brandon, is he ...?'

She nodded down the hall. 'Asleep. They didn't touch him but he saw it all.'

'Did the attackers say anything, talk to each other?'

'Dunno, I wasn't there was I? Tyson's jaw's strapped up now but he never mentioned anything to me. Crystal's in intensive. They reckon she might lose the baby.' Karina stubbed the cigarette out and fumbled in her packet for a replacement. 'Cryssie loves being a mum; she's trying to do the right thing. It's just that dickhead bloke of hers.'

Cato looked around the desolated room. 'Where are you staying?'

'Here. The mates I had faded away when they heard about this. Don't want any of this shit round their doors as well. Who would?'

Cato summoned a taxi on his mobile. It was late afternoon and still hot, the street was empty. Karina escorted him to the door.

'We don't deserve this you know. Just because we live in state housing doesn't mean we don't have the right to feel safe. Those Murdoch pommie cops aren't gonna do anything are they?'

The taxi pulled up, the driver peering warily at the smashed house, the limping Chinaman, and the hard-faced woman sucking on her cigarette.

'I'll look into it,' said Cato.

'Yeah, thanks.'

As the sun sank into the Indian Ocean, Lara Sumich sat on her balcony eating a tuna salad and swigging a stubby of Rogers. Down below, a mob of teenagers screeched and jostled in the Round House car park. A bottle smashed, followed by whoops and laughter. She thought about the student Samuel Ho, scarred for life and scared to seek redress. Lara went back inside, closed the French windows and flicked on the air conditioning. Colin Graham was playing family man again tonight but that was fine, she didn't need him. The little plot he had concocted over lunch at Zorba's may or may not work but it would almost certainly put the old man and his brood in harm's way. She'd pointed this out to Graham on the drive back to Fremantle but he'd just smiled and reminded her that you can't make an omelette without cracking a few eggs.

Madge the Jack Russell stopped howling at the moon when she heard the sounds of things dropping into her backyard. Bite-sized things. Things that smelled good. Worth eating. She ate one, then another, then one more.

14

Tuesday, February 2nd.

Cato was woken by a furious knocking. He started to roll out of bed in his usual way but was brought up short by the strain on his stitches. He moved gingerly, dressing slowly, as the knocking persisted.

'You've poisoned her, you sick bastard.'

It was Felix, his face red with tears. Behind him: a stern young woman wearing a RSPCA shirt. Behind her were two uniform constables from Freo cop shop. Noelle and Norma, the octogenarian matriarchs of the street, hovered close by: hearing aids locked on target.

Cato ran his hand through his hair. 'What seems to be the problem?'

'As if you don't know,' hissed Felix.

Cato looked back at the uniforms to see if they could shed light on the matter. They shrugged, the younger one stifling a grin.

The RSPCA woman spoke up. 'This gentleman's pet dog became violently ill overnight. We have reason to believe it was deliberately poisoned and we understand that you have a history with the dog. Sir.' The last part spat out like an unsavoury meatball. 'We will be conducting tests and may need to speak to you again. I must warn you that we always prosecute in matters such as these. Sir.'

'Is the dog dead?' asked Cato, trying to keep the hope out of his voice.

'No. No thanks to you,' snarled Felix.

He left, along with the RSPCA woman. Noelle and Norma gave Cato a disappointed look and shuffled away. The uniforms remained.

'You'd better come in,' Cato said.

They did.

'God's gift? You found him yet?'

'Not yet, no.' Lara gave DI Hutchens a convincing look of grim determination. She'd been checking her emails: mainly circular drivel including a week-old one from Cato with an attachment of ten pages of local crime stats. She'd scanned it, recognising a name in one of Cato's priority action recommendations. She knew his game, swamp them all with guff, and piss Hutchens off – she'd have done the same in his shoes. Delete.

'You need to get out there and use a bit of shoe-leather, Lara. It's not as if Freo's crawling with mad, homicidal African ex-child soldiers.'

'We're on the case, boss.'

Hutchens must have heard the edge in her voice. 'DS Graham isn't still wasting your time on Jimmy Tran, is he?'

'We're exploring all options. Keeping an open mind.'

'Don't.' He disappeared into his office.

Lara tapped her way into the network to check overnight incident logs for any traces of Dieudonne. It was already after nine: Colin Graham was late in today. The reports showed the usual: drunks, domestics, car theft, a suspected poisoning of a family pet, a king-hit outside a pub in Freo, vandalism. A meth lab explosion in Munster. She spotted something and smiled: could it be that simple?

A burglar interrupted in White Gum Valley. Description, twenty-ish, slightly built and dark-skinned. The attending officer asks: Aboriginal? No, blacker than that, the old man says. African for sure, he knew the difference. The bugger had waved a funny toy laser gun at him but the pensioner hadn't been fooled. He'd summoned his wife from the kitchen to call the cops. The would-be burglar must have decided two pensioners was more grief than he needed and took off. Was the burglar in a car? No, on foot.

Lara double-checked the existing records for Dieudonne. No, he didn't seem to have a driver's licence. That didn't mean much when most weeks they were picking up twelve year old kids for grand theft auto. But maybe in this case it was simple and it was true, Dieudonne didn't drive and he'd just been spotted in White Gum Valley. The clincher was the 'funny toy laser gun': odds-on it was her missing taser. Why didn't he use it? Maybe there was a conscience in there somewhere: old people were one step beyond. Lara brought up a map of Fremantle and surrounding suburbs on her screen. So how does being on foot or public transport affect Dieudonne's rampage through society? Cato's Safer Streets email had just given her an idea. She grabbed her car keys and headed out the door.

Cato could see that his visitors wanted to believe him. He was one of their own after all, and a bloody hero at that. A stabbed bloody hero. He played it up, sitting forward in the chair, wincing. The gist of it was that Madge had been found slumped against the back fence, twitching, whining, with smelly liquid at either end of her. As far as Felix was concerned, Cato was prime suspect so his was the first door they'd knocked on.

'I'm not going to deny the dog pisses me off with the bloody yapping,' Cato said. 'But it's a much longer stretch to trying to poison it. More than my job's worth.' He opened his arms in supplication. 'Feel free to search the place for incriminating evidence.'

The younger uniform ummed sympathetically. 'No need for that, mate.' But the older, quieter colleague lifted his hand and they exchanged a glance. 'Well, maybe a quick once-over might be good, if you don't mind.'

'Be my guest.' Cato nodded and made a mental note of the name and number of the older transgressor. He hadn't come across him yet; maybe he was new to Freo cop shop. They checked the cupboards and fridge but they were pretty much bare. 'No meatballs there,' said Cato.

'Who mentioned meatballs?' said the quieter more dangerous one.

Cato ignored the comment and reminded them that he hadn't had the time or inclination to shop since his stint in hospital. 'Eggs, sour milk, tomatoes with black spots: more chance of poisoning myself,' he joked, closing the fridge door. They smiled on cue. Cato made a show of limping in bravely suppressed pain as he continued the tour. He waved them out to the backyard. 'Help yourselves to the shed. You'll probably find some snail pellets there but I've heard they're not so reliable.'

'Maybe that's why poor little Madgie survived,' said danger man.

Their rummage of the shed produced no smoking gun and they left with a promise to keep him informed of developments. It was midmorning and Cato hadn't even started on his TO DO list. He checked his reflection in the mirror, sniffed an armpit and decided he needed a shower. His mobile chirped. Hutchens.

'What you been up to, Cato?'

'Boss?'

'You're on the overnight log. Dog poisoning. I thought you were meant to be an invalid?'

'I am.'

'Was it you?'

'Course not.'

'Good. No time for silly buggers. When you due back?'

Cato put some stiff upper lip into his voice. 'Soon as possible, boss.'

'A week? Two?'

'Difficult to say.'

'You putting in a claim? Talked to the union yet?'

'Hadn't given it any thought.'

'Better had, could be worth a bob or two, mate.'

'Will do. Thanks.'

'Look after yourself. We'll see you when we see you.'

End of conversation. DI Hutchens coming over all attentive and caring? Cato looked at the screen: call duration, thirty-eight seconds.

It didn't take Lara long to find him. He was the only grown-up among a cluster of teens sitting in a cloud of cigarette smoke on the low brick wall of Wilson's Car Park in Cantonment Street. The Fagin of Fremantle – Lara's favourite snitch, now that Santo was dead. He was whispering in the ear of a greasy-haired girl who must have been all of thirteen.

'Got a moment?' said Lara.

He turned and gave her a cheesy – not a good look with so many teeth missing. 'Detective Sumich, how you going?' He sauntered over and bent his head to the car window.

Lara nodded back towards the teenager jealously scowling in their direction. 'Let me guess: you were just encouraging her to go back to school, complete her education and lead a good life.'

'Good as.' He climbed in, bringing with him his BO and the sour smell of something vaguely ammonic. 'Where are we going?'

'You'll see.' Lara pulled away from the kerb. Fagin, real name Jeremy Dixon, wound his window down a crack and pushed the seat back to accommodate his long, white, spotty legs. 'Boardies don't really suit you, mate,' said Lara.

'Yeah, right. Noted.'

'Did you know you and your little oompa-loompas are on our radar?'

'Why's that then?'

'Somebody's been looking at the local crime stats. You're an anomaly.'

'Yeah?' He seemed quite impressed with himself.

'You might want to pull your head in for a while.'

'Ta, for that.'

Lara headed along past the port, under the old traffic bridge, the river glistening on their left as the big white cabin cruisers glided downriver for a day at Rotto. She could see out of the corner of her eye Fagin wondering, waiting for an explanation. She didn't help him out. They passed the Swan Yacht Club: millions of dollars sitting idle on multi-storey boat racks. Then up to Preston Point Road, past the mansions overlooking the river and the hazy heat shimmer of Point Walter spit.

'Miss it, Jezza?'

'No.'

'So you don't get home much, to see the folks?'

'What do you want, Detective? Only, I've got a bit on today.'

'I know, I saw her. Thirteen? Fourteen? There's a law against that you know, Jez. Of course you do, Daddy being a judge and all.'

Fagin's eyelids fluttered and then suddenly there it was, the long-repressed western suburbs drawl. 'Is there a point to this?'

Lara opened the glove box and flicked the file photo onto his lap. 'Seen this guy anywhere?'

'Yeah, it's Tupac. Can I go now?'

'His name's Dieudonne. He hangs out somewhere on your patch: White Gum, Hilton, Hammy Hill maybe. Get your artful dodgers to keep their eyes out.'

'What's in it for me?'

'A nice warm feeling that you're doing something good for your community?'

'Lovely. Got it. What else?'

'A tip-off before the next raid.'

'Make it the next three.'

'Deal.'

They were back out on Canning Highway. Lara pulled into the car park at the Leopold Hotel and let him out. He leaned down into the passenger window and smiled wistfully, expensive orthodontics a distant memory.

'Why can't you just leave me alone, Lara? You've had your pound of flesh ten times over.'

'I remember you at primary school, Jez. Showing me your willy in the toilets. Telling me about your dad and what he was doing to you. I'll never forget that: even if you want to. She winked, a genuine connecting friendly one. 'La lotta continua, eh mate?'

Cato had intended to take a stroll along South Beach, to keep moving and try to speed up the recovery. It was less than a five-minute walk from his house but by the time he reached a bench overlooking the water he felt exhausted. He'd phoned Murdoch Detectives to try to find out more about Karina's home invasion. The attending officer was a Liverpudlian called Des who'd arrived during the Great Pommie Recruitment Drive of 2006. They were acquainted.

'Cato, mate, up and about already? Can't keep a good man down, eh.'

Pleasantries exchanged, Cato asked his questions and Des quickly lost interest.

'Did you look into the kid's supplier?'

'Mate, a skanky druggie bashing's not high on me list, you know? Too much paperwork and too little reward. Anyway I'm flyin' home next month. It's too hot here, too many flies, and you can only ever watch the football in the middle of the bastard night. I've had it.'

'Bon voyage,' said Cato.

It was early afternoon and only a handful remained outdoors. They were probably European backpackers, soaking the UV rays into their bare bodies as if melanomas were what other people got. A few were cooling off in the water, although, by the winces and arm rubbing, it was evident that the stingers were out in force. Oily black-brown blobs glistened at the shoreline, sea hares: he'd read about them in an old *Australian Geographic* at the hospital. A sun-hatted toddler bent down and prodded one with her plastic spade. Beached as.

Cato shielded his eyes against the glare and looked out to sea where a huge section of oil rig was being towed into port. After the hiccup of the global financial meltdown, the boom was back and it wasn't just about red dust this time. The dwindling, trouble-prone world energy supplies had sent shivers down the spines of the gas-guzzlers. Luckily it seemed that wherever you poked a stick in WA you were likely to strike oil or gas or both. Deliverance. Exploration licences were being handed out like Minties on Australia Day. Pristine world-heritage-listed coral reefs, ancient dinosaur trackways, Margaret River vineyards, prime farmlands. No sacred places or sacred cows anymore. The only areas you couldn't dig were the affluent western suburbs where the politicians and leaders of industry lived. Even that could turn out to be negotiable. Cato shifted in his seat. Gas. Would the country whose success once rode on the sheep's back base its future prosperity on the methane from a sheep's fart? So what if it meant sacrificing all that you loved to the gods of the bottom line? When something is there for the taking you'd be a fool to leave it for anyone else.

He fingered his knife wound tentatively. The boom in amoral

ultra-violence was harder to grasp. Too often now, petty slights concluded with some poor bastard in intensive care, or the morgue. Over-reaction had replaced walking away. Turn the other cheek and you were likely to have a stubby buried in it. But maybe it wasn't so hard to fathom after all: the role models were hyperventilating politicians and shock jocks, dummy-spitting mining magnates, tantie-chucking sports stars, and cops who surrounded an unarmed Aboriginal man and tasered him repeatedly to show who was boss. Everybody needed to take a deep breath and count to ten.

Cato looked up; the oil rig seemed to move so slowly. The boom might be over before it docked.

The afternoon dragged. Lara looked out through the windows of the detectives' office at the sun beating down on the heat-weary residents of Fremantle. She walked over to the water cooler and filled her glass. Where was Colin Graham and what was he up to? He'd sent her a text.

duty calls, gangs bzns, c u l8r

The operation with the old Greek was set for tonight. They were teeing up a meeting between Christos and Jimmy Tran. Christos was to be wired for sound. Lara still couldn't see any connection between an old man sick of paying protection money and the death of an undercover cop but this was being run primarily as a Gangs Op so it was out of her hands. Either way, they needed to make sure nothing went wrong or the old Greek would pay, dearly. Graham was off being enigmatic and Lara was twiddling her thumbs. The initial burst of energy and independence she'd felt during the morning had evaporated like a pool of spit in the midday sun.

She reviewed the Santo case again. His job was stirring the pot and gathering intelligence, according to Graham, but as for who Santo was reporting to and precisely what he was working on; that remained a mystery. She replayed her own dealings with Santo. The last time they'd met was just a week before she found him with his throat slit. They'd had a beer at The Orient down the West End. The bar was full of Notre Dame students and Lara had dressed as if she was one of them, instead of a cop. Santo looked like a low-life pusher so he also fitted in. No special occasion, just a catch-up to see if there was anything in the offing. After an unusually quiet few weeks over Christmas she was desperate for any intelligence, even from him.

'Got anything for me, Santo?'

A headshake and that thin reedy voice. 'Very quiet right now, Lara.'

'Nothing at all? It's the holiday season. Somebody's got to be getting some stock in somewhere?'

'They took their deliveries pre-Christmas. Those trucks I told you about that were coming in off the Nullarbor in November.'

'OC were already onto that, Santo, and they showed up empty.'

'Really?' A bemused frown.

'Really. Look, I just want a bit of low-level skinny on the locals to tide me over. Couple of runs on the board to keep my boss happy. Got a performance appraisal coming up soon.'

Santo had smiled at that one. 'Wish I could help you, Lara.'

'No January sales for the Australia Day barbies? No year tens looking to make a big impression in term one?'

'There's a kid up at the high school you could take a look at. Fancies his chances. He'll be year eleven by now, Pancho something or other.'

'Cutting in on your territory is he?'

'He just needs saving from himself, that's all: too young to be ruining his life.'

'That's it?'

'That's it.'

They clinked glasses. 'Cheers,' said Lara. Her last words to him.

Those trucks that came in empty off the Nullarbor. Did he suspect her of the tip-off? Had it been a plant in the first place to test her? Lara was aware of rumours of an undercover unit whose sole job was to weed out internal corruption. Maybe after Hopetoun she was on a watch list. Colin Graham would know what Santo had been up to. Whatever it was he wanted from her, it seemed she also needed him. Co-dependence, the essence of many a beautiful dysfunctional relationship.

15

Cato had made a few calls to some old colleagues, now retired. He was about to meet one of them in a Red Rooster out on South Street. It was the kind of place he was unlikely to see any of his current workmates; they favoured McDonald's. Cato stepped into the bright, air-conditioned fast-food netherworld. He nearly didn't recognise the old man sitting in a corner booth with a paper cup of cappuccino and a copy of *The West* open on the cryptics page.

'*Great Greek warrior longs to be sick inside.* Eight letters.' The voice was a low rasp, a rusty file on prison bars.

Cato bought a Fanta and sat down slowly as his knife wound adjusted to the new position. 'Keeping the Alzheimer's at bay, Andy?'

'I'm in better shape than you by the look of things.' Andy Crouch was already on the verge of retirement when Cato first joined DI Hutchens' detective squad a lifetime ago, long before Cato's disgrace and exile to Stock Squad. Crouch would be pushing seventy by now. He looked old: hair as white and thin as a bride's veil. 'Read about you in the paper, how's the gut?'

'Fair to middling,' said Cato. 'How's retirement?'

'I'm not a gardener, I hate exercise, and I can't stand the grandkids. Cryptics and the odd whisky are the only things left to live for.'

'Cheer up. You haven't got much longer. Death's just around the corner.'

He folded the paper. 'What can I do for you, young Philip?'

Crouch was the only one in the Job who called Cato that. His name. He was also the one who'd given him two bits of advice to live by. One, take up cryptic crosswords: all you need to know about detecting is there. Two, don't let Hutchens own your soul.

'DI Hutchens,' said Cato.

'Surprise surprise.'

'You and he were a duet once?'

'Best thief-takers in Armed Robbery.'

'It just hasn't been the same since they brought in that rule about not dangling suspects by their feet from the windows of Curtin House.'

'Oh, there's still a few who keep the flame of righteous justice burning.' The wistful smile faded. 'What do you want to know?'

'One of his pet informants, a bloke named Gordon Francis Wellard.'

'Doing life in Casuarina?'

Cato nodded confirmation.

Crouch coughed something unpleasant into a hankie and examined it. 'What about him?'

'He's a nasty piece of work. From what I can see he showed up on record regularly until about the mid-90s, when I assume he came under Hutchens' wing. Then nothing until the last few years when he was done for murder. During that gap of about ten years I can't believe he just quit being bad. So did he reform under the guiding hand of Mick Hutchens, or did he keep on doing his nasties with protection from the DI?'

'That's quite an allegation, Philip.'

'I know.'

'Why the interest?'

'There's another case: a missing teenage girl. Wellard's the prime suspect.'

'Why?'

'He's the stepfather. He's been bragging about it, winding up the mum. Claims to know where the body is buried.'

'Sick bastard. But I'm still not sure what you're getting at. Did the mispers case happen during those intervening years?'

Cato nodded. 'Towards the end. About two years before the murder arrest.'

'So why are you digging up ancient history on your boss?'

'It might lead us to digging up the girl.'

'How come?'

'Geez, you can tell you were in the Job. I came here to get

information out of you and I'm the one answering all the questions.'

'Funny that. So, how come?'

'Two things. Somebody has been sending packages to the girl's mother. About the missing daughter. Taking the piss.'

'Charming.'

'And there's something about the way Wellard and Hutchens communicate.'

Crouch suddenly seemed more interested. 'Yeah?'

Cato was on his guard now. Was it some remnant of loyalty towards his boss or was it fear of Crouch dobbing him in? 'I don't know. Sometimes Wellard's the one that acts like he's in charge, not the DI. Maybe I'm imagining it.'

'So what do you want from me?'

'You and the DI were partners. Mates.'

'Not mates.' A firm shake of the head. 'Partners.'

Duly noted. 'Firstly, do you know of any accomplices from Wellard's early days who might be helping him out now?'

Crouch's eyes narrowed behind his bi-focals. 'Can't you get all that off the computer at work?'

Cato patted his gut lightly. 'Sick leave. This is under the radar.'

'Why?'

'Why do you think? The DI isn't going to be happy about me checking up on him.'

'Trust me not to tell him, do you?'

'I have to.' Cato wondered if he was talking his career down the drain. 'So, accomplices?'

Andy Crouch appeared to give the matter due consideration. 'Did you look at the family? Bad seeds tend to come from a dodgy pod.' He put his cup back on the table and wiped the froth from his lip. 'He had a big brother. Kevin, I think his name was. A real hard case, made Gordy look like a cheap imitation.'

'What became of him?'

'Dropped out of sight.'

'Any particular reason?'

'Probably, but damned if I know it.' Crouch tapped his forehead. 'Memory not so good these days.'

Cato didn't believe him but let it go. Crouch was going to make him work for this. 'Anyone else?'

'Nah. If I think of anyone I'll get back to you.' Crouch drained and crumpled his coffee cup.

'So, on the other matter, would Wellard have anything on Hutchens?' said Cato.

'Such as?'

'Haven't a clue, that's why I'm asking.'

'But you've been wondering. Go on, try me.'

'What about turning a blind eye? Letting Wellard get away with stuff in exchange for information?'

Crouch gave this one a bit more thought. 'Maybe, but I think he'd still keep him on a tight leash. Anything too serious, I doubt he'd have let it go. Mick Hutchens is a tricky bastard but he does know the difference between right and wrong.'

Cato was happy to accept Crouch's assessment: he wanted to believe it too. 'Yeah, probably.'

Crouch started to gather his things. 'What are you getting yourself into here, Philip?'

Cato tried a reassuring grin. 'Don't know. I'll keep you posted.' He nodded towards the cryptic on the table. 'Achilles.'

'What?' said Crouch.

'*Great Greek warrior longs to be sick inside.* Aches-ill, Ach-ill-es.'

Cato had done a project on him at high school. A man whose name embodied the grief of a nation and whose all-consuming rage over petty slights led to the needless slaughter of thousands. Talk about over-reactions: if anybody needed to learn a bit of tolerance, perspective, and cheek-turning it had to have been Achilles.

'You wanted to talk to me, old man?'

Jimmy Tran's voice sounded extra tinny through the headphones. The surveillance van was a sweatbox and Lara was falling out of love with Colin Graham's breath in the confined space. They'd shared a takeaway pizza during the wait: the extra anchovies and garlic bread on the side hadn't been a good idea. They were parked just down the road from Zorba's restaurant.

Two cars full of Gangs Ds nearby. The sun had just set, casting a sulphurous glow over the rooftops of Northbridge. The neon flickered. The Shanghai food hall was filling up and a pale balding man sauntered as casually as possible out of a sex shop where you could see live shows if you put your money in the slot.

'Yes, Jimmy.'

'Mr Tran.'

'Mr Tran.' Christos's voice sounded wheezy but after forty cigarettes a day for the last sixty years, it would. For all that, there was steel in it. This was a man who had had enough.

'What can I do for you?' Quiet. Mocking.

'I can't afford to keep paying you at this amount, Mr Tran. We have nothing left for ourselves.'

'We have an agreement, Christos.'

Lara looked at Colin Graham. He hadn't volunteered anything about his precise whereabouts for the day, just summoned her to Curtin House and said it was on. He and a colleague from Gangs had briefed Christos and wired him up. This was definitely their operation; DI Hutchens wasn't invited.

'I set this place up for my family, my children, my grandchildren.' Christos broke off for a smoker's cough. 'At this rate there will be nothing left.'

'We have an agreement.' Scraping of chairs, people rising to leave.

'Mr Rosetti said you would help me.'

A silence. 'Say that again, old man?'

'Santo, he ...'

'How do you know him?'

'He eats here many times.'

Lara noticed a sudden stillness in Colin Graham. That was the information he'd held back from her. He'd learned that Christos knew Santo and he knew that if the old man mentioned that name tonight it would provoke a reaction. He probably hadn't warned the old man about what kind of reaction.

'And you talked to him about our business relationship, Christos?' Jimmy Tran sounded disappointed, and dangerous.

'That is meant to be confidential.'

Christos didn't retreat. 'He said you and he were friends, good friends. He said you were a reasonable man. A fair man.'

'Good old Santo,' said Jimmy Tran. 'Did you know the cocksucker was dead, Christos?'

'Yes, I knew that, Mr Tran. He came to see me that last night. He ate here.' A pause. 'He said he was going to meet you.'

It was like all the air had been sucked out of the surveillance van. Lara felt droplets of sweat run from her temples, down her neck.

'Do you mean something by that, old man?'

'I don't want to end up like him, but I'm sorry, I cannot go on paying.' Christos's voice had firmed up.

'You know, Papa, if I didn't know better I'd think you were trying to provoke me. Why would you want to do that?'

Lara's sweat turned cold. Graham's eyes had glazed over. Jimmy Tran's voice got louder as if he was leaning right in to Christos's hidden microphone.

'Santo was right. We *were* very good friends. And I am a reasonable man, I'll get back to you on your proposal, Christos.'

Lara ripped off her headphones. 'We need to pull Tran in and get Christos and his family somewhere safe.'

Colin Graham seemed drowsy and distant. 'Pull him in for what, Lara?'

'He's blown us. He knows.'

'We don't know that for sure and there's nothing to arrest him on, yet.'

'I should never have agreed to this.'

'Your agreement wasn't necessary, love.'

'You fucking patronising bastard.'

Graham lifted a placatory hand. 'Hold your nerve and keep the faith, Lara. If Tran does come back to get Christos and we're there waiting, then we really do have him, don't we?'

'Have you asked Christos how he feels about being the tethered goat?'

16

Wednesday, February 3rd.

Lara had just come back from her early morning run when her phone buzzed. It was Colin Graham, whispering on his mobile: in the background the sounds of family breakfast and kids getting ready for school. They would be the kids from his previous marriage. Six, eight, and ten – nicely spaced.

'Christos has gone missing.'

'What do you mean?'

'He didn't come back from the early morning vegie run.'

Lara closed her eyes and rubbed her forehead. 'I thought we were meant to be watching him. Protecting him.'

'Somebody screwed up.'

Understatement of the year. 'He's a dead man and you as good as killed him.'

'*We're* in this together, Lara. I'll pick you up in half an hour.'

'Where are we going?'

'Chateau Tran. I've got the ninjas out again.'

Conversation over. In a daze she turned on the shower and stepped under. Lara had always believed she had the guts to do whatever it took: she'd prided herself on that. She'd grown up with it, listening to her parents' conversations around the dinner table. Who Daddy had knifed that day to ensure he won: some unsuspecting innocent who was in the way of his ambitions. Mum congratulating him. *Well done, darling.* Colin Graham as an extension of her daddy fixation? How banal. Meanwhile the innocents were still getting slaughtered. She had to find a way of extricating herself from this with minimum damage to her prospects. If that meant doing the right thing then so be it. She just had to work out what the right thing was.

After a restless and sore night, Cato woke late. He sealed the house against another hot day, took his coffee and sat down at his computer to start looking for Gordon Wellard's brother. Google and Facebook offered up more Kevin Wellards than you could poke a stick at, but nothing to suggest any of them was the right one. Cato had a hunch that Kevin probably wouldn't be a Facebook kind of guy: he phoned Andy Crouch.

'When did you say Kevin Wellard dropped out of sight?'

'Morning Philip. How you feeling? Gut on the mend?'

'Great Andy, thanks.'

'I'm good too. It's looking like another beautiful day.'

Retirees. Cato cleared his throat. 'Kevin Wellard?'

'In a hurry, huh? Last I heard of him was maybe mid-1990s. He would have been in his thirties.'

'Left town? Dead?'

'Haven't a clue, mate. Out of sight, out of mind. Anything else?'

'Did the brothers get on?'

'Dunno. Blood's thicker than water though isn't it? Family's just like any other institution, a little loyalty can go a long way. Have a good day.'

Thus spake Andy Crouch.

If Kevin Wellard was dead then maybe there was a death notice in *The West* but their online archive only seemed to go back as far as July 2004, ten years too late. The state death registry required official ID and paperwork, even for police investigations. The kind of stuff he was chasing needed either the official apparatus or at least for him to be more mobile. As he was still flying solo he'd just have to go to a library, get on the microfiche, and plough through old newspapers. Today something that simple felt too hard. He'd become reliant on the ready access to information, to technology, to legal and physical backup. Cato was due back at work on Monday, or longer if he needed it. In the meantime he'd do what he could. He decided to toughen up and go to the library.

'Who?' said Jimmy Tran, voice muffled because his face was pushed into the gravel by a TRG boot.

'Christos Papadakis. He runs Zorba's restaurant in Northbridge.' Colin Graham was crouched down beside him, sweat beading his forehead.

It was just past nine in the morning and already the temperature had hit thirty-five. Another fire had been lit about two kilometres east of them and the wind was sending it their way. There were media warnings of the need for evacuations in the face of a catastrophic fire risk. They didn't have time to mess about. 'You need to tell us where he is, Jimmy.'

'Can't help you,' came the squashed reply. 'Haven't a clue.'

Lara looked at the other prone men on the ground. One was conspicuously absent. 'Where's Mickey?' Mickey Nguyen, the man whose ankle she'd stomped on.

A shrug from Jimmy Tran, not easy face down under a ninja boot.

Colin Graham had his gun out, the muzzle prodding the corner of Tran's eye. 'Jimmy, if any harm comes to that old man, I'm coming after you.'

'So, am I under arrest or not?' Tran giggled. He already knew the answer.

Lara left Colin Graham to his devices: there was an alert out on Mickey Nguyen, and Jimmy and friends had been dusted off and released. Colin Graham's superiors in Organised Crime had listened to the previous night's recording and they had concurred: firstly the wire was unauthorised, secondly there was no explicit threat. The old man was simply a missing person, they concluded, one who had only been gone for a few hours. In the absence of compelling evidence of foul play, there was nothing to link his absence to the Trans. Graham had been predictably outraged but Lara just added it to the growing weight of her guilt. The only consolation for her now was that the Tran compound was directly in the line of the bushfire. She hoped the whole place would be razed to the ground. She drove up the freeway to see Mrs Papadakis. Colin Graham had given Lara a funny look as she pulled away: three parts hurt, two parts suspicious. Or was it the other way around?

Zorba's had a handwritten sign on the door, 'Closed – private family matter'. Lara knocked and tried to peer into the gloom beyond. The door was opened by a bulky, bearded man in his forties, maybe one of the sons. She showed him her ID.

'Yes. What do you want?' A blink of watery eyes. 'Have you found him?'

'No. Sorry. Can I come in?'

He opened the door wider and walked away. Lara closed it behind her. Mrs Papadakis was seated at a table at the back of the restaurant, surrounded by her middle-aged children and their spouses and offspring. Some looked fearful that Lara was the bringer of bad news; others glared or ignored her.

'Why are you here?' said Mrs Papadakis.

Lara wasn't sure. She brought no news, had no advice or solace, she had nothing to offer. 'I came to see how you are.'

Mrs Papadakis fluttered her hands at her children. 'We want him back. We want you to bring Christos Papadakis back to his family. Do you understand that?'

Lara nodded.

'My husband brought us here for a better life. He made this restaurant. He worked hard. He paid those animals to leave us alone.' A despairing shake of the head. 'And he stood up to them.' There was a choked male sob in the background.

Lara listened to the words in their past tense. Already it was a eulogy. 'I'll bring him back to you.'

She could see they didn't believe her, or if they did they feared the double meaning.

Cato was upstairs in the State Library scanning microfiche editions of *The West* for any traces of Kevin Wellard during the 1990s. It was a long haul. Allowing for Andy Crouch's memory, Cato added a few years leeway either side of the timeframe. By the time he'd skated his way through the late 1980s and early 1990s he was an expert on the unfolding disaster of WA Inc. On he went, eyes blurring at the small print, a dull ache radiating from the back of his head. Then he found it: November 1996, a Saturday in the middle of the month.

In memoriam. Kevin Paul Wellard 1959–1996. Beloved son of the late John and Mary. Brother of Gordon. We'll meet again. Miss you mate. Gordon.

Kevin was dead, at the age of 37. If he was an accomplice to his brother's misdeeds then his role was over by 1996 – around the same time as his little brother dropped off the criminal records. Kevin couldn't be the one sending the *FINDERS KEEPERS* letters to Shellie.

Cato had the page printed and left the library. He made for the railway station and a homeward bound train. The CBD was a forest of high cranes and the skeletons of new buildings. Cato spotted the outline of at least one skyscraper he knew to be funded by drug money and several others where the builders and security firms were fronts for bikie and other criminal enterprise. The Perth city motto was 'Floreat', Latin for 'flourish' or 'prosper'. It figured. Even some of the more legitimate dwellings were the results of wealth laundered over two centuries from stolen land, wages and minerals. Perth's skyline might be constantly shifting but underneath the city remained the same: a grubby little fiefdom of robber barons.

Cato bought his train ticket and took the escalator down to the Fremantle Line. His phone beeped: a text from Jake.

can i come over this weekend?

Texting his father, midway through a school day? Cato wondered what was wrong. He texted back:

sure, will talk to mum

and then he rang Jane.

'Hi.'

'Hi.'

'Just had a text from Jake. Wanting to come over this weekend.'

A moment of silence. 'Really? Are you well enough?'

'Yeah, fine. Might not be up to shooting any hoops but we'll work something out.'

'Okay.'

'Everything okay?' said Cato.

'Yep.' When she said it like that it meant no.

'Okay, so when do we do it?'

'I'll drop him over on Saturday morning and pick him up same time Sunday?'

'Sure.'

Jake was upset about something and Cato had been blind to it. Instead he had become obsessed with the twisted world of Gordon friggin' Wellard. He needed to get his bloody priorities straight.

Senior Fire Officer Bevan Foley still had occasional nightmares about his experiences during the Black Saturday inferno in Victoria. He'd seen enough horror to last a lifetime. This wasn't as big but it was still a potential killer. It had swept through three Baldivis properties, destroying one and badly damaging another. This third was lucky just to lose a couple of outlying sheds. They'd been at it since daybreak and he was stuffed. All because of some little fuckwit with a box of matches. The wind had finally shifted and the helicopter water-bombers had punched a big enough hole to allow them to get the bastard back on a leash. Foley and his team just needed to damp down these sheds and then another crew would relieve them. Then he could have a shower, a beer, and a sleep. The main shed had partly collapsed inwards: the Colorbond walls buckled and blackened. Through the gaps, thick oily chemical smoke indicated something none too healthy still burning inside. Probably tyres.

Another few minutes and they were able to pull the door back to get a better sense of what they were dealing with. He'd hoped the burning tyre smell was from a pile of old spares but it looked like there was a vehicle in there, a 4WD, probably once worth a bob or two. As the acrid smoke cleared further, he realised there was another smell: like a barbecue left unattended. And there was somebody in the driver's seat.

17

Lara watched as her boss dispatched orders and lesser mortals with obvious relish. By contrast, DS Colin Graham looked like he would rather be somewhere else.

As soon as the body had been spotted, the firemen had called it in. In the wait for permissions and protocols the fire had come to life again briefly but now, properly extinguished, they were able to extricate the charred corpse from the driver's seat.

'Aw fuck.' A fireman stepped back from the rear of the blistered Prado.

Lara exchanged glances with Graham.

DI Hutchens lifted his chin. 'What?'

'There's another one in the boot,' said the fireman.

Hutchens fixed a beady on Graham. 'Any ideas, Col?'

Graham shrugged. 'All of the Trans and associates are accounted for, except Mickey.'

'And at this stage we're guessing he's the chauffeur. So we have a spare body. Curiouser and curiouser. What do you reckon, Lara?'

This was her chance to come clean, distance herself from DS Graham and his dangerous games. Do the right thing by the Papadakis family. 'No idea, sir.'

The fireman leaned in closer to the body in the boot. 'Jesus. You might want to check this out.'

DI Hutchens sauntered over for a look. 'Aw fuck.'

'Nails?' said Lara Sumich.

'About forty of them,' confirmed Hutchens, reading from an email. He closed his laptop and switched his attention to DS Colin Graham. The door to the DI's office was closed and the blinds were drawn. It was well after home time but nobody was going anywhere soon. 'So Col, we have a problem.'

'Sir?'

'Running side errands with your Gangs mates and poor old Mr Papadakis.' He flicked his hand at his computer, where the email had been. 'What do you reckon we should say to the family?'

Colin Graham folded his arms and slumped back into his chair. 'Sorry?'

If Lara had had a gun in her hand she probably would have shot him. 'I'll go and see the family, sir.'

'Both of you will.' Hutchens levelled his gaze back at Graham. 'Then you'll come back here, write a full report of your activities over the last seventy-two hours and have it in my inbox before you finish for the day.' They stood to leave. Hutchens had his eyes down studying a desk diary but his finger was pointed at Graham. 'Sergeant, I am initiating disciplinary proceedings against you. You're off this investigation. Once you've notified the family you are to return to your usual duties with Gangs and await further instructions.' He raised his head and looked at Graham. 'You're a disgrace. Get out of my sight.'

Lara turned to follow Graham.

'Not you,' said Hutchens.

She stayed.

'Can you give me a good reason why I shouldn't be disciplining you too?'

'No.'

'Did you help set it up or were you just along for the ride?'

'The latter. Sir.'

'It showed poor judgement.'

'Yes sir.'

'He's a prick and he's sloppy and he'll take you down with him when he goes. You want that?'

'No.'

'Then be warned.'

Heading north on the freeway, she couldn't bear to look at Colin Graham. Lara was driving: the passing traffic a blur, the tension in the car a thick choking presence. She cracked open a window to a warm breeze scented with fuel and bush smoke. 'So what *do* we say to Mrs Papadakis?'

'The usual. We're very sorry for your loss.'

'Prick.'

'Grow up, Lara. You're a cop. Shit happens. Deal with it.'

'We made this shit happen.'

'We. That's right. And *we* still have a long way to go to get to the other side of this. You got that?'

'What do you mean?'

'United we stand, divided we fall.' Graham reclined his seat, yawned, and closed his eyes. 'Give me a hoy when we get to the Greek.'

'Cato?' It was DI Hutchens.

'Yes?'

'How you feeling?'

Hutchens attentive, again: twice in as many days. What was he after?

'All the better for hearing you, sir.'

'No need for the sarcasm, mate, I only asked.' There was hurt in Hutchens' voice. Genuine.

'Sorry, yeah, on the mend, thanks.'

A pause. 'Remember that day we were out bush with Wellard and Shellie?'

Cato tensed. 'What about it?'

'Remember the pig with the nails in it?'

18

Thursday, February 4th.

Lara woke up late. She'd ignored the alarm set for her morning run. Her limbs felt heavy and it was an effort to even open her eyes. She crawled out from under the sheet.

The encounter with Mrs Papadakis had been predictably ghastly. While the woman had anticipated the worst, that wasn't the same as having it confirmed. The wailing and keening had seemed primeval to Lara whose upbringing had been essentially emotion-free. Colin Graham, to her surprise, had risen to the occasion: he'd oozed sympathy. It had been so effective that the family seemed to forget it was actually his machinations that had killed their patriarch. Their dark wet eyes seemed instead to probe Lara for coming around all shiftless and guilty and making promises she couldn't keep. Was that why she felt like shit?

Or was it the fear that the affair with Colin Graham was dead? In the last few days her fascination for him had lurched over to revulsion at what he seemed capable of: yet still there was this longing for what she felt only a week ago. It went beyond the sex; inventive as he was, he wasn't irreplaceable. Flushing Colin out of her life also meant flushing away her immediate hopes of a ticket into Gangs. But it was more than that too. Lately people kept getting the better of her. She'd misread Santo, and now Graham too. Was she losing it? *It*. Control over her life and her destiny.

'Stupid bitch,' she said aloud.

After the visit to Christos's family she'd dropped Graham in the city. Lara had returned to the office to file her report. Graham hadn't attempted to coach her as to what it should say. He knew he didn't need to. *United we stand*. She flicked on the kettle and chucked a teabag into a mug. Her report said Christos Papadakis, after years of paying protection money to the Trans and after forming a close personal bond with the now deceased officer Santo Rosetti, had volunteered to be wired for a meeting with Jimmy Tran in order to help gather evidence of Tran's involvement in the murder of Rosetti.

He came to see me that last night. He ate here. He said he was going to meet you.

Was Santo really intending to meet Jimmy that night or was it a line fed to Christos to wind Jimmy up? If the former then she needed to know what the planned meeting was about. Her report concluded that Tran was now believed to be behind the subsequent abduction and murder of the old man after somehow becoming aware of the wiretap. It was recommended that Tran and his associates be arrested and questioned over the murder.

Divided we fall. DI Hutchens had kicked Graham back to Gangs and was initiating disciplinary proceedings against him. Lara suspected Graham could look after himself, but what would Hutchens do with her? He'd already given her a second chance after the Hopetoun affair. She couldn't see his goodwill stretching much further. Her phone went.

'Lara?'

'Boss?'

'Autopsy on the old Greek. Ten o'clock.'

'Will DS Graham be attending?'

'No, he fucking won't.'

It had been a while since Hutchens had talked to her like that. Like she was just the same as everybody else.

Cato sat in his Volvo station wagon in the car park at Casuarina. He had phoned ahead for an appointment and made it sound like official business even though he was still meant to be on sick leave.

'Nasty business you had the other day. Surprised you're up and about so quickly.' Superintendent Scott seemed distracted, conducting two or three conversations at the same time: all the better, thought Cato.

'The longer you stay down, the harder it is to get back up again,' Cato had replied manfully.

He was fairly confident that the Super would, sooner or later, make a crosschecking phone call to his boss DI Hutchens. In some ways that was the aim: the boy who kicked the hornets' nest. The Wellard accomplice track was a dead end, at least for now, until Cato returned to work and had access to databases and such. In the meantime he thought he'd try shaking things up a bit. He checked the dashboard clock. Visiting time.

'Just the two of us? Nice and intimate.' Wellard took a seat as directed.

Cato had persuaded Superintendent Scott to allow them some privacy. He'd hinted that he wanted Wellard to be able to open up and say things he may not be able to say in front of the guards, or the DI, he'd added enigmatically. Cato had met the Super's look with a carefully crafted one of his own that suggested anything and said nothing. The hint that Cato might be working against DI Hutchens had no doubt tickled Scott and the wish had been granted. All's fair in love and turf wars. There was still the backup of CCTV surveillance on the room and Scott would cover his arse by contacting the DI after a diplomatic amount of time had elapsed – enough for him to hear and record any dirt that might come in useful at some point in the future.

'You, me and these four walls, mate.'

'And the camera and the microphones,' said Wellard, playing bored. 'Found my Briony yet?'

'No, any ideas?' said Cato.

'Nah, not today.'

'Good, we've got that out the way then.'

Wellard perked up; apparently there was a new game afoot. 'Where's Mr Hutchens today?'

'Busy.'

'I can imagine. Lot of bad people out there.'

'Few in here too.'

'That's for sure. Any developments on your little Finders Keepers case?' He'd used two fingers from each hand to do the parentheses mime. Eyes twinkling merrily as he tried to provoke Cato.

'Nothing,' said Cato. 'Some crank probably.'

'Reckon?'

'Have to be. Nothing normal about teasing some woman about her dead kid is there?'

'S'pose not.' Wellard tilted his head. 'So why *are* you here?'

'I want to know about you and my boss. Apparently you go way back.'

Wellard glanced up at the winking red light on the wall. 'This official?'

'What do you think?'

'I think you might be straying from the path. Wandering in the wilderness.'

'Why's that Gordon?'

'You tell me. Why are you going off on your lonesome?'

'Okay. I think you know something about my boss and you're holding it over him.'

Wellard seemed to like that idea. 'Really? What makes you think that?'

'The thing is, I watch you and the DI together and it's not like your usual master–servant relationship. He's meant to be in charge but you don't act like it. See what I'm getting at?'

A frown. 'No, you've got it wrong,' said Wellard. 'I'd never be a servant.'

'What are you then? Equal partner? Colleague? Or is it you that's in charge?'

'If I'm *in charge*, how come I'm in here?'

Good point.

'I haven't worked that out yet. Maybe you thought you'd become untouchable but you got it all wrong.' Cato smacked his forehead. 'Eureka! Is that it? You're just an idiot like all the rest?'

Wellard yawned. Exaggerated. He was no longer enjoying himself. He was twitchy. Score one.

'What's wrong, mate? Have I touched a nerve?'

Wellard closed his eyes for a moment, like he was gathering in his frayed edges, folding them over, tucking them under. 'I can see now why Shellie likes you.'

Wellard had reverted to the old game plan. Running out of ideas already? 'I like her too, Gordy. She's pretty special.'

A blink at the word 'Gordy'; he didn't like it. Score two?

'I think Shellie appreciates that you have the gift of empathy,' said Wellard. 'You're a parent too. You can imagine what it would be like to lose a child.'

'Is that meant to be a threat, Gordy?' Another flinch. Cato recalled his conversations with Andy Crouch, he'd called him Gordy too, comparing him with his big brother. 'While we're on the subject of family, you must miss your brother. Kevin was it? I read it in the paper.' This time it was Cato who curled his fingers mockingly in inverted commas. *'We'll meet again. Miss you mate. Gordon.'*

Wellard slammed his hand on the table. 'Back off, chink.'

Score three. 'Quite a temper you've got there, Gordy. You need a cool head to prevail in a man's world, though. Kev never really took you seriously, did he?' Cato shook his head. 'Short fuse like that. You'd be a liability in a tight corner.'

Wellard looked up at the camera. 'I'd like to go back to my room now. I'm finished here.'

'What was it that triggered you on your honeymoon with Shellie? Eggs too runny? Air conditioning on the blink? No sugar in your tea?'

'I said I'm finished here.'

'You're not as special as you think, Gordy. Gatecrashing vulnerable people's minds isn't an art; it's bullying and cowardly. You're no different from all the other dickheads in here who have no perspective or self-control. If you think this is all a game, then it's one you've already lost. You're in here and you're never coming out alive, Gordy.'

Wellard's hand lashed out and smacked Cato hard across the left cheek.

Cato returned the favour, opening up Wellard's lip. Wellard lunged across the table, fury and blood on his face, spittle around his mouth. Cato stood and stepped back out of his reach.

'Cool it, Gordy. Nothing personal, mate.'

The door opened and in walked Superintendent Scott with a

broad smile, an outstretched hand, and two burly guards. 'Detective Kwong, your boss is worried about you. He reckons you should still be at home in your bed.' An arm went around Cato's shoulder and he was guided towards the door.

'He attacked me. I want to press charges.' Wellard dabbed some blood from his lip. Fury quashed, replaced by fear, hurt, and victimhood. Impressive. 'It's all on camera.'

'Yes, Mr Wellard, it is,' said Scott. 'And you started it.'

'Still want to make a complaint.'

'No worries, we'll get you a form.'

Cato caught Wellard's eye as he was shepherded away by the two guards. 'Maybe you can tell me all about your big brother next time. Real tough nut, I hear. Staunch. See you soon, Gordy.'

Wellard failed to hold Cato's gaze. It felt good to have got under the bastard's skin. It felt good to win.

'Forty-two of them, eighty-five millimetres long, fired into the back of the head and along the spine at point blank range from a standard cordless, gas-charged nail gun.' Professor Mackenzie wiped some grime from her spectacles. 'Widely available for sale or hire: Bunnings, Mitre 10, Home Builders, you name it. My hubbie's got one, never uses the bugger though.'

'Fucking animals.' Hutchens shook his head.

'And I suspect Mr Papadakis was probably alive for most of the ordeal.'

Lara felt like throwing up. The charred carcass lay curled on the steel table, foetal in its final agony. Melted body fat had congealed in the creases and crevices. Organs, tissue and other samples glistened in bowls and bags on a nearby bench. The nails were lined up and numbered on a sheet of plastic. Photographs had been taken to show where a certain numbered nail had been positioned in Christos's body. The smell of blood, offal and over-cooked meat was overpowering.

Hutchens glanced her way. 'You okay there, Lara?'

She straightened up. 'Fine, sir.'

'Nasty one this, eh?'

'Yes, boss.'

'Whoever's responsible, we're going to make them pay. Right?'

'Right.'

'Which brings us around to the other corpse,' said Professor Mackenzie.

'Mickey Nguyen,' said Hutchens. 'Deep fried.'

They turned to the second table and the shrivelled remains of the Tran henchman.

'Was that what killed him?' said Lara. 'The fire?'

Hutchens gave her a glance as if to say, duh.

'As far as we can tell, so far, yes. There don't appear to be any other wounds or inconsistencies.'

'So the Trans torture and kill Mr Papadakis. Somewhere off-site we presume, as a police raid that morning found no sign of him or Mickey at the compound.' Hutchens strolled around looking thoughtful like a TV detective. 'Then later that day, after the police depart, and with an approaching bushfire, Mickey is ordered to dispose of the body. Tragically, he is caught by the speed of the fire and trapped in the vehicle. Perishing in the inferno.'

'That's your department, Inspector.' Mackenzie squinted in the harsh light. 'I'm getting a wee headache from all ...' she waved a hand at the bodies, 'this.'

Hutchens turned to Lara. 'Is that your reading of it, Lara?'

'The fire moves so quickly he doesn't even have time to drive out of the shed?'

'Not unheard of. Read the Black Saturday Report.'

Lara turned to Mackenzie. 'Any drugs or alcohol in his system?'

'No traces so far but, particularly in the case of alcohol, the heat could have evaporated it.'

Lara back to Hutchens. 'Do we bring the Trans in yet, sir?'

'May as well,' he sighed. 'Although I suspect that until we get any other evidence, Jimmy Tran is going to flick-pass all the blame to Meltdown Mickey.'

That's exactly what he did, accompanied once again by his well-heeled young lawyer, Damien.

'Mickey, he's mad as. Gets a bit Freddy Krueger you know? A real loose cannon. Terrible way to die though, eh?'

Hutchens flicked through the skimpy file in front of him. 'And what did you and your brother Vincent do between the time our officers visited you, and the fire coming through? A period of approximately four and a half hours.'

Jimmy furrowed his brow. 'We were a bit shaken to tell the truth. Those TRG guys can be pretty rough and scary. We sat around and had a few beers to settle our nerves then we packed our valuables and evacuated as instructed by the fire authorities. We were out of there by early afternoon.'

'And Mickey?'

'As we told your officers yesterday morning.' A yellowy gap-toothed smile towards Lara. 'We hadn't seen Mickey since the previous day.'

'When was that?'

'Last thing Tuesday night.'

'After your meeting in Zorba's with Mr Papadakis?'

'Oh, how do you know about that?'

'You were being followed. The meeting was recorded.'

Tran turned to his lawyer, seemingly perturbed. 'Is that legal, Damien?'

'Probably best to just answer the question for now, Mr Tran,' said Damien.

'Yeah, what he said,' said Hutchens.

'Mickey said he was heading off to the snooker hall in Northbridge. See some mates.' Tran tried to look sad for a moment. 'Last time we ever saw him.'

'Until he turns up in the Prado in your shed.'

'That's right.'

'And the elaborate security system, CCTV, et cetera you've got round your place. That'll confirm all that, right?'

Damien the Lawyer leaned forward. 'It's not up to my client to prove his account, Inspector. It's up to you to prove yours.'

'Thanks for reminding me what my job is, son.'

'Pleasure.'

Hutchens switched tack. 'What about Mr Papadakis, when was the last time you saw him?'

Tran smiled. 'If you were following me around and recording me I assume you already know.'

Damien intervened. 'As a matter of disclosure, Inspector, I assume you'll be providing us with copies of your surveillance material?'

'Assume what you like. Your client hasn't been charged with anything yet.' Hutchens shifted his menace back onto Tran. 'The question?'

'The last time I saw the old man was in the Greek restaurant.'

'When?'

'When our meeting finished. Seven o'clock or something.'

'You were very angry with him,' said Lara.

'Was I? I don't recall.'

'During the conversation with Mr Papadakis he mentioned to you that Santo was on his way to meet you.'

Tran shifted in his seat. 'Did he?'

'You know he did, that's when you got angry with him. You asked the old man if he was trying to provoke you. What was Santo coming to talk to you about and why did mention of it annoy you, Jimmy?'

'I don't recall. Maybe if I get to listen to your recordings it might trigger a memory.' His amusement had worn thin. 'Are you sure you're not just imagining it, Lara?'

'Detective or Officer Sumich will do fine.'

'So will *Mister* Tran, Officer.' Lara could see now the man beneath the jovial mask. The man who could screw a bottle into a student's face, who could chop the hands and feet off a traitor, slit the throat of an enemy. 'Respect is a two-way street, madam. Don't you think?'

And then the smile returned and so it went on. Jimmy knew nothing about what happened to Papadakis. Mickey must have done it. Bit mad and all that. Why? Dunno. Jimmy and Damien looked ready to leave.

'Just one more thing,' said Hutchens.

'Yes.' The lawyer rolled his eyes.

'Mr Tran, have you had any previous dealings with DS Graham?'

Lara studied a distant spot on the wall. Tran looked at his lawyer.

'What does this have to do with your inquiry, Inspector?' said Damien.

'It's a question for your client. Is he going to answer it or not?'

'What do you mean by dealings?' Tran's mind visibly ticking over.

'Arrests, social gatherings, squash ladders, book club. You tell me.'

Tran smirked. 'He's not my type.'

'So have you had previous dealings with DS Graham or not?'

'Surely all that would be a matter of record, Inspector?' said the lawyer.

'The formal stuff would. Arrests, interviews, et cetera.'

Tran shook his head. 'I think you're barking up the wrong tree, mate.'

'How do you mean, Jimmy?'

'Woof, woof.'

They left. But Lara had discovered some things along the way. Her question about the planned meeting with Santo had rattled the cage and provoked a tetchy squawk out of Jimmy Tran. And the DI, for some reason, was interested in Colin Graham's dealings with the Trans. What was that about?

Cato took the call from DI Hutchens as he was passing Adventure World on his way back from Casuarina.

'What the fuck were you doing out there?'

'Hello, sir.'

'Answer. Now.'

'I'm feeling a lot better, sir. Reckon I'll be back in the office on Monday.'

'Not if you're suspended you won't. Answer the question.'

'I've had time to think during my time off. Been developing a few theories about the Wellard thing.'

'What "thing" is that then?'

'He knows more than he's telling us.'

'No shit, Sherlock.'

'That's why I want to get back to work. Follow up a few lines of inquiry.'

'No need, I've got the Wellard "thing" all in hand. But you can sit at your desk and put together a Safer Streets Action Plan if you like.'

'Now you're talking. Tomorrow okay?'

'You're taking the piss again aren't you? Don't stretch my patience, mate.'

'What's happening?'

It was Colin Graham on the phone. He sounded remarkably chirpy for someone on the cusp of disciplinary action. Lara looked up to see if DI Hutchens was in earshot. No, his door was closed. 'We interviewed Tran and let him go.'

'Let me guess, Mad Mickey dunnit?'

'Pretty much.'

'Are you home this evening?'

'Why?'

'I thought I might drop round.'

The voice dripped the promise of sex as if nothing had changed in the last few days. Now was the time to tell him where to go and to get back her life.

'Yes, I'm home,' said Lara.

'Look forward to it. See you then.'

The phone died. Lara looked at the screen like it would somehow provide her with a clue as to why she'd had a sudden rush of blood to her head. But then again it wasn't her head where it had rushed to. Saying no to Colin Graham couldn't be that hard could it? She wondered how different she really was from those pathetic women who always seemed able to give their bad bastard just one more chance. Anyway it was a win-win: they could review those matters that had triggered the strong reaction in Jimmy Tran. Maybe there was still hope yet for nailing him and emerging from this looking good. And maybe they'd have some great sex.

Her phone buzzed again. No caller ID.

'Detective Sumich?'

'Yes?'

'Jeremy.' Fagin, she hadn't recognised his voice.

'Yes?'

'I think we've found Tupac.'

She gripped the phone tighter. 'Where is he?'

'There's a boarded-up Homeswest house in Willagee. I'm over the road from it now.'

19

There was an amber haze over Willagee when Lara pulled into the car park in the grim shopping strip. The street was full of young Noongars: kicking a footy, arguing, laughing, jumping the footpath on BMXs, or just sitting and staring. The sun floated low, the heat hanging in the air. A mob of teenagers lounged against the wall outside the deli, sharing hot chips. Across the road, ibises prodded the grass in the graffiti-sprayed primary school. Across the road the other way, a Homeswest house was ringed by a temporary builders' fence. One front window was boarded up; on the other window the board was hanging loose. Beer cans and other rubbish carpeted the front yard, and the spray-painted writing on the wall let everybody know that Lance was a fucken dog.

So where was Fagin? Lara looked up and down the shopping strip but could see no trace of the tall, awkward figure. He would stand out on these streets like an ailing flamingo among pit bulls. Maybe he was in one of the shops buying smokes or selling drugs to some kids. Perhaps he was recruiting a few more Artful Dodgers. She glanced at the teenagers; they met her look and started snorting at each other like pigs. She couldn't imagine any dodgers more artful than these. She suspected they'd send a rank amateur like Fagin on his way quick sharp. She tried phoning him and was put through to message bank.

'I'm here. Where are you?'

The light was fading fast. Was Dieudonne home in that abandoned house with the wooden curtains? Given his track record, she should really call in the TRG but she'd had too many false starts lately and couldn't afford another cock-up. Besides she didn't have the authority to summon them even if she wanted to. Still, an extra backup body, even one as ineffectual as Fagin, would be better than nothing. He wouldn't have gone in there alone would he? No, she dismissed the idea. Then she thought she saw a flicker of movement at the window where the board was hanging loose.

She tried phoning DI Hutchens but he wasn't answering either. She sent him a text giving the time and location: she could always explain it away later if nothing came of it. There was another flash of movement, a glint of light in the dark eye of the window. Lara grabbed a torch from the back seat of her car and walked towards the house, keeping her gun holstered for the time being. A street commotion was the last thing she needed right now. She felt the eyes of half a dozen teenagers boring into her back.

Lara pushed a section of the builders' fence aside and walked through. The sun was gone and the afterglow receding, leaving only shadows and silhouettes over Willagee. The noise level in the street seemed to have suddenly dropped. The front door was securely boarded up and the only apparent way in was either through the loose board on the window or possibly a side or rear entrance. She decided to try the latter first. Now she had her gun out and cocked.

Lara's approach was far from noiseless. With every step she crunched broken glass or kicked a can. She became aware of a strong smell of putrefaction. She flicked on her torch. A large black plastic bag of rubbish had split and flies hovered around chicken bones. She came to the back door and nudged it with her foot. It was open.

'Ah sick, eh, she's got a Glock.'

'Hey sis, what you doin'? No blackfellas for you to shoot in there.'

The hot-chip teenagers had followed her over the road and were standing out front by the fence finishing up their snack. Lara kept her voice low, level, and not unfriendly. 'Guys, do you reckon you could go back over the road? Wouldn't want you getting hurt.'

'Nah, here's good. Front row seats. Who you after?'

One of his mates jostled him. 'We know who you after, bro. You in love with the lady monarch.' They hooted.

Lara ignored them and went inside.

The first room was the kitchen. Her torch swept over the walls, more graffiti; Lance the Dog wasn't well regarded in here either. A smell of piss and shit and something else. A bathroom and toilet: a dripping cistern, linoleum sticking to her feet. Lara advanced down the black hallway. At each door she stopped and scanned the room with her flashlight and her gun. Two bedrooms, empty, more opinions on Lance, and what looked like human faeces in the corner. That other smell getting stronger.

Two more rooms to go. The first smaller, a child's bedroom, surprisingly clean compared to the rest of the house. Her torchlight played across a mattress, sleeping bag, pillow, a bottle of water and a small wooden crucifix leaning against the wall. Three books neatly stacked: a Bible, Conrad's *Heart of Darkness,* and a Harry Potter. There was a noise behind her.

Lara whipped around but there was nobody there.

Somebody grabbed her ankle. She yelped and dropped her torch. Its light found Fagin with blood spouting from his neck and face.

Fagin died on the way to hospital. He had lost too much blood from the gashes in his neck. That was the smell she hadn't been able to identify among the others: the cloying perfume of the slaughterhouse. As the body bag closed over Fagin's face, Lara thought she saw a kind of serenity that had not been there since primary school. Since before his father started coming into his bedroom at night. DI Hutchens turned up, took one look at her and told her to go home. Under the shower she couldn't rid herself of the smell of piss and shit and blood or the sight of Fagin by dropped torchlight. When Colin Graham buzzed the intercom from outside she ignored him and stayed beneath the jets of steaming water.

20

Friday, February 5th.

Cato was at his office desk early. Today it was not expected to get over 34°C and there was the promise of a proper sea breeze by noon. The handful of fires that had flared, died, and flared again around the metropolitan area over the last fortnight were finally out or under control. He wondered why neither his boss nor Lara Sumich were in yet. Was it that death in Willagee he'd heard about on the news that morning? The body count seemed to be way up this summer. It tended to happen in heatwaves. Maybe the slight break in the weather would bring relief there too.

Cato clicked a couple of keys and summoned Wellard's records from the system: he'd been convicted of assaults, usually against women, drugs charges, some burglaries, and at least two reported rapes. One rape victim had been left so traumatised by the level of violence and degradation inflicted on her that she attempted suicide within three months. In her statement she recalled Wellard threatening her: 'You're lucky I'm in a good mood today, darling. The last one never woke up.'

If that meant what it seemed to mean, at least one more body was out there somewhere. This was at least ten years before Briony Petkovic and Caroline Penny. The comment had been followed up by police in a subsequent interview with Wellard but not pursued any further. He couldn't be linked to any of the missing persons who might fit the bill. He'd served blocks of a few months here and there for the lesser offences and three years each, concurrent, for the rapes.

A psych report, commissioned while on remand at Hakea awaiting sentencing for the Caroline Penny murder, noted Wellard's disturbing lack of remorse or empathy and a highly manipulative personality. No shit. It had been signed by a Dr Marissa Jenkins.

Cato tried phoning the number and was told she had since left the department and handed her caseload to a colleague.

'Any forwarding contact?'

'She's backpacking in South America.'

'Nice,' said Cato.

'After what she'd been through, I'd be out of here too.'

'Really?' said Cato, sensing a loose tongue. 'Why's that?'

'She took extended leave not long after dealing with some guy in prison. Messed her head up big time. Nightmares. Heebie-jeebies. The lot. He was a complete psycho freak apparently.'

Guess who?

As Cato had already gleaned, Wellard was a nasty piece of work at least until around the mid-1990s when he came under the benevolent guiding hand of one Detective Senior Constable Michael Hutchens. Then clean as a whistle for the next decade or so before he went all funny again, killing his girlfriend Caroline Penny and earning a mention in connection with the earlier disappearance of his teenage stepdaughter Briony Petkovic. So did Wellard go into hibernation for those years when he disappeared off the database? The man's violent, controlling temper was a matter of record; it seemed implausible that he'd managed to simply switch it off between 1996 and around 2005. There were a number of options: he stayed good, he changed his name, he left the state, or he had someone watching over him – a guardian angel.

One way to track Wellard's movements during that 'down time' was to follow Hutchens' career over that same period and look for traces. Accessing such information from the system, if it allowed Cato to at all, would leave a trail that Hutchens would no doubt sniff. It was a dangerous step, the career-ending kind. Cato's hand hovered over the keyboard.

'How's the gut?'

DI Hutchens' voice was right beside his ear. The jolt sent a spasm through Cato's midriff. 'On the mend,' he said through gritted teeth.

'Back on the case I see?' Hutchens pointed over Cato's shoulder at the screen and tutted disapprovingly. 'But we don't need

Wellard's résumé to know he's a sick fuck. Check your inbox, lots of lovely Safer Streets stats for you to massage instead.'

Lara Sumich crossed Cato's line of vision: ashen, dark-eyed, slumped shoulders. He'd never seen her like that before.

Hutchens put a finger to his lips and shook his head at Cato. Don't go there.

'The joker who put you in hospital has been at it again,' he said.

'The African?' said Cato.

'Dieudonne's his name.'

'Willagee?'

'That's the one. He slit some dero's throat and Lara found the guy. Turns out she knew him.'

'Nasty.'

Lara returned from the kitchen with a cup of something and sat at her desk without acknowledging either of them.

'While I think about it, I also want you to look into any links between that pig we found and the death of Mr Papadakis.'

'Pig?' said Cato, absorbing the news that Dieudonne was still out there doing bad stuff with a knife.

'That nail-gun thing I mentioned to you. Get the files out, compare and contrast.' Hutchens shook his head. 'Three dead in as many days. Is it me or is the world going to hell in a handbasket?'

Cato held off poking around in DI Hutchens' past life. He wanted to keep his job for now. There was something concrete and settling about being back at work. Desks, phones, paperwork, bureaucracy: the paraphernalia of the institution. He had never expected to find comfort in all that stuff. Safer Streets. Cato wandered over to Detective Constable Thornton's desk and pulled up a chair. The young man smelled like he'd just come off a big night and, with his hand shaking, took gulps from a two-litre bottle of Coke.

'Chris, looking good.'

'Oh, you're back,' he said, as if Cato had been on holiday instead of stabbed.

'Fine. Thanks for asking. How's Safer Streets shaping up, mate?'

'Boring as bat shit.' The voice was high, nasal, and carried an inflection of being smarter than everyone else. Obviously Thornton was too good for this and it was only a matter of time before everybody recognised it. 'Did you get the latest stats? I cc'd them to the DI and you.'

'How about you talk me through it?'

Give him his due; the boy had the jargon down pat. He was indeed destined for higher office – maybe Policy or OHS. Thornton droned on with his analysis and recommendations for the key points of an action plan to be presented at the next task force meeting. Cato tuned out and observed the comings and goings in the office. Whenever he did reconnect to the high-pitched whine he felt the urge to slap his neck for a non-existent mozzie.

'So what do you reckon?'

Cato realised that Thornton was talking to him. 'I think you're doing a great job, Chris, and I'm going to recommend to the DI that you see it through.'

'Arsehole.'

'You don't get it, mate. This is just the kind of bullshit that gets people fast-tracked. That's why the boss had me on it first.' Cato winced and touched his wound lightly. 'But ever since this I just don't have that, that ...'

'Vim?' said Thornton, stifling a Coke belch.

'Exactly.' Cato winked at him. 'Losers and plodders see boring bat shit; winners seize the moment.'

'Yeah,' Thornton straightened in his seat and took another galvanising swig. 'Yeah, right.'

Cato waved at Thornton's computer screen. 'Meantime, got another job for you.'

'What?'

'Nail-gun injuries. Check all the hospitals in the state. Any unusual nail-gun injuries in the past, say, six months to a year?'

'What's an unusual nail-gun injury?'

'Multiple, in a pattern, up the spine.'

'Jesus.'

Lara Sumich had used the traumatic circumstances of the last twenty-four hours as her reason to go home by late morning and DI Hutchens didn't argue the point. She felt washed-out but on edge. She jumped at sudden noises, desk drawers slamming, phones ringing. Her concentration was cactus. Colin Graham was either the first or last person she wanted to see right now. But there he was downstairs at her door, looking suitably concerned into the security camera, and she was the one who'd made the arrangement in the first place. She buzzed him up.

She'd planned to confront him about the horrific and needless death of Mr Papadakis, to question him about the real aim of Santo Rosetti's undercover investigations, to tell him she'd had enough. Instead she just held onto him as he stood on the threshold; her face buried in his chest, breathing in his smell. Then she was tugging at Graham's belt buckle and his shirt. He responded, matching her urgency. They went straight to the bedroom and fucked: she straddling him, taking control, if only this one last time. When she finally came she brought with her all the tears left unshed this past week. Then she slept.

When Lara woke Colin was already alert and watching her. 'What time is it?' she yawned.

'Just gone three.'

'How long have you been awake?'

'Not long.' His left hand absently stroked her breast, his wedding ring grazing her nipple.

'You haven't told me much about your wife.'

He smiled. 'She's none of your business.'

Fair enough. Lara decided to move onto the things that mattered. She left out the recriminations over Papadakis: that would be dealt with by any disciplinary proceedings.

'What was Santo investigating?'

Graham shifted position, lying on his back, hands behind his head. 'Drugs, bikies, Trans, low-lifes. The usual.'

'Jimmy Tran got jumpy when I reminded him of the bugged conversation: Christos saying Santo was headed for a meeting with Jimmy the night he died.'

'Did he explain himself?'

'No. Was Santo really going to meet Jimmy or did you just get Christos to say that as a wind-up?'

A tilt of the head. 'You give me more credit than I deserve. No, I didn't plant it and I don't know what the meet was about.'

'Who else might know, apart from Jimmy?'

'Lots of questions, your pillow talk isn't as romantic as it used to be. I wasn't Santo's handler, Lara, I was part of a management team that assessed what he brought to us. I wasn't in on the detail of his day-to-day operations.'

'Who was?'

'That's probably above your pay grade.'

She could feel herself getting annoyed. 'We have to be able to trust each other, don't we Colin?' A benevolent smirk but he was keeping his mouth shut. She tried another tack. 'Nothing else on the agenda?'

'Like what?'

Lara hesitated. From here on in she would be drawing attention to her own misdemeanours, offering up her weaknesses for Graham to exploit, even further. Her fingers played across his stomach. 'Was Santo looking at any of his own side?'

Graham brought one of his hands from behind his head and rested it on the nape of her neck. 'What makes you think that?'

'He was one of my informants. My dealings with him were ... unorthodox.'

'Your informant? You never knew he was UC?'

'No.'

A chuckle. 'So how do you mean, "unorthodox"?'

In for a penny. 'Bullying, threats, manipulation, blind eyes here, raid tip-offs there, favours against rivals. That sort of thing.'

His hand stroked her neck. 'Standard MO for a good detective, I'd have thought. I don't think you've got too much to worry about. Like I've said before, Lara, you'd go down well in Gangs.'

She felt a warm flush of relief. 'I was getting worried. He'd given me a big tip about some trucks off the Nullarbor that went nowhere. I wondered if he had me down as dirty when they rocked up empty.'

Graham rolled on top of her and she spread herself to accommodate him. He placed a finger over her mouth. 'Shush now,' he said.

Midafternoon, Cato strolled over for a very late lunch at the food hall. He felt vulnerable among the crowds, harbouring an unreasonable fear that some stranger was going to walk up and punch him hard on his knife wound. One bit of good news had come through by phone late-morning; test results showed he was free of hep C and any other potential nasties from sharing a dagger with Santo Rosetti. Things were looking up.

Cato found a free table and sat down with a seafood laksa. Adjacent to him a stocky young woman in nurse blues stood to leave, abandoning her half-read *West*. Cato leaned across and swiped it. The headline worried about the impact of a threatened mining tax on the fragile livelihoods of the state's billionaires. The Forbes rich-listers reckoned a combination of over-taxing, union bullies, and high wage demands would lead to them shifting operations to Africa where they knew how to do business. Two dollars a day they reckoned. The Premier was a tad alarmed and promised to see what he could do.

On one of the inside pages it was reported that the couple hospitalised after the recent drug-debt home invasion in Willagee had lost the child they were expecting. Cato phoned Karina.

'I'm sorry about Crystal and the baby.'

'Yeah.'

'Is she going to be okay?'

'Probably, but she won't be having any more kids. Found out anything yet?'

'No, sorry.'

'Lot on your plate I expect. Don't worry about it, what's the point anyway?'

The connection died. Cato had once again lost his appetite and the crossword blurred in front of him.

Ant lies at odds with tease. Nine letters.

His phone buzzed. It was Hutchens. 'Where are you?'

'The markets, having lunch.'

'Lunch? It's after three. You on bankers' hours or something? Eat up. Got a job for you.'

'You do know I'm on restricted duties. Injury and all that?'

'Yeah, yeah don't worry it's a fairy desk job.'

'What's the urgency?'

'I've got a deadline and I'm your boss.'

Cato's laksa was starting to congeal. Coming back to work so soon wasn't the best idea he'd had lately. 'Give me ten minutes.'

He killed his phone and tapped the pen against his teeth. The crossword came back into focus. *Ant lies at odds with tease*, an anagram. *Ant lies at*. Tantalise.

Cato went to sit in the naughty chair but DI Hutchens got him to close the door first.

'Tell me what you know about your mate Colin Graham.'

'Why?'

'Because I want some dirt on him.'

'Not sure that's appropriate. Sir.'

Hutchens squinted menacingly. 'What do you mean?'

Cato didn't flinch. 'Facts and evidence. Hearsay won't get the result you're after.'

Hutchens coughed. 'Intelligence. Not the same thing.'

Cato sighed. 'I'm out of the loop with what's been happening with DS Graham, both currently and in the years since I last worked with him. If you want my professional opinion on a colleague you'll have to fill me in a bit more. Even then I reserve the right to keep my opinions to myself.'

'Alright. I think Graham is dirty. I think he's trying to take over my job. And I think he's fucking Lara Sumich.'

'Which of those do you want to nail him for?'

'Unfortunately only one of them is a disciplinary issue so we'll proceed with "dirty".' Hutchens filled Cato in on what had been happening: the Jimmy Tran fixation even when alternative evidence, such as the knife in Cato's gut, suggested otherwise. The Papadakis fiasco. 'And to cap it all he's a smug prick.'

'Reckless, yes, but I haven't heard or seen anything to suggest he's dirty.'

'Yeah, fucking shame. That will only get him a slap on the wrist. I've lodged the Reckless report but I need some Dirty to really nail the bastard.'

'Sorry I can't help you there.'

Hutchens grunted. 'What about your time with him in Gangs? Any whispers?'

As far as Cato was concerned, DS Graham was guilty of little more than being a Hutchens clone. 'Nothing untoward.'

'Untoward? What kind of a fucking word is that?' Hutchens chucked his pen across the desk in a hissy fit. 'Go and park yourself at your computer. Have a look at DS Graham's history. See if you can spot anything "untoward".'

'No. You want him, you chase him.'

'You promised you'd be a team player when I took you back.'

'I've never *not* been a team player. I took everybody's fall last time, remember?'

'Pretty please? Mate? Just a quick scroll. I wouldn't be asking this if I didn't have reasonable grounds.'

'So share them.'

'I inquired about Graham further up the food chain. They all blanked me. It's a sure sign, mate.'

'So there's no evidence to back up your spurious claims but you see that as proof?'

'Instinct. Look Cato I really need you to help me out here.' A pause and a manipulative grin. 'Go on, you know you want to.'

Cato could feel himself folding. 'Why me?'

'You've worked with him and you see patterns others don't. Maybe it's those crosswords you do. You've got the gift, mate.'

'Yeah, right.'

'I need it for Internals by first thing Monday.'

And it was now Friday, late arvo. 'So you want me in on the weekend?'

Hutchens looked pained. 'You've had over a week off and it's only desk work.'

A week and a bit off for a stabbing, maybe he could get himself shot, and swing a fortnight? Cato remembered he had Jake coming for an overnighter. 'I can't do anything until Sunday, got the boy over.'

'Sure, buddy. Family's important. Sunday's fine. Long as you deliver.'

Playing the family card hadn't done the trick. Cato tried to think of another way out of this thankless task. 'Won't my browsing trigger alarms in the system?'

Hutchens scribbled something on a yellow post-it. 'My access code, your eyes only.'

Cato slipped the post-it into his shirt pocket. As Miss Grabowski, his old piano teacher, used to whisper in his ear as her hand guided his over the arpeggio: God moves in mysterious ways.

Lara felt energised. Graham had gone home to his family and it didn't bother her one bit. They'd fucked each other's brains out and she was ravenous. She scanned the fridge and freezer for signs of nourishment and settled on frozen lasagne. Not her usual attention to dietary balance but what the hell. She popped it in the microwave.

She needed to get back to being a cop. Graham had eased her mind about Santo Rosetti: it didn't look like she was on his radar. She'd queried why Colin was so upbeat and optimistic under the circumstances.

'Circumstances?'

'Hutchens. Disciplinary proceedings.'

'Sideshow.' Another one of his enigmatic smirks.

'Tell me. I can see you're dying to.'

'Gangs have been upping the ante on the Trans. In the last few days the gooks have lost half a kilo in a car stop, had a meth lab blown up, and had one of their dealers hospitalised in a home invasion.'

'Your doing?'

'Not directly: courtesy of a few leaks to traffic division and the Apaches. I always like to have a Plan B.'

'How does that help, apart from making you feel a whole lot better?'

'Piss them off enough, they'll make a mistake.'

She recalled Hutchens' interest in how much contact Tran and Graham might have had. 'It's personal with you, isn't it?'

'Hmmm?'

'You seem to put a whole lot more energy into nailing the Trans than you do any of the other gangs out there.'

'It helps to go to work with a spring in your step.'

The microwave beeped. Lara scraped the steaming food onto a plate. So who killed Santo Rosetti and why? If Jimmy Tran was theoretically clear, for now anyway, then Dieudonne was the key. The African had shown himself to be erratic or at least unable to walk away from provocation: getting involved in fights in Fremantle cafes, drawing attention to himself at the fireworks on Australia Day, stabbing Cato. Yet the murder of Santo was anything but erratic. The cubicle door had remained locked from the inside, meaning the killer was calm and calculating enough to climb over the partition leaving behind a deliberately confusing scene. Was Dieudonne, the former child soldier, that smart? Or was he only obeying orders? Maybe the trail still led back to Jimmy Tran after all.

21

Saturday, February 6th.

There was a knock at the door. Cato had been awake since before six: restless and disgruntled, fretting about his son and the job – in that order. That was progress at least. He shuffled to the door and opened it. Constable Quiet-and-Dangerous and his mate from the Madge Poisoning Squad.

'Morning, sir.'

Cato held out his wrists in handcuff-me mode. 'Fair cop.'

'Very funny, sir. May we come inside?'

Cato ushered them in. 'Has there been a development?'

'Of sorts.'

Cato gave Q-and-D the expectant look he was expecting.

'The vet confirms that there were traces of meat-like substance and poison in the dog's stomach.'

'Really?'

'However, as yet we have been unable to identify the poison or the origin of the meat.'

'There's a few shops around here. Did you check the IGA? Woolies?'

'There appear to be a number of disgruntled neighbours,' said Constable Quiet-and-Dangerous, 'of which you seem to have been the most vocal and most forensically aware.'

Forensically aware. What was this, *Criminal Minds*? 'And?'

'And you remain a key person of interest.'

Somebody's been reading the Ace Detective's Manual, thought Cato. Chapter Nine – Pressure the Prime Suspect into a Fatal Mistake. 'What do these other disgruntled neighbours say? Any of them have foul deeds in mind?'

'That's confidential.'

Cato showed them both to the front door. 'Keep me posted guys. Cracking this case could be your ticket into the Ds.'

'Particularly if there's a sudden vacancy,' said Constable Q-and-D, settling his uniform cap back on his head and squinting into the sunshine.

'What do you think?'

Lara had just finished outlining her theory to Colin Graham. She'd taken him away from his weekend of domestic bliss. They had an hour, that's all, he'd said tersely. She'd laid out the Dieudonne–Jimmy Tran scenario over a coffee at The Blue Duck at Cottesloe, halfway between their Floreat and Fremantle homes. The sea sparkled flat and blue and children frolicked where a great white had taken a morning swimmer a few years back. The cafe was full, everybody summer-casual and most of them expensively so. There was enough of a busy breakfast hubbub to mask the details of their conversation. 'Col?' she pressed. 'Thoughts?'

'Maybe,' he said. 'But we can't go back to Jimmy without some knockout evidence.'

'He still hasn't explained what his semen was doing in Santo's mouth.'

'So they're good friends. It's a nice bit of gossip but it doesn't give us anything to hang Jimmy with.'

'They were intimate. That night.'

'Tran doesn't deny that. He's a well-known pillow-biter. Word around the traps is that he likes his couriers to give him blowjobs and pretend they like him. It's his special little way of exerting control.'

'A hell of a way to maintain cover.' Lara wondered what Mr and Mrs Rosetti would make of that aspect of their son's job description. 'But we've now narrowed the window of their likely encounter down to a specified time in the Birdcage.'

'Jimmy said he was there for a couple of hours. It's still a big window between blowjob and murder.'

An old woman at the next table gave them a look, half-disapproving, half-inquisitive. Lara dropped her voice further. 'But the photo you showed me on that mobile from the club, Santo with his arm around Jimmy's shoulder. I noted the time it was taken. That was less than half an hour before Jimmy said he left the club.'

'And?'

'And while I've done a quick trawl, we haven't gone through all those phones properly looking for the African yet: or the CCTV for that matter. Our focus has been Santo and the Trans. We should be looking at who Dieudonne is tied up with.'

'So all we need is some footage of Jimmy Tran ordering the African to kill Santo and hey presto.' Graham smiled mockingly.

'A week ago you would have been hot to trot on anything that pointed you in Jimmy Tran's direction. Now you're as sceptical as DI Hutchens. What happened, Col?'

Graham drained his coffee. 'Hutchens is trying to have me sacked, I've had a gutful of Jimmy Tran, and I prefer to be called Colin, not Col.' He gathered his things. 'Family commitments. Sorry.'

Jane and Jake rolled up just as Constable Quiet-and-Dangerous left.

'Work?' said Jane, glancing at the departing cop car and handing Cato an overnight bag. There was no disguising the coolness in her voice even if her expression seemed serenely neutral. Her hair had been cropped and styled. Her clothes seemed more fitting. The new job and new boyfriend suited her. Cato felt a pang of loss.

'Of sorts.' Jake sidled up and Cato caressed the top of his head. 'How was your week?'

'Good,' said Jake.

'Great,' said Cato. They waved Jane off. 'Same time tomorrow.'

Jake slung his things into the spare bedroom and they settled out back with a cold Milo and a pot of coffee. Cato tried to study his son without seeming to.

'What's been happening with you, then?' he said breezily.

'Nuthin' much.'

'School going okay?'

'Yep.'

'How you getting on with Simon?'

'Fine.'

'Mum?'

'Everything's fine. What's with the questions?' A scowl and a slurp of Milo.

A tactical retreat was in order. 'So, what do you fancy doing today? Beach? Pool? Movies?'

A flick of the hand towards Cato's gut. 'You can't do much with your injury.'

'Movies then?'

'Okay.'

Two or three hours in air conditioning sounded just the job. They settled on yet another Marvel superhero movie and when they came out later they both agreed it kind of sucked.

Lara spent Saturday afternoon trailing around shops south of the river that had sleeping bags, pillows and bedding for sale. To try to narrow it down she kept to within about a ten-kilometre radius of Fremantle on the assumption that Dieudonne was still on foot or public transport. It was pretty loose as deductive reasoning goes, but you had to start somewhere.

She flashed pics of him and left them with storeowners in a succession of soulless suburban shopping precincts but her expectations were low. If he really was a murder suspect and this was a proper manhunt, then the area should have been saturated with uniforms, public transport CCTV would have been trawled, et cetera, et cetera. But it seemed to be a low priority. Was it because his victims were a drug pusher and a dero? So the drug pusher had been an undercover cop and the dero was actually the son of a District Court judge, but those facts remained taboo. Nobody wanted to go there for various reasons: Santo Rosetti was possibly poking his nose into dirty cop business and the powers-that-be wouldn't have wanted a secretive intelligence unit opened up to public scrutiny. Santo's parents had been visited by HQ brass to ensure they helped keep a lid on who he really was. Meanwhile Jeremy Dixon had played Fagin to a band of child thieves who plagued the suburbs. Lara could almost see HQ's point: there were better places to focus public attention and limited resources.

'Yeah, he was in here yesterday.'

'What?'

The shop manager, a heavy-set woman covered in bling, prodded the picture of Dieudonne. Her badge said *Francesca*. 'Him.'

'You sure?' Lara pushed the photo closer.

'Yeah. Never forget a bod. He was ripped, love. Bit short, but ripped.'

It was a leisure and camping superstore on Leach Highway in Melville. Lara checked the walls and ceiling. 'CCTV?'

'Yeah, we got it. What's he done?'

Lara ignored the question. 'When was he here? What did he buy?'

'Yesterday afternoon, nearly closing. A sleeping bag. I said to him, "What, just for you, all alone?" He could have come home and shared my waterbed. Hubby's not back from the mine until next week. We could have made beautiful waves together.' She laughed like a sewer. 'So what's he done, then?'

'He's wanted for questioning in relation to a number of serious crimes. If he comes in again would you call me?' Lara handed her a card. 'Meantime, maybe I could have a look at the CCTV?'

'Mad, bad and dangerous to know, huh? My kind of man.'

You don't know the half of it, thought Lara.

For dinner, Cato and Jake had fish and chips from the shop around the corner on South Terrace. They even tried a carton of mushy peas for the novelty value.

'Doesn't taste so bad,' said Cato. 'Kind of like warm green mud.'

'Looks like snot,' said Jake wrinkling his face in disgust.

Cato turned away briefly and when he faced Jake again he had a smear of mushy peas under his nostrils. 'Got a hankie?'

'Aw yuck.' Jake collapsed into giggles.

They cleared away the chip papers. Jake lay on the couch reading an Artemis Fowl while Cato sat before the piano. He chose a Satie, *Gnossienes.* It was soothing yet he was aware that something melancholic had settled over the two of them. Towards the end of the piece Cato became aware of a squeak and a muted sob behind him. Jake was crying. He went over, sat beside him, hugged him close.

'What's up?'

'Nothing.'

'Come on.' A shake of the head buried into his side. Jake's shudders gradually subsided. He whispered something. 'What was that, mate?'

'I want our family back.'

Cato felt his heart break. He searched for some words. 'I know you do, bub, but your mum and I can't live together anymore.' What was the other thing you were always meant to say in these situations? 'But you know that we both love you, don't you?'

No response.

Cato lifted his son's face to look into his eyes. 'You do know that, don't you?'

Jake nodded and looked away, unconvinced. He reached a hand towards Cato's knife wound. 'Are you gunna die?'

Cato hugged him close again. 'Not for a long time.'

22

Sunday, February 7th. Midmorning.

The City of Fremantle sits within the Aboriginal cultural region of Beeliar. Its Noongar name is Walyalup, the place of crying, and the local people are called Whadjuk. The Whadjuk used to hold their funeral rites here: the deceased would be buried in the sand dunes and the singing and mourning would start so that the dead could go on their next journey into the spirit world. Jake had told Cato all about it last night after another hug, a reviving Milo, and a 'Chopsticks' duet on the piano. It had been part of his research for some homework – 'My Town'. So Fremantle had always been a place for crying and funerals. It figured, thought Cato, particularly the last few weeks.

Cato was glad to have the office to himself. He was also unexpectedly glad to have some work to occupy him. Jane had picked up Jake, and Cato found a moment to give her a potted version of what passed between them. Relief softened her features, filled her eyes.

'I thought it was about Simon.'

'Not specifically, no. He just wants what he can't have and he thought if he said that, then the sky would fall in.'

'Poor little bugger.'

'Yep.'

She'd given Cato a hug and left. It was the first connection and warmth between them in many months. He realised he'd missed it. He couldn't deliver on what Jake wanted but at least he now knew that his son still liked snot jokes. Cato was beginning to feel like a parent again for the first time in a long while.

Shellie Petkovic crowded into his thoughts: she'd had parenthood brutally snatched away from her. Cato switched on his computer. He flipped open his wallet and plucked out the post-it with Hutchens' access code. It was meant to authorise him to dig the dirt on Colin Graham on his boss's behalf but it would also enable him to tiptoe through Hutchens' own career without tripping any alarms in the system. Cato could now check, one last time, if there was anything in the Hutchens–Wellard relationship that might help him make more sense of the undercurrents in this case.

He navigated his way in. The file recorded, in dry terse prose, Hutchens' rise through the ranks from police academy, through time on the streets in uniform, country postings, various investigation branches as a detective, and his early successes and promotions in the Armed Robbery Squad under Andy Crouch. These, according to Crouch, were the early days of Hutchens' dealings with Gordon Francis Wellard. Were those early successes and promotions due to him being a good cop under a good mentor like Crouch? Or did luck come in the form of Wellard and, if so, at what price?

Case one. Four TAB hold-ups during a wintry fortnight in July, the perp wielding a sawn-off to relieve the bookies of over half a million in total. During the fourth hold-up, in the northern suburb of Balcatta, the duty manager decides to have a go and gets the gun barrel shoved in his teeth. He shits himself before being clubbed senseless. After a tip-off, Hutchens, Crouch and a heavily armed team lie in wait for the fifth TAB hold-up in Malaga. After an exchange of fire they nab their man. He is wheeled away on a stretcher with gunshot wounds to the upper legs. Detective Constable Michael Hutchens is commended for his bravery in confronting the armed gunman and acting quickly to protect the safety of the public and his colleagues. A coded reference number was given for the informant but when Cato tried to access the name he was denied. So even Hutchens was locked out of *that* level of the system. Cato wrote the reference number down and pressed on.

Case two. Nine months later. Newly promoted off-duty Detective Senior Constable Hutchens apprehends a youth holding up a twenty-four hour convenience store in Belmont: weapon of choice, a blood-filled syringe. Another commendation notes it was pure good luck that he happened to be there at 2.45 in the morning given that he wasn't working or living anywhere near Belmont at the time.

And so it went on. From Detective Senior Constable to Detective Sergeant. Sometimes tip-offs, sometimes fortune, sometimes good coppering, and often just plain criminal stupidity. Sometimes that same informant reference number and sometimes not.

On to Detective Senior Sergeant Hutchens and then Inspector and the spectacular screw-up on an innocent man framed for murder that led to Hutchens' posting to Albany, and Cato's exile to Stock Squad. The files contained nothing specific to link Hutchens and Wellard except the same coded reference that may or may not be him.

So what qualified Gordon Wellard to be Hutchens' informant? His criminal history was tied up in petty drug offences, assault, domestic violence, rape. How would he have the inside dirt on upcoming armed robberies? Something nagged at Cato. Andy Crouch on big brother, Kevin. *He was a hard case. Made Gordy look like a cheap imitation.*

Cato diverted off into Kev's criminal history in the archives – dead he might be, but his crimes lived on in cyberspace. That was more like it: standover and extortion, firearms offences, armed robberies, and very bad company. Big brother was moving in exactly the right circles. So Gordon's jewels of intelligence most likely came from Kevin. Gordy Wellard was just a messenger boy.

Cato returned to Hutchens' career file. The dates were wrong. Some of the possible tip-offs occurred well after Kevin's death in November 1996. He re-checked the informant source codes. The same ones that peppered the file before Kev died continued into his afterlife. So if little brother Gordy was one of those informers perhaps he'd ingratiated himself with the really bad boys to continue the supply of information. Or Cato's theory was simply wrong and Kevin hadn't been the real snitch. Either way it didn't get him any closer to understanding what was going on between Hutchens and Gordy Wellard now. In the meantime Cato decided to push on and go for a late lunch and a short day; he closed the Hutchens and Wellard files and opened up Colin Graham for inspection.

Colin Graham's career history read very much like that of DI Hutchens: maybe that's why the DI had taken a strong dislike to him. The usual ingredients had seen Colin Graham also rise steadily in the ranks. The only surprise was that he hadn't actually got any further. He didn't seem to have put a foot wrong. By that reckoning he should have been at least Senior Sergeant or Inspector by now, instead of plain old DS. His career seemed to have stalled for the last three or four years, yet he was still getting results and commendations. The most recent was two years ago. A raid on the Marangaroo home of a high-ranking drug dealer with Eastern States loyalties had resulted in a shoot-out. The dealer died. DS Graham was exonerated by an internal inquiry and later commended for his swift and decisive action to defend the lives of his colleagues.

Where most high-flyers used various departments as stepping-stones towards the top jobs, Graham seemed to have landed in the Gangs section of Organised Crime and stayed there. Maybe he'd found his niche, liked it, and didn't want to move.

Cato recalled their time together in Gangs. Graham was a sharp operator: charming, funny, cold, threatening, one of the boys, a lone wolf, bent, straight. A man for all seasons. Had Cato trusted him? Yes. They'd been in a number of hair-raising situations together and Cato had never not-believed that he could rely on his partner to help get them out safely. Dirty Harry and the Jedi, childish blokey nicknames for each other. But Cato's fond reminiscences of *dos hombres* leading the fight between good and evil didn't really help DI Hutchens achieve his aims. Was Cato really going to let himself be dragged into this? Both Hutchens and Graham were big enough to fight their own battles. Cato scrolled through the remainder of Graham's file as a prelude to wrapping up for the day.

And then he spotted a familiar name.

23

Monday, February 8th. Morning.

'Cato. In here. Now.'

DI Hutchens' desk looked nice and tidy. The phone was parallel to the edge allowing a three-centimetre border. There was an A4 note pad and biro in the centre approximately ten centimetres in front of the DI's elbows: in-and-out-trays in the top left and right corners: a closed laptop just to his left and a half-drunk mug of coffee just beyond his right hand. Up on the filing cabinet to his right, a picture of Mrs Hutchens at a posh function in a plunging neckline.

'Boss?' said Cato.

'Shut the door behind you.'

He did.

'Sit down.'

Ditto.

'What are you playing at?'

'Hmm?'

Cato wondered how Hutchens had busted him so quickly. He'd half-expected Hutchens to follow where he'd been in the database so before he logged off he'd attempted to leave a false trail. It wasn't foolproof and it relied on Hutchens being lazy, preoccupied, and not too tech-savvy. Any of those was a fair bet on most days but the look on Hutchens' face suggested that Cato had underestimated him.

Hutchens leaned back in his chair and waved his hand in front of him. 'Look at my desk, what do you see?'

'Very neat, sir.'

'No fucking Colin Graham report, that's what.'

'Ah,' said Cato, relieved at possibly dodging a bullet.

'Ah,' said Hutchens.

Cato cleared his throat. 'His record is spotless, sir. Never put a foot wrong. Nothing to report.'

'Nothing?'

'Nothing concrete, nothing of consequence.'

Hutchens' eyes narrowed. 'Explain yourself.'

'He had a professional run-in with Santo Rosetti a few months ago.'

'Really? That's interesting. Tell me more.'

'I reckon you know it already. It's a five-minute job to scan Graham's record. Even a busy bloke like you would have found time for that.'

'Humour me,' said Hutchens.

'Claim and counter-claim on a botched raid. Each blamed the other. A couple of shipments of ice in two trucks go walkabout, a prominent Perth identity escapes charges, and Gangs suspects a mole in their midst. You're figuring on using that to try and tie Col to Rosetti's murder?'

Hutchens shook his head and tutted. 'But we'd need facts and evidence for that, wouldn't we?'

'And you want me to go looking for some, on the quiet.'

'It's what you do best, Cato.'

'And whether or not I find any, mud sticks: especially if there's a parallel disciplinary inquiry. Keeps him from sniffing around your job, if that's what he's doing.'

Hutchens eyes twinkled. 'I hadn't thought of it like that.'

'What if I say no?'

'Why would you?'

'It's my job to investigate crime, not dob on colleagues.'

'What if he really is implicated in Rosetti's murder?'

'It's Lara's case; she can work it out. Or bring in the Internals.'

'I've already got the Inquisition looking at him for the Greek fiasco. It's all around the office: Graham's fucking Lara, she's not objective right now.'

Objectivity: not Hutchens' strong point either. Cato said nothing.

'It's not like you're over-stretched, Cato. Restricted duties until you've fully recuperated. And I've received your email recommending DC Thornton be allowed to run with Safer Streets. Given how busy you might be in the immediate future, the answer's a provisional yes.' Hutchens smiled encouragingly. 'You might even crack the Rosetti case. How would that look?'

Cato tried another avoidance tactic. 'I'd need resources. Lots. You can't do something like this on your own.'

'Sure you could. All you need to do is look closer at what Rosetti was investigating before he died and get more details on the tiff they had. I've got a number for Rosetti's UC handler, that's a starting point. If anything comes of it, IA will put in all the resources it needs.'

Cato tried a last desperate act. He grimaced. 'I'll give it a go but my injury's been playing up lately. I might have come back to work a bit too early.'

Hutchens looked concerned. 'Sure. Take it easy, mate, nice and slow. Don't bust a gut.'

Lara saw the expression on Cato Kwong's face as he emerged from Hutchens' office. She felt unexpectedly sympathetic.

'How's it going?'

He looked cornered. 'Been better.'

'The gut?'

'On the mend.' He patted it gingerly.

'What are you working on at the moment?'

'Paperwork. Reports. Stuff.' He pointed to his wound. 'Not up to much at the moment.'

'Poor thing.' She surprised herself at how genuine she sounded. He seemed a bit taken aback too. 'If there's anything I can do to help, let me know.'

'Sure. Thanks.' He disappeared behind his partition.

The office was like that these days. Hutchens was in siege mode and his example had infected the rest. Everybody was heads down, bums up and cards close to chests. In some ways she preferred it like that. She heard Cato murmuring on the phone. Lara could see Hutchens staring at her through his open office door. The stare turned into a summons.

'Boss?' She stood at the threshold, hip cocked.

'Come in and close the door.' She did and took a seat. 'Where are we at with Rosetti, the Trans, Papadakis, the dero. Remind me. It's all getting a bit ...' He flapped his hands uselessly.

Lara knew how he felt. She summarised the main points. 'Jimmy Tran denies murdering Rosetti, as you know, and the blood evidence on the knife used to stab Cato implicates Dieudonne.'

'Check.'

'Tran also denies any responsibility for the death of Mr Papadakis and suggests Mickey Nguyen was responsible, acting under his own volition.'

'Volition. Nice word. Check.'

'Mickey burned to death so we can't ask him.'

'Which leaves the dero. What's happening there?'

'Forensics finished with the Willagee house over the weekend. There was a sleeping bag and some books, I'm betting they were Dieudonne's. So if our man was there, and the "dero" – his name's Jeremy Dixon by the way – told me he was, then he'll have left traces. Dieudonne doesn't seem that worried about clearing up after himself.'

'Strange.'

'Why?'

'Well if it *was* him that did Rosetti, he went through all that palaver with the locked cubicle door and other smartypants stuff. Since then he's been like a bull in a china shop. What do you reckon, Lara?'

'The same thought occurred to me over the weekend.'

'And?'

'Maybe he was under specific orders for the Rosetti killing to muddy the waters but since then he's been doing his own thing?'

'Orders from who?'

'Jimmy Tran?'

'You're determined to get Jimmy aren't you? What's your evidence for a connection between him and the African?'

'None so far. I was going to re-examine the CCTV and the mobile phone footage, ditto the witness statements, maybe reinterview club staff and patrons. We were looking for Santo and Jimmy first time round. Can I ask you something, boss?'

'Fire away.'

'In the interview with Tran the other day you seemed to be interested in a past history between Graham and the Trans. Why?'

Hutchens scratched his nose. 'I'm just wondering if there's something personal in Col's obsession with Jimmy.'

Lara conceded the point with a nod. 'Either way, the key to this is Dieudonne. We need to find him.'

'Need any help?'

About time. 'Is there a reason this hasn't been getting the attention it deserves, boss?'

'How do you mean?'

She counted on her fingers. 'Rosetti, Dixon, Papadakis, Nguyen. Four dead in a fortnight and it's as if we're not that fussed. I've seen more resources go into a Northbridge juvey round-up. It's like we're setting ourselves up to fail.'

'Why would we want do that?'

To put me in my place maybe? Lara shrugged.

A warning frown, he'd read her mind. 'Lara, this job's tough enough without carrying around a bloody great chip on your shoulder. If I didn't have faith in you, you'd still be in Albany chasing bogans. We have Major Crime, area Ds, and uniforms doing the donkeywork on Papadakis and Nguyen. The other two, we already know whodunnit – Dieudonne. We've got pressure from above to be discreet about the UC aspect with Santo. It's a balancing act and I'm doing my best. So, I ask again, who do you want to help?'

Lara realised she'd better pull her head in. Resources allocation and case management were not in her job description. 'Well DS Meldrum is in charge and I'm sure he'll come to you if we need any more bodies, boss.'

'Both you and I know that Graham was running the case and the whole time Meldrum has been twiddling his thumbs. Leave him to his Rotary talks. Get Cato to help you with the office stuff: the CCTV, the mobes and the statements. You get out there and find the fucker.'

It made sense. She didn't even feel her usual territoriality about letting Cato near her case. So why, when she closed the door on Hutchens' office, did she feel like she'd just been had?

Cato hadn't looked at any pictures, and tried not to think about the man who had become known as Dieudonne. Now he was there in front of him, a blurry CCTV image on Lara's laptop. Cato had the musky smell of him in his nostrils, the breath, the gleam of teeth: the feel of his wrist tendons as they fought for control of the knife.

Do not struggle, my friend. Accept it.

Cato was sweating. The room swirled.

'You okay?' Lara, looking concerned.

'Yeah.' Cato swallowed down his rising nausea. 'So he was in a camping shop at the weekend. What now?'

'He's been good at staying off the radar. Maybe he picked up a few camouflage tricks in the Congo. He bought a cheapo sleeping bag with cash then caught a bus on Leach Highway heading west. Got off again at Freo Station.' She clicked her fingers. 'Poofff. Thin air. Frankly I don't know where to start.'

'And you think he's being run by Jimmy Tran?'

'It's an idea.'

'Tried asking Tran where this bloke is?'

'You serious?'

'Why not?'

'And Hutchens thought you'd be able to help me.' She closed her laptop grumpily. 'Any other ideas, hotshot?'

'You got a number for Jimmy Tran?'

'You *are* serious aren't you?' She gave him the number.

They found the Tran brothers at an outside table at the rear of Little Creatures down by Fishing Boat Harbour. Late afternoon on a weekday and it may as well have been prime-time Friday night: the beer barn was packed to its high rafters. Out on the harbour, crayboats and trawlers creaked on their moorings and seagulls squawked for attention. There was an aroma of salt, oil, hot chips and beer in the lacklustre breeze. Jimmy and Vincent had dressed up, clean shirts with collars, boardies and trainers. In their 'going-out' gear, Lara noticed how similar they looked. Vincent, although younger, was a slightly bigger and more muscular version of his brother.

'Business meeting?' said Lara, waving her fingers at their attire.

They ignored her. She introduced Cato. Vincent, the strong silent type, just stared and unwrapped a stick of gum. Jimmy Tran studied Cato and cracked a smile. 'We met a few years ago I think?'

Cato shook hands with the Trans. 'Life treating you well, Jimmy?'

'Can't complain.' Jimmy glanced at Lara. 'Even if I wanted to.' Cato took drink orders and headed for the bar. Jimmy watched him go. 'Hospitable. Friendly. Respectful. He's an improvement on DS Graham.'

'You think so?' said Lara.

'So what's he here for? Speakee the lingo with the natives?'

'He's helping me out.'

'Where's DS Graham?'

'Unavailable.'

'Pending a disciplinary hearing.'

'You're well informed.'

'I make it my business to be.'

'We need your help, Jimmy.'

'If you're after favours it's "Mr Tran". Remember?'

She played along. 'Mr Tran.'

He snorted and raised a Rogers to his lips. 'You can't afford me.'

Cato returned with two new Rogers for the boys, a pilsener for Lara, and a lemon, lime and bitters for himself. He chucked in a packet of Nobby's Nuts for good measure. 'Cheers.'

Jimmy was clearly bored with Lara, he latched onto Cato instead. 'You the tracker or something?'

Cato acted like he didn't get it. 'Sorry?'

'What's the Chinese equivalent of a coconut?'

Cato smiled. 'It didn't work when I was in Gangs, Jimmy. Not going to work now, is it? We wouldn't want to insult your intelligence.'

Jimmy seemed to like that. 'So what are you after and what's in it for me?'

Lara unfolded the pic of Dieudonne and slid it over the table.

'Can you tell us where to find him?'

Both Trans leaned over for a look. Jimmy lifted his head. 'Who is he?'

Lara looked him in the eye and realised this was one of those rare occasions when Jimmy Tran was probably telling the truth.

Cato studied the back of Superintendent Scott's head. He needed a haircut and a neck shave and there was a pimple struggling to the surface. It was an anomaly in an otherwise carefully groomed image. A faulty fluoro flickered in the corridor and Scott pointed it out to a passing staff member.

'Get somebody onto it, today.'

A smell of large-scale cooking in the air: spag bol for dinner. Cato's stomach rumbling at the thought of prison food? He'd never have imagined it. As Lara had driven them away from Little Creatures, she'd seemed preoccupied.

'So the Trans don't know the African either?' Cato prompted.

'Doesn't look like it.'

At the crossroads there was an interlude of passing Fremantle scenery: sunburnt backpackers spilling out of the Norfolk Hotel, an old Noongar limping across the road and made to hurry by a BMW convertible running the amber. 'What's Colin's thoughts?'

Grumpy gear change. 'He's off the case. Doesn't matter what his thoughts are.'

'Right, sure.' Cato could see a pulse in the skin at her left temple. He didn't envy the pressure she would be under to find Dieudonne, and now an extra pair of hands had been taken away from her because of Hutchens and his office politics. Cato found it hard to believe there could be any substance to the DI's machinations. 'Hopefully that'll get sorted out soon. We can't afford to let the Cols of this world sit idle. Dirty Harry'll bounce back soon enough.'

'What's with the nickname?' said Lara.

'It's what I called him when we worked together a few years ago. He lives on the edge but he gets results.'

They pulled up outside Freo cop shop.

'So you're old mates then?'

Cato recalled another conversation in a Red Rooster. 'Not mates really, more like partners.'

Then Superintendent Scott had called him on his mobile. 'Wellard wants to speak to you, alone. Says it's urgent.'

'Tell him to write me a letter. I'm not in the business of pandering to people like him.'

'Yeah, that's what I told him, more or less. He said it's about his brother. Thought you might be interested.'

Cato was. 'Is he still frothing at the mouth?'

'Nah, we've been feeding him the happy pills since then. He's a pussycat.'

Cato took his seat in the interview room.

Wellard's lip had a fresh scab but apart from that there were no obvious signs of their previous encounter. 'Why are you interested in Kev?'

Something was bothering Wellard. His eyes were glazed but his facial muscles were working overtime and he kept glancing up at the camera. Maybe they needed to up the dosage on the happy pills.

'You asked me to come here, Gordon. I'm not here to answer your questions. What is it you want to tell me about your brother?'

'Kev's dead.'

'I know, I read it in the paper. November 1996.'

Wellard blinked and chewed his fingernail. 'Whatever. I want to know who killed him.'

'What makes you think somebody killed him?'

'He disappeared. Didn't come back.'

'Now you know how Shellie feels.'

'This isn't about her, it's about me.'

'Not as far as I'm concerned. Anyway, Kev's old news, we're talking fifteen years or more. You need to build a bridge, mate.'

Wellard sniffed, looked pissed off. 'They're out to get me.'

'Who?'

'Dunno. Been getting funny looks the last few days. Something's goin' on. Ever since you came to see me last time. Did you mention Kev as a threat to me?'

'Feeling a bit vulnerable?'

'Gofuckyerself.' Cool, cocky ice man had reverted to a whining teenager.

Cato looked at the clock on the wall. 'Time for my dinner. Enjoy your spag bol; hope nobody puts anything in it.'

'What does Mr Hutchens say about me?'

'He reckons you're a waste of oxygen. No use to him any more.'

'He wants me dead, doesn't he?'

'You're not the centre of his universe, Gordy.' Cato rose to leave. 'I've got a bit on today, mate. You invited me here. You're wasting my time.'

'I bet he knows who killed Kev.'

'Why would he?'

A sly smile. 'There's lots he knows that he's not telling.'

'That makes two of you. Look, maybe he does know but unless you're offering anything in return we're not interested.'

'What about Briony?'

'No more mind games, Gordy. No more outings. No more deals. If you want to tell us where she is, draw a mud map and get the Super to fax it through.'

Cato settled in for an evening of Indian takeaway and trash TV. He'd just left another message on the number Hutchens had given him for Santo Rosetti's UC handler, a bloke called 'John'. Time to call it a day, eat some fast food and watch *The Biggest Loser*. There was a knock at his front door. It was Shellie. With a bottle of red wine.

'Hi,' said Cato. 'Everything okay?' Stupid question.

Shellie brushed past him, collected two glasses from his kitchen and sat down in the armchair he'd saved for himself. She sloshed some cleanskin shiraz into the glasses and shoved Cato's and the plate of curry across the table. 'Cheers. Don't mind me.'

'What are you doing here, Shellie?' She shrugged and took a great interest in *The Biggest Loser*. 'Shellie?'

She took a slurp and banged her glass back on the table. 'You haven't a fucking clue.'

It didn't seem to invite a reply.

Shellie tapped her forehead. 'You live up here. Maybe you have to because of your job. Everything's a mystery, a game, a bloody puzzle.' She took another slurp, eyes blazing.

'Shellie, I ...'

'Shut up and listen.'

Cato muted the TV and did as he was told.

'I still see Bree. Out on the streets, in shops ... around.' She held the glass to her cheek. 'Sometimes she's fifteen with that bloody ugly lip stud. Sometimes she's a young woman, an office worker or a student or something, making her way in the world. Once I saw her and she was still only six, in her tutu and fairy wings.' Shellie's eyes brimmed and she laughed bitterly. 'How fucked up is that? Sometimes I lie in bed in the morning waiting for Bree to come and jump on me like she did when she was three.'

Cato searched for words but couldn't find any. Shellie was right: he didn't have a clue. Faced with this raw grief he felt useless.

'Everything I do, everywhere I go, every day, she's there and she's not there. Sometimes I think I'm getting better, normal, managing you know? Other times, like now, I feel like I'm going mad. Or I want to join her.' Shellie refilled her glass, a shaking hand lifted it to her lips. 'I brought that bastard into her life.'

'You couldn't have known what he was like.'

'No? Maybe deep down I did. Maybe I'm the one who's really to blame for all this. Who knows?' Shellie put down her glass and stared directly into Cato's eyes. 'Wellard's telling me it's "finders keepers", he's saying Bree belongs to him and he won't give her back. What would you do?'

'Did another note turn up?'

'No. Answer my question.'

'I don't know,' said Cato.

She drained her glass and stood to leave.

'You can't go, not like this.'

'What are you offering? A shoulder to cry on? A comfort fuck?' She shook her head and made for the door. 'Once bitten.'

He reached out a hand. 'You need to get help.'

She turned. 'Fuck off. I'll decide what I need.'

Cato had no answers. Maybe Wellard would send through his

mud map in the morning and it would all be over. On TV there was a close-up of a chubby surprised face. A big loser had just learned he'd been eliminated.

Cato was woken by his mobile. He groaned. He'd been in the middle of a not unpleasant dream involving Shellie Petkovic and some antiseptic ointment. Under the current circumstances, his erotic fixation with her was cause for significant ethical concern. All the same, nice dream. The caller was Hutchens and it was just gone 5.45.

'You awake?'

'No.'

'Good, we need to go out to Casuarina. Up for it?'

'No. I've been stabbed. It hurts.'

'Somebody's topped Wellard. You interested now?

24

Tuesday, February 9th. Dawn.

They'd made short work of Gordon Francis Wellard. A sharpened, tape-reinforced toothbrush had been rammed into his right eye and, according to the on-site medic, had penetrated the brain. Just to make sure, somebody had stamped on his head several times. There was blood all over the kitchen floor and crime tape keeping the scene off-limits. Breakfast was being bussed in from a catering service out near the airport, plastic cutlery and all. The Casuarina inmates were in lockdown – it would be room service only today.

Cato looked at his boss. DI Hutchens was transfixed by the image of Wellard curled up in the corner beside the fridge.

'Who did it?' said Hutchens.

Superintendent Scott cleaned his spectacles on his tie. 'Bikies. It looks like there were two and the CCTV identifies them as Apache associates. We have them isolated and under watch and their cells have been taped off.'

Hutchens grunted. 'Sequence of events?'

'Alarm raised at 04.52. My officers were called by a prisoner from the kitchen breakfast roster who found him. They attended and initiated a Code Red. We immediately summoned paramedic staff from the hospital block. They arrived within a few minutes and confirmed death. You'll be wanting the logs and the names of those involved?'

'Sure,' said Hutchens, 'and the CCTV, and the visitors and phone logs all in good time. Any motives yet?'

Scott sniffed. 'Apart from the fact that everybody thought he was a sick puppy who didn't know when to stop yapping? No.'

Cato thought about his last meeting with Wellard yesterday.

They're out to get me ... Been getting funny looks the last few days. Something's going on.

Gordon Wellard was right. Something had been going on and someone was out to get him. Cato looked up at the camera mounted on the wall in the corner where Wellard lay. It pointed away from the body towards a serving counter. There was a second camera on the wall above the counter, looking back into the kitchen area. A third sat dead centre on the ceiling.

'There's somebody monitoring the security vision all the time?' asked Cato.

'Sure, we can take you to the control room whenever you like.'

DI Hutchens shook his head. 'Later.' He marshalled some minions to do witness interviews. Hutchens tapped Cato on the shoulder. 'You're with me. I want to talk to these pesky injuns now.'

'The Apaches? Which one first?' said Scott, summoning a jailer.

'The stupidest,' said Hutchens.

'That'll be Danny Boy,' said Superintendent Scott.

Danny Mercurio was a bikie from central casting. Dodgy facial hair, built like the brick proverbial, tattoos, et cetera. He was sitting in an interview room in his prison-visit greys: there were two screws hovering just outside the door and the recording equipment was on.

'Which were you: toothbrush or headkicker?' inquired Hutchens.

'Nuthin' to say.' Mercurio's voice was higher than Cato expected, like maybe he'd swallowed a jockey.

Hutchens sized him up. 'Headkicker, I reckon. Toothbrush needed a bit of finesse: right on target. Can't see you having the necessary hand–eye coordination.'

'Where's my lawyer?'

'Mr Hurley's stuck in traffic on the freeway.'

'Sat'dy mornin'?'

Hutchens nodded. 'I know, the road system's shithouse isn't it? Need some of that Royalties for Regions money in Perth, I reckon.'

'Saying nuthin' without the lawyer.' Mercurio folded his arms and stared at the ceiling.

Hutchens aped the gesture. 'What would you be saying if he was here?'

'Nuthin'.'

'Due out soon aren't you? Another few months.'

'No comment.'

Danny's mate was reading from the same script. Kenny Lovett also had nothing to say and wasn't fazed by the fact that, with just a few months left to serve on his sentence, he seemed set for a much longer stretch. Kenny dismissed, Cato and Hutchens retreated to the staff canteen, nursing coffees and waiting for the bikies' lawyer, Henry Hurley. The rest of the morning would no doubt be a frustrating and time-wasting series of 'no comment' sessions. Cato was aware of a healthy enmity between Hooray Henry and his boss, dating back to their encounter on the Hopetoun case, perhaps earlier. Hutchens had treated himself to a bacon and egg toastie from the self-service food warmer and was examining the insides closely.

'Do you reckon they spit in the food?'

There was nobody around apart from two tired-looking corrections officers. 'On their wages I reckon I would, yeah.'

'I meant the prisoners, dickhead.'

'I can't see staff allowing them anywhere near these kitchens, boss.'

Hutchens risked a bite and chewed thoughtfully. 'Why have those gorillas just opted to spend the rest of their lives in a cage? I know they're not too bright but this is something else.'

'They really took a strong dislike to Wellard?'

'Who wouldn't? But this smacks of an obligation. Either the pay-off was well worth the extra time, or the consequences of not doing it were a whole lot worse.' Hutchens' mobile buzzed, he checked the screen. 'The prick's here.'

Cato assumed he meant the lawyer.

If Dieudonne wasn't working for the Trans, then who was he working for? Lara dunked a peppermint teabag in her cup and returned to her desk. She decided to review the CCTV footage, the confiscated mobiles, and the witness statements for any traces of him. Cato and Hutchens were tangled up in the Wellard case at Casuarina so there would be no one looking over her shoulder today.

It was midmorning by the time she'd worked her way through the statements. None of them alluded to any Africans although there were passing references to the Vietnamese guys, the Trans and Mickey Nguyen. That was strange. If Dieudonne was there then he should at least have been noticed by the bouncers or the door bitch; how many Africans did they get in the club on a Thursday 80s retro night? Unless, of course, he was privy to the rooftop door that the Trans had used that night. The CCTV footage was inconclusive. The front door camera had zilch but there were a couple of figures passing the dance floor cameras that may or may not have been him. Lara noted the timecodes with a view to having the images enhanced by the techs. It was now lunchtime. Her neck and shoulders were tight from hunching over the screen; she needed a break. Her mobile trilled – caller ID, Colin Graham.

'Dirty Harry himself,' said Lara. 'How's it going?'

A pause. 'Good. You?'

'Good,' said Lara.

'Sorry about being grumpy on Saturday, lot on my mind.'

'Poor sausage.'

'Thought I might pop over later?'

'When?'

'Early evening?'

'For how long?'

'Long enough.'

She thought about it for a second. 'Okay.'

'Great. See you then.'

Lara realised she was hungry.

As expected it had been a fruitless few hours with the bikies and their lawyer and by the end of the morning Cato's knife wound was giving him grief so they called it a day. Unusually solicitous, Hutchens encouraged Cato to go home and rest for the afternoon. In the car park, the DI zapped the locks and Cato tugged the passenger door open. It was time to come clean.

'I spoke to Wellard yesterday afternoon.'

'You did what?'

'You heard.'

The solicitousness had been replaced by a growl. 'And?'

'He wanted to talk about his brother.'

'Arsehole's dead, that makes two of them.'

'He reckons you know how Kev died. He was looking at offering up Bree in return.'

'That right? Did he tell you where Bree was, then?'

'No.'

'Surprise.'

Cato decided to drop it; he wasn't going to get anywhere today. 'So what about Shellie?'

'What about her?'

'Shouldn't she be told?'

Hutchens unfolded the heat shield from the windscreen and tossed it on the back seat. 'Drop by and see her in the morning if you're up to it. The squad can put together the timeline and the statements and such this arvo. I'll find something for you to do after you've talked to Shellie.'

'Okay.'

Hutchens registered the recalcitrant tone. 'What's up?'

Cato reclined his seat a notch to ease the discomfort. 'I thought you'd be all over this like a rash. You seem ...' Cato searched for the right word. 'Relaxed?'

'Hardly, I've got enough on my plate already. But he's solved a lot of problems by carking it.'

'Shellie might beg to differ.'

'You reckon?' Hutchens ignored a few road rules and checked his mobile for messages while he drove.

The remaining punters from that night at the Birdcage had been traced and interviewed and a half-dozen more mobiles sequestered for possible evidence. From the new batch, fourth mobile in, Lara found him. The phone belonged to a Dutch backpacker and she'd taken a photo of her mates with their drinks raised and arms around a couple of surfie dudes who had a just-got-lucky look about them. Dieudonne was passing right of frame and the flash had frozen him. Blue VonZipper T-shirt, eyes focused on something to his left outside of frame. The same calm he showed at X-Wray Cafe. No mistake.

So we've got you on the premises on the night, and then later in possession of a knife with Santo's blood on it, thought Lara. A bit more finessing and he would be their man. They just needed to find him, that's all. Motive. Did they need one? Increasingly it counted for little these days: just look at the headlines. Two teenage girls strangle their friend and dump her in a wheelie bin. 'She was up herself.' A man stomps his flatmate to death. 'He looked at me funny.'

Lara worked her way through the rest of the mobiles. On the last one he was there again: in the background of another sculling and cleavage shot. Less defined than the previous pic but this time given away by the same VonZipper T-shirt she'd identified earlier. He was talking on a mobile phone, its blue-white light illuminating his right cheek. Would he be on the records of any of the telcos? If so, they might be able to track him. She started making the calls.

'He's dead.'

Cato didn't take up the DI's offer of an afternoon off. Instead he'd downed some painkillers, topped up his blood sugar levels with a pie and a Cherry Ripe, and paid Shellie a visit.

Shellie's brow furrowed. 'How? When?'

'This morning. Killed by one or more fellow inmates.'

Shellie filled two coffee mugs with hot water. What was that look on her face? Wistful perhaps? Regretful? Relieved? 'I'm glad Gordon's dead, it makes it all a bit easier.' She handed a coffee to Cato.

'Pity he didn't give up Bree first,' Cato said.

Shellie nodded automatically. She led them both outside to the patio table. 'Sorry for last night. Sometimes it all gets too much and I need to let off steam. You copped it.'

'No worries.'

'So what happens next?' she said, not seeming to care about the answer.

'We put the case together, prosecute the perpetrators, move on.'

'You sound like a report. "Perpetrators".'

'Sorry.'

'Are you?'

Every question, look, or gesture felt like a trap today. Cato wished he hadn't said yes to the coffee, he wanted a quick, cowardly getaway.

'Will there be a funeral?'

Cato hadn't thought about it. 'Probably, eventually.'

'Let me know when.'

'Why? I thought you'd want to keep well away.'

She shook her head. 'I'd like to see the bastard off the face of the earth. It's the least I can do. For Bree.'

Funerals. That reminded Cato of something. 'Did Wellard ever talk to you about his brother?'

'Kevin?'

'Yeah. He died.'

'Drowned.'

'That right? I didn't know the details.'

'Mundaring. The dam. Why?'

The informer tip-off dates that didn't make sense. The last visit, yesterday. *He disappeared. Didn't come back.* Something was beginning to take shape but it depended on the answer to Cato's next question.

The internet cafe was a good place to hide. He was surrounded by teenage gamers, young men in hoodies and baseball caps, opting to spend their days of summer in this stuffy hole. They used foul language and they looked at him like they were better than him. Why, thought Dieudonne, because you are white? Because you are Australian? He recalled the gang who'd surrounded him on Australia Day, measuring him up: little black man, easy target they thought. They fell away like frightened children when he stood up to them. Maybe these hoodie boys would also try to find out for themselves. Let them. His blood was up.

It was both a strange yet familiar sensation for Dieudonne: being hunted. In Kivu he had been both predator and prey. Usually it was a simple affair: follow tracks, sniff the wind, look for smoke, listen for sounds. Move in, terrorise, kill, leave. Here in Australia there was all this clever technology. Cameras that follow you everywhere, phones that track you. He wondered how many of those gadgets would be powered by the magic dust, tantalum? He closed his emails, typed in the word and clicked the search button. The first page told him what he already knew: tantalum is very precious and very important. They use it to make the electronic games that all the children play and to make the mobile phones that everybody says they need. Life in Kivu was cheap, cheaper than one grain of the rare earth that made all those toys and gadgets for a grasping greedy planet.

Another click. Wikipedia told him that the dust the world digs out of the big hole near his village was named after Tantalus, the father of Niobe, the goddess of tears in Greek mythology. Dieudonne chuckled to himself. One of the gamers straight across from him looked up.

'Choo laughin' at?'

'Nothing to do with you, my friend.' Something about Dieudonne's tone of voice and blank expression told the young man not to take the matter further. The gamer ducked his head and returned to his online killing spree.

Tantalus was a rich man, his wealth came from mining. Like many ancient Greek mythological figures he had both mortal and divine parents. Tantalus was welcomed to Zeus's table in Olympus, home of the gods. But once there, like a gatecrasher at a suburban party, he misbehaved and stole the food of his hosts to bring back to his people. Worse still, he revealed the secrets of the gods.

The gods were furious so Tantalus offered up his son as a sacrifice to appease them. He cut the boy up, cooked him, and served him up in a banquet for the gods. The gods found out and were even angrier. Tantalus was then punished after death, condemned to stand knee-deep in water with perfect fruit growing above his head. If he bent to drink the water, it drained below the level he could reach, and if he reached for the fruit, the branches moved out of his grasp. Eternally tantalised to temper his greed.

Dieudonne loved the story: it was like those the old people of the village would tell before the militias came. It had cannibalism, human sacrifice, infanticide: atrocities he was all too familiar with. The militias, the businessmen, the government officials; they all passed through his village and took whatever they saw: food, women and girls, boys for fighting, lives. They took the dust. They always wanted more and they would never be satisfied.

Dieudonne once again studied the boys around him, their eyes locked on the screens, faces twitching, transported into a cartoon world where only the quick and strong survive. A world where blood gushes and guns roar. Would they be so brave faced with the real thing? Technology. They craved it. They believed it was the answer to all of their problems. They were very wrong. He logged out and went to pay his hire fee. He smiled at the aggressive game-boy: it could be seen as a peace sign or a provocation, he didn't care. He'd grown up knowing you can slaughter a nation in less than a week using only machetes. Hunted. With all the technology in the world it had taken them nearly two weeks to even catch his scent.

The instructions were to do it tonight. He needed to sharpen his knife.

At home after an early finish and a recuperative nap, Cato had put in a call to Andy Crouch to follow up his thoughts on Kevin Wellard. The retiree's phone was switched off so that line of inquiry would have to wait. Meanwhile Cato had the post-mortem reports and photos on Christos Papadakis and on the pig found in bushland at Beeliar. The images were fanned out across the kitchen table. Cato made sure he finished his dinner before getting them out and it was just as well. Spaghetti bolognese sat warm and heavy in his stomach: he hoped it would stay there. The night was still and balmy and traffic throbbed along the main drag that connected to the bottom of the street. The smell of frying meat wafted up from the corner burger joint. Next door, Madge was clearly on the mend:

barking, albeit feebly, at the waning moon. For some reason that had reminded Cato to get around to the subject of the nail gun.

Around forty nails in each case: following the line of the spine, one either side, spaced approximately according to where the vertebrae would be. Then, in both cases, bunched around the base of the skull was another deadly bloom of between ten and twenty nails: among these, at least one would have been the eventual killer. According to the pathologist, the sequence of placement along the spine meant that Christos Papadakis would have endured a torture of medieval agonies prior to death; same with the pig. In both cases the nails were the same size and, given the corresponding patterns, had probably been fired by the same person with the same gun. Prime suspect: Mickey Nguyen, one seriously sick puppy.

Had he done this before? Cato scanned an email from DC Chris Thornton listing hospital admittances for nail-gun injuries in the last twelve months. They averaged two or three a month. Most were fingers and hands but one poor bloke managed to blind himself when he checked too closely on a malfunctioning Senco. There were two instances of deliberate or malicious abuse: an apprentice hazing incident in Geraldton left one young man with a plank attached to his left foot, and a disaffected youth in Bunbury used one to self-harm. No reports anywhere of unusual patterns up the spine.

The pig had no doubt been used for practice then buried at the locale Wellard had led them to. The coincidence factor was huge but why was DI Hutchens so interested in pursuing it if both Nguyen and Wellard were dead? Cato decided to try the direct approach first: he prodded his mobile.

'So what's the point?' said Cato after outlining his observations on the two cases. 'Mickey and Wellard are no longer with us. It's a coincidence, but is it a priority?' He could hear soft music in the background, Burt Bacharach. Cato pictured dimmed lights or candles, chilled wine, Mrs Hutchens in a negligee. Maybe he was projecting.

'Is this urgent?' DI Hutchens was very territorial about his personal time. It was a one-way street; everybody else could get stuffed and fit in with his plans.

'I guess not.'

'You need to look at your work and life balance, mate. You're getting too obsessive. You need a girlfriend or something. Speaking of which, how did Shellie take the news?'

Cato ignored the jibe. 'Kind of shocked, sir.'

'Right, yeah, shame. Look, talk to me about nail guns tomorrow, mate, maybe read a good book or play that piano of yours. Get your mind off things.'

Lara Sumich had just stepped out of the shower and was drying herself when her door intercom buzzed. She'd luxuriated under the powerful jets, enjoying the warmth on the back of her neck as it soothed away the effects of several hours at a computer screen. The telcos were insisting on paperwork authorised at a higher level before proceeding with any of the high-tech tracing stuff they do: even then they weren't promising anything. The buzzer went again and Lara squinted at the tiny screen next to the unlock button but could only see a shoulder.

'That you, Col?' She received a tinny incomprehensible grunt and hoped he hadn't reverted to his grumpy state of a few days ago. She wrapped the towel around her head, buzzed him up, left her apartment door ajar and padded naked into the kitchen to get some wine out of the fridge.

Lara slipped on a pair of knickers and a T-shirt but she didn't expect them to stay on for long. She admired her reflection in the lounge room window: nudging the big three-oh and still looking damned good if she didn't say so herself. She began teasing her hair out to make it look beddable when a figure appeared behind her. It wasn't Colin Graham.

Dieudonne shut the door behind him and slotted the deadbolt. He had a big knife in his hand. Lara turned to face him. Her service Glock was back at the station in the locker. Her backup baby Browning was in her undies drawer, seven or eight metres away in the bedroom. Dieudonne hadn't moved. He wore baggy cargoes and another VonZipper T-shirt, red this time. He was about ten centimetres shorter than her and with less arm-reach – but the knife gave him a bit more.

'Hi Dieudonne. Is that how you say it?'

He nodded and smiled. It was a beautiful smile, like a child's.

'What are you doing here?'

No reply. Big knife, locked door. Silly question. She had to stay calm and focus when what she really wanted to do was scream like a girl and throw up.

'Cat got your tongue?'

Dieudonne looked puzzled, then smiled again. He seemed to be admiring her furniture, specifically her shelves. 'So many books!'

'Of course, you're a bit of a reader aren't you?' She waved a hand generously. 'Help yourself.'

Lara was edging towards the kitchen, where her knives were. It was nearer than the undies drawer. Dieudonne was slowly shuffling to block her way. Where was Colin Graham when you needed him?

'I'm thirsty. I need a drink of water.' She started to walk naturally and purposefully towards the kitchen. 'Do you want some?'

Dieudonne marched up to her, left hand raised to grab her hair, and right hand swinging with the knife in a backhand slash aimed at her throat. Lara swatted away his left arm, danced back from the swinging arc of the knife, then punched him in the face as hard as she could. He was dazed, his nose was pouring with blood, and he looked humiliated and angry. Lara smacked a nicely chilled bottle of Cloudy Bay sauvignon blanc across his forehead. Dieudonne dropped like a stone. She made sure his lights went fully out by pounding him a couple of times with the heaviest pan she could find. Lara wasn't sure if she'd killed him but didn't particularly care. She searched his pockets and got a pleasant surprise.

'You brought my taser back, how sweet.'

She flipped open her phone and summoned assistance.

25

Wednesday, February 10th. Morning.

Dieudonne was in hospital under police guard, suffering from concussion and a possible hairline fracture of the skull. News media were clamouring for a file picture of the photogenic kick-ass officer and for further details of Lara's capture of the wanted man. Around the office it was slaps on the back, big smiles, good news week. Lara was at her desk, hunched over the phone.

'Where were you?'

'Family emergency: Dylan got sick.' Dylan, Colin Graham's youngest, by his previous marriage.

'You couldn't have called or texted?'

'He's fine. Thanks for asking.' That was Colin for you: attack, the best form of defence. 'Anyway I was just calling to check you're okay.'

'Yeah, good.' She relented. 'Thanks.' She wondered whether or not she should say the next thing. 'When are you coming over?'

'I'll see if I can get there tonight. So what's happening with the African?'

'How do you mean?'

'Anything to tie him to the Santo thing?'

'Early days, we didn't get to do much talking yet. He's the strong silent type. We'll run the usual tests. We've also got his phone.'

'Yeah? Good stuff, should help clear up a few matters.'

He sounded falsely bright and encouraging. Lara felt a mini-rush of sympathy for him: sick kids, demanding wife, under the disciplinary spotlight. 'How are *you* going?'

'Good, yeah.'

'Any developments?'

'Nothing I can't handle. Been summoned to a meeting with the Internals again today. Apparently all the paperwork is in.'

'Anything I can do?'

He chuckled. 'You've already done more than enough, sweet-heart.'

Hutchens was right: it was mainly Danny Mercurio who was the headkicker although his mate Kenny got a few in as well. Kenny must have been the one wielding the sharpened toothbrush, although by then Gordon Wellard was on the floor and out of frame while Kenny leant over him, administering the coup de grace. It was quick, brutal, and very effective and caught on three different CCTV angles. The assassins had not made any attempt to hide their identities. Indeed it seemed to Cato that they made a point of ensuring the viewer could tell exactly who'd done it, pausing side by side to look up into the camera over the serving counter before walking away. The attack had taken two minutes and twenty-three seconds.

Ten seconds after the killers have left, the kitchenhand walks into frame to find the body. He couldn't fail to see the killers leave. He crouches down for a few seconds to take a closer look and seems calm as he picks up the wall phone and raises the alarm. Meanwhile the officer on duty in the CCTV monitoring room coincidentally and conveniently is distracted by a phone call, logged in at ten seconds before the attack occurs and logged out at ten seconds after it's all over. It explains why nobody came rushing to stop them. Cato rewound to where Mercurio and friend posed for the camera and froze the image. Was he reading too much into it? For all of this to work it needed split-second timing and collusion between inmates and jailers. Cato grimaced; he knew how much DI Hutchens hated conspiracy theories.

'It's not *Ocean's Eleven*,' snapped Hutchens. 'Split-second timing, my arse. We're talking low-level bikie scum and screws who can't wipe their bums without an instruction manual.'

It was a rather uncharitable view of his colleagues in Corrections but DI Hutchens wasn't well known for his generosity of spirit. They were in the waiting room at the mortuary. The Professor was busy on an overnight car crash but she'd be with them asap. Cato kept his mouth shut while his boss fumed. Hutchens was tetchier than usual today, despite the capture of Dieudonne.

'Look, Wellard's given somebody the shits, and Dumb and Dumber stepped up for the job. End of story.'

'They were both due out later this year,' Cato reminded him. 'Now they're looking at life.'

'Like I said, Dumb and Dumber, these people rarely think about consequences. Look at the statistics. Master criminals and fiendishly clever plots just don't figure. I agree that they've stepped up to do a job and I'd like to know who it's for, but I don't buy the collusion shit. That's going too far.'

'So we steer clear of Corrections staff for now?' asked Cato.

'We steer clear of Corrections staff, full stop.'

Cato looked at his boss for any signs of an agenda. Inconclusive. 'Sure,' he said.

They were saved by a summons from the pathologist's assistant, a surfie-type with a scorpion tattoo on the inside of his wrist.

'Lead on, Igor,' said Hutchens.

'Ha friggin' ha,' the assistant muttered.

Professor Mackenzie hadn't come across anything like it before. 'It's quite an impressive way to kill somebody. A combination of force and almost pinpoint accuracy.' She nodded in admiration. 'Killing a man with a toothbrush to the brain. That's creative, resourceful, very classy.'

Hutchens was less impressed. 'Was that what did it or was it the stamping on the head?'

Mackenzie waggled her scalpel thoughtfully. 'Six and two threes? The intracranial bleeding from the toothbrush would probably have led to death all by itself. But the stomping certainly sped things up and added a degree of certainty.'

'I wouldn't normally associate these guys with finesse and class,' said Cato.

'Ach, there's no telling what a man can achieve when called forward in his hour of glory.' Mackenzie's assistant finished putting labelled bags of organs back inside the body ready for the closing sutures. 'My report will be with you in due season, Inspector. Was there anything else, gentlemen?'

Hutchens gave her a grumpy shake of the head. Cato lifted a finger.

'If you've only got a margin of a minute or so to work with, is this the best way of killing somebody in this situation?'

Mackenzie slipped off her butcher's apron. 'I'm not an expert in prison assassinations but I can think of at least half a dozen quicker, easier, and more reliable ways of killing somebody with limited time and means. A sharpened toothbrush through the eye to the brain isn't high on my list.' She ran her arms and hands under the tap and grabbed some paper towels. 'But very theatrical, don't you think?'

Dieudonne's prepaid phone turned out to be with Optus and it looked like any top-ups were cash transactions in Optus shops. Lara had put in a formal request for any CCTV from their outlets in the metro area corresponding with the top-up days and times. She also asked for a printout of all calls made and received along with the locations of those calls. If the printout duplicated the info they'd already taken from the SIM card then it would just be the one number calling him, or being called by him. That number was also being checked out and was probably a cash prepaid too. None of the clothes they'd taken from Dieudonne bore traces from any of the crime scenes he was associated with. For any decisive DNA or forensic evidence they needed to see if he left anything of himself on the victims or at the loci – that would take longer to trace. It would also help to have access to his current bolthole, but they hadn't been cleared to talk to him yet.

It was early afternoon. Lara had only had a few hours sleep once Dieudonne was removed from her apartment and the techs had finished with it. The earlier adrenalin rush had dissolved into a creeping fatigue. She called the hospital yet again and was advised that they could probably expect to get access to their man the next day, all things being equal. Lara zapped an email to that effect through to DI Hutchens and checked her in-box. Good news. All clear on the blood tests, she hadn't picked up anything nasty from Dieudonne's much-used knife: apart from a pain in the arm of course. She decided she'd earned the right to an early finish and a power nap before, hopefully, Colin Graham called around this evening. She had some pent-up emotional energy to use on him and wanted to be in good shape for it.

Lara's email pinged. There was a match on the mobile number Dieudonne kept getting calls from. Again Optus, prepaid, with cash top-ups. Registered seven months earlier in the name of a Leon Johnstone who gave an address in Rockingham. The ID proof had been in the form of a Medicare card and a driver's licence number. Lara plugged the DL number into the system and found no match. It was fake. She sent a reply back seeking the precise location of the Optus outlet that had taken the registration and a request for any CCTV footage from that day. Lara put her power-nap plans on hold and set out for Little England.

Leon Johnstone's address was in a cluster of grim brick and tile units, two streets back from the Rockingham foreshore. Lara could see down the street through gaps between the units and the back of a real estate agency, a thin strip of Indian Ocean, startling blue to match the sky above. The turbo ute and Monaro in the adjacent carports spoke 'bogan' in mile-high capital letters – bold and underlined. Cigarette butts and empty packets skittered in the sweltering easterly. The wheelie bins were packed to bursting with empty stubbies, cans and pizza cartons. There was a sour and dusty quality to the air. Lara rapped on the front door of Unit 4. Heavy metal music thumped through the open window next door. No answer. Maybe Leon couldn't hear because of the fucking Foo Fighters. Lara rapped again. Nothing.

'Whatchawant?'

The bearer of the gravelly voice was the neighbour, a woman of indeterminate age in a straining Cougar singlet. Lara flashed her ID. 'And you are?'

'Sheree.' Sheree lit a cigarette and nodded her streaky locks in the direction of next door. 'Nobody there, been empty for months.'

There was a flatness to the vowels, a distant memory of northern England.

'You sure?'

'I'm not stupid.'

'Okay. Do you know who owns these places?'

'Some dick up in Claremont. That mob on the corner manage it.' She pointed at the real estate agency Lara had noticed earlier. 'Manage my arse. They do fuck-all except take our money.'

Lara handed Sheree a business card and asked her to get in touch if ever anybody did show up.

'Filth, huh? Yeah, right.' Sheree grunted and retreated back indoors.

Lara rummaged through the designated letterbox for Unit 4 but there was only junk mail. She tried squinting in through the curtained windows but it was too dark to discern anything of consequence. Next stop, the real estate agent.

'Yes,' said Carl from Tudor Dreams Realty, checking his computer screen, 'that unit is rented out to Mr Leon Johnstone.'

The only contact details were the mobile number Lara already had. Carl wore golfing pastel shades and his accent was further south in England. The office overlooked Rockingham foreshore, the sandstone dolphin statue, the fake Tuscan architecture, the naval base shimmering over at Garden Island, and the Indian Ocean just beginning to ripple with the hint of a late sea breeze.

'According to the next-door neighbour, nobody has lived there for months.'

Carl shrugged: it multiplied his chins from three to five. 'Mr Johnstone's rent is up to date.'

'Really? How's it paid?' Lara tried to lean over the counter and look at the screen.

Carl tilted it away from her. 'That has to be confidential at this stage unless you have a warrant.'

Lara resisted the temptation to bury his face in the computer. 'Is it a monthly cheque, or EFT deposit, or cash? You can tell me that surely. This is a serious crime we're investigating here.'

Carl thought for a moment. 'It was paid six months in advance, cash.'

'Is that usual for a place like that?'

'A place like what?'

How about bogan rathole? 'The budget end of the market,' said Lara.

'None of my business as long as the rent is paid.'

'Do you have spare keys for the property?'

'Yes, but again I suggest a warrant.'

'Of course, but I have reason to believe that Mr Johnstone may in fact be inside and seriously ill or even dead. As such I need to effect an entry as a matter of some urgency. I could just go and kick the door down but your cooperation and a key might be less damaging.'

'Are you serious?'

'Deadly,' said Lara.

'Ladies first.'

Carl stepped to one side to allow Lara to cross the threshold of Unit 4. There was a musty, unlived-in smell and a fug of baked-in heat. If Leon Johnstone existed then he sure as hell didn't live here now. Next door the Foo Fighters were at full throttle. Lara wanted to thump on the wall but suspected it would be to no avail. Carl looked a bit distressed.

The place was furnished, cheaply, and had all the basics a transient boarder would need: crockery, cutlery, bedding, towels, et cetera. All appeared to be unused. There was an open plan kitchen and dining area, a lounge with a TV, two bedrooms, bathroom and laundry and a small courtyard at the rear with a couple of withered plants. Ex-geraniums. The general colour scheme was overwhelmingly beige.

'Anything else I can assist you with?' By the expression on Carl's face he clearly hoped the answer was negative.

'No.' Lara handed him a business card. 'If Mr Johnstone or anyone else shows up in connection with this place call me, please.'

They parted company. Before she started the car, Lara phoned Leon Johnstone. She got a message telling her he was either turned off or out of mobile range. Chucking her phone onto the passenger seat, Lara relished the promise of an evening in the company of Colin Graham.

After a late lunch topped up with another couple of painkillers (he was developing a taste for them), Cato cited his injury and took his work home. Once there, he opened his backpack and took out the Wellard papers he'd acquired that day. Witness statements, phone logs, visitors log, duty rosters, background files on inmates connected with the inquiry. He spread them out on the bed, flicking the fan down to one to keep the sheets from blowing away, and lay down for a read.

Mercurio and his mate Kenny Lovett were in for firearms and drug possession offences, and a serious assault charge in Lovett's case. Both were due for release in the second half of the year. Next item. The officer who was meant to be monitoring the CCTV screens but was summoned away for a conveniently timed phone call had an unblemished record and even a couple of commendations to his name. On paper he seemed clean. Maybe Cato was once again just chasing shadows and it was all as simple as Hutchens said. No conspiracy – what you see is what you get.

Cato unfolded the visitor log printout for the two weeks preceding the murder and scanned the names. The bikies received visits from their wives, girlfriends, and known associates. No surprises. Wellard received visits from Cato and DI Hutchens in various permutations. Cato was dimly aware of a dull ache around his midriff and a wave of afternoon drowsiness. It would be nice to slip off to sleep.

No chance. He was wide-awake now.

Fourth from the top of page two: the afternoon of Friday 5th, four days before Wellard's murder. A visit to Stephen Mazza, the kitchenhand who had found Wellard and dialled for help. The visitor was Ms Michelle Petkovic.

26

Cato felt brave enough to go for an early evening swim at South Beach. It was busier than he expected and certainly busier than he remembered from previous summers. Families had brought along picnics and fish and chips while the orange sun sank below a purple ocean, the surface brushed by a weak south-westerly. Kids raced in and out of the shorebreak, balls and frisbees floated through the air. Cato's gut clenched in fear of accidental contact with the world. Physical vulnerability was a new sensation for him. He sank into the cool water and wondered how long it would take for those fears to subside. He scanned the silhouettes along the beach and heard the shouts and squeals of the children and the relaxed chatter of the adults. How long before he felt like them again?

He'd phoned his boss and passed on the news about the prison visitor's log.

'Shellie Petkovic?'

'Yep.'

'Fuck.'

'Mmmm,' said Cato.

There'd been a pause and a flapping sound like flags in the wind. Nice, his boss had found time for a sunset sail. Maybe he was networking. 'Go and see her in the morning. Be a bit sharper. Not so much of the social worker any more, Cato. Bring her in if you think it helps.'

'Could be a perfectly reasonable explanation,' offered Cato, unconvincingly.

'Yeah, Danny and his mate could have been a couple of Florence Nightingales performing emergency brain surgery. Let me know how you go.'

Cato dipped his head and dived down to grasp a handful of sand from the ocean floor. He let it slip through his fingers and filter back into the water. Surfacing, he did a few tentative freestyle strokes to test the elasticity of his stomach muscles. It all felt tight and tender but he could also feel that this was doing him good. He resolved to do more. Maybe he could come over here every morning before work, or every evening after, and do a few laps from one groyne to the other. Regain that balance he needed in his life. Cato pushed aside those negative thoughts of other failed resolutions. He ducked under one last time. A cool breeze swept across the surface of the water. He shivered and swam to shore.

Lara's bedroom window was open: the breeze lifted the curtains, and the subdued revelry of a Fremantle evening floated past. Lara and Colin lay cupped together. Beyond the Round House the ocean broke on the night sand. He kissed the back of her neck.

'I'm worried about you.'

She clutched his hand tighter to her breast. 'Why?'

'Why do you think? That madman coming into your home, he could have ...'

'I'm okay.'

'Has he told you what he was doing there? I mean, why you? And how?'

'We haven't been able to speak to him yet. I nearly killed him apparently.'

'Remind me not to surprise you with a knife.'

'Yeah, pity about the wine though. I could go a drop now.' She could feel him stirring again. He pressed into her. She reached behind to encourage it. 'Now I know why they call you Dirty Harry.'

'You and Cato been comparing notes?'

'Yeah, he only gave you seven out of ten in bed.'

'What about you?'

'Oh, eight maybe?'

He pressed her face down into the pillow, nuzzled against her nape, tugged at her hips. 'I don't know what I'd do without you.'

There was a missed call on Cato's mobile when he got home from the beach. Andy Crouch. Cato returned it and they exchanged the usual retiree-extended pleasantries before getting down to business.

'Kevin Wellard drowned in Mundaring Dam, late 1996.'

'That right?' said Crouch.

'No body recovered.'

'It's very deep, I believe.'

'Given his history, I think Kevin was Hutchens' informant. Gordy was just the messenger boy.'

'I can see why you might think that, Philip.'

'You knew, that's why you nudged me in that direction.'

A pause and a measuring of tone. 'Your point?'

'Kevin drowned in November, but according to the files the Squad was still getting good tip-offs for several months after that. Kevin didn't die did he?'

'Interesting theory.'

'You guys hid him, gave him a new name, new life, new town. Were his mates getting suspicious? Where did you put him?'

'Nothing to do with me, Philip.'

'Who then?'

'Remember the cryptic clue you solved for me?'

'Achilles?'

'That's the one. Very apt. Maybe you should ask your boss about his weak spot.'

27

Thursday, February 11th.

'You look nice in that shirt.'

Not a bad opening gambit for a conspiracy-to-murder suspect. Shellie sipped a glass of iced water and gazed at Cato. They were sitting in her back courtyard. The sun hadn't yet climbed high enough to pierce the shade. The space was no larger than a ping-pong table but it was cool and the freshly watered plants gave off an aura that was lush and sultry.

'Thanks,' said Cato.

It reminded him of a previous occasion when she'd seemed transformed: just a few days after the T-probe incident. Bright, hypnotic. She'd put it down to a change of attitude. *I've decided that arsehole isn't going to run my life anymore.* So did she start to put her plan into action a week or so later?

'Shellie, why were you visiting Stephen Mazza at Casuarina last Friday?'

She put her drink down on the glass table. 'None of your business.'

'Bullshit, Shellie, he was the one who found Wellard dead just a few days later. You've got motive, he's got means and mates. How do you know him?'

She paused, formulating her answer. 'He's an old boyfriend. We used to be close. I needed somebody to talk to.'

Cato shook his head. 'Gordon messes with your mind big-time at Beeliar. Next thing we know you're calling on your old flame in Casuarina. Bingo – Wellard's history.'

She stared at the foliage clinging to the Colorbond fence.

'Then the night before his murder you show up at my door. Acting all ... strange, emotional.'

'Heaven forbid.' She laughed bitterly. 'I was upset. I was trying to make you understand what it's like.' A tear rolled down her cheek. 'I didn't have the bastard killed, much as I might have wanted to. You can think what you like.'

'It's gone beyond what I think, Shellie. You're officially a suspect now.'

'So are you arresting me?'

'No, not yet.'

'You know the way out, then.'

Back in the office, Cato reviewed the Wellard case files once again but now his focus was Stephen Anthony Mazza. Cato could see from the photo why Shellie might have once gone for him; he was not a bad-looking bloke. He didn't look like your Casuarina stereotype – the inbred inmate covered in tatts, teeth like tombstones. Mazza had a firm jaw, strong face, mop of curly dark hair, eyes not too close together. Mazza looked like a sensitive new-age tradie who had strayed: calendar material, Mr April with a pipe wrench. This was the man Shellie said she poured her heart out to. Did she still carry a torch for him? Cato found himself feeling slightly jealous. Silly, but there it was.

Mazza was serving four years for drunk driving which had resulted in a crash and death. He was due out at the end of the year. He didn't seem an obvious candidate for a hardcore place like Casuarina, in with all the very bad boys. Cato wondered why Mazza wasn't in a lower security pre-release joint like Wooroloo or Karnet. Was he a difficult prisoner? Had he upset somebody?

Mazza's statement. He was heading to the kitchen around 4.50 for a five o'clock start. Just as he arrived, he noticed two figures leaving but only saw them from the back and was unable to identify them. Big, they were. He found Wellard almost immediately and raised the alarm. End of story. It was all very neat; if that's the way you wanted things. For Corrections and for Hutchens, each overstretched and under-resourced, it would be a temptation to accept it at face value and wrap it all up. For Hutchens, there would be the added danger of questions being raised about the Beeliar Park charade and the waste of time and resources on a manipulative dipstick like Wellard. No wonder he wanted to avoid Cato's conspiracy theory and not look too closely at any suspicion of Corrections collusion. Would justice be served by seeking out the truth behind Wellard's murder? In a strict philosophical sense, probably yes. In day-to-day reality, no. A shadow fell across Cato's desk.

'What happened with Shellie?' Speak of the devil.

'She said Mazza is an old boyfriend. She needed a heart to heart. The rest is none of our business.'

'My arse,' said Hutchens. 'Bring her in.'

'Why?'

'What do you mean, why? We want to know if she arranged to have Wellard topped. You losing the plot, Cato? Gone soft?'

'You said yourself, Wellard was a prick. Who cares?'

Hutchens tutted. 'It's our job, Cato mate. We can't let our emotions or personal agendas get in the way of our professional duty.'

That was rich, coming from him. 'So you're happy to bring in Shellie and put her through the wringer to find out what happened but if it touches Corrections we lay off? To hell with that, you either want the truth or you don't.'

'Who the hell do you think you're talking to?'

Should he apologise or stand his ground? 'Sorry. Sir.'

'Fucking right you are. I'd appreciate it if you did what you were told for a change.'

'So you want me to bring Shellie in?'

'Yes.'

Fagin's body had been released by the pathologist and he was to be dispatched from this world via Fremantle Crematorium. The send-off was attended by a handful of street people. The greasy-haired thirteen year old, who may or may not have been his girlfriend, picked at a scab on her wrist while the duty priest talked about lost sheep. Outside, gum trees blistered in the late morning heat. Lara swept her gaze across the congregation: she recognised a few faces, people she'd busted along the way for petty theft and drug offences. These were Fagin's family: just as well, for there were no signs of his actual relatives. He had been comprehensively disowned and erased from their comfortable Cottesloe lives. Every time the priest referred to him by his proper name, Jeremy, the Artful Dodgers nudged each other and giggled. This 'Jeremy' was not the bloke they knew. Clarrie, a long-limbed Noongar didge busker, played for a few minutes in final tribute and then Fagin's casket rolled through the red velvet curtain and everyone filed out. Lara wanted to be as far away as possible.

'You caught that cunt?' It was the thirteen year old. She lit a cigarette and blew the smoke out quickly like she was still learning how to do it. She offered a hand, awkwardly formal. 'Chelsey.'

Lara shook it. 'Lara.'

'I know, Jez told me your name. So, you got him? I saw it in the papers. The African, is that him?'

Him. Dieudonne: the smiling assassin. 'We are questioning somebody, yes. But it's early days.'

'What's that mean? He going to prison or not?'

'I hope so.'

Chelsey shook her head, unconvinced. 'You think we're shit. You won't do nuthin'.'

Lara felt the need to make this skanky little no-hoper believe her. 'I will.'

'Yeah, right,' said Chelsey.

Lara checked her phone and found a message from Hutchens.

DD is awake and receiving visitors

Dieudonne had a room all to himself in Fremantle Hospital. He also had two armed and very alert police officers at his door. Lara was once again struck by how slight he seemed. The doctor in charge had refused DI Hutchens' earlier request to have the prisoner handcuffed to the bed. At the time the DI had tried his best to be diplomatic and persuasive.

'Mate, you're a fucking idiot. If you knew what this guy was capable of, you'd have him strapped to the gurney with a Hannibal Lecter mask on.'

The doctor was Sri Lankan; he didn't seem to get the cultural reference and anyway had indicated he'd already seen enough of this 'heavy-handed police repression' where he came from. Handcuffs, he said, could interfere with emergency medical procedures and the armed guards should suffice. He also insisted on staying in the room to observe the 'interrogation' as he called it. Dieudonne was hooked up to the usual drips and monitors but apart from bloodshot eyes and some suturing on his head, he didn't seem in too bad a shape. There was a library book on his bedside table: Tim Winton, *Cloudstreet*. DI Hutchens pulled up a visitor's chair on one side of the bed and Lara stood on the other.

'How you feeling?' Hutchens enunciated a little too loudly, as if Dieudonne was deaf as well as African.

'Very good, thank you sir.' The voice was soft, polite and respectful and accompanied by a smile.

Hutchens dropped the decibel level and pointed at the book. 'Keeping up the reading, I see.'

'Yes.'

'Goodonya. Missed out on school a bit, yeah? Making up for lost time.'

An affirmative nod from Dieudonne, 'The hairy hand of God, sir.'

Hutchens was none the wiser. 'Do you know why you're here?'

Dieudonne lifted his hand and pointed. 'My head.' He looked at Lara and smiled again. 'She hit me.'

The Sri Lankan doctor stiffened and glared at Lara. She decided to put him straight; she wagged a finger at Dieudonne. 'You shouldn't have tried to stab me, mate.'

Dieudonne gave a little laugh.

DI Hutchens opened a file on his knee. 'There's a number of matters we need to talk to you about, Dieudonne. Is that how you pronounce it?'

He nodded. 'Very good.'

Lara hoped the DI wasn't going to attempt a long interview under these conditions. When Hutchens closed his file again she realised he wasn't.

'But in the meantime I'm formally arresting you on suspicion of the murder of Jeremy Dixon and Santo Rosetti and the attempted murder of Detective Senior Constable Philip Kwong.'

'Don't forget the assaults on me, sir, at X-Wray Cafe and in my home.'

'Yeah. Her too,' said Hutchens. He turned to the doctor. 'Can we have him now?'

The doctor shook his head. 'He is not in any condition to be released to you yet. We have to do more tests to confirm that there is no brain damage and to make sure his condition has stabilised.'

'When then?' said Hutchens.

'I'll give you an update tomorrow, Inspector.' The doctor left.

Hutchens muttered something undiplomatic under his breath and turned back to Dieudonne. 'There are armed police stationed at your door and around the hospital. They have authority to shoot you if you present a danger to them. We'll be back to see you tomorrow, mate.'

'Very good,' said Dieudonne through that dazzling smile of his.

'Am I under arrest?' Shellie Petkovic's question was to DI Hutchens who was leading the interview, but her eyes were on Cato.

'Not at all, we're just having a chat. Trying to clear a few things up.' Hutchens smiled reassuringly. 'So, tell me why you were visiting Stephen Mazza, Shellie.'

Hutchens was enjoying being in the thick of things: it had to be better than budget meetings and Safer Streets strategising. The interview room was the same colour as the decor in the detectives' office: baby-shit yellow according to one of the baggier-eyed constables trying to juggle work and new parenthood. Even without air conditioning, the thick stone convict-built walls held a chill of their own. Shellie shivered in her thin cotton T-shirt. 'He's an old friend. I wanted to talk to him about stuff I was feeling.'

'What stuff was that, Shellie?'

She shrugged. 'Wellard. Bree. The business out in the bush.'

'Do you mean down at Beeliar Park?'

'Yes.'

'What were you feeling?'

Her eyes flashed. 'What do you think?'

Hutchens leaned forward. Father figure. 'Shellie, I'm sorry. I know it's not easy but it's our job to find out what happened. I need to understand the nature of your talk with Mazza.'

'Why?'

'Because it's our job to find out who killed Gordon Wellard and why.'

'Like it's your job to find out who killed Bree, and why, and where she is?'

'It's not that simple, Shellie.'

'It is to me.'

'The sooner you answer the questions, the sooner you can go.'

Her shoulders slumped in resignation. 'I was feeling like shit. I wished Wellard was dead. I was sick of everything. Is that what you're after?'

'What was Mazza's response?'

'He said I needed to let go.'

'That it?'

'Yes.'

'You were in there for an hour and that's all he said?'

'We talked about other things. Old times. News and gossip.'

'Did you ask him to kill Gordon Wellard?'

'No.'

'Did he offer to take care of Wellard for you anyway?'

'No.'

'This doesn't look good you know, Shellie.'

'Are we finished?'

Cato was sent back to Casuarina to have a chat with Stephen Mazza.

'Shellie and you go back a long way, then?'

'That's right,' said Mazza.

The tradie-gone-bad image was accentuated by a five o'clock shadow. He looked like he was managing to keep himself in reasonable shape inside. It could go either way: some came out lean and mean and others came out looking like Kung Fu Panda. Cato sucked his stomach in.

'So what did you talk about when Shellie came to see you?'

'Old times, where she was at, stuff she was going through.' He opened his palms. 'Life in here.'

'Specifically.'

'Word for word?'

'As best you can.'

'She asked how I was going. I said not bad, considering. I asked how she was going. She said fucking awful. She told me all about that bullshit with Wellard in the park. Whose brilliant idea was that?'

'Not mine,' said Cato. 'Go on.'

'You lot, messing with people's lives. It's not on.'

Cato cleared his throat. 'What did you say to her when she told you about that?'

'What I just said then: it's not on.'

'Anything else?'

'Wellard's a piece of shit. She needed to try to forget him and move on. He was never going to give her what she wanted. He liked having that power over her.'

'Did you offer to sort him out for her?'

'No.'

'Did she ask you to kill him?'

'No.'

'Did you arrange to kill him anyway?'

'No.'

'The morning you found Wellard, tell me what happened.'

'It's in the statement. I started work in the kitchen around ten to five. I saw two blokes leaving as I arrived but I couldn't identify them because they had their backs to me. I found Wellard. Raised the alarm. That's it.'

'How far away from you were those two blokes?'

'Fifteen, twenty metres maybe?'

'Hair colour, height?'

'Dark. Big.'

'What dealings had you had with Wellard prior to that?'

'None.'

'He was on duty in the kitchen too. Same roster. You must have had some contact.'

'You can work with people without talking to them or being their mate.'

He wasn't wrong there, that pretty well summed up Cato's professional life. Mazza went on. 'He was a cocky, sleazy little prick. Nobody liked him. Nobody talked to him. You want a list of suspects? Try everybody in here.'

Cato was aware of the guard shuffling by the door.

Mazza looked down at his hands. 'I didn't have anything to do with it. Are we finished now?'

Superintendent Scott personally escorted Cato to the exit.

'How'd it go?' he said thumbing back in the general direction of Stephen Mazza.

'Sticking pretty much to his statement. His story matches with Ms Petkovic's. They're old friends. She needed a shoulder to cry on. Nothing more.'

Scott shook his head. 'That was an ugly business out at Beeliar. Poor woman. We did advise your boss against it.'

Cato glanced sideways at his companion. 'Win some, lose some. I'm sure DI Hutchens had her best interests at heart.'

'Undoubtedly.' They were at reception. A flunkey passed a package to Scott which he then offered to Cato. 'The CCTV disks from the outside cameras – you only have the interior stuff, so far. Thought it might be useful.'

The man was a regular customer service guru, thought Cato, maybe he'd once worked at Bunnings. Scott offered his hand for shaking. 'If there's anything else I can help with, don't hesitate.'

Cato had plenty of questions for Superintendent Scott but, according to orders, they were off-limits. 'There is one thing that puzzles me.'

'Fire away.'

'Mazza. Given the nature of his crime and the closeness to his release date, I would have expected him to be in a lower security facility by now.'

Scott nodded. 'You're right, he should be. Most people would be busting a gut for a transfer out of here. Staff included.' He smiled, only joking, really.

'But Mazza?' prompted Cato.

'Every time it looked like he was due to ship out, he arked up. Trashed his cell, assaulted somebody, disobedient to staff. He's spent a lot of time out the back in Chokey.' The punishment block. 'It's like he had a particular reason for wanting to stay here.'

28

The shrubs lining the freeway were parched and weary. Cato turned the air con up a notch and flicked on the radio for some distraction. He settled on a golden oldies station: Billy Fury was only Halfway to Paradise. So near yet so far away. Fury, paradise, dissatisfaction: it reminded Cato of the terms of reference for the Stiffies task force. He shuddered at how close he'd come to being lumbered with that.

Every time Cato felt on the verge of grasping some insight into the Wellard case it crumbled like a dried flower in a sudden gust. As he took the off-ramp at South Street his phone trilled. ID blocked.

'Kwong?'

'Who's this?'

'John.'

'I know a few Johns. Which one are you?'

'You called me. About Santo.' The number Hutchens had given him, Santo's handler.

'Oh, right.'

'You want to meet?'

'Sure. Where and when?'

'How about now, that Maccas coming up on the right?'

Cato looked in his rear-view and saw a bloke in a ute talking on a mobile. The bloke lifted his finger from the wheel in a country salute. 'Cute trick,' said Cato. 'See you in there.'

John returned to the table with two Quarter Pounder meal deals. 'My shout.'

'Thanks,' said Cato. John had the build and ruddy complexion of a farmer and his ute had out-of-town plates: Dardanup. Cato pointed his chin at John's grubby Elders polo shirt. 'You in disguise, then?'

'No, I'm on leave. Helping out at the family farm.'

'And you took time out to follow me around. I'm honoured.'

Farmer John dipped his head. 'It's my job.'

They both picked at their burgers and fries, slurped on their Cokes. Cato realised he was becoming overly dependent on other people's air conditioning. He could have sat there all day eating processed food and tuning out the hyped-up kids and their snarling mums. 'Santo?'

John glanced furtively around the joint. 'What about him?'

'What was his job?'

'Cop. Intelligence. UC.'

Cato had another fry and waited.

'Specifically, you mean?' said John, after a rattle of ice.

Cato nodded.

'Drugs. He was mixing it with the major suppliers in Perth. You'll have heard of the Trans and the Apaches?'

'No, who are they?'

'Funny cunt.'

Cato swallowed another couple of fries. 'We've been looking at the Trans for his murder but lately it's shifted over to this African bloke.'

'Dieudonne.'

'How come I'm not surprised that you already knew?'

'Intelligence. It's what we do.'

'How about instead of me telling you what we all already know, you tell me something I don't?'

John chomped the last of his burger and dabbed at his mouth with a napkin. 'Bad apples.'

'Dirty cops?'

A terse nod in reply.

'Who?'

'That would be an infringement of the rules of natural justice and grounds for an unfair dismissal claim.'

Code for 'getting warmer'. Cato took the hint. 'Was Santo getting close?'

'He seemed to think so.'

'How many people knew what he was doing?'

'At least one too many.'

'Colin Graham was in the loop. He was the one who told me Santo was UC.'

Farmer John flicked a fly away from his face and said nothing.

'Graham and Santo had a run-in a few months ago: a botched raid or something. What was that about?'

John scraped some dirt from his fingernails.

'Was Santo looking at Graham?' said Cato, exasperation creeping into his voice.

'To the best of our knowledge, DS Colin Graham is an outstanding officer with an exemplary record.'

'I'll take that as a yes, then.'

When Cato got back to the office he found an email from Hutchens. The boss was out at some strategy meeting up at Adelaide Terrace HQ but wanted to meet with Cato later on – nothing specific, for a general 'update', he said. Sounded ominous. His phone buzzed.

'Cato?' It was Colin Graham. Spooky timing.

'Col. What can I do for you, mate?'

'Fancy catching up for a beer?'

'Sure. When?'

'Tonight? The Seaview? Eight-ish?'

'Okay.'

'Mine's a Fat Yak. See you then.'

'Everything okay, Col?'

'Hunky-dory mate, why wouldn't it be?'

'I heard you were in a bit of grief.'

'Lara tell you?'

'Nah, the boss.'

'Thought he might. Hutchens was going through my career history at the weekend. Vindictive old bastard.'

Cato felt himself flush. 'How do you know?'

'Mate in IT section. A real whiz, owes me favours. So, Seaview at eight?'

'Right.'

Cato felt the lunchtime burger settle heavily in his gut. The DI might not have tracked his movements on the database but Colin Graham certainly had. Fair enough, Graham wasn't being paranoid; somebody really was out to get him.

With difficulty, Cato put Graham and the meeting with Farmer John to the back of his mind and focused instead on Mazza, Shellie, and Wellard. He spent the next few hours collating the material needed for the prosecution brief on the Wellard murder: the CCTV footage showing the bikers all over him, the statements from said bikers, from Stephen Mazza, Corrections staff and management, and the attending medicos and associated roster logs for timings. The visitor and communication logs, the photographs, the forensic reports. It was a useful exercise. He tried to crystallise the main points that nagged. A few days before Wellard's death, Shellie visited an old friend, Stephen Mazza, in Casuarina. Mazza was the first man to find Wellard dead after Danny and Kenny had finished with him. According to the Superintendent, Mazza seemed to be doing everything he could to stay in a prison wing where he really didn't belong. Was that so he could stay near Wellard? Add all that together and, at face value anyway, Shellie had motive, means, and opportunity to have Wellard murdered.

Other things didn't add up too. The stageyness of the murder, bikies posing for the security cameras, prison staff conveniently distracted, and Mazza's calm demeanour upon finding the body. Was this an orchestrated inside hit? A nod and a wink and a look the other way wouldn't be too hard to arrange and everyone would be reasonably confident that nobody would look too closely at the death of such a reviled character, particularly with two big buffoons taking the fall.

Shellie's creepy letters. Was there an accomplice, somebody out there who knew what happened to Bree? Prime suspect, Gordy's big brother Kevin, a dead man who maybe didn't die after all.

'All done?' Hutchens was back from his meeting and pointing at the pile on Cato's desk.

Cato looked at the bundle representing Shellie Petkovic's fate. 'Yes, but still a few loose ends.' Among other things, he hadn't got round to reviewing the external CCTV from Casuarina.

'Great. It's a start.' Hutchens hefted it off Cato's desk and stalked back into his office, kick-closing the door behind him.

The Sri Lankan doctor finished shining his light into Dieudonne's eyeballs and checking his vital signs. He bowed forward to speak to his patient. 'The results from this afternoon's tests should be back by tomorrow morning. Apart from a slightly high temperature you seem to be doing very well. We'll keep you in here for one more night just to make sure.'

Dieudonne could see the yellowy film in the doctor's eyes, the puffiness of exhaustion. He smelled the breath of a man who spent too many hours indoors. The doctor patted the back of Dieudonne's hand, made a note on the chart and whispered instructions to the nurse. He didn't notice that he'd left his pen on the little table at the end of the bed.

'Thank you, Doctor,' said Dieudonne.

'Talked to John lately?' Hutchens had summoned Cato for the non-specific, general end-of-day catch up.

As a rule, Cato's boss didn't do 'non-specific' and 'general'. He always had an agenda. 'You know I have.'

Hutchens closed his laptop and sat back, hands behind head. 'And?'

'Santo was looking at dirty cops.'

'Really?'

'Really.'

'Graham?'

'John retains the utmost confidence in Detective Sergeant Graham and cites his exemplary record of service.'

'Gee, he's really fucked isn't he?' Hutchens could hardly contain his glee.

Cato hid his distaste. 'Does Lara know about any of this?'

'Not to my knowledge.'

'Shouldn't she?'

Hutchens tilted his head. 'Why?'

'He's now potentially a suspect in a case she's investigating. It might help.'

'She's too close. He might get tipped off.'

'If he's theoretically capable of having one colleague killed, maybe he could theoretically do it again.'

'Nah, Col's a prick but he's not a killer.'

Col, tracking their movements through cyberspace, calling up out of the blue for a beer. 'You seem very sure of that.'

'He hasn't got the guts.'

'Since when did killing require courage?'

Hutchens smiled. 'I'll keep an open mind. Good work, Cato, keep on digging.' Woof, thought Cato. He assumed he was dismissed and rose to leave. Hutchens lifted a hand. 'Been reading the brief and thinking about Shellie and those mystery packages.'

'Yeah?'

'Convenient isn't it?'

'What is?'

'It's just that we never did find an accomplice and we never worked out who sent those packages to Shell. But within a couple of weeks of them starting up, Wellard's dead. What do you reckon?'

'Still not sure where you're headed with this, sir,' Cato lied.

'It's a distraction. It's like saying, "look over there". And it worked. On you anyway.'

'You reckon Shellie sent them to herself?' Cato played incredulous.

'How hard would it be Cato, for fuck's sake.'

'She put on a very good performance when she received them.'

'Obviously. You're her number one fan.'

'Wellard's done this before, his mate Weird Billy last year, remember?'

'Maybe that's what gave her the idea.'

Cato rubbed his eyes. He felt weary, his injury was throbbing, and he was getting a bit sick of all this. 'There's another scenario.'

'Yeah, what?'

'Wellard had a brother, Kevin. He supposedly died back in 1996 but a body was never found.'

'Go on.'

'There's speculation he didn't die.'

'Speculation?'

'Yeah.'

'Who's been doing the speculating?'

Cato decided to keep his chat with Andy Crouch a secret. 'Me.'

'Did Shellie tell you about the brother?'

'Yes.'

'And she gave you something to speculate about did she?'

'In part, yes.'

'Focus on being a copper, Cato. Facts and evidence. Shellie's leading you around by your todger and it's most unseemly.'

Cato and Colin lifted the Fat Yaks to their lips. It was ten past eight and the pub was almost empty. The Seaview was one of those bars that seemed to have survived the yuppification of Fremantle. It had kept its old name and didn't do tapas. The Irish barmaid gave Cato his change, yawned, scratched her nose stud, and returned her attention to the soccer match replay on the flat screen. Wigan Athletic and Blackburn Rovers were grinding out an enthralling nil-all draw from the previous weekend.

'Wouldn't be dead for quids,' said Colin, in answer to Cato's inquiry after his welfare.

'Good to hear.'

'You? How's the gut?'

In truth, Cato was feeling crook. His wound felt hot and tender and the gap between doses of painkillers had shortened as the day wore on. A pint of Fat Yak right now was probably not the best idea. 'Been better,' he said.

Colin nodded sympathetically. 'How's the case?'

Which one, thought Cato, the Wellard murder, the missing teenager, or the covert investigation into you? 'Wellard?'

'Yeah, sounds like a real piece of work.'

'You heard he got topped?'

'Not much I don't hear,' said Graham.

'Apaches, looks like. Open and shut.'

'They're the best cases when you're flat chat and worse for wear.'

'True,' said Cato.

They both nodded meaningfully at this shared insight and drank some Fat Yak. On TV a player got tackled and dropped like he'd been shot. He played dead for a few seconds then got up and trotted away when the referee ignored him.

'Lara keeping you in the loop on Santo?' said Colin.

'No, not really. It's her baby. I've got enough on my plate.'

'Right, yeah. Your meeting with the Trans didn't play out then?'

'Meeting?'

'You and Lara, Little Creatures.'

'I see suspension hasn't kept you out of the loop at all, has it?'

Colin grinned. 'The Trans get followed everywhere they go. Hutchens might not be interested but Gangs is, always. They keep me posted.'

'Anything I need to know?'

'We suspect Santo was in bed with them.'

'The Trans? In what way?'

'They knew he was a cop. They kept him on a leash, probably threatened his mum and dad with unspeakable atrocities if he didn't play ball. He was feeding them high level intelligence on the Apaches.'

'Is that fact or supposition?'

'Think about it. A motley collection of skinny-arsed misfits outgunned and outnumbered by the Apaches. Yet they've been running rings around them for the last twelve months.'

'Maybe they're smarter?'

'Wouldn't take much,' Colin conceded.

'So why do you think they would have killed Santo, then? They're ahead in the game. Bit too valuable surely?'

'Nobody's indispensable, Cato.'

'I would have thought the Apaches had more motive to kill him if what you say is right.' Cato steadied himself against the bar; either the alcohol or his wound, or both, were affecting his balance. 'No, it doesn't make sense.' Cato softly belched some Fat Yak. 'And even if the Trans did do it, where does the African fit in? He's the one connected to the murder weapon. Yet the Trans put up a pretty good show of not knowing him at all. Strange, eh?'

'Yeah? Maybe the African has nothing to do with it after all?'

'Oh, I doubt that,' said Cato as his injury throbbed. 'I've been up close and personal. He's very capable and all the evidence is starting to point his way. Now we've got him, Lara just needs to find out who he's been working for and then everything'll fall into place.'

'Cheers to that,' said Colin.

They clinked glasses and Blackburn had a goal disallowed.

'This IT pal of yours,' said Cato. 'Would he do me a favour too?'

'Sure,' said Colin. 'Anything for a mate.'

They clinked glasses again and Cato explained himself.

Dieudonne could tell from the view out of his window that he was up high. That meant he had to go down many floors to get to ground level in a building he did not know. That was the first thing. He also knew from the last two days that whenever there was a change in the tubes or wires connecting him to the machines there would be some kind of alarm noise, a beeping. That was the second thing. The third problem was the two guards outside his door. It was an interesting situation.

The alarm noise on the machines: he heard them going off all the time, not just his own but others too. The nurses got sick of it but it was their job to check them just to be sure. Dieudonne unclipped one of the wires that was monitoring his heart. The alarm sounded. He waited a few seconds then reclipped it. Two nurses came in: the young dark pretty one and the tall one with the angry eyes. Behind them was one of the police officers, looking nervous with his hand just above his gun. The nurses checked everything but couldn't find the problem.

'Sorry.' Dieudonne gave them one of his smiles and they left.

By the fourth time they were muttering bad words and tapping the monitor with their knuckles. The police had grown bored and no longer cared.

By the fifth time they turned the machine off, assuring him that they would check him regularly until one of the porters wheeled in a replacement later.

After evening visiting time this floor of the hospital got a lot quieter. The tall nurse came to check his pulse, temperature and blood pressure using the old-fashioned ways because of the broken machine.

'All good.'

'Thank you nurse.'

'No worries, mate.' She turned to leave.

'Nurse can you do me a favour please?'

'Yeah, what?'

'It is very hot. Can you leave the door open please? Also I am worried that you might not hear me if I get sick and the machine is turned off.'

'Big sook, there's nothin' wrong with ya.' But she checked with the police at the door and it sounded reasonable to them. The one with the red hair said it gave them a clear line of sight to keep an eye on him. So, now the door was open and the nurse would not be back for at least an hour, maybe more.

Under the watchful eyes of Red-hair, Dieudonne dozed peacefully. After a while all the lights in the ward and side rooms were dimmed and the hospital settled into overnight mode. Dieudonne pulled the bedcovers up ready to sleep. Beneath the covers he disconnected the tubes and wires. Red-hair read a magazine with Angelina Jolie on the cover while his friend, who had her back to Dieudonne, played a game on her mobile phone. It sounded like Angry Birds.

'Coffee, Deb?' said Red-hair.

'Yeah. My shout or yours?'

'Yours, tight-arse, and get me a Kit Kat while you're on.'

'Fat bastard.' She stood up, checking her wallet for cash. 'Back in a sec.'

'Miss you.'

Red-hair was alone. He stood to stretch, did a small fart, scratched his buttocks and sat down again. This time in his friend's more comfortable chair, which had a proper armrest. He now had his back to Dieudonne.

29

Friday, February 12th. The small hours.

Lara got the call just after midnight. She'd been in the deepest sleep she'd had for weeks. She was at the hospital fifteen minutes later. DI Hutchens was already there and Duncan Goldflam and his crew had the area taped off, marked up, and were doing their geek thing in the blue paper suits and facemasks. Cato Kwong was there too; he was pale and looked like he was in pain. He was interviewing a tall nurse with dark hair and wild eyes. On the floor outside the doorway to Dieudonne's room there was a lake of blood. Lara knew already that it belonged to a man she had been introduced to earlier in the day, Detective Constable Aidan Murtagh. She'd made a sympathetic comment about his bloodshot baggy eyes and he'd shown her a picture of his baby daughter. On the white wall above the pool of blood was a line of crimson spray. The man's distressed colleague, DC Deb Hassan, was being interviewed by Meldrum. There was no sign of Dieudonne.

'What happened?' said Lara.

Hutchens told her the basics. 'The little bastard rammed a ballpoint pen into Aidan's carotid artery and fucked off.'

'Just like that?'

'Give or take, yeah. Aidan may or may not live. He's being operated on now. S'pose if something like that's going to happen to you then this is the best place for it.'

'What do you want me to do, boss?' said Lara numbly.

'Find Dieudonne and kill him.'

'That an official order?'

'Give or take, yeah.'

All the streets adjacent to the hospital were blocked off, uniforms were banging on doors and dog teams were jumping fences and scouring backyards. The chopper was hovering with searchlight and infra-red. The police radio channels were a bedlam of babble and static. Lara checked her watch: nearly 1.30 a.m.. DI Hutchens and a squad from Major Crime were coordinating things from an Incident Room at Freo cop shop with a direct feed from the Mission Control street camera monitoring centre up in Maylands. Cato, Meldrum, and Goldflam's forensic team were running the crime scene. The manhunt for Dieudonne was getting the full treatment but Lara suspected it would count for little with this particular individual. She'd linked up with a touring TRG crew and found herself seated next to Darth Vader, the same man she'd professionally humiliated at the raid on the Tran's compound all those days ago.

'How you doing, love?'

'Lara's the name,' she said testily.

'Dave.' He offered a hand like a shovel. She shook it. 'Piece of work, this bloke, eh?'

'Yep,' said Lara.

'Reckon we'll find him?'

'Fingers crossed.'

'That's the spirit.' Dave winked at his colleagues and checked his equipment while Lara looked out the window and breathed in the heady aroma of gunmetal and testosterone. Her mobile went off.

''Sup?' It was Colin Graham.

'Everything. Dieudonne's attacked a colleague and escaped.'

'Jeez.'

'I know. Where are you?'

'Home.'

'What's that noise in the background?'

'Washing machine.'

'Bit late?'

'Tan's a bit OCD sometimes, domestic goddess and that.'

Lara bit back an unkind comment. 'Coming out to play?'

'Wouldn't miss it for quids.'

A patrol car screamed past, full lights and sirens. 'So Gangs have been called in?'

'Not yet, as far as I know, but I'm sure we'll be happy to make up the numbers.'

The radio in the TRG van crackled. 'Sighting up by Beaconsfield Primary School,' said Dave.

'Got to go,' said Lara. 'Keep in touch.' She flipped her mobile shut and held onto the sissy handle as the ninjas took the corner at eighty. There was something funny about that phone call but she couldn't figure out what it was. She checked her Glock as Beacy Primary loomed dark on the hill above them.

Cato popped another couple of painkillers. His gut was playing up and he felt like he was running a temperature. He'd changed the dressing a couple of hours ago when he got back from the pub. The wound that, for the last couple of days, seemed to be healing nicely was now red and inflamed. He resolved to head back to the doctor in the morning and have it checked. Besides he was already in the right place if it turned really bad. His injury wasn't the only thing troubling him. The conversation with Colin Graham had also triggered alarm bells but the follow-up could wait. This was more urgent.

The interview with the nurse offered a few clues about Dieudonne's modus. He'd obviously worked out that the monitors would give a warning if he disconnected himself so he'd tricked them into turning the machinery off with a succession of false alarms. Conferring with DS Meldrum who, despite his reputation as a plodding clockwatcher, had shown himself to be meticulous in his questioning of the second officer, it was clear that Dieudonne had seized the moment while one of them had disappeared to the vending machines. He'd snuck up from behind and plunged a biro into Murtagh's neck. The nurse had told Cato she thought she recognised the metallic casing as one of the type favoured by Dieudonne's assigned registrar, Dr Jayawardene.

'Metal's best,' she said. 'A Bic would probably splinter on impact.'

Preliminary examination of CCTV covering all floors, lifts, and the hospital entrance suggested that Dieudonne had coolly walked out the building waving a pack of cigarettes taken from DC Murtagh as a pretence that he was just going out to join the smokers. Nobody batted an eyelid. Thirty seconds later the alarm sounded but by that time he had disappeared into the dark streets.

Cato left Meldrum and Goldflam to wrap up things at the crime scene and headed back to the office just a couple of hundred metres around the corner. The night was balmy with a soft breeze floating in from the east. Police cars and vans whizzed off in various directions, some with lights and sirens to signify their urgency. He came to the roundabout with its statue of footy legend John Gerovich reaching high for the ball. Cato stopped: his stomach was on fire and sweat beaded his forehead. The horizon tilted, the ground turned liquid. He leaned against the entrance to the Freo Markets, vomited a yellow spray and slid down the wall to lie with his cheek against the cool footpath. Cato closed his eyes, wishing for sleep, for death, for any kind of release. When he opened them again he saw a pair of feet. Not his own.

About a dozen squad cars ringed the perimeter of Beacy Primary, some had trained their spotlights onto the school grounds. The school was on a hill overlooking South Freo and the Indian Ocean: inky-black in the middle of the night except for the winking green and red navigation lights of the Gage Roads shipping channel. The TRG van pulled up at the main school entrance on Hale Street. There were a series of single-storey buildings arranged in quadrangles at two levels with the second further down the hill adjacent to a covered assembly and playground area. Dave the TRG man found a sergeant and asked him what was going on.

'Report from a local resident of somebody sneaking around the school buildings. Came in about twenty minutes ago.'

'Description?'

'Dark skinned. Carrying a stick or possible weapon of some kind.'

Dave put on his helmet and brought the night vision goggles down over his eyes. He cocked his machine gun and his comrades did the same. Lara checked her Glock again. Dave raised a forefinger.

'Not this time ... Lara.'

The TRG spread out and moved down the hill making manly hand signals to each other. There was a noise coming from an alcove near the school library. The ninjas closed in on the source. A quick scuffle of boots, a thump, a yelp and a splintering sound. They emerged with their quarry a minute later. Lara recognised him immediately: it was Clarrie, the didgeridoo player from Fagin's funeral. He was handcuffed and bewildered, and his didge was in two pieces.

'Can't a bloke get a bit of sleep in peace? Wadjela nazi arseholes.'

'Shut it,' said Dave.

'Fucking monarch,' said Clarrie.

'Looks a bit crook, mate.'

'Yeah, he does, doesn't he?' said a second pair of boots. Cato couldn't bring himself to lift his head and see who all these talking feet belonged to. Everything was blurred, the world tossing and turning, his stomach on fire.

'Let's get him in the car.'

'You take him; my back's stuffed. I'll get the doors.'

Cato felt himself lifted and carried like a small child. Except that the breath on his face was not that of his father or mother but of somebody who smoked a lot of mull and had a taste for bourbon and coke. Cato was within about fifty metres of the back gates of the cop shop. If anybody was there and looked out of one of those office windows on the first floor they could see him. See this, whatever it was. A car door opened. Cato tried to protest but when he opened his mouth all he did was spew again.

'Aw shit. D'ya have to do that, mate?'

Cato folded onto the back seat and gagged.

'We got a bucket?' The voice came from the front seat.

'Don't sweat. We'll just hose the whole lot out afterwards.' Cato didn't like the sound of that. 'Now floor it before some bastard sees us.'

30

Friday, February 12th. Early morning.

DI Hutchens had summoned a squad meet in the Incident Room for 4 a.m. All across Fremantle and surrounding suburbs, doors were being knocked, dogs were straining at leashes, the chopper and plane circled, and police vehicles chased shadows in the hunt for Dieudonne. Lara had persuaded Darth Dave to let Clarrie go and reluctantly he'd agreed.

'Not a good night to be sleeping under the stars, mate,' she'd said. 'See if you can find a friend.'

'What about me didge?' Clarrie had said, holding up the two splintered halves.

She'd given him her business card. 'Come and see me about it in a few days. Bit busy right now.'

Hutchens asked Duncan Goldflam to summarise his findings to the assembled throng. There was a tense hush as Goldflam described the details of the attack and the emergency first aid on DC Murtagh.

'Because of the heavy finger pressure put on the artery to stop the blood, he lost supply to the brain. Result – a stroke. They don't know yet whether that damage is permanent.' Goldflam's mouth was a thin, angry line.

Murtagh's mobile was missing and Dieudonne was the prime suspect for that too: it had been added to the signal trace list. Goldflam sat back down, shoulders slumped, eyes bloodshot.

All the CCTV in the vicinity, public and private, was being examined for any signs of Dieudonne. His photo would be in the morning paper, on news websites, and his description on the radio. As usual, a fair percentage of the reported sightings were a massive waste of time and resources but they couldn't afford to ignore any of them. They came from jittery geriatrics, attention-seekers, nutters, and grudge-bearers.

'Daylight in another hour,' said Hutchens checking his watch. 'It'll be harder for him to hide then. Drink lots of coffee, matchsticks under the eyelids, we keep at it until we find him.'

Lara's mobile vibrated. A text from Colin Graham:

meet me in hungry jacks.

The meeting was breaking up. Lara was summoned to Hutchens' office with a raising of the managerial eyebrow.

'Got a job for me, boss?' said Lara.

'Twist arms, look under rocks, that kind of thing. Use your instincts, think laterally, and keep me posted. Speaking of which, you seen Cato anywhere?'

'Drink this.'

It tasted like water with soluble aspirin. Cato drank it and hoped it would stay down. He tried opening his eyes and was surprised to find the dizziness and nausea had subsided. All he needed now was for the pain to go away. The room was small and sparsely furnished with a cheap pine three-piece, a glass-topped coffee table stained with smears and cup rings. There was the bitter tang of cigarettes and ashtrays although no immediate evidence of the presence of either. It was like they'd made an attempt to tidy up before he dropped round; like students for a rental inspection.

There were two of them: by their voices, the same ones who'd picked him up. They occupied the armchairs either side of him and nursed a mug of something each while Cato was curled on the sofa with a rug smelling of his vomit. They looked like they came from the same gene pool as Kenny and Danny, the bikies from Casuarina. One had a goatee and the other wore a stud in his left eyebrow. Goatee took a sip from his mug and studied him. Eyebrow Stud cleaned his nails with a fork: at his feet, a battered and oil-stained sports holdall.

'Where am I?' said Cato.

Goatee plucked a stray hair off his tongue and shifted in his seat like his back was bothering him. 'Myaree.'

A nondescript suburb east of Fremantle: Cato was none the wiser.

Through vertical blinds that may once have been cream-coloured, Cato could discern a gradually brightening sky and hear the birdsong that heralded a new day. He wondered if it was to be his last. 'Why?'

'Because,' said Goatee.

'What do you want from me?'

'All in good time.'

Cato tried discreetly to feel if his phone was anywhere on him.

'This what you're after?' Goatee fished Cato's mobile out of a pocket. He put it on the coffee table. 'You've got four messages and four missed calls: all from Hutchens. Your boss, right?'

'Yeah. He'll have people out looking for me by now.'

Goatee and Eyebrow Stud shared an amused look. 'From the radio traffic sounds like they're a bit preoccupied.' Goatee took another sip from his mug.

The aspirin was starting to take effect, it must have been industrial strength or homemade. Cato was beginning to feel well enough to care whether he lived or died. He had an image of Jake in his mind and an unbearable sadness choked him. He closed his eyes and when he opened them again he felt the sting of tears.

Eyebrow Stud stopped scraping his fingernails and wiped something off the end of his fork. 'I think we should put him out of his misery.'

He unzipped the holdall at his feet and pulled out a nail gun.

For just after 6 a.m. on a weekday morning, Hungry Jacks was doing a brisk trade. Police dragnets were obviously good for business. Colin Graham was seated next to a window looking out on Essex Street and the old redbrick TAFE building. He was halfway through a breakfast wrap when Lara joined him.

'You eaten?' he said.

'Not hungry.'

Graham looked fresh, clean-shaven and bright-eyed. He looked like he'd slept properly in the last twenty-four hours. He took another bite. 'You look a bit weary.'

'Got a lot on right now.'

'Any leads?'

'I wouldn't be here if we had.'

'Thanks a lot.'

'What do you want from me, Colin?' His laid-back, centre-of-the-universe, sense-of-entitlement thing was pushing her buttons this morning.

'Hutchens got you doing anything in particular?'

'No, he's leaving me to my own devices.'

'Doesn't sound like the control-freak Hutchens I know.'

'Takes one to know one.'

'Tetchy. Maybe we can hang out together for a few hours?'

'Not a good time, Colin. I want to catch this bloke.' She rose to leave. Graham put his hand over hers.

'I might be able to help you with that.'

'How?'

He wiped his mouth with a paper napkin and crumpled it into a ball. 'I know things other people don't. Trust me.' He took a set of keys from his pocket and pressed unlock. The lights flashed on a police-pool Commodore parked outside. 'Hop in.'

'Two bits of information.' Eyebrow Stud laid the nail gun on the coffee table.

'What do you want to know?' Cato tried to keep his voice steady.

Goatee grinned. 'Not from you. For you.'

'What?'

'We have two bits of information for you.'

'Go on.'

Eyebrow Stud nodded at Goatee. 'Go on, show him.'

Goatee stood up, wincing as his back spasmed. He lifted his shirt to reveal a hairy beer gut. Then he turned around.

'Wow,' said Cato.

There was a line of five puncture wounds down the left side of Goatee's spine. Cato had seen those kinds of wounds before. Goatee dropped his shirt and sat down again. 'A run-in with the Trans, middle of last year. I'd been out on the piss and was on my way home, alone. They picked me up, shoved a gun in my mouth, and took me for a ride down to Baldivis.'

'Sounds a bit direct to me,' said Cato. 'Good way of starting a war. That wouldn't be good for business.'

Goatee appraised Cato. 'Looks like you're perking up and getting that brain of yours ticking over. I heard you were a bit of a deep thinker.'

'Yeah? Who from?'

Goatee ignored the question. 'I don't know why they did it. Maybe they were bored or stoned. Maybe they're just psycho, or fucking idiots. Either way I'm glad they stopped and I'm glad they weren't on target: a millimetre here or there and I'd be stuck in a wheelchair now.'

'Why did they stop?'

'Jimmy came home. Shouted at them in Vietnamese. He's a bit smarter than the others.'

Cato recalled the hospital nail-gun reports. Goatee's injuries didn't feature. 'Who fixed you up?'

'Bloke in private practice. On a retainer. Confidentiality guaranteed.'

That figured. 'Why haven't you sorted it out your own way?'

'We did. A few weeks later we threw one of their boys off the pedestrian overpass at Leederville.'

Nice. 'So what do you want me to do?'

Goatee shifted in his seat and grunted. 'Your job. Arrest the prick and take his nail gun off him.'

'Mickey Nguyen's already dead. Burnt to a crisp.'

'Who said it was Mickey?'

They were heading down the coast road past the McMansions at Port Coogee and towards the shipyard at Henderson. Carnac and Garden Islands floated on a sheet of blue glass: ahead of them, the smokestacks of Kwinana. Lara caught the acrid ammonia tang from the alumina refinery.

'Where are we going?'

'Following my nose,' said Graham.

The police radio chatter indicated no let-up in the false sightings and wild-goose chases. 'I don't think Dieudonne would have got this far on foot without being spotted. We're a good fifteen k out of Freo now.'

'I've got a hot tip.'

Lara had a growing sense of unease. Was she just overtired? Something nagged at her memory. The phone call she'd taken from him around 1.30 just before they got to Beacy Primary.

So Gangs have been called in?

Not yet as far as I know, but I'm sure we'll be happy to make up the numbers.

'Did Gangs get called in?'

Graham shrugged. 'Makes sense.'

Either they did or they didn't. Either he was in this officially or he wasn't.

'You still suspended?' Lara tried to make the question seem casual and conversational.

'All hands on deck. Why?'

The answer was quick, airy, and she was pretty confident it was a lie. It triggered an avalanche of half-memories and misgivings: Dieudonne turning up at her apartment the same night that Graham piked out citing a sick kid, the insistence on pursuing the Trans even though there was compelling evidence pointing at Dieudonne.

'I was just wondering. There was a news-media blackout: so how did you know what was going on when you phoned me?'

'Grapevine. Jungle drums. Twitter. You know what it's like.'

That noise she'd heard in the background of his phone call, supposedly from home. She knew now. It wasn't the washing machine, it was a hovering helicopter, like the ones over Freo looking for Dieudonne. Graham hadn't been at home when he phoned her; he'd been just around the corner.

'Dieudonne called you, didn't he? You helped him escape.'

'What was the other thing?'

Cato was still digesting the implications of the first tip-off but he wanted to get this over with and get the hell out of there. He knew now they weren't going to harm him, not this time anyway. They intended to use him. The real agenda behind these pearls of information was anybody's guess but he'd worry about that later. The pain relief was wearing off: he was beginning to feel feverish and nauseous again and the wound was back in full throb.

'Wellard,' said Eyebrow Stud.

'What about him?'

'We didn't stab the prick. All we meant to do was give him a good kicking.'

'Why?'

Eyebrow Stud shrugged. 'He gave Kenny a funny look. Who cares?'

'You said, "all we meant to do". So it was planned?'

'Bit hard to be spontaneous in there, mate. Course it was planned. But the plan was assault, not murder. We're not that stupid.'

Cato kept his thoughts to himself. 'That's out of my hands. The paperwork's being prepared and will be sent to the prosecutor.'

'Kenny and Danny don't mind doing the extra time for assault, that's fine, but not the stabbing.' Eyebrow Stud leaned in, sharing his mull breath with Cato. 'Shellie's been through a lot, I know that. You're close to her, she trusts you. Tell her and her boyfriend they need to put our boys in the clear.'

'Or?'

Eyebrow Stud picked up the nail gun and tapped Cato on the knee with it. 'Or somebody is going to get hurt, very badly.' He frowned at Cato. 'Speaking of which, we better get you to a hospital, mate.'

Lara now knew where they were headed. Her gun was on the back seat in the holster clip. She'd removed it for comfort, as you do, when you're set for an hour or two in the car searching for a killer. As you do when you're with people you think you can trust.

The look on Graham's face said she shouldn't make any sudden movements. But could he stop her? His focus was driving. Her right hand drifted towards the seat belt buckle. Out of nowhere his elbow crunched into her nose. The pain was blinding. He had her now by the back of the head and was ramming her face against the dashboard. She felt her nose break. She struggled but his grip was more powerful than she'd expected. Lara lashed out with her right hand trying to find his face, his eyes. He pulled over to the side of the road and placed a gun muzzle in her ear.

'Stop now, Lara. Or I'll do it here.'

She stopped. She felt a trembling consume her. Graham clamped the blue light onto the car roof and set it flashing.

'When I tell you to, open your door and step out of the car.'

He pressed the button to release the lid of the boot. He got out, keeping his eye and the gun on her, then gave her the signal to move. There was still surprisingly little traffic around. Any attempt by her to get attention would be neutralised by the flashing blue light: cop business, butt out. He waited for a suitable gap in the traffic before lifting the boot lid and gesturing for her to climb in. She lay down as instructed. It felt like a coffin. He told her to roll over and face away from him. Lara took a last look at the sky, and at the face she'd once kissed hungrily. She rolled over, closed her eyes and waited for the shot.

Cato was left at the A&E doors at Fremantle Hospital just before seven. At the admissions counter he flashed his ID and explained his circumstances to the duty nurse. She buzzed him through and gave him a bed to lie on until the next doctor was free. While Cato waited he ignored the warning signs and used his mobile to phone DI Hutchens.

'Cato, about time, you and Lara some kind of tag team?'

'What?'

'First you go walkabout, now her. She's not answering my calls either. A bloke could start taking this personally you know.'

When Lara regained consciousness she had a blinding headache and the back of her head and her face felt sticky. Blood. There was a stuffy, oily smell: she was in the boot of Colin Graham's Commodore and the car had stopped. It was stifling in there. Was that how she was going to die, suffocating like a dog in a car on a hot day? Shooting would be more humane. There was a lot of noise outside: the relentless thump of thrash music. It confirmed her theory of where she was being taken. It was the Foo Fighters and the volume had been turned up to eleven.

31

Cato was in a side ward, dosed up on antibiotics. The stab wound was infected and inflamed and he wasn't going anywhere for at least the next twenty-four hours. He was attached to drips and monitors and he felt like he could sleep for a month. His mind wasn't having any of it, though. Thoughts and emotions jostled for attention: all urgent, all compelling. One increasingly stood out from the rest: a nagging cold fear for the safety of Lara Sumich.

Dieudonne had still not been found, even with the assistance of broad daylight, massive resources and saturation media coverage. The longer he went unfound and the longer Lara remained out of contact, the more likely it was that the two situations were connected. Sure, Lara had shown herself to be resourceful in her last encounter with the African, but had her luck run out? DI Hutchens stood at the end of Cato's hospital bed looking like a man caught in a rip without the energy to swim back to shore.

'I'll hear all about your adventures in Bikie Land later, mate. Just wanted to check you're okay. It's bloody madness out there.'

Cato nodded. 'Add Lara to the news story. Get the Neighbourhood Watch busybodies looking out for her too. You've got nothing to lose. For all we know, if we find one we might find the other.' Hutchens had lost his glazed look but Cato hadn't finished. 'Is Colin Graham dirty and, more importantly, is he dangerous?'

'You finally coming round on that one then?'

Cato sighed. 'This isn't some white-anting office politics game anymore. We had an opportunity to warn Lara about him and we didn't.'

'Jesus, Cato, you don't really think ...'

'I don't know what to think but I fear the worst. Col invited me for a beer last night. He was trying to find out what we know and at the same time trying to muddy the waters. Colin's dissembling:

it's what he's always been good at. Tell Farmer John the time for being coy is over. We need to know what's really going on.'

Hutchens' gaze travelled over the tubes and wires and medical machinery and came to rest on Cato's face. 'How come you're the one with all the bright ideas and you're lying there, cactus, with all this spaghetti coming off you?'

Lara was curled up on the couch in Leon Johnstone's grungy unit in Rockingham. Next door, the heavy metal was at full tilt; it didn't do much for her thumping head. Her hands and feet were bound with plastic cable ties: arms pinned behind her back, numb from restricted circulation. Colin Graham sat in an armchair opposite her, a police Glock resting in his upturned palm. There were a couple of mobiles on the coffee table: one of them would be for his 'Leon Johnstone' alias, showing a missed call from Lara a couple of days ago. That's what had tipped him off that she was closing in. Graham checked his watch for the fifth time in as many minutes.

'Expecting somebody?' said Lara.

No reply.

'How long have you known Dieudonne?'

Still nothing. He was disengaging. That suggested he was mentally readying himself to kill her. It also suggested that this didn't come easily or naturally to him. By contrast, Dieudonne could serve you a winning smile and sever your arteries in the flutter of an eyelash. Life and death were all the same to him. He'd grown up in the slaughterhouse of the Congo: it was the only existence he'd ever known. Nothing personal, no deceit or greed. Colin Graham? He'd grown up comfortable, well fed, safe: and he'd turned into a callous, self-absorbed sociopath. How might Dieudonne have turned out if he'd had Colin Graham's chances in life? She recalled Santo Rosetti in the toilet cubicle in the Birdcage, Fagin in the house in Willagee, DC Murtagh's blood in the hospital corridor. Lara's new-found empathy and insight would come to nothing: she was going to die to the sound of the fucking Foo Fighters.

'Santo was investigating you.'

Nothing.

'You invited yourself into the murder investigation to make sure it pointed in the direction of the Trans.'

Nothing.

'Is that why you fucked me?'

A half-smile. 'That was a bonus.'

Not fully disengaged yet then. 'So you're in with the Apaches?'

'For now.'

'How does it work?'

'The usual way: I provide information and influence and help bury the competition. In return I get paid, handsomely.'

'Enough to cause all this bloodshed?'

'Absolutely. But it's more than that. I can influence and shape events, I get to be master of my own destiny instead of a cog in the machine.'

La-la-la, thought Lara. 'Why didn't you just have Dieudonne kill Jimmy Tran? Bit more direct surely?'

Graham shook his head. 'Tit for tat, knock one Tran down and another stands up. And it didn't get rid of the problem of Santo. The best thing was to take him out and blame the gooks – two birds, one stone.'

'You can't keep killing your way out of this.'

An apologetic smile. 'You're right, Lara. I'm running out of options, but I can't think of any other way right now.'

The room was getting stuffy. Graham reached for the remote and zapped the air conditioner onto high. Lara heard a footfall and became aware of a shadow of movement in the corner of her eye. Dieudonne had appeared at the kitchen counter: once again he had a knife in his hand. Next door the thrash music stopped for a few seconds, there were some raised voices, and then the Foos started up again.

DI Hutchens had rediscovered his mojo. He'd reined in some of the wilder goose chases and redistributed the resources to follow up new leads on the plucky and photogenic missing police officer, DSC Lara Sumich. Hutchens also had a designated team trying to track down DS Colin Graham and his white Commodore and right now they were busy tearing apart the man's home and private study much to the consternation of his pregnant wife.

With DC Murtagh in intensive care and a missing officer in peril, the Commissioner had made it clear that Hutchens had carte blanche, resource-wise, and had even offered him some superintendents and other top brass to help coordinate things. Hutchens had said thanks for the former but no thanks to the latter.

Lara's, Graham's, and DC Murtagh's mobile phones were all being monitored to try to get a location fix. At this stage all seemed to be switched off with SIM card and battery removed. Somebody knew what they were doing. The coincidence of them all being untraceable confirmed and exacerbated Hutchens' fears, particularly as the last fix they had on all three phones was in Fremantle around dawn.

Hutchens could have done with the familiar face and the lateral brain of Cato Kwong right now. Kwong's deduction about Graham had been on the money. Farmer John, as Cato called him, confirmed that they had been investigating Graham for over a year. A catalogue of botched raids, leaks, and large cash deposits into a family trust account suggested he was in with the Apaches.

'They pretty much paid for the house in Floreat,' said Farmer John.

'Don't suppose the fuckers fancy buying me a weekender in Yallingup do they?' said Hutchens acidly.

'Depends what you're offering.'

Lastly, yes, Graham was considered to be dangerous. He was believed to be personally responsible for at least one hit for the Apaches two years back – to prove his credentials to them.

'A raid in Marangaroo on an Eastern States–linked dealer.' John said. 'The way we heard it, Col effectively executed the guy but instead of sacking him the brass gave him a fucking commendation.'

Why UC thought it was okay to hold that kind of information close to their collective spook chests was anybody's guess but Hutchens intended to have Farmer John strung up by his nuts when this was all over.

A message was handed to him relaying the transcribed contents of a phone call from somebody called Sheree in Rockingham who wouldn't give her last name but told the operator to shut up and listen. Apparently the unit next door was meant to be unoccupied but the air conditioning was on and there was a car parked outside. So what? Yeah, but the point is that cop chick was here only a few days ago asking about this place. What cop chick? The one in the photo on the telly right now.

'Do your job properly this time, please,' Colin Graham said as he left.

Dieudonne smiled and fingered the stitches where the Marlborough sauv blanc had caught him. Graham hadn't looked at Lara on his way out. Trussed up like the proverbial turkey, she had no chance of bettering Dieudonne this time. The only positive was that Dieudonne had shown no particular signs of being a sadist. All his work so far had been quick and effective even if it did entail redecorating everything within a five-metre radius.

'How much does he pay you?'

A puzzled look.

Lara nodded in the direction of the departed Graham. 'Your boss.'

Dieudonne shook his head. 'Money is not the issue. I am a soldier. He is a commander. We understand each other.'

As a foundation for a relationship she'd heard worse. What had been the foundation of her relationship with Graham? Monkey and organ-grinder, maybe. Puppet and puppeteer, and all along she'd deluded herself that she'd been in control.

'You know he'll kill you too, don't you?' Lara said. 'Once he no longer has any use for you.' His bright wide smile said, 'What's your point?' Lara knew there was no mileage to be had there. 'Where did you get your name?'

A frown.

Lara wondered how long it was since he'd been asked to think about the time before his killing career started. 'Gift from God. Your mother must have given you that name. Fathers tend to name after themselves as a way of showing proof of ownership.'

Lara wondered where she'd dug that up. Maybe she'd read it in a magazine in a waiting room somewhere. 'Your mother must have been a stunning looking woman.'

'Do not talk about my family, please. You know nothing of them.'

There was an edge of anger to his voice and she decided to abandon the Psychology 101. The volume on the Foo Fighters had dropped. Lara could yell out and attract the neighbour's attention now and they might even hear her: after all, what was the worst that could happen? Dieudonne was going to slit her throat anyway. But if that was certain then it was also certain that he would do the same to Sheree and anyone else who got in his way.

Next door's music had stopped altogether. It was mercifully quiet. Shadow and movement past the front window suggested Sheree and family were off out somewhere. Lara's eyes teared up at the thought that these were her last minutes on earth. It seemed so unfair. She'd taken for granted that she would have a long life and at some point she might even have kids and get married: now, in the face of death, it suddenly seemed important. She wanted to take her never-to-be kids around to her parents' place and have them call them nanna and grandad and remind the oldies of what family life could be. She wanted to go and see Mr and Mrs Rosetti and tell them some good things she'd found out about Santo. She wanted to deliver Dieudonne and Colin Graham to justice for Santo's murder. She wanted to try to make amends to Mrs Papadakis for dragging her husband into this sorry mess. And Fagin. She wanted to call upon Jeremy Dixon's father and make him pay for ruining his son's life. It wouldn't happen; she'd stuffed up and was about to pay the ultimate price. Tears were streaming down her face now at all the lost promises of her too-short and too-bitter life.

Dieudonne looked at her curiously. Maybe in his experience regret and grief had been irrelevant luxuries. Maybe it all just happened too quickly and they never had time to beg. He moved behind her, pulled her head back to expose her neck. He laid the blade against her throat.

'Do not struggle. Just accept it.'

'Please,' she begged, through blinding tears and dribbling snot.

The room was silent now. No music pounding through the walls. No air conditioning. No fridge hum even. 'Please,' she said, one last time.

32

When Cato woke he no longer felt feverish or nauseous and the pain from his infected wound had subsided. He checked the clock on the wall: early afternoon. He took a punt on it still being Friday. Hospitals could be like casinos and shopping malls; once inside you lost all sense of time, space and reality. Had Cato really been abducted by two bikies and taken to Myaree? Myaree. No, you don't dream that kind of thing.

Where to start? The nail gun. Cato didn't imagine those wounds in Goatee's back but, according to him, it wasn't the handiwork of Mickey Nguyen. Nguyen's death in the bushfire with the nail-gunned Mr Papadakis in the boot of the car, and little in the way of forensic contradiction, had quickly wrapped up that nasty little case. Now, if Goatee was to be believed, the murder of Christos Papadakis had to be re-opened. The problem was that Goatee himself was never going to stand up in court as a witness; outlaws didn't do justice that way. Cato believed the bikie's story but proving it in court would be a different matter.

Item two. The prison bikies, Kenny and Danny, were happy to own up to kicking the crap out of Gordon Francis Wellard. They had no real choice given the CCTV corroboration but, according to Eyebrow Stud, they played no part in administering the fatal coup de grace. If the suggestion now was that somebody else did the toothbrushing then the obvious candidate was Stephen Mazza: he was the only one else on CCTV who came close to Wellard's body. At the moment when Mazza was kneeling down and supposedly checking Wellard's welfare, the victim had fallen below the frame of vision. So it was possible that Mazza seized his opportunity to finish him off.

The real nail-gun murderer had been offered up as a trade for a closer look at Wellard's death and the roles of Kenny and Danny. It was win-win for the Apaches. They might get some sentence relief for their boys and, as a bonus, bring extra grief to their rivals. Their insistence on Cato's cooperation on the matter had been reinforced with a tap on his knee with the nail gun: whether it was a real threat or just a melodramatic flourish, Cato wasn't keen to find out.

Hopefully by the end of the weekend he'd be back in action and he could follow up on the Wellard killing. He could pass the Papadakis nail-gun tip on to Lara Sumich, as that was her case. That, of course, assumed Lara would come out of this alive.

Three floors below, Lara Sumich lay in the emergency department. She was receiving attention to some of the facial cuts and the broken nose resulting from Colin Graham repeatedly mashing her face into the car dashboard. There was another nasty gash on the back of her head where he'd pistol-whipped her as she lay facing away from him in the boot of his Commodore. She had pleaded for her life and been given it back. Dieudonne was interrupted by explosions, shouting, and all hell breaking loose. When the smoke had cleared in the Rockingham unit, the first voice she heard was that of Dave the TRG man.

'You all right there, Lara?'

Dieudonne was disarmed and facedown on the kitchen lino, four men-in-black kneeling on him with one repeatedly administering the taser. It was probably overkill but, at that precise moment, Dieudonne's human rights weren't a big issue for Lara. The front door was off its hinges and bright Rockingham sunlight streamed through the gap. She'd never seen anything so beautiful.

Now that they had Dieudonne in custody, the very public manhunt had been wound down. A more discreet one was still underway for Colin Graham. The notion of a rogue killer cop on the loose was just a bit too much for the faint hearts in the PR department at HQ so they were keeping it all hush-hush. This time, though, Dieudonne would get the full Hannibal Lecter treatment: handcuffs, straitjacket, padded cell, muzzle, sedation – whatever it took.

'He can howl at the moon all he friggin' likes,' said Hutchens.

The DI had given Lara back her mobile. Confiscated by Graham, it had been left behind in the Rockingham unit in his rush to be gone. The techs had already downloaded all they needed from the SIM and confirmed Graham's prints were on it.

'If he tries to contact you we want to know, right?'

Lara had nodded her assent to Hutchens but that wasn't the same as a promise. With Colin Graham still out there, she wasn't allowed to go home. She'd been booked into a hotel and could count on an armed guard at her door; not that it had meant much in the case of poor DC Murtagh.

33

Saturday, February 13th.

'Where do I begin?'

The boss policeman had a thin file of papers in front of him on the desk. Dieudonne had expected it to be thicker given the number of people he had hurt or killed in the last few weeks. Maybe the file was some kind of prop, or trick, and the important thing was the camera up in the corner with its little red light. Dieudonne was wearing a paper suit as his clothes had been taken away for scientific testing. They had also taken blood and hair samples, swabs, and fingerprints. The suit made him itchy.

He was flanked by two women: Evonne the Translator was a big Kivu woman who reminded him of his mother: except that she seemed very afraid of him. He didn't really need her to translate but she might be useful to hide behind if things turned difficult. The other was an Indian woman who was his lawyer. Her name was Amrita.

The policeman looked very happy to see her. 'Miss Desai, weren't you in Albany with Legal Aid?'

'I transferred back.' She flashed a big ring on her wedding finger. 'And the name's Gupta now.'

The other person in the room, apart from Mr Hutchens, was a fat man called Meldrum. Dieudonne wondered where Lara was: he expected her to be here. Maybe she was still hurt or too sad. He remembered her crying and begging just before the police raid: it wasn't the first time somebody had begged him for their life but it was the first time it had affected him since his mother. Maybe he wasn't the iron-willed soldier he thought he was. Maybe this country of sunshine and riches was turning him soft.

The boss policeman had said all of their names, where they were, time and day and the red light on the camera was blinking.

Dieudonne put his hands on the desk and let it be known that the handcuffs were uncomfortable. The lawyer lady understood immediately.

'Inspector, is this really necessary?'

'I'm afraid so, Mrs Gupta, and if I were you I wouldn't leave any pens lying around either.'

'What precisely is the purpose of this interview? I assume you have sufficient evidence to go ahead with formal charges so we can adjourn to a more appropriate time and,' she waved her red fingernails at the handcuffs, 'more appropriate circumstances.'

'You're right, we do have enough evidence to charge but we're also hoping your client can assist us with our urgent inquiries into an ongoing matter. His associate is still at large and we'd like to get him locked up too.'

'If it was so urgent why didn't you pursue the matter yesterday? You had my client in custody by late morning. You had an afternoon and evening to follow up your "urgent" inquiries.'

'Paperwork, Mrs Gupta, sad but true: a policeman's lot is not a happy one. And, to be fair, everybody was a bit knackered after driving around all night trying to find this cu–, your client.' The boss policeman cleared his throat. 'We also had to debrief from a life-threatening hostage situation and a number of my officers remain traumatised after the savage attack on their colleague on Thursday night. All in all ...'

'Let's proceed then, shall we?' The lawyer tapped her pen on her notepad impatiently.

The boss policeman looked like he wanted to kill her. 'Yes, let's.'

Cato was allowed to go home from the hospital by midmorning. The infection was on the way out and a box of antibiotics would fix what was left. Stepping out of the taxi in front of his house, the warm sun felt good on his shoulders. There was plenty to chase up from his little excursion to Myaree but he was content to leave that until office hours on Monday. For now, he had a weekend free. He'd heard on the cab radio the news that Dieudonne was now in custody and he'd had a text from DI Hutchens to the effect that he was busy right now but would be in touch, Lara was fine, and Cato should rest up.

He paid the cab driver, unlocked his front door and opened all the windows to let in some air and light. Cato had just filled a plunger of coffee when there was a knock on the flywire. It was his neighbour, Felix, and behind him stood Constable Quiet-and-Dangerous. Behind him, Madge the Jack Russell yapped and pissed on Cato's geraniums, again. Cato aimed for Zen.

'Morning,' he said.

'Morning, sir.' Constable Q-and-D stepped out from behind Felix. The neighbour had a strange look on his face. 'Do you have a moment?' said Constable Q-and-D.

'Sure.' They all trooped back to Cato's kitchen. All except Madge: Cato firmly closed the flywire on her and was rewarded with an annoyed yap. 'Coffee?'

Constable Q-and-D gave the thumbs up. 'Lovely, thanks, white and one.'

'Is it fair-trade?' said Felix.

'No.' Cato poured for two and looked at the constable. 'Let's have it.'

'There's been a development, sir.'

'A DNA breakthrough? A witness has come forward? A copycat?'

'Very amusing, sir.'

Cato handed the coffee over. 'This is my day off, mate. I'm crook. I've been chasing mad axemen. What do you want?'

'To apologise,' said Felix with a sigh.

Constable Q-and-D explained. Apparently the poisonous substance found in Madge's system wasn't snail pellets or Ratsack. 'Sea hares, sir.'

'Come again?'

'Sea hares. Those blubbery lumps that get washed up at the beach sometimes.'

'Sea hares?' said Cato.

'There have been some recent cases of dogs eating them and getting sick later. They're poisonous apparently. Neurotoxins.'

'Really?' said Cato.

Felix gave a shuddery breath. 'Madge was at the beach that day.

She got off the lead. Some of those things had been washed up. She must have ...' Felix folded his hands in on each other. 'Sorry.'

Constable Q-and-D drained his coffee. 'My apologies also, sir, but you understand I had a job to do.' He tried to give Cato a meaningful brotherhood-type stare but Cato blanked it. 'We won't take up any more of your time, sir.'

Cato ushered them out of his house. Madge yapped at her master's return. 'Constable,' said Cato.

'Sir?'

'Do me a favour and formally advise this gentleman of his obligations under the Dog Act of 1976. You are familiar with it, aren't you?'

'Yes. Sir.'

'I'll leave it with you, then.' Cato smiled and closed the door on them. Sea hares. The near-perfect crime. Why hadn't he thought of that?

They had Dieudonne on a long list of charges, some pending further forensic examination. Murders of Jeremy 'Fagin' Dixon, DC Santo Rosetti; attempted murders of DSCs Philip Kwong, Lara Sumich and DC Aidan Murtagh; assault and wounding charges, deprivation of liberty, kidnapping, resist arrest, escape custody, theft, overdue library books. He was a one-man crime wave. Hutchens studied the wiry young man on the other side of the desk. He seemed childlike both in physique and manner. The big brown eyes, the winning smile, thin wrists, nervous mannerisms. He looked like he needed mothering. Hutchens had seen his like before, many times: complete absence of remorse, no moral framework. Why would he? The poor bastard had been taught the finer points of butchery by the age of ten. But the people who harnessed that horror for their own profit: now that really was evil.

'Tell me how you know Colin Graham.'

'Who?'

'Detective Sumich has already told us that you know each other, that you were both in the property in Rockingham yesterday morning, and we have mobile phone records linking you.'

'Sorry.' He looked at the translator, pretending he didn't understand. The translator translated for him and sent a reply back on his behalf.

'He says he does not know the name of the man you talk about. He never met him before.'

Hutchens sniffed. 'Have it your way. We're going to lock you up for a very long time. At the end of that, if you're still alive, we'll most likely send you back where you came from. Protecting Colin Graham isn't going to save you. He certainly won't lift a finger to help you, sunshine.'

The translator relayed that to Dieudonne. 'Sorry,' he said again.

Amrita Gupta put the lid back on her expensive-looking biro. 'Is that it for today, Inspector?'

'You might want to have a chat with him about doing the right thing.'

Amrita looked at Hutchens like he was born yesterday.

Lara Sumich woke in a strange bed and took a moment to remember where she was: room 4-something-or-other, Esplanade Hotel, Fremantle. The room was standard Hotel Anywhere décor but comfy enough all the same. She checked the bedside clock, just after half-ten: she'd slept all the way through from yesterday to this morning. Her various facial injuries stung, and her head and re-set nose throbbed. Lara switched her mobile back on. She briefly pondered the notion of food and dismissed it, opting instead for bottled water from the mini-bar. Her mobile beeped. Messages from friends and family: some aware of what she'd been through in the last few days, others not. A text from Hutchens:

rest up c u monday.

A missed call and voice message from an unknown number. She dialled messagebank.

Hi Lara, we need to talk when you've got a moment. Let's catch up soon.

The call had come through about an hour ago. It was Colin Graham, acting like they were still lovers.

Lara took a shaky sip from the water bottle and sat on the bed. He obviously had heard from news reports that she was still alive but did he know where she was? She went over to the door, opened it and peeped out through a two-centimetre gap. A fresh-faced uniform looked up from a jet-ski magazine.

'Morning. Anything I can do for you?'

'No, thanks. Just checking.'

'No need to worry. We're here.'

'Right,' she said and closed the door.

Colin Graham had seen her coming a mile off; knew she favoured bad boys. His confidence and whiff of danger was part of the turn-on but while she'd picked him early as a bit of a bastard she'd read him as no more than a dodgy cop who got results. Dirty Harry. Somebody like her but more experienced. Somebody she could learn from, aspire to, have fun with, fuck. Somebody she could use to advance her career. Somebody she could handle. She got that wrong. Lara knew she was urgent unfinished business but now, with Dieudonne locked up, was Colin Graham cold enough to do his own dirty work? Lara looked at the mobile sitting on her bedside table. She looked at it for a long time.

For a Saturday the office was busier than Cato had expected. Even though the manhunt had wound down, a number of officers were catching up on paperwork and reporting obligations, or milking what remained of the overtime allocation. Cato was on a roll. After the Dog Poisoning Task Force had left with their tails between their legs, Cato turned his attention back to the main game. He decided that Wellard's murder and the various versions of whodunnit were a sideshow. The real victims here were Shellie and Bree. Cato's priority was to find the last resting place of Briony Petkovic.

Cato spread out the relevant files on his desk and logged on to the system. He went back to the beginning. Who was where and when, on the day that fifteen year old Bree went missing? From his earlier reading of the files, nobody seemed to have mapped out a precise timeline for that day and nobody really took it seriously, until very recently. Bree was a troubled kid, Wellard was a low-life, and Shellie was his moll: they all deserved each other. That was the subtext of the care and attention lacking from this particular missing persons investigation.

Cato started comparing notes between Bree's case and that of Caroline Penny. Drugs, alcohol, violence and abuse featured heavily in both. But Cato was looking for other kinds of patterns. On the day she disappeared, Bree had phoned her mum, Shellie, and during that last phone conversation she had mentioned that she was with Gordon Wellard but didn't say where. She hadn't seemed unduly upset or worried about anything. When later questioned by police, Wellard had admitted that he had seen her earlier that day but then she had gone off with some friends in the evening and he hadn't seen her since.

Fast forward about three years. On the day Caroline Penny disappeared, she had phoned her mum back in Wales. That phone call had triggered alarm bells, firstly because it was late morning Perth time but still only middle-of-the-night Aberystwyth time. Secondly, according to her mum, Caroline certainly *was* upset and worried about everything. When later questioned by police, Wellard had admitted seeing Caroline earlier that day but that they had an argument and she had gone off with some friends that afternoon and he hadn't seen her since. Same shonky story – gone off with friends, dunno where she is. But this time his story fell apart after the untimely discovery, two days later, of Caroline's body by an early-morning walker out with the dog.

Caroline Penny had been found in a grave in Star Swamp not far from the unit she and Wellard were sharing in Scarborough. Cato brought up Google Maps on his screen and studied the route and distance from the unit to Star Swamp. Approximately eight kilometres, around ten to fifteen minutes drive in usual traffic conditions. Cato noticed there was a choice of other bush reserves in the general area, some of them nearer than Star Swamp. Why did he choose there? Privacy perhaps. Vehicle access. Or just plain chance? That also begged the question of why Wellard had chosen Beeliar Regional Park as the venue for his nasty mind games with Shellie. Cato was confident that Beeliar Park was not where Bree was. He had seen the look on Wellard's face when the cadaver dog had signalled its find. Gordy was more surprised than anybody to see the nail-gunned pig. He wasn't expecting them to find anything.

Cato stood amongst the gums, paperbarks and waist-high grasses of Star Swamp as flies droned listlessly in the late afternoon heat. The swamp was dried up at this time of year; in fact he doubted it had been swampy wet for a long, long time. Cato held the file map in front of him. X marked the spot where Caroline Penny's body had been found. It was about two metres off the walk path through the bush. The path led to a small car park; one of several on the perimeter of Star Swamp but this particular one was at the quieter end of the street bordering the reserve. Wellard would have had to carry Caroline's body approximately thirty metres from the car to her final resting place. If it hadn't been for an inquisitive labrador he might even have got away with it.

According to the pathologist's report, Caroline Penny had been dead for about thirty-six to forty-eight hours when discovered. A forensic entomologist had studied the maggots and other insect life to estimate that Caroline had been buried within about twelve hours of her murder. The timing of the phone call to her mum in Wales put the window of her passage from life to death at about two hours around lunchtime later that same day. Maybe Wellard was just driving around with a body in the boot waiting for nightfall, looking for a good place, and here it was. But if so, it made more sense to try the reserves nearer to home or go even further afield to the better-known dumpsites up in the Gnangara pine plantation or the hills of the Darling Range. No, the location of this dumpsite suggested a degree of premeditation and foreknowledge. Wellard had seen this place before and he had seen it through the eyes of somebody wanting to hide a dead body. So was Bree somewhere here too?

A young mum strolled past with her toddler: a little hand inside a big hand, a world of wonder, love and safety. She hurried on at the sight of Cato standing alone in the bushes just off the path, deep in thought. He couldn't blame her.

34

Monday, February 15th.

'Myaree? What the fuck they take you there for?'

Cato told him. They were in DI Hutchens' office with the door closed.

'So those dickheads think they can just abduct one of my officers off the streets and get away with it?'

'Looks that way.'

'We'll see about that.'

Cato was used to Hutchens huffing and puffing. In the meantime he had some news to pass on to his boss. He outlined the Wellard end of the story first: the denial of Apache involvement in the actual toothbrushing.

'They would say that, wouldn't they?'

Cato shrugged. 'Something about it rang true.'

'Looked into their eyes did you? Saw into their souls?'

'I'm passing on a message: what do you want to do about it?'

Hutchens did a Dickensian harrumph. 'We need to revisit the forensic reports, focus on the toothbrush. My memory of it was that there were no traces of anybody on it: except Wellard of course. Then go and see Mazza again, put it to him.'

'Will do.' With everything else going on, Cato realised this probably wasn't the best time to be raising the issue of Star Swamp, cadaver dogs, search teams and ground-penetrating radar. He didn't imagine DI Hutchens would be too keen after the fiasco at Beeliar and the poor internal PR it had brought him. Nor did Cato want to put Shellie through any more false hope: he had to have more to base it on. 'There was something else.' He told Hutchens the story about the nail gun.

'Fucking hell,' said Hutchens. He looked out of his partition window onto the slowly filling detectives' room. 'Better get Lara in here.'

Lara was already sick of living out of a suitcase. She'd been to her apartment with an armed escort to pick up some clothes, toiletries, books, laptop and a few other essentials and returned to the hotel via a circuitous route. Colin Graham may or may not have been watching her place and may or may not have trailed her back to the hotel. He was certainly experienced enough to have done so without her knowing but she remained unmolested for the rest of the weekend and there had been no further messages from him. She was well rested now, ready to come back to work and keep her mind occupied. Easier said than done: her thoughts and reflexes felt dull, her head empty yet cluttered at the same time. Cato and Hutchens were looking at her expectantly.

'Vincent?' she said. Jimmy Tran's kid brother: quiet, brooding, second-fiddle type and, according to Cato's new bikie friends from Myaree, handy with a nail gun.

'Yep,' said Cato.

'Not Mickey Nguyen.'

'No,' said Cato.

'Does this Goatee bloke have a proper name?'

'I'm sure he'll be in the system somewhere and I'll recognise him. But he's an old-school outlaw, not the cooperative testifying type. We'll need other proof.'

DI Hutchens glanced at Lara. 'Revisit the case notes for Papadakis and the pig for a start. See if the trace evidence matches anything we have on Vincent. Bring him in to get more samples if needed.' Hutchens tapped his chin in thought. 'Any other agenda going on here, Cato?'

'I assume they're trading off Vincent for us revisiting the Wellard case,' Cato said.

'Could be that simple, they're not well-known for doing complex.'

'It's interesting that they knew Vincent was a tradeable commodity right now.'

'What way?'

'Well the nature of Papadakis's death and the link to the pig, neither are public knowledge. They had an inside line.'

'Colin Graham?' said Lara.

Cato nodded. 'Most likely. The Apaches grabbed me within a few hours of my beer with Col. He'd have tipped them off that I was the one they needed to talk to and told them what to offer in return.'

'Any news on Graham, sir?' said Lara.

'Nada,' said Hutchens. 'You?'

This was the moment to let them know about the weekend message: to be a team player, to take them into her confidence. She shook her head. 'No, nothing.'

Cato flicked through Professor Mackenzie's pathology notes on Wellard: the catalogue of kicking and stomping injuries, the toothbrush. DI Hutchens' recollection of the notes was right. While there was trace evidence between attackers and victim; no DNA, fingerprints, or anything else connected Danny or Kenny to the toothbrush itself. But neither had anybody looked at the possibility of matching it to the witness first on the scene, Stephen Mazza. In an ideal world that might automatically have been done, but the compelling CCTV coverage of the bikie attack on Wellard had closed investigative minds to other scenarios. As Colin Graham had reminded him, there's nothing like an open-and-shut case when you're flat chat. And the victim happens to be someone like Wellard.

The more Cato thought about it, the more it fitted Mazza. Creative, resourceful and classy, the pathologist had said. All relative, but Mazza had to be a better contender for the description than the hapless boot boys, Kenny and Danny. Still, without any actual evidence it counted for nothing. A jury was far more likely to convict the bikies based on the CCTV of the attack, their lack of cooperation, and a history of poor bikie PR. Unless Stephen Mazza put his hand up for it, Kenny and Danny would probably do the extra time for Wellard's murder. Cato wasn't going to lose any sleep over that. Kenny and Danny were bad bastards and keeping them locked up for one reason or another was in the public interest. Either way, all suspects for the murder of the understandably maligned Wellard were already in jail; that had to be some kind of justice.

As for where Shellie Petkovic fitted into all of this, that was anybody's guess. Cato's brain had hit overload. He needed more coffee.

Suitably recharged, he took the opportunity to tie up one of the many loose ends. He slotted the first of several disks of external CCTV footage from Casuarina for the days leading up to Wellard's death. There were cameras placed strategically around the perimeter of the prison pointing both inwards and outwards. Cato was interested in the ones that covered the car park and the entrance to reception. Superintendent Scott had helpfully included log sheets identifying each camera location, dates and times, and which disk to find it on. Nothing jumped out at him either on the day of Wellard's murder or the day before. He was working his way back to the day of Shellie's visit to Mazza, the preceding Friday. If nothing else it would tick some procedural boxes in the event of a prosecution move on Shellie. Sometimes this job really sucks, thought Cato.

Friday, visiting time. This disk showed the angle of a camera placed near the connecting road into the car park and looking back towards the jail. Cato was looking for Shellie's dark blue Hyundai Excel. There were intermittent comings and goings, delivery vans, prison transport vehicles, cops – marked and unmarked. In the twenty minutes leading up to visiting time the pace picked up and more cars arrived. An hour or so later they all left again. So where was Shellie?

Cato switched to the camera placed near the entrance to reception and fast-forwarded to visiting time. Yes, there she was, walking into reception, and an hour later leaving again. But the car she arrived in was out of frame: obviously not her own. Maybe it was broken down and she had borrowed one or somebody had given her a lift. She hadn't mentioned it but then again she hadn't actually been asked. Cato plugged in another disk: this one for a camera covering both the car park and reception entrance: lots of cars arriving, lots of people walking in. When Cato finally picked out Shellie he rewound slowly to find which car she came in. It was a black 4WD, a tad upmarket for her budget. Shellie got out of the passenger side and the chauffeur accompanied her inside. The images were too blurry and distant and the angles wrong. Cato didn't recognise the driver, a large male with head bowed wearing sunnies and a baseball cap, so he tried to zoom in and at least get a read on the numberplate. He wrote it down and ran a check. Five seconds later the owner details flashed up on the screen. The name was flagged as an ongoing person of interest. Cato clicked the flashing icon.

'Bloody hell, Shellie,' said Cato softly, 'what have you done?'

As far as Lara was concerned, Vincent Tran could wait. Going after him wasn't going to bring Christos Papadakis back to life or undo the pain in the old Greek's family. The priority was Colin Graham. The DI's chat with Dieudonne over the weekend had delivered nothing. The smiling assassin had appeared briefly at a weekend sitting in the Magistrates Court and been remanded in custody to Hakea.

Colin Graham was out there somewhere and he had made contact with her over the weekend. It was the only lead she had. The search team, coordinated by a bloke called John (from some special UC squad according to Hutchens) had hit a brick wall. John had taken up residence at a spare desk, the one Colin Graham had commandeered while he was around. He was talking quietly on his mobile and his eyes scanned the room, resting briefly on Lara before moving on. Lara's choice was whether or not to involve Hutchens or the UCs in her next move. Logic said yes: Graham was dangerous and he wanted her dead. But he also had nowhere to run. She was his last hope or last loose end, and he was her unfinished business. It felt personal.

'How you feeling?' John pulled up a chair beside her desk. It squeaked under his rugby player's bulk. He held out a hand. 'I'm John.'

Lara shook it. 'Hi. A lot better thanks.'

'You've been through the mill lately.'

'Yeah, a bit.'

He looked around and leaned in closer. 'It doesn't need to be this way, you know.'

'What way?' Her defences were up.

'Guts and glory. We're here to help.'

'Who's we?'

'You're not alone, Lara. Just know that. If you need backup just ask for it. We're listening in and we know you're in contact with him. Use us. We can be your safety net.'

She said it again. 'Who's we?'

'Not Kwong or Hutchens if that's any comfort. Look, in our section we tend to make it up as we go along. Ends and means, all that stuff. I can see you're like that too. I can work around that.' He squeezed her shoulder. 'Here's my mobile number, plug it in and save it.'

Her mobile buzzed. John had sent her a text while they were talking.

use us – or go down with him

She flushed. 'Are you threatening me?'

'Friendly advice, take it.'

A short time later Lara's mobile buzzed again. A thumb on the button and the words came up on the screen.

2nite @ 9 @ end of capo dorlando – come alone

35

'Been in the wars, Stephen?'

DI Hutchens put on his concerned expression as he gestured towards Mazza's bandaged and splinted right hand and a blistering scald on his neck and face.

'Accident in the kitchen.'

Cato could picture it, boiling water laced with sugar or flour to help it stick. Moonshine napalm.

'Nasty,' said Hutchens with no great feeling. He tapped his teeth with a biro a few times. 'We're all getting a bit sick of this, Stevie.'

Cato nodded in agreement. It wasn't just a puppet nod like all those backbenchers behind their political leaders at Question Time; it was heartfelt. Cato really was getting sick of it all. He hadn't yet told his boss about Shellie's Casuarina chauffeur. Or about the two emails that came through just before they set out on the freeway: one from the lab with the results on Shellie's envelopes, another on Cato's private hotmail address from Colin Graham's dodgy IT mate.

A mild frown from the strayed tradie. 'Sick of what?'

'Driving backwards and forwards between here and the office through all that traffic and those ugly suburbs,' said Hutchens. 'And all just to try and get a bit of sense out of you lot.'

'Who lot?'

'You, Kenny, Danny.'

'Still not with you. Kenny and Danny are nothing to do with me.'

'Wellard. The toothbrush. It was you, wasn't it?'

An eye flicker; the game had changed. 'That's a new one.'

'Answer the question. Did you stab Wellard with the toothbrush?'

'Why would I do that?'

Cato cleared his throat: a signal that it was his turn. 'Bree and Shellie deserve better than this, mate.'

A half-smile from Mazza. 'Meaning?'

'Kenny and Danny stepped up and did the right thing. They kicked the bejesus out of Wellard. They made no attempt to hide or deny what they'd done. They were proud of it. It was a matter of honour. If they'd done the toothbrush they would have admitted it, but they didn't. Where's your honour, Steve? If you did Shellie a favour and you think Wellard got what he deserved, then man up and admit it.'

'Admit what?'

Cato waved his fingers at the injuries Mazza was carrying. 'The Apaches are going to keep coming after you, maybe after Shellie.' Cato recalled the tap on the knee with the nail gun. 'After anybody they think can help them get what they want. I don't think Shellie should be caught up in this crap given everything else on her plate.' Cato sat back and folded his arms. 'And I think Bree deserves a more honest championing of her cause.'

Mazza's face darkened. 'That right?'

'You know it is.'

Lara hadn't been for a run for a few days. What with being bashed and abducted and staring death in the eye a bit lately, her heart hadn't really been in it. She was also still living at the hotel and theoretically under police guard from the desperate fugitive, Colin Graham. But she needed to get her body moving. She'd left work promptly at five, driven straight into the secure undergound car park at the hotel and five minutes later was pounding away on the gym treadmill. Around her a motley collection of toned, semi-toned, and seriously flabby conference delegates and travelling salesmen shadow-boxed with mortality. Some gave her strange looks and, when she caught her reflection in one of the full-length mirrors, she realised why. Boxer's nose, panda eyes; she'd forgotten that she was no longer a serious contender for Australia's Next Top Model. In some ways she relished her difference, her immersion in this mad, bad dangerous world. So much for her death's-door promise to herself to settle down and be a nice girl. Her mobile throbbed, a familiar number. She stopped the treadmill.

'Did you get my message?' Colin Graham.

'Yes.'

'You'll be alone?'

'Sure. You have my word.'

'You're being sarcastic aren't you?'

'What do you think?'

'I think I'll be watching and if I don't like what I see it's all off.'

'What's all off?'

'I'm doing this for you, Lara. I'll surrender to you, just you.'

The phone died.

Would he really surrender or was it a trap? Graham's life and career were wrecked and he faced a solid twenty years inside. Not a nice prospect for a cop: they'd be queuing up for a pop at him in Casuarina. His options were limited. He could kill her and go out in a blaze of glory like a Ned Kelly wannabe. No, that wasn't his style. Or he could surrender and try offering a bigger prize than himself to negotiate a spot in witness protection. That was more like the Graham she'd come to know. Mr Plan B.

Lara restarted the treadmill and pressed the buttons for an uphill run. Why had she allowed herself to be consumed by such a nasty piece of work? Surely by now her judgement was based on something more sophisticated than pure fuckability. Apparently not. All along she'd thought she could match him but she'd been way out of her league. That settled it. Colin Graham was *her* mistake and she wanted to rectify it. He might think he had a number of options as to how all this might end but Lara intended to present him with just one.

By the end of the interview, Mazza still hadn't fessed up and it remained a stalemate. But they had obtained fresh blood, skin, hair and saliva samples from him to crosscheck in the Wellard murder case. Mazza could explain the presence of his DNA on the victim as resulting from his close proximity as he knelt down to check for signs of life before calling for assistance. It would depend on the amount, type, concentration and precise location of any such traces as to whether it could be explained away in that fashion. They were back on the freeway, heading north. The sun dropping, shadows lengthening. Hutchens finished off a call to Lara.

'Yeah, we'll leave Dieudonne until tomorrow now. I've had enough of dickheads for one day. What you up to?' Some measured husky tones from the other end. 'Right. Take it easy. See you then.' This less strident, more concerned Hutchens was on display a lot lately. Was he mellowing? Maybe this was a good time to bring up the subject of Star Swamp. Cato gave it a go. Hutchens nodded and ummed.

'So you reckon that because Wellard knew where the car parks were when he dumped Caroline Penny, he must have been there before and so that's probably where Shellie's kid is? That right?'

'Sort of.'

'Bit thin maybe? Couldn't he have just been there on a picnic and remembered where the car parks were?'

'Wellard? Picnic?'

Hutchens ignored that. 'And on the strength of this you want earthmovers, cadaver dogs, ground radar, and maybe a couple dozen uniforms and SES volunteers?'

The traffic was banking up at the Leach Highway turn-off: road works and rush hour. Lots of drivers with that resigned look of not going anywhere soon.

'Keep that beautiful mind of yours ticking over, old son. Meantime let's see if we can get Mazza wrapped up.' Hutchens stabbed the radio button and Drivetime came on.

Cato decided it was time to come clean on the Shellie thing.

Capo D'Orlando Drive is about halfway between South Beach and Fremantle city centre and heads west off Marine Terrace to bisect the marinas of Fremantle Sailing Club and Fishing Boat Harbour. Further out along the drive, nearer to the harbour gateway to the Indian Ocean, the pleasure craft of the moneyed give way to rows of rusted and paint-chipped deep-sea trawlers and cray boats. A large car park patterned with burnout rings marks the boundary of where pleasure ends and industry begins. Finally, right at the tip of the drive: a rocky man-made promontory for anglers or those who simply want to gaze at the horizon.

At just before nine o'clock on a Monday night there was no one about. Ten minutes earlier the last dog walker had ambled home with her fat old kelpie. Half an hour ago the last tinkering boatie realised he could delay no further his return to the bosom of his family. A black Falcon ute had roared up the drive at full doof, done a couple of burning spins, chucked a stubby out the window and departed. The sun was long gone and a stiff breeze snapped at the masts on the sailing boats. Streetlights cast pockets of sickly yellow on the nearly empty car park. Colin Graham opened a window and sniffed the salt, oil and fish in the breeze. He reclined his seat a notch and re-checked his police-issue Glock.

Lara had decided to walk. She'd given her minder the slip: yawning and feigning an early night, she'd then used her mobile to phone hotel reception to get them to page him, using the distraction to slip out a side exit via the hotel bar. She'd left her TV murmuring in her room as continuing evidence of occupation and slipped the Do Not Disturb sign on the outside handle. Lara shivered as a breeze swept through. She wavered now between High Noon determination and a nauseous feeling of peering over a crumbling cliff.

She knew Colin Graham would have got there early to try to seize the advantage and she could see him now, sitting in the Ford Laser, staring at the road and waiting. The car park gave him a clear view of anybody approaching down Capo D'Orlando Drive. That's why she'd come even earlier and on foot. She was already behind him. In choosing this spot for a rendezvous Graham had already limited his options. It would be relatively easy for the police to seal off the promontory once he was on it and pick him up in their own time. Graham must have known this; maybe surrender to Lara really was his sole intention: or maybe he had an ace up his sleeve. As insurance, Lara had notified John, designated coordinator of the Graham search team, to be on standby. His 'arms-length' status made him seem a better bet than Hutchens or Cato in the event of a false alarm. Of course she might be wrong about that. There was also his implied threat: *use us – or go down with him.*

Lara was sitting on one of the boulders at the promontory staring meaningfully at the horizon. The dog walkers, the amblers and the anglers had left her alone. The cuts and bruises on her face would have added to the image of the lonely, wounded woman seeking solace and meaning in the dying light of the day. Lara checked her pistol and the cuffs clipped to her belt loop. She looked at the time on her mobile: 8.50. The civilians were gone, she was now able to move in. She summoned her resolve.

36

Shellie Petkovic was back in the interview room at Freo cop shop accompanied by Rebecca, the tired legal aid lawyer. Cato had laid it all out for Hutchens during the remainder of the journey back from seeing Mazza. The numberplate on Shellie's mystery chauffeur to Casuarina had thrown up a red flag, person-of-interest. Bryn Irskine, AKA Eyebrow Stud, Sergeant-at-Arms with the Apaches.

'Dearie me,' said DI Hutchens.

That alone was enough to bring Shellie straight in for more questions. When she found Hutchens and Cato on her doorstep it was like she'd been expecting them.

Hutchens led the interview, Cato in attendance and plugging any gaps he spotted. In contrast to the previous occasion, Shellie made a point of focusing on Hutchens and tried not to meet Cato's gaze. It turned out that she and Eyebrow Stud had both gone to school together. He and Shellie's little brother, half-brother to be precise, had both joined the Apaches when they left Collie High. Shellie's kid brother, Gary, had since died in a motorbike accident. Eight years ago on a wet day in August, he'd come off and rolled into the path of a truck on Stock Road. As far as Eyebrow Stud was concerned, Gary was a fallen comrade, and if Gary's sister needed help they were obliged to give it. In short, he was happy to organise for the boys inside to give Wellard a kicking.

Cato had crosschecked against the visitors log and it all added up. With her Hyundai in for a service, Shellie and Irskine had car-pooled on that prison-visiting day: he to have a chat with Danny Mercurio, she to pour her heart out to Stephen Mazza. Call it a veterans and families welfare service, explained Cato to his boss. Nice, kind of like the RSL, Hutchens had postulated.

'So did you specifically say you wanted Wellard dead or just that you wanted him hurt?' Hutchens had on his gentle, understanding voice again.

'I didn't care.' Shellie was by now no doubt wondering how much trouble she was causing Irskine. 'I told Bryn what Wellard had done. Said I was sick of it all. He said he'd take care of it. Maybe they were just going to bash him but it all went too far?'

Hutchens tapped the file. 'Might buy that if it wasn't for the toothbrush, Shell.' Shellie shrugged her reply. 'So what precisely was Mazza's role in this?'

'Nothing. The bikies did it.'

'But he found the body, Shellie. It's all a bit cosy isn't it?'

It got worse. There was the question of the mystery *FINDERS KEEPERS* packages. The lab results had shown that traces of Shellie's DNA and some fibres linked her to the envelopes, not surprisingly, as she had handled them. But more importantly significant traces showed on the sheet of paper in the first package that she claimed to have been too upset to look at or touch. Shellie's DNA was already in the system for elimination purposes as part of the ongoing investigation into her daughter's disappearance. If they were to take a full finger and hand print sample from her now it would confirm everything. But perhaps it was just the look in Shellie's eyes that said it all.

Shellie confessed to making up the *FINDERS KEEPERS* letters. She had resolved after that day out at Beeliar Park that she wanted Wellard to pay. The letters were a half-arsed diversionary tactic: the genuine ones from Wellard's mate, Weird Billy, a year earlier had given her the idea and helped provide a bit of credence. The idea was to keep the police focus on Wellard and obscure her true intentions – revenge.

'Did you really think you could get away with it, Shellie?' Hutchens seemed disappointed with her naivety.

She glanced Cato's way. 'It worked for a while.'

Cato flinched at the confirmation that he'd been dudded like a lovelorn probationary: the tremulous phone call, the sobbing into his chest – all worthy of an Oscar. DI Hutchens, to his credit, managed to keep a straight face throughout. Maybe Hutchens just had a more realistic approach to human nature: sometimes good people do bad things for good reasons. And vice versa.

Under whispered guidance from the lawyer, Shellie's answers grew muddier. Fair enough. With the bikies still in the frame, on CCTV at least, the police would have to do a lot more yet to prove a direct link between her wishes and Wellard's demise. But Cato hoped he'd get at least one more straight answer.

'What made you think of those words, "finders keepers"? Was that something Wellard said?'

A smile through brimming eyes. 'No. It was something Bree used to like saying, a game we had. I'd hide lollies around the house and pretend to be annoyed when she found them all before me.'

That last night before the murder, Shellie on his doorstep with a bottle of wine, she'd bared her soul.

Wellard's telling me it's 'finders keepers', he's saying Bree belongs to him and he won't give her back. What would you do?

Or was it a coded confession of her intentions?

Shellie was charged with a range of procurement and conspiracy offences in relation to Wellard's bashing, along with wasting police time and perverting the course of justice. She was processed and locked up to face a court appearance the following morning. If they managed to join the evidentiary dots between her and the bikies and Mazza, the charges could be upgraded. Meanwhile the TRG would be sent in to pick up Eyebrow Stud from bikie HQ.

Hutchens straightened out his files and papers. 'Good work, Cato.'

'Thanks.'

'The simple answers are usually the best, mate. All your conspiracy theories about accomplices and collusion, all bullshit in the end, eh?'

Cato wasn't proud of himself and didn't appreciate his boss's gloating. 'Fair enough, Kevin Wellard wasn't the mysterious accomplice. But it still doesn't explain how he was providing tip-offs to you, via Gordy, long after he supposedly died.'

'Ancient history, mate, and not relevant to the matter at hand.'

'Really?'

Hutchens opened a door for Cato to walk through, 'Something on your mind? Spit it out.'

'Gordon Wellard acted like he had something on you. I think it was to do with his brother. I think Kevin is still alive.'

'I think you need to take a couple of Bex and have a good rest. Like I said, Kevin Wellard is ancient history and you need to let sleeping dogs lie, mate.'

Cato outlined the results of the search he'd asked Col's IT mate to do based on the coded informant reference. 'Gordon Wellard was given false papers and sent off to Thailand. The word was out that he was a snitch and there was a price on his head. He came back eight years later, just a few months before he met Shellie. Maybe he was homesick, maybe he got word that the coast was clear. God knows what he got up to in Thailand but that's why he dropped off the system here.'

Hutchens' eyes narrowed. 'How do you know this shit?'

Cato ignored the question and the menace. 'Kevin joined him in Thailand not long after. As extra insurance, Kev's death was faked: mock funeral, notice in the paper, et cetera. Gordy was in on the act. I still don't know what happened to Kev yet or where he is now. Watch this space.'

'You're on very thin ice here, mate. I'm warning you.'

'If you want me to stop digging tell me what happened to him. I know he didn't die in November 1996, he was talking to you beyond the grave and there was no body found.'

Halfway along the corridor Hutchens ushered Cato into an unused room and closed the door. 'Believe me, once and for all, Kevin Wellard *is* dead.'

'How do you know?'

'Because I saw what they did to him.'

Hutchens came clean. Kevin had returned to Australia early, a few months before brother Gordon. The people who'd put out the original contract were now either dead or locked up for life. The game had changed and a new generation ran things: young guys who didn't know or care about Kevin Wellard. Or so he believed.

'A fortnight after he got back we found his head in one of the canals in Mandurah,' Hutchens said. 'The rest of him was in plastic bags buried on a farm near Toodyay. Anonymous tip-off. We kept it quiet. He couldn't be seen to die twice could he?'

'The scores were settled: Kev was the one they wanted, the real traitor. Gordy was nothing to them. The coast was clear for his return. Am I right?'

'Good as,' said Hutchens.

'You didn't tell Gordy? He suspected you over Kev's disappearance.'

'Mate, by then even I knew how much of a nasty prick Gordy was. I've invested too much in him and ignored all the warning signs. Sure, I let the bastard stew. Good riddance to both of them.'

'You wanted to talk.'

'Lara, so good to see you.' Graham's hand drifted down to his side.

She dug her pistol in behind his ear. 'Keep your hands on the wheel where I can see them.' She snapped one cuff around his right wrist and the other to the steering wheel.

'You're very good at this.'

'Thanks.' She patted him down, found his gun, chucked it into Fishing Boat Harbour and pocketed the car key. So far things were going very smoothly. It didn't feel right.

'I'm sorry about how everything turned out, Lara.'

'Not sure how to read that, Colin. Sorry, as in remorseful for doing bad things, or sorry it all went wrong for you?'

A self-deprecating chuckle, 'Both, I suppose.'

Lara scuffed a heel on the oily bitumen. 'So how does it all end?'

'Is that what this is? An ending?'

A car rumbled up Capo D'Orlando. Lara didn't turn to look but it sounded like the souped-up ute from earlier.

'Surely you were never expecting to walk away from this were you? What makes you think I haven't got a van of TRG waiting for you up the road?'

'Ah, but you haven't, have you Lara? I've come to know you.

You're just like me, you want it all.'

'Meaning?' she bristled.

'You've got a best and worst case scenario. Best: I surrender and you take me in alone and get all the applause. Worst: the cavalry are on standby if things go wrong.'

'You're very sure of yourself.' And that was truly beginning to worry her. Colin seemed to be reading from UC John's script. Were they in cahoots? She steadied her nerves. 'So what are *your* scenarios?'

'Worst? You succeed in arresting me, with or without help. I end up in protective custody for a few months while my lawyer plea-bargains me into the witness program for the price of a few names. I then live out my life in Beavertown, Ontario, with a couple of Mounties in the spare room.'

'Best?'

'The key witnesses against me disappear, leaving a very thin case and an embarrassed WA Police Service. I help them out, take early retirement and put all my super into a B&B in Tassie.'

'Key witnesses being me and Dieudonne?'

'That's right.' Graham raised his eyes to the rear-view mirror. 'Ah, prompt as ever.'

Figures materialised in a pool of light at the far end of the car park. There were four of them: Lara recognised two who'd been identified by Cato from file mugshots as the ones who'd abducted him. She didn't know the others but she was guessing that they too were Apaches. Colin's little insurance policy: Plan B. The one who Cato had called Goatee, for obvious reasons, walked stiffly ahead and the others followed a pace behind. The other familiar face, Cato had called him Eyebrow Stud, carried a large can of something. Lara suspected it was petrol – was that intended for her? The remaining two had sawn-off shotguns.

Lara zapped her pre-arranged alarm text to UC John then pointed her Glock at Goatee. He smiled and put his hands up, taking in the scene: Lara with a gun and Colin Graham handcuffed to his steering wheel.

'Nice touch. Maybe we weren't needed after all,' said Goatee.

'What?'

'Looks like you and me have got what's called a confluence of interests.'

'This is official police business. This man is under arrest. You guys should turn around and go home. Now.'

'Got any ID?'

No, she hadn't.

'Thought not.' Goatee puffed out his chest and went mock theatrical. 'So we, as upright concerned citizens have noticed what seems to be a crime in progress and we've come to the rescue.' He thumbed over his shoulder at Graham. 'This poor bloke clearly needs our help.'

Graham rattled his handcuff merrily for attention. 'The key's in her pocket, guys. Let's take her and get out of here.'

One of the shotguns was edging to her left; she waved him back in with her pistol. On the other side, his compadre edged to her right. She repeated the action. Eyebrow Stud had set his can on the ground and sat on it, looking bored. Then he seemed to make a decision, stood up, walked over to Graham and began dousing him with fuel.

'Oh, Jesus no.' Graham jerked his handcuffed hand uselessly. 'What the fuck is this? We had a deal.'

Eyebrow Stud ignored him and continued pouring.

'Stop now,' yelled Lara.

'Nearly finished,' said Eyebrow Stud, tapping the bottom of the container. The two shotguns were levelled at Lara.

'Final warning,' said Lara.

Eyebrow Stud smirked. 'That's what my mum used to say to me. All the time.'

Petrol fumes filled her nostrils. Colin Graham's eyes beseeched her. A sudden gust clinked metal against mast on a nearby catamaran. The shotgun barrels twitched. Lara's knuckles whitened on the trigger.

Lara had intended to arrest Graham and bring him in. She'd miscalculated, badly. Both of them had. Their so-called best and worst case scenarios counted for nothing. Was she prepared to die to save Colin Graham's life?

Goatee dropped his hands and turned them palm upwards in a gesture of conciliation. 'Love, I don't think you're going to use that thing.' He took a step forward. 'Even if you did you'd probably do me a favour. I've got constant chronic back pain and I'm jack of it. These guys?' He waved in their general direction. 'They're live fast, die young types. They've all got "Such is Life" tattooed on their dicks. Except for poor little Dennis there, he only had room for "Such is".'

The shotgun to Lara's right muttered, 'Ha fucking ha.'

Eyebrow Stud had finally emptied the can. Colin Graham was whimpering. Goatee turned his back on Lara and walked over to Graham. 'Sorry, Col mate, it's nothing personal. It's just that you've become a bit of a fucking liability.' Then he lit a match.

There was a whoosh and a howl of agony.

Goatee stepped back from the flames and turned to face Lara. 'Go home. While you can.'

37

Tuesday, February 16th.

'Handcuffed?'

The question came from John. Cato noticed he'd smartened himself up, had a shave, lost the farm boy threads and looked a lot more like a career cop. The man was certainly in better shape than Cato, who'd rocked up red-eyed after a sleepless night: a combination of Madge, a knife wound, and spiralling thoughts about Shellie Petkovic and the Wellard brothers.

It was just past sunrise, there was a fresh blue-tinged clarity to the light over Fremantle. The streets were waking up, the coffee shops beginning to hum; magpies chortled and cockies complained. The TRG had already radioed back that Bryn Irskine, Eyebrow Stud, was not at bikie HQ. An alert was out on him but, for now, there were more pressing matters. They had been summoned to DI Hutchens' office to talk about the burning car and its charred occupant, now confirmed as Colin Graham.

'Right hand, to the steering wheel,' said Goldflam.

'Were the handcuffs police issue?' said Cato.

'Yet to be confirmed but it looked like ours.'

'His?' said Farmer John.

Goldflam yawned. 'Maybe.'

Duncan Goldflam was in the middle of providing a bullet-point summary of the forensic first impressions. DS Molly Meldrum looked chuffed to be in the same room as the big kids. Lara Sumich sat in the corner with dark rings under her eyes and a faraway look.

'Anything else?' said DI Hutchens.

'Petrol, lots of it,' said Goldflam, 'An empty can a few metres away. No prints. Melted remains of two mobile phones and a laptop: will get more to you on that as soon as I can. Semi-charred wallet with average amount of cash, cards, photos of loved ones.' Cato noticed

Lara looking bleakly out the window. 'House keys in left pocket, no car keys in the ignition. In the boot: the remains of a holdall with a few changes of clothes and some toiletries. That's pretty much it.'

'Thanks Dunc,' said Hutchens. 'Molly?'

Meldrum opened his notebook. 'A call came in within an hour of the emergency response. A local had heard the sirens and saw the activity. She'd been walking her dog down that way around 8.30 p.m. and noticed a car parked in the area. She'd remembered it because when she got further down Capo D'Orlando on her way home, another car, a ute, had gone speeding past and the occupants were, quote, "playing very loud horrible music and shouting expletives". She'd noticed the occupant of the Laser shaking his head in sympathy with her.'

'Description or rego on the ute?' Farmer John, chin resting on knuckle.

Meldrum scanned his notes. 'Black, one of those modern city-type utes apparently. She didn't catch the rego. We'll be reinterviewing her this morning, we'll show her some pictures of various makes.'

'Anything else?' said Hutchens.

'A boatie, around about the same time as dog woman, also noticed the parked Laser and the ute doing a doughnut before it departed. He reckoned it was a Falcon, newish.'

'So the ute left the scene and isn't relevant?' said Farmer John.

'Possibly not,' said Meldrum.

Lara took a sip of water.

'That it?' said Hutchens to Meldrum.

'Yes. I've got uniforms and DCs ready for a doorknock kicking off in about half-an-hour.'

'Better let you go then.' Hutchens smiled encouragingly. 'Solid work, Molly.'

Meldrum blushed and walked out of the room two centimetres taller. That left Cato, Farmer John, Lara and DI Hutchens. Cato was heartwarmed to see DS Meldrum get his moment in the spotlight but remained bemused by the choice of him on a job like this. The first he'd heard of Colin Graham's spectacular demise was a 4.30 a.m. phone call from Hutchens. As far as he could tell, Lara was in the same boat. They'd been sidelined: leaving Hutchens, Farmer John, Duncan Goldflam and Molly Meldrum in the know and acting on it since last night. Why?

'Any thoughts?' said the DI to no one in particular.

'Suicide?' said Farmer John.

'Please explain,' said Hutchens.

'He's been rumbled, his life has turned to shit, his hired African is locked up and about to dish the dirt. Writing on the wall. Petrol, match, whoosh.'

'Handcuffs?' said Cato.

'Insurance, in case he bottled out and changed his mind. He did it himself and threw away the key.'

Hutchens looked thoughtful. 'The ute?'

'Distraction. Red herring.'

'Nice and simple,' observed Cato neutrally.

Hutchens nodded, noncommittal. 'Lara? You're very quiet.'

Lara's eyes dulled and she shifted in her seat. 'I think John's probably on the money, sir.'

'Go and get some rest, Lara.'

The DI's office had been cleared. It was just the two of them. 'Sir?'

'You're a wreck. You're on the verge of cracking up. You need some professional help.'

'Thank you, sir.'

Hutchens closed his laptop and swivelled in his chair to face her. 'You've had to be rescued by TRG, you've been attacked in your home by Dieudonne, there's the Papadakis thing, and you've witnessed the death of that dero.'

'His name was Jeremy Dixon,' she said.

'Yeah. And now this.' Hutchens shook his head. 'You're traumatised. You need time out.'

'I'll be fine, sir.'

'I'm not advising you, Lara. I'm directing you. I'll get Human Resources to contact you with a psych appointment or something.'

'What about Dieudonne, and Vincent Tran and the nail-gun thing?'

'We'll take care of it; you take care of yourself.'

She didn't have the strength or inclination to argue.

Next it was Cato's turn in the DI's office behind closed doors. He watched Lara gather her things and leave. That dark-eyed, hollowed-out look reminded him of Shellie Petkovic. Cato went in and shut the door behind him.

'Coffee?' Hutchens thumbed over his shoulder at a tray on top of a filing cabinet: half-filled plunger, cups and milk jug, even a plate of biscuits.

'Don't mind if I do.' Cato grabbed a cup and an Anzac and sat down.

'Thoughts, maestro?'

'On Colin Graham?'

'Anything else happened in the last few hours?'

'Yeah, right.' Cato took a sip: it wasn't half bad. 'Farmer John seems keen to keep it neat and tidy.'

'What's your point?'

Cato shrugged. 'Bit early to be closing our minds to other possibilities.'

'Go on.'

'Murder? Maybe Graham's associates got round to thinking he was more trouble than he was worth.'

'Suicide is better PR.'

Cato munched on the biscuit. 'In what way?'

'Well the Commissioner's got the choice of *Rogue Cop Murdered by Bikie Pals* or *Veteran Cop Suicide Tragedy*.'

'Pithy. Ever thought you were in the wrong job, boss?'

'Never.'

Cato flicked some crumbs off his lap. 'Your call: PR is above my pay scale. So what now?'

'As you say, let the spin doctors at HQ come up with the story. We'll stick to collecting the evidence. Duncan can do his sifting and testing, Molly can do his asking and unless anything to the contrary comes in, we might let sleeping dogs lie, for now.'

That term again. You couldn't move around here these days without tripping over sleeping dogs. 'Okay,' said Cato.

Hutchens glanced out of the window at nothing in particular. 'Lara's got the rest of the day off. Maybe longer.'

'Good idea, she's been through a lot lately.'

'You up to absorbing a few of her jobs?'

'Like?'

'Vincent Tran and the nail gun; helping me with ongoing chats with Dieudonne?'

The idea of sitting in a chair opposite the man who'd pushed a knife into him didn't really appeal. 'DS Meldrum couldn't help out there I suppose?'

'Meldrum has important work to do, not finding any evidence that contradicts the suicide theory.'

Cato swallowed the last of his Anzac and pretended he hadn't heard that.

Hutchens flipped open his laptop and looked busy. 'We'll head out to Hakea in an hour to see Dieudonne. Grab some brekky while you can.'

Lara lay in bed, her window open to the sounds of Fremantle. Her limbs felt dull and heavy: her chest tight from holding back the flood. She wanted to cry, she wanted to die, worst of all she wanted to quit the job. Hutchens and UC John obviously wanted to sweep Colin Graham under the mat as a suicide. It suited them and it kind of suited her too. It explained away the handcuffs she'd snapped on his wrist, closing off his escape and sealing his fate.

Lara had done as instructed by Goatee. She'd walked away with the flames crackling in her ears, the glow flicking her shadow skittishly on the bitumen, the low murmurs of Graham's killers. And did she also hear, or just imagine, Colin's groans from within the furnace? They'd passed her on the drive out, in their black low-slung Falcon ute, Goatee encouraging her to get a move on.

'Fireys'll be here soon. Don't want them to catch you in the vicinity do you? Might need to do a bit of explaining.'

'You can handcuff me any time you like, sweetheart.' It was 'Such is' Dennis from the back seat.

A laugh and they were gone. Lara had crouched behind a wall as the fire engines and the first patrol car raced by. In her state, returning to the hotel was out of the question.

She'd gone home and showered to remove any odour traces of smoke or petrol and put her clothes and sneakers in the washing machine. She'd sat waiting for the inevitable callout to the scene. It never came and she fell asleep until an early morning summons from Hutchens.

On her way in she'd stopped by the hotel and collected her things. Events were moving too fast for her bodyguard on the door. He'd heard the manhunt was over and was still trying to work out why Lara wasn't tucked up in her room. She didn't bother to enlighten him.

Putting Meldrum on the case had been a clever move, ensuring the official version prevailed. Lara was content to play along. She'd seen the look on Cato's face though; he'd be a different prospect altogether.

Lara knew what had really happened. The Apaches had been Graham's insurance, or at least that's what he believed, but they'd turned on him. The question was whether they'd thought of it all by themselves. Goatee had said something early in the encounter, a reference to the handcuffs on Graham. *Nice touch. Maybe we weren't needed after all.* Both Hutchens and UC John seemed keen to whitewash the affair and that made her think that one or both of them were involved in some way. It had to be John: he was the one in the loop and he'd failed to respond to her emergency summons. Colin had been absolutely confident of the outcome and the chosen location because John, either directly or via the Apaches, had spoon-fed him that confidence. Lara had been offered up to Colin as an apparent sacrifice and that's why he never saw the double-cross coming. She had been UC John's tethered goat. How was that for karma?

A crowded interview room at Hakea prison: guards, an African woman, a lawyer with her back turned as she rummaged in a briefcase, and of course Dieudonne. Across the table: Cato and DI Hutchens.

'You guys have met, haven't you?'

Hutchens – a laugh a minute. Cato wanted to shove a knife in *his* gut to see how funny it felt. 'Very amusing, sir.'

'I meant you and the lawyer.'

The lawyer stopped rummaging, turned and offered a hand. Cato remembered her: Amrita, from Legal Aid; she'd given him grief aplenty in the Great Southern. He stuck out his hand and played professional. 'Miss Desai, keeping well?'

She shook it. 'Yes thanks and it's Mrs Gupta now.'

'Congratulations.'

'Thank you, Detective, Kwong wasn't it?'

'Still is.'

They took their seats with two corrections officers visible on the other side of the glass door. Dieudonne sat between Amrita Gupta and the large African woman who Cato assumed was the interpreter.

'Evonne.' She offered her hand for shaking too.

Dieudonne was in handcuffs and his prison-visit greys, his face alert and interested. The equipment was checked and names, dates, times, and places announced. Amrita Gupta took an early opportunity to record her continuing displeasure at Dieudonne's handcuffs and DI Hutchens took an early opportunity to remind her that he was a dangerous fucking nutter.

'Excuse the strong language, Mrs Gupta. It's an expression of my state of unease.'

Amrita pursed her lips.

Cato felt Dieudonne's eyes boring into him: there was no particular gloating or psyching going on, just an apparent curiosity. *Do not struggle, my friend. Accept it.*

Hutchens ahemmed his intent to proceed. 'You'll be glad to know we've located Mr Graham, Dieudonne.'

'Mr Graham?'

'Yes, he's dead. Burnt to death in a car last night.'

Dieudonne's eyes widened for a nanosecond, Amrita breathed sharply. 'These shock tactics are outrageous and uncalled for.'

'Sorry.' Hutchens switched his attention back to Dieudonne. 'Anyway mate, it looks like you're on your own now.'

'Own?'

'Yes. So there's nothing to stop you giving us a full statement regarding your involvement in all these matters.' Hutchens waved a hand across his open file. 'And it may even work in your favour in sentencing if the court is made aware of your cooperation.'

'Cooperation.'

Hutchens looked at the interpreter. 'Is he repeating everything I say because he doesn't understand or because he's trying to wind me up?'

'I'll ask him if you like,' said Evonne. There followed a brief exchange. She turned back to face Hutchens. 'He's winding you up.'

'Glad you're having fun, mate. Are you going to help us out today or are we just going to leave you buried in here and get on with our lives?' Hutchens flipped his file shut.

'What do you want to know, Inspector?' Dieudonne, in clear stentorian tones: like he was giving the valedictory for the Year 12s at Scotch.

'Lovely.' Hutchens re-opened his file and picked up a pen. 'How about you start at the beginning and keep going until the end and we'll see how we go?'

'For that we need to go back to the day Commander Peter came to my village and ordered me to kill my mother.'

Hutchens groaned. 'Fuck's sake, go on then, let's hear it.'

38

'Like Lord of the fucking Flies on acid.'

'Well put, boss.'

They were driving on Nicholson Road in Canning Vale: flat, bare paddocks and the occasional rusty car body. It was late morning by the time Dieudonne got to the point and by then DI Hutchens was beside himself with impatience. The oral storytelling tradition of Dieudonne's forebears had a pace and rhythm that was a tad languid for Hutchens' taste. The Congo had been a bloodfest: it made Dieudonne's antics in Fremantle look like a visit to the petting zoo. The wonder of it was that he was not a complete gibbering basket case.

'Papa was already dead and my baby brother was on the fire – neck broken, brains leaking into the flames. After the gang finished with my mother and sister, the leader handed me the machete and told me I must prove my loyalty to him.'

Hutchens grimaced. 'And what was all that blather about tarantulas?'

'Tantalum, sir.'

'Yeah, that. He's got a real bee in his bonnet about it.'

'They mine it in the Congo. Rare earth, very valuable. It goes into our mobile phones. It's part of the reason for the non-stop killing over there. Whoever controls that territory controls access and reaps the rewards.'

'How do you know all this shit?'

'Radio National.'

'Fuck's sake.' Hutchens shook his head in disgust.

Cato had been transfixed by Dieudonne's recounting of the Greek mythological tale of Tantalus; a mining magnate of his day, doomed to be forever dissatisfied, to have all his wants and needs just beyond reach. Dieudonne, espousing like a reclusive scholar.

'Depending upon which story you read, his fate was either a punishment for greed, theft, betrayal, or for the atrocities of human sacrifice and infanticide. All of those things are very common in Kivu.'

Evonne the Translator had nodded sadly in agreement.

Colourful and tragic as Dieudonne's early life had been, the story wasn't really relevant for them until he arrived in Australia and was taken under the wing of DS Colin Graham at a police youth club in the northern suburbs.

'PCYC a recruiting centre for assassins, would you believe it?' said Hutchens.

'Makes a change from ping-pong and basketball,' said Cato.

Dieudonne was initially paid by Graham to do some debt-collecting and enforcing here and there but his obvious willingness to go the extra yard meant that he was destined for higher things.

'What did you get out of it?' Hutchens had asked. 'Money? Drugs?'

'A bit of money, for living only. No drugs. He offered me something far more valuable.'

'Go on.'

'Belief in myself. Like when I was with Commander Peter.'

'Brilliant,' muttered Hutchens, 'the Poet Warrior meets the Floreat Maharishi. Bingo.'

Dieudonne had upgraded to official hit-man status with the Santo Rosetti killing. He'd followed Santo into the toilets and overheard the sexual encounter between Rosetti and Jimmy Tran from the adjoining cubicle. Once Jimmy had zipped himself up and made his exit, Santo had decided to stay there and pop some pills: to steady his nerves maybe. Dieudonne moved in. If the opportunity hadn't presented itself there and then, he said, he would have trailed Rosetti out of the club and done it somewhere else.

'And the business with the locked cubicle door was Colin's idea to give us extra stuff to think about: ad-lib instructions over the mobile.' Cato slowed for a stoplight. 'Yet it was Colin who gave us the early tip-off about Santo being UC?'

'Drip feed, mate. He would know questions would be asked if he didn't deliver the basics. He fed us just enough to stay credible. But I'm wondering why Col seems to have kept Dieudonne a secret from his Apache associates if most of the work was on their behalf?'

'Maybe he had future plans that didn't include them.'

Hutchens snorted. 'Got that wrong, didn't he?'

'All of that testimony on the record doesn't help the HQ spin doctors with their "veteran cop suicide tragedy" stuff,' observed Cato.

'That's their problem. I'm just an honest copper doing my job, Cato mate.'

Cato didn't detect any irony; he kept his eyes on the road.

'Sorry, Lara love, nothing personal. It's just that you've become too much of a fucking liability.'

Lara struggled to free herself but the handcuffs rattled against the steering wheel. She saw the match flare and the look of regret in Colin's eyes. Beep-beep. Somebody was trying to send her a text but she couldn't get to her phone because it was on the back seat of the car with her gun. Beep-beep. Lara woke up gulping for air. Her phone beeped and vibrated on the bedside table. A missed call and voice message.

Hi Lara, this is Melanie Kim. I've received a message from DI Hutchens to contact you about our Stress Management program. Can you call me back on ...

Melanie Kim could wait. Stress management? There were a couple of bottles of Marlborough white in the fridge. No. Too cold and thin and probably a bit sharp. She needed warm, thick and sweet right now. Chocolate. She needed chocolate. Comfort food of the gods and her staple fallback in troubled times. She padded out to the kitchen and wrote CHOC!!! on the shopping list magnetised to her fridge. Then she double underlined it.

Stress management. Exactly how do you manage those dreams where you watch your ex-lover burst into flames? Over and over again. She could have done with a few handy tips for dealing with that tightness in your chest when you recall the lid of the car boot closing on you. Maybe there was a pill that exorcised that metallic smell of freshly sprayed blood from your nostrils.

She should have stopped them but she didn't. And now she had to pay with the dreams and flashbacks of Colin Graham's last agonies, trapped by *her* handcuffs. Even after what he'd done to her she couldn't wish that on any man. Lara had meant to do the right thing: arrest him and have him face justice, the civilised way. Instead she'd hesitated and he lost his life.

Stress management? That implied a future in the job.

Cato arranged for the Dieudonne interview to be transcribed for the prosecution case notes and spent the remainder of the morning catching up on paperwork. The closing discussions with the African and his lawyer suggested an early guilty plea to expedite the process. Dieudonne was happy enough in prison: he had a sense of belonging to a community with rules and a pecking order and he had no fears for his own safety.

'They will have to be very many, very fast, very tough, and very good to hurt me.' He'd smiled and shrugged his narrow shoulders. 'What is the worst that they can do? Kill me?' There was an added bonus: access to books and education courses. Dieudonne could finally get to finish his schooling. 'My mother had great expectations of me. That is why she named me her gift from god. She taught me to read. Now maybe I can finally repay her.'

Dieudonne's recounting of the story of Tantalus reverberated. Colin Graham: betraying secrets and sacrificing colleagues, all for earthly gain. Was he now in a subterranean Hades embarking upon his eternity of torment? Cato doubted it: the man was just charcoal remains waiting to be bagged and tagged. But it wasn't just about Colin Graham. It seemed to Cato that the rage and blackness he encountered every day in his job was usually some variation on the twisted tale of Tantalus: greed, betrayal, human sacrifice, infanticide. He thought of Karina Ford's unborn grandchild, bludgeoned to death even before seeing the light of day, and all over a pathetic drug debt.

This was a Tuesday afternoon in Fremantle, Australia, yet

sometimes it felt like chaos was just a wrong look, a brain snap away. One day: a beautiful, sun-kissed and laid-back paradise – God's own. The next: a vicious, amoral, 'nothing personal' vacuum. The Big Empty. A state that had built itself around a one-word motto, 'Floreat', prosper – and never looked back. It was a place Dieudonne now called home. For all the contrast in wealth and privilege between the two societies there were commonalities: two resource-rich nations, a sense of entitlement for those who plundered those resources, and sometimes a savage lack of empathy for those who wished only to live their lives in peace and safety.

Hutchens popped his head around the door. 'Thought you might like to know. Shellie's out on bail, magistrates hearing adjourned for a couple of weeks.'

'Bryn Irskine?'

'Still looking.' Hutchens disappeared again.

Paperwork. The prison bikies' next court appearance was due within two weeks. The Vincent Tran tip-off had been offered as a counter-balance to the Wellard bashing case to get the two Casuarina stompers out of the frame for murder. Clearly the Apaches wanted a game-changer from Cato before then. He didn't have a clue where to start. Maybe lunch first.

By midafternoon Lara was going stir-crazy and her eyes kept returning to that note on the fridge door. CHOC!!! She decided to go and get some but it had to be seen as part of an orderly plan and not a panic response to a disgusting base impulse. She drew up a full list of a week's worth of groceries with meals planned out for the next seven days. Balanced nutritional meals with plenty of fresh vegetables, crunchy salads, fruit. And chocolate.

She drove over to the Woolstores, parked and grabbed a trolley. Lara had caught a glimpse of herself in the rear-view mirror and was aware that her face still carried bruises and abrasions from her recent adventures. Fellow shoppers looked at her and looked quickly away. Battered spouses must get this every day, she realised. Maybe she had more in common with the Shellie Petkovics of this world than she was game to admit: blind faith in a violent, controlling and manipulative man. Result – a world of hurt. Maybe she should have come down in her police uniform and they could have shaken her hand and given her medals instead of those pitying glances.

Chocolate. Lara knew where it was but she went in the opposite direction. Queen of Denial. She packed her trolley with nature's bounty: crunchy salad; ripe, shiny, juicy fruit; wholemeal bread. Fresh fish packed to the gills with omega-3. Fruit juice, wholemeal pasta, chicken, herbal teabags, bircher muesli.

CHOC!!! One aisle to go.

She almost deliberately went past and then, as if struck by a second thought, or a reminder that she'd promised to buy something for a friend, she edged towards the chocolate, tense and wary, as if approaching somebody armed with a knife. *A spray of arterial blood across a white wall.* Above her, piped muzak, instantly forgettable. Pity her bloody daydreams weren't the same.

CHOC!!! Row upon row of the stuff: plain, dark, mildly dark, fruity, nutty, fruity and nutty, peppermint, caramel, she didn't know where to start. She picked one block, looked at it, put it back. Another. A hand gripped her below the knee. *Fagin crawling along the floor, blood gushing from his neck.* She looked again: it was a toddler thinking Lara was his mum and scared now because he was wrong.

'You okay there, sweetie?'

The mum gathered her toddler up in her arms and repeated the question, but to Lara this time. Lara stood holding onto her trolley, heart pounding, reaching for breath.

39

Cato had returned from lunch with a half-filled cryptic and a fully filched *West*. The headline featured the launch of the Premier's Safer Streets campaign: a slogan, *Reclaim Our Streets* – the vigilantes will like that one, thought Cato; a photo of a parent of a one-punch killing; an education program including TV ads; a promise of stricter penalties; and a new hard line from the police. Cato wondered how much harder they could get when they already had batons, tasers and dogs. Shoot on sight? What it really needed was a change in the way we all think and act. Easy. Got ten generations to spare?

He followed up on the DNA and other samples taken from Stephen Mazza to see if there had been any progress. The lab was snowed under with a backlog of samples from all the volume crime that had been added to their workload. The powers-that-be had reasoned, correctly, that your average punter tended to experience crime usually as a victim of the lower level but far more pervasive volume offences: burglaries in the suburbs, car thefts, vandalism, assaults. It was Safer Streets writ large: lift your game and your clear-up rate on the things that matter to them and you have happier taxpayers and voters. As a result DNA and other forensic testing, previously the reserve of murders in Mosman Park, was now also applied to burglaries in Bassendean. The predictably massive increase in workload was never going to be adequately matched by the more moderate increase in resources allocation.

'Friday week do you?' mumbled a flat voice at the other end of the phone.

Kenny and Danny were due in court on the Tuesday after that; it was cutting it fine if anything bigger and more urgent happened in the meantime and shunted it down the list. 'No chance of a fast track?' said Cato.

'That is the fast track. Everybody else has to wait until at least April. What's the emergency?'

Cato explained about the Wellard case and the upcoming court appearance of the bikies but left out the personal bit about the nail-gun tap on the knee.

'Let's get this straight. You want me to drop everything to run some tests that may or may not help clear some scungy bikies who are up for killing a pervert rapist murderer in Casuarina? That right?'

Cato didn't get the chance to confirm that was the nature of his request. The phone connection hummed discouragingly.

His mobile beeped. It was a text from Jane.

ok 4 jake this wknd?

It was lucky that the previous weekend's manhunt and Cato's Myaree abduction hadn't interfered with their shared custody arrangements. So, all things being equal, it should be fine to have his son over.

sure

he texted back. Almost immediately another reply from his ex-wife's nimble fingers:

will drop him friday @ 6 and back sunday 9am.

Domestics sorted, Cato's mind returned to bikies and nail guns.

'You busy?' It was DI Hutchens standing in his office doorway.

Only on a matter of urgent and knee-shattering importance.

'It can wait,' said Cato. He sauntered into his boss's domain. DS Meldrum occupied one guest seat, Farmer John another. Cato took the only one left.

Hutchens nodded at Meldrum to proceed. There was a sheen of sweat on the well-fed face and dark patches around the armpits; Meldrum must have been outside doing some work. 'The doorknock has thrown up something interesting.'

'I'm all ears,' said Cato. Farmer John yawned: he appeared to already know what this was about.

'Mr David Rose. Lives alone in one of the Biscuit Factory units. He was fishing from the rocks at the end of the mole up to about an hour before the emergency services callout. He recalls the black ute showing up and doing a couple of burnouts just as he was packing up his gear.'

'Yep,' said Cato.

'He also remembered there was someone else at the end of the mole about the same time he was there. A woman. And she wasn't fishing.'

Cato nodded. 'Sounds suspicious. Go on.'

'His description of her, particularly of the cuts and bruises on her face, matches our own DSC Lara Sumich.'

'I thought she was acting funny this morning. That explains it.'

All eyes turned to Farmer John.

'Explains what?' said Hutchens.

'The off-the-planet, shell-shocked look. Poor kid must have seen the whole thing.'

Poor kid? It wasn't the image Cato had come to associate with Lara Sumich. 'Just "seen" the whole thing, or been part of it?' he said.

'You serious?' DI Hutchens clearly didn't fancy the sound of that. The paperwork would be the end of him.

'Why not? He abducted and tried to murder her so she had a strong motive. She was there when it happened. If we can establish any connecting physical evidence then we're in business.'

'We're in trouble, more like. Fuck's sake Cato, I know you two don't get along but this is a bit much.'

Farmer John's head lifted at this new bit of intra-office gossip but he didn't pursue it; like any good intelligence man he'd be storing it away for a rainy day. Hutchens tapped a pencil furiously against the edge of his desk.

Cato decided to turn the thumbscrew. 'Colin Graham would have had a gun. Has anybody wondered why it was never found? Maybe Lara took it off him; maybe we should send some divers into the harbour for a look. If I was contemplating suicide I'd be keeping my gun. Eating your Glock has to be better than self-immolation. And if you did an inventory of Lara's locker and kit supply you might find she's short one set of handcuffs. Who knows? The least we should be doing is pursuing this as a line of inquiry.'

Farmer John appraised Cato. 'We should probably ask Ms Sumich to explain herself,' he conceded.

'Shit,' sighed Hutchens, 'you think there's a light at the end of the tunnel and it turns out to be a fucking express train.'

Lara wasn't sure how she got home from her panic attack in the supermarket. She dimly recalled that at some point a cherubic ranga-curled youth in a polo shirt gave her a glass of water while several people looked at her as if she was on drugs. The same youth, his name badge said *Liam*, had helped process her shopping through the checkout. Liam had even gone and chosen some chocolate for her. The shopping was still in bags on the kitchen counter, waiting to be put away. It had been there for a couple of hours. Lara sat on the couch watching daytime TV, the bar of chocolate in her hands: Mildly Dark with Almonds. A mug of sweet milky instant coffee cooled at her feet. She had visions of herself in a few weeks: a big, greasy blob of lard. On TV it was *Deal or No Deal*: all those decisions and Lara couldn't even choose a bar of chocolate for herself. For all that, she was about to pick the blue-haired nanna with briefcase 21 when her door buzzer went. She swore and stumbled over to the video monitor screen above the entry button.

'Yes?'

'Lara?'

'What do you want?'

'You and I need to talk.'

'What about?'

'What you were doing down on Capo D'Orlando Drive last night.'

Lara closed her eyes and rested her forehead against the cool wall. She pressed the button to let him in.

'We have a problem.' UC John planted himself at her kitchen table.

'Who's "we" this time?'

'The boss, Meldrum, Kwong.' A pause. 'You and me.'

'What's the problem?'

'We know you were there. That makes you at least a witness, maybe even a suspect. Somebody saw you on the scene during the timeframe. There's also a CCTV camera mounted on a light pole near the trawlers and the toilet block. We haven't checked it yet but who knows what we might find. There's also the matter of the handcuffs to be investigated, plus the records of your mobile phone communications with Graham.'

'And?'

'And I know you didn't kill him.'

'Of course you do. You already knew I was there. You were meant to be my "safety net".'

'That's right.'

'So why didn't you respond to my emergency text and why haven't you told Hutchens what really went on?'

No answer.

Lara glanced over at her unfinished slab of Mildly Dark. 'You tipped them off.'

'Tipped who off, Lara? You're not making any sense.'

'Oh fuck off, I don't need your games, I had enough of that shit with Colin.'

'Look Lara, I know you've been under a lot of stress lately and that you're about to undertake trauma counselling.'

'Who says?'

John leaned forward over Lara's kitchen table and patted her hand. 'I'm here to help. There's a few bits and pieces to tidy up but once done we can file Colin Graham away and all get on with our lives.'

'That easy, huh?' she said dully. 'What about me? What if I decide to come clean? Does that put a spanner in your works?'

'Feeling guilty about him? Don't. He was going to hand you over to the Apaches as a plaything before they killed you. If I hadn't convinced them otherwise, you'd be wishing you were dead by now.'

'You didn't just turn them though, did you? You set the whole thing up, even the location, nice and quiet at that time of night, and you got word to him that it would be just me.' She shook her head, disgust and admiration in equal parts. 'And he believed you.'

'He believed his mates. They told him I was also in their pocket. I'm almost hurt that he bought it. Here's me thinking I came across as squeaky clean.'

'That's why he was so confident,' said Lara. 'And I was the bait. Ends and means, huh?'

John stared at the tabletop, measuring out his words. 'Santo Rosetti was a mate of mine. He was a good officer. He lived every day with the fear and danger of his cover being blown: every day with scumbags for companions until you begin to forget whether you're one of them or not.'

Lara wondered about that daily destruction of your sense of self and how long she'd last under that kind of pressure. She remembered the looks in the supermarket, the assumptions that the bruises on her face were there because she was one of life's losers. The kind of looks and judgements she too had foisted on Santo and on Cato's mispers mum.

'You let them kill him. Aren't we meant to be better than that?'

'It was in all our interests.' John shrugged. 'Santo Rosetti was betrayed by a colleague, somebody he needed to be able to trust. In our game you show no mercy. Graham got what was coming. The alternative was having him laugh at us all the way through the courts and ending up with a reduced sentence and a cushy job in the library at Karnet. Believe me Lara, it was for the best, and now we just have to tidy this up.'

'What if I don't play ball?'

'We could hang you out to dry.'

'I doubt it. You want this to be as neat as a pin. I've been through all sorts of shit these past few weeks. The newspapers love me. I'm a hero.' Lara broke off a square of chocolate. 'So, what's in it for me?'

'What do you want?' said John.

She gave it some thought, told him, and then they worked out what to do next.

The sun floated on the horizon for a few seconds before melting from view. From his vantage point on the parapet of the Round House, Cato turned his back on the ocean and looked east up High Street and the rooftops of the West End bathed in the sunset glow. Cato had decided he needed to right a wrong; he felt guilty about being such a hard-arse. This had been a violent and blood-soaked few weeks and Lara Sumich had been at the centre of much of it. Right now she didn't need the kind of scrutiny he'd just unleashed upon her. He was on his way to tip her off when he'd seen Lara's visitor enter the apartment building. He'd bided his time with a stroll up to the historic lookout. Now, twenty-five minutes later, her visitor was leaving. So what was it that Lara Sumich had been cooking up with Farmer John?

40

Wednesday, February 17th. Morning.

'We need you to clarify what you were doing there, Detective Sumich.'

DI Hutchens didn't look comfortable in the role of Inquisitor today. That was good, thought Lara, he'd be keen to get it over with, keen for an exit strategy. Hutchens was doing the talking, Meldrum the transcribing, and John was there in case he was needed. No tapes yet and no formal caution. Also no Cato: he'd been sent off to get some coffees and to get on with other duties. He hadn't kicked up a fuss like she would have: he'd just smiled at Hutchens and John and given Lara a wink on the way past. That spelled danger to her.

'During the day on Monday, I received a text message from Colin Graham seeking a meeting with me at Capo D'Orlando Drive at 9 p.m. that night.'

'Why didn't you inform us?'

'I believed I had the trust of DS Graham and that I had the best chance of bringing him in if I was able to go alone to the rendezvous and persuade him.'

'Are you serious? This was after he abducted you, assaulted you, and left you to be killed by Dieudonne?'

'Yes sir, I can see now that it was a poor judgement call.'

'Fucking right.' Hutchens lifted a warning finger to the scribbling Meldrum. 'Don't write that, dickhead.'

'What made you think you could persuade him this time?' said John.

'It was my belief that Graham himself was not capable of seriously harming me. He had Dieudonne to do that kind of thing. He previously had numerous opportunities to kill me but never did it. As such I believed I was relatively safe.' Meldrum was struggling to keep up, tongue poking through. 'I also believed that during the course of our investigative work together we had bonded to some extent. I also believed that he wanted to surrender, as his options by then were severely limited.'

'You believed a lot but most of it was wrong,' said Hutchens.

'Unfortunately, yes sir.'

Hutchens had that dropped-penny look: the rehearsed answers, the practised delivery. He'd twigged that somebody had tipped her off, he just didn't know who; yet. He gave John and Meldrum searching looks but didn't linger on Meldrum too long. He barked out across the office, 'Cato!'

Cato appeared with a cardboard tray, five coffees and a ready smile: like he'd been expecting the summons. He closed the door and Hutchens brought him up to speed.

'Very interesting, sir,' Cato agreed.

'Carry on, Ms Sumich. You arrived down at the marina and then what?'

Lara re-composed herself and took a sip from the cardboard cup. 'I arrived early and spent some time at the end of the mole enjoying the view and the sunset over the ocean.'

'Lovely,' nodded Cato.

The DI sent him a warning glare. 'That would have been about seven-ish?' said Hutchens.

'That's right, something like that.'

'Still a good couple of hours before your rendezvous.'

'Yes.'

'And you just sat on the rocks admiring the view, in the dark, until meeting time?'

'Obviously I made sure I was very early so that I could recce the scene and assess the risks.'

'Where did you stash the petrol can?' said Hutchens.

Lara lifted a hand to her mouth. 'Surely, you don't think ...'

'Think what? That you ambushed lover boy, cuffed his hand to the steering wheel, poured petrol over him and set him on fire?'

'Why would I want to do that?'

'I wonder,' said Hutchens.

John raised a hand like he'd just had an idea. 'There's a CCTV camera down there overlooking the car park. Have we checked that yet?'

Meldrum stopped scribbling. 'Out of order. And even when it's not it's usually angled and framed on the toilet block looking for perverts.'

'Really? Shame,' said John.

'So tell us your version, Detective.' Hutchens was beginning to look bored.

'By about 8.45 the area was pretty well deserted, a fisherman at the end of the mole had packed up and gone not long after 8.00. There was a woman walking her dog about then too. A black ute had come up and done a couple of burnouts in the car park and then left.'

'Was Graham's Laser parked up by then?' said Cato.

'Yes, although at that point I didn't recognise it as such.'

'At what point did you recognise it as such?' said Hutchens.

'Never. Not really. Not until we were given the news the following morning.'

'What do you mean?'

All eyes were on Lara. 'I got spooked. I had a strong gut feeling that I'd miscalculated and that this was a set-up, an ambush. I think the hoon ute did it. I felt my life was in danger and I got out of there.'

'If you were scared why didn't you call in backup?'

Lara steadfastly looked anywhere but at John. 'I was aware I'd already done the wrong thing by not reporting the planned meeting. I feared I'd get into trouble.'

'So you didn't see or speak to Colin Graham?'

'No, sir.'

'You didn't handcuff him to his steering wheel and set him on fire?'

'No, sir.'

'You expect me to believe that?'

'Yes, sir.'

'Do you mind if we inspect your kit locker, Detective Sumich?'

'Not at all, sir.'

The locker inspection confirmed no handcuff shortage. Lara was sent home again to continue her stress leave.

'And when Melanie Kim calls with your counselling appointments I recommend you play ball.'

'Absolutely, sir.'

Cato, Meldrum, Farmer John and Hutchens reconvened.

Hutchens slammed his office door, slapped a file down on his desk and slumped into the chair. 'She's been tipped off. Which of you did it?'

'What makes you think that?' said Farmer John.

'I didn't come down in the last shower.' A twist of the head. 'Cato?'

If there was a time to ask Farmer John what he was doing visiting Lara yesterday evening then this was it. Instead, Cato took a leaf out of John's book, staying quiet, hoping to get added value from it later. 'Not me, sir. Remember I was the one who originally drew attention to her possible culpability. Tipping her off now would be illogical.'

Hutchens shook his head. 'Culpability? Illogical? Thank you, Mr friggin' Spock. How about you, Molly?'

Meldrum's pencil jumped and his lower lip quivered. 'Me? No. Never.'

'Nah, I can't see it either. That leaves you, John.'

John shrugged. 'Can't help you, sir. Maybe she's just had a bit of time to think. She's a smart cookie. Knew there were possible witnesses putting her at the scene. She could work it out for herself.'

'The handcuffs?' said Cato.

John smiled. 'Just proves that she was innocent and that your theory of the missing cuffs was fanciful speculation.'

'Got me there,' said Cato.

Hutchens opened a file and flicked through the papers. 'Would all this bullshit stand up to more formal scrutiny?'

Cato recognised the signs: Hutchens already knew the answer to his own question.

Farmer John helped him out anyway, just in case. 'The evidence against her is thin and her story is hard to contradict. She's also been placed under extreme stress in the course of her duties and an internal inquiry might be seen as victimisation. In the end, Colin Graham is a case of good riddance to bad rubbish. It's a no-brainer really. I suggest we drop it.'

'All agreed then?' said Hutchens, opening his laptop and inviting them all to get lost.

All neatly sewn up. Lara had obviously seen and known more than she was admitting to. Had Lara killed Graham in revenge for his betrayal of her, or did Farmer John set up the killing as payback for the murder of his colleague Santo? It probably amounted to some permutation of those scenarios. Cato knew he really should care more but Colin Graham was no innocent and it looked like he'd got what he deserved. Cato could settle for that. It was beginning to have parallels with the Wellard case: a nasty piece of work getting his just desserts and, for Cato, a feeling of ambivalence over the relative truths of each matter.

It was now Wednesday and Cato needed some kind of development to keep the bikies off his back ahead of the upcoming court appearance. Maybe he could just explain to the Apaches that there was a bureaucratic delay at the lab but that he really was onto it. Then again forensic evidence was not the point. They knew they hadn't done it and they knew who really had. Science wasn't the issue, honour and honesty was. They just wanted Stephen Mazza to stand up and be counted. On impressions to date, Cato had the feeling that Mazza was usually a stand-up kind of bloke. So why not now?

Cato logged in to the system and brought up Stephen Anthony Mazza. He scanned the case details again: no previous record until a drunk-driving incident that killed the three occupants of the other car, an elderly couple and a grandchild returning from a day out at the zoo. Mazza had pleaded guilty and made no attempt to cite any mitigating circumstances for a sentence reduction. He'd copped it sweet, four years. But once inside it seemed like he was determined to make life tougher for himself. He could and should have spent most of his sentence in a low-security prison but he'd decided to make himself a management problem.

Cato already knew this from previous readings but was there anything hiding in the detail that could shed new light? If the theory was that Mazza deliberately arked up in order to be kept in Casuarina with Wellard, then it implied that Mazza had a lethal grudge against Wellard and that he was prepared to make some personal sacrifices in order to wreak his revenge. Believing Wellard to be responsible for Bree's disappearance or death could inspire that kind of grudge. It also suggested that Mazza took a long-term view of the problem: he was patient enough to wait and pick his moment despite probably having several opportunities over the preceding months and years. So what made this moment the one he chose? Possibly the opportunity to hide it behind somebody else's crime. Or perhaps it had just taken that long to sharpen the toothbrush and get his nerve up.

Something else was forming in Cato's brain. Back a step. A lethal grudge, a long-term view, personal sacrifice. This was theoretically about his ex-girlfriend's daughter. Yes, he might have been prepared to do whatever it took to help out Shellie but this man was prepared to go through hell to achieve his goal. Did Stephen Mazza have a much more personal stake in the death of Wellard? As Cato re-read the case file through that prism he began to see things more clearly.

41

Lara sat outside the Spearwood home of Mr and Mrs Rosetti. The old man was ignoring the summer hosepipe ban and watering the front yard while his wife swept the driveway. It was heading for lunchtime and it really was too hot to be doing something so futile, but that was just Lara's point of view. She hadn't gone home as instructed by the DI. She knew there was no danger of them looking too closely at her for what happened to Colin Graham. John had wrapped all that up: topping up her quota of handcuffs, feeding her an explanation of her part in events, making sure the CCTV coverage of the car park was destroyed or unavailable. He was a real Mr Fixit. But there were some things she couldn't abrogate to others.

Mr and Mrs Rosetti both looked up as Lara walked down their garden path. Of course they remembered her and welcomed her inside for a cool drink. They sat in a darkened room with photographs of Santo on the sideboard – his life from cradle to grave. Lara told them some of what had really happened: of his courage and high regard among his colleagues, the constant dangers he faced as an undercover officer, of his important role in trying to combat the scourge of drugs and gang-violence, how they could be very, very proud of him.

'We've always been proud of him, Lara.' Mrs Rosetti's eyes were shining.

'Of course,' said Lara.

'And now we can finally bury him, after three weeks!' Mr Rosetti tried to hide his anger. 'But they won't give him a full police funeral. No, "Top Secret" they say, so he doesn't get a hero's send off like he should.'

Mrs Rosetti placed her hand over his to calm him. 'A family funeral is fine. It's what he would want.' Mr Rosetti shook his head.

Lara looked once again at the photo of Santo graduating from the Academy: fresh-faced, clean-cut, full of hope and pride. She said her goodbyes; they patted her hand and thanked her and they all smiled through their tears. As she drove away they waved and recommenced the futile sweeping of the already clean driveway and the watering of the front yard in the blinding sun.

Until the results came back, Cato couldn't be sure and there was no point in taking it further unless he was on firm ground. He needed some clout to hurry things along.

'Let's hear it.' DI Hutchens glanced up from his budget reports or whatever it was that occupied his time these days.

Cato outlined his latest theory on the Mazza–Wellard–Petkovic affair.

Hutchens nodded. 'The case is with the prosecutors and the few loose ends will be tied up in due course. It's dropped down my priority list. Why are you still worrying your pretty little head about it?'

He knew the DI needed something new so he told him about the nail gun and the threatening tap on the knee in Myaree.

'Why didn't you mention this earlier?'

'Not sure, sir.'

'Were you concerned that I might think less of you?'

'Well. I ...'

'You were right. I think you're a fucking dickhead. You don't let these people get away with threatening you. You tell me and we go around there and kick their arses. Who do they think they are?'

'Your loyalty and protectiveness is heartwarming, sir, but a show of force isn't necessarily going to neutralise that threat. If anything, it might even convince them they're onto a winner.' Cato was also aware that, despite Hutchens' previous bluster on the matter, nothing had actually happened in regard to Goatee and Eyebrow Stud. 'Still no sign of Irskine, then?'

'No, who'd believe such a big ugly bastard could disappear into thin air?' Hutchens cracked his knuckles in an abstract, menacing way. 'Does make me wonder why, if he knew her, he didn't just talk direct to Shellie. Why get you to ask her and Mazza to put the boot boys in the clear? Why go all around the houses? It doesn't make sense.'

'Maybe he did ask her direct and she didn't listen?'

'If I was a feeble little sheila and the bikies were threatening me, I'd listen.'

Cato ignored the thinly veiled insult. 'Maybe when we find him we can ask him to share his thinking with us. Meantime we need to keep things moving.'

'What do you suggest?'

'A hurry-up from you to the lab would suit all our purposes. We get nearer to the objective truth of the matter and they know where they stand in time for the court appearance.'

'So we give them what they want, basically?'

'Yes.'

'Interesting concept. Forgive me for not being as intellectually astute as you but I still don't grasp the part where we teach the fuckers a lesson.'

'I'm sure you'll think of a way, boss. It's just a matter of whether it needs to be now or later.'

'Well, as you're a friend and a colleague you can go ahead and give the lab a gee-up from me while I meditate on the possibilities.'

'Thanks, sir.'

'Don't mention it. Ever.'

Cato called the lab with a Hutchens-enforced hurry-up then left the office and went down the road for a late lunch. He grabbed a couple of samosas and a fruit juice from a health-food shop, walked down to Esplanade Park and found a shady spot under a Norfolk pine. He checked first for any danger from above. The heat swelled. Kids in the play area sauntered listlessly from swings to monkey bars and back again with no enthusiasm. Cato leaned his head back against the tree and closed his eyes.

Somebody was kicking the soles of his shoes.

'Wakey, wakey.'

Cato opened his eyes. There was a shadow over him, two in fact. Once his vision adjusted to the glare, he recognised them: his bikie friends from Myaree.

Cato tried to stand but Eyebrow Stud crouched and placed a firm hand on his shoulder. 'No need to get up.'

He didn't try. 'Bryn. Just the man we've been wanting to speak to.'

'Bryn? Nobody calls me that, except my mum.'

'I hear you and Shellie Petkovic know each other. Old school pals from Collie.'

'Yeah?'

'And we'd like to have a chat with you about that.'

'Call my lawyer. Make an appointment.'

Goatee came closer and leaned against the trunk of the tree, his knee millimetres from Cato's face. 'Meantime, how are your inquiries progressing?'

'As well as can be expected.'

'What's that mean?'

'We're pursuing several lines of investigation.'

The knee scraped Cato's cheek. It was encased in grubby denim and smelled of oil, ashtrays and sweat. 'I heard you were a funny cunt, a way with words.'

Cato noticed they were attracting nervous glances from passers by. Well, they would: two big bikies crowding up on some comparatively puny Chinese office worker in a park in the middle of Fremantle in broad daylight. Cato wondered if anybody would bother to raise the alarm or whether they'd mind their own business while he got stomped to a pulp.

Goatee lit a cigarette and flicked the match at Cato. 'My advice to you, mate, is to quit the comedy and pull your finger out. We've got a court case coming up and we want to have some certainty by then.'

Certainty, a real commodity of late: mining magnates wanted it, beachfront developers wanted it, even outlaw bikies. It was an expensive commodity too; ordinary people couldn't afford it.

'Why the urgency? There'll be a few court hearings before any actual trial.'

'There'll be no trial. We'll be looking at a guilty plea on assault, a few months on the existing sentence, and Bob's your uncle.'

'Guilty plea? That sounds like cooperation to me. Isn't that against the Code?'

Goatee pulled hard on his ciggie. 'Business is business. We decide what the Code is and when we abide by it. All you need to do is play your part and nobody gets hurt. Well, no civilians anyway.'

Cato felt Eyebrow Stud's breath close to his ear. Was he about to bite it off?

'You might think we stick out like sore thumbs, mate, but we've managed to creep up on you twice now. Third time ... unlucky.'

Cato thought it would be a good idea to keep his mouth shut. It worked. Eyebrow Stud patted him on the shoulder, Goatee winked, and they both left. Cato put a call through to the TRG to tip them off about Eyebrow Stud's general whereabouts but knew he'd be long gone before they got here.

Cato guessed that the Apaches wanted certainty on their two soldiers in Casuarina because they were gearing up for another turf war in the not-too-distant future and needed all the numbers they could muster. He had a pretty good idea who the enemy was too.

'Hold the front page.'

DI Hutchens was predictably unimpressed. Farmer John was in on the meeting too.

'Still here, John?' said Cato. 'With Graham wrapped up I thought your work would be done.'

'It was, but your boss wanted some advice on a matter close to home. Personal threats against our officers need to be taken seriously.'

'Is that your area of expertise? I thought you were Intelligence?'

'And that's exactly what you've just brought us.'

'Hardly earth-shattering though. The Apaches and the Trans are always going at each other. Surely you already had wind of this?'

'Good to have as much objective verification as possible,' said John. 'It does sound like they're planning something more than a border skirmish though.'

'Border skirmish?' said Cato.

'The tit for tat the last few weeks: tattoo-parlour arson, meth-lab explosions, home invasions, dealer bashings. Col and his Gangs mates have been busy stirring the pot.' John grinned. 'That's one thing we will miss him for.'

'Col set up the Willagee bashing?' said Cato.

'He was behind it but the Apaches did it. Kept the wheels turning. Good result.'

Cato went over to the window, looked out at the sunshine. 'Does beating an innocent pregnant teenager into a miscarriage count as a good result these days then? Prick.'

John examined a bit of loose skin on his thumb. 'I'll let that pass, given the strain we've all been under.'

Hutchens gave Cato a warning glance. 'So if they're factoring in Kenny and Danny's release dates that means it's a good six to nine months away.'

A nod from John.

DI Hutchens yawned. 'I think I might be washing my hair that night.'

Cato turned from the window. 'Their chat with me in Myaree makes more sense now though, doesn't it?'

'Explain.'

'Sure they can put the hard word direct on Shellie to help clear their boys inside, but we're the ones with real clout. And we're the ones who can do something about weakening the Trans by arresting Vincent. You generals can decide what to do with all that.' Cato turned to leave Hutchens' office. Farmer John stood aside to let him pass.

'Cheers, Cato,' he said.

Cato gave no reply.

They finally caught up with her late in the afternoon. She was watching TV: some really obese guy showing people how to cook a healthy dish; he somehow lacked authority. The phone trilled.

'Lara! At last. It's Melanie Kim.' A pause. 'Human Services? Stress Management Program?'

Lara mouthed an expletive. 'Hi, Melanie.'

'How are you doing?'

It was a simple and innocent enough question but Lara could feel the panic symptoms returning. For a while there earlier she'd thought it was all going to be okay. She'd held it together while they grilled her at the office. She held it together while she lied to the Rosettis about the usefulness of their son's death. She had even begun to think that the meltdown in the supermarket was just a one-off and things were on the up again. But now big fat tears ran down her face and her voice cracked, 'Good.'

'It doesn't sound like it. Look I've got an appointment pencilled in for you for Friday but maybe we'll bring it forward to tomorrow. How does 9.30 suit?'

'Fine.'

'Okay, here's the address, have you got a pen and paper handy to take this down?'

'No.'

'No problem, I'll SMS it to you. We'll see you tomorrow, okay?'

On TV the dish came out of the oven, it was a kind of pasta bake with vegetables, tuna, and low-fat cottage cheese. There was a close-up of the guy forking some into his mouth. Lara looked at the empty chocolate wrappers on the floor and the cold unfinished cup of instant coffee on the table. She got to the toilet just in time to spew. As she hunched over the bowl and tasted the bile in her throat she wondered bleakly if there would ever be a time when all of this would be over.

Back in the office in the communal kitchen, Cato flicked on the kettle. He wasn't sure what to make of Farmer John. He might be a ruthless bastard but he didn't think the man was corrupt. Then again, he'd never thought so of Colin Graham either. They were both involved in areas, Gangs and Intelligence, where there was perhaps more potential for temptation and conflicts of interest. Cato replayed in his mind the part of the conversation in the park that set him wondering.

I heard you were a funny cunt, a way with words.

Goatee's description. He could have heard it from Col Graham or Farmer John. Col was in with the Apaches anyway and John no doubt had access to them, it was his job. But it was John who'd used that familiar term that first day they met in a Maccas on South Street.

You'll have heard of the Trans and the Apaches?'

No, who are they?

Funny cunt.

Cato wasn't a great believer in coincidences. Plus Cato's dealings of late had been far more to do with John than Col Graham. So let's take a cognitive leap and assume Farmer John is talking to the bikies. Did that make him corrupt or was he just using them to achieve certain ends? Cato could try asking him. There were a number of possible outcomes: if John *was* corrupt then Cato could end up dead, or if John was playing a strategic game with the bikies then he could just tell Cato to mind his own business. Or John might even make a clean breast of it. Cato reckoned it at fifty-fifty on options one and two and snowball's on number three. He'd had worse odds. He left his tea untouched, went over to his boss's office, knocked and entered.

DI Hutchens looked up, mildly irritated at the interruption. 'Not now, Cato.' He registered Cato's determined expression. 'What do you want, then?'

Cato nodded towards Farmer John in his usual chair. 'I want John to tell us all what's really going on. I want to know why he visited Lara yesterday evening and whether that had anything to do with her having a ready answer for all of our questions this morning. And while he's on, maybe he could explain the nature of his relationship with the Apaches.'

Hutchens sat back in his chair and folded his arms. 'John?'

John did come clean, up to a point. He admitted passing on the Capo D'Orlando rendezvous details to the Apaches. Lara had chosen to let him know of her plans and for him to be her backup. Interesting. She'd trusted him over Hutchens and Cato. John claimed he hadn't anticipated them actually killing Graham but it didn't bother him that they had.

Hutchens shook his head. 'Couldn't you have just organised for our mob to pick him up instead? Maybe land him a smack or two yourself if that was important?'

John looked semi-rueful. 'It seemed more certain of a just outcome, more arm's-length this way.'

'Arm's-length my arse. We're implicated now. This is a crime, mate.'

John shook his head. 'I wouldn't worry about that too much.' He then outlined his briefing to Lara and his tampering with CCTV evidence to help support the Graham suicide theory.

Cato repeated what was becoming his mantra. 'The handcuffs?'

'Lara was in the process of arresting Graham when the Apaches turned up. She was a witness, not a participant. But yes, it was her handcuffs that made sure Graham couldn't get out of there once it all kicked off.'

'No wonder she feels like shit,' observed Hutchens. 'So can you show good cause why I shouldn't just do the right thing and pass all this on to a higher power?'

John laid his hands on the desk. 'Busted. Two witnesses. Do whatever you need to do. But don't you think I would have cleared it with someone further up the food chain first? I'm confident the higher powers would prefer you to stick to the suicide scenario. And the handcuffs? Well that just gets poor Lara into trouble, doesn't it?' He smirked. 'The right thing? I hope both your careers are worth it.'

Hutchens was toying rather menacingly with a letter opener. Cato leaned forward. 'Between these four walls, I'm inclined to agree with John, sir.' The letter opener glinted in the late afternoon sun. 'And I think there's an opportunity for us here.'

Hutchens laid the sharp instrument back on the desk. 'Well, well, Mr Truth and Justice, do go on.'

42

Thursday, February 18th.

The water at South Beach was flat and clear. The sun was not long up but already there were pods of swimmers cutting the surface fifty metres out in deeper water. Cato dipped his head for a look at what was going on below. A few herring skittered away to the deep and some seaweed floated past. Along the sandy bottom the contours created by the steady movement of waves and tides left a mesmerising pattern. It was so peaceful and other-worldly: the water lapping and ticking, rays of sunlight, flickering shadows. A sense of calm and of time slowed down. Cato lifted his head and took a breath. He really should do this more often.

They had moved swiftly on Cato's suggestions. John had reluctantly conceded that, yes, the Capo D'Orlando CCTV footage apparently 'out of order' at the time of the Colin Graham killing could be magically resurrected if necessary. That – along with witness testimony from Lara – could put the Apaches into the kind of trouble they didn't need when they were on a pre-war footing so it made for good leverage. The first priority was to get them to back off from their personal threats against Cato and to patiently await the outcome of the forensic tests on Mazza in relation to the Wellard murder. Tick, sorted.

Next, Irskine would still need to come in for questioning on the Shellie–Wellard matter. If he and his lawyer cooperated and volunteered for interview the likelihood was that it would turn into an inconclusive he said – she said. That was expected and, in relative terms, acceptable. The victim was Wellard, so who cared? But appearances still counted, Irskine needed to play the game.

The main agenda item was a bigger ask but it might just be timely. They would know by midmorning whether it was on. Cato dived down again, enjoying the feel of his arms and legs moving strongly underwater and a new looseness around the wound that signalled a return to wellbeing. Ahead of him a baby stingray, tan coloured and speckled with light blue spots, lifted from the sand and glided out into the shadows. Moments like this helped dissolve those dark thoughts about society going to the dogs. Life really was beautiful sometimes. Cato resurfaced – all was well with the universe. Then a stinger, transparent body no bigger than a thumbnail, wrapped its long tendrils around Cato's upper arm and jolted him back into the real world.

There was a nice painting on the wall: an abstract mix of daubs and splashes in restful colours. Framed certificates too. The blinds were down but twisted to filter the morning sun in diffused horizontal lines. Polished jarrah floorboards with a large thick expensive rug in swirls of deep dark reds and ambers. A desk with obligatory laptop and a happy family photo. Finally, a filing cabinet and the two comfortable visitors armchairs separated by a low coffee table. Lara occupied one chair, Dr Melanie Kim the other.

'I didn't think it was actually you I'd be talking to, I thought you were just a ... the ...'

'Secretary?' said Melanie, 'I get that a lot.' She was older than Lara had expected. The voice had sounded young on the phone: confident but young. In fact the shrink was nearer to forty. She looked like she went to the gym regularly and she filled out her casually expensive clothes with the kind of easy grace and poise that comes from a certain kind of upbringing. The same kind as Lara's.

'So what made you take on a job like this?' said Dr Kim.

Lara tried to remember. 'Partly a rebellion against my parents, I suppose.'

'In what way?'

'Privilege. Expectation. My mother would prefer me to do something nicer than police work. My dad has always seen me as ten percent less than the son he really wanted. Clever. Pretty. A bit of a try-hard. I think he had in mind for me a short, successful career in the arts. But really just biding my time until I churned out some children, hopefully a grandson as consolation. Cop?' She shook her head. 'Never.'

'Bit harsh?'

'You haven't met him.'

'I meant harsh on you. That's a lot of pressure you've put yourself under.' Kim tilted her head. 'So is the rebellion working? Are you winning?'

'The chip's still on my shoulder but I do like the job.'

'What do you like about it?'

'I like beating the bad guys.'

Kim looked alarmed. 'Beating?'

'As in – getting the better of. Winning.'

'Who are the bad guys?'

'It changes. Sometimes it's dickheads on the street, sometimes they're in the office.'

'You see your colleagues as the enemy?'

'Not all. But I don't entirely trust them.'

'Why not?'

Lara shrugged. 'It's what I've been taught. In the end I'm Daddy's little girl.'

It was on. Word came through half an hour ago: they had what they needed, on the dotted line. This time though it was intended to be low-key. DI Hutchens had baulked at another full-scale TRG raid after the first two failed to deliver the required results. Instead they were in unmarked Commodores parked in a couple of bays at Phoenix Shopping Centre on Rockingham Road. Cato and Hutchens in one, Farmer John and a burly associate in another, plus two more carloads cruising the nearby streets and waiting for orders. Two lock-up paddy wagons were also on standby. The Trans were under surveillance and were to be picked up at a time and location of Hutchens' choosing.

Cato's gamble had paid off. The idea was to use the leverage they had over the Apaches not only to get them to back off on their personal threats against him but also to tidy up the nail-gun murder of Christos Papadakis (along with a supplementary pig cruelty charge). Getting Goatee to tell his tale on record had been the big sticking point but now there was a new pragmatism to their Outlaw Code of non-cooperation. Brokered discreetly by Farmer John, the prospect of effectively taking the Trans out of the game without the need for an all-out war was win-win for everyone. Except the Trans of course. That morning Goatee, real name Titus Galsworthy – no wonder he went bad and became a bikie – had provided a signed statement and agreed he would submit to a medical examination at some unspecified future date.

'Vinnie is toast.'

DI Hutchens couldn't hide his glee that he was wrapping up a murder and, in effect, doing Gangs' job for them. The notion that he was also getting into bed with one side – well, that was another matter. Cato was ambivalent: it was all his idea in the first place so he couldn't complain about the moral niceties. He thought about Karina's pregnant teenage daughter, held down and beaten with baseball bats by the very men they were doing deals with. Cato had that ugly tight feeling in his gut again: an unnerving sense that his karmic chickens would come home to roost. He'd had the feeling ever since he exited the water at South Beach earlier that morning with a stinger rash around his upper arm like a bogan tattoo waiting to be inked.

All the shopping centre entries and exits were covered. Everybody was armed and vested. The Tran brothers were being trailed inside by a couple of Farmer John's UCs. The idea was for a quick walk-up, four to each man: outnumbered and outgunned, they were to be bundled into the vans and driven off, minimum fuss and drama. It seemed that on Thursdays the Trans always paid a visit to their semi-legitimate money laundering outlets in the southern suburbs.

'Phoenix fucking Shopping Centre,' said Hutchens, filling the silence.

Cato wasn't sure whether his boss was seeking a reply.

'Big fucking W,' Hutchens muttered.

Was this the DI's take on commerce and existentialism? Rather than be subjected to a long expletive-riddled list of local retail outlets, Cato decided to join the conversation. 'Looks like it's going to be another warm one, boss.'

'No shit?'

The rising heat and the protective vest gave Cato the sweats, big-time. Hutchens too looked like he was suffering. Waiting, wondering, and sweating: life on the frontline of the fight between good and evil in Western Australia. Hutchens' Hawaii-5-0 mobile throbbed.

'Both of them?' A pause. 'Unaccompanied?' Another pause. 'You sure they're unarmed?' He covered the mouthpiece and turned to Cato. 'Call everyone into position, surf's up.'

Cato got onto his mobile and did as he was told. No radios in case they were being monitored. There was a sudden rise in testosterone, adrenalin and tension. Cato breathed deeply to steady his nerves. A series of texts came through to Cato's and the DI's phones simultaneously. Everybody in place. Only now did Hutchens use the radio.

'Let's go,' he said.

Afterwards, Cato wasn't sure where it all started to go wrong. They caught up with Jimmy and Vincent just outside the newsagent's on the main concourse. In retrospect everything assumed a dream-like quality: time playing tricks, stopping and starting, evaporating and re-forming.

A handful of punters queuing up for Slikpiks for the weekend lotto draw, a child of indeterminate sex wailing and straining against the straps keeping it in the pusher. The Trans in mid-conversation, Vincent laughing at something Jimmy just said. DI Hutchens stepping forward with his ID on display.

'Morning Jimmy, Vincent, we'd like you to come with us. Nice and calm, mate, okay?'

Jimmy taking in the situation, mind clicking into gear, smile just holding. An old lady crossing his path, squinting at her shopping list.

Maybe this was where it started to go wrong.

Vincent Tran revealing that he isn't actually unarmed.

Producing a butterfly knife that he holds to the throat of the passing pensioner.

Cato pulling out his pistol, holding it two-handed, focusing on Jimmy while colleagues lock on Vincent. Somebody screaming and a scattering of footsteps as a space opens around them. The toddler still wailing. The pensioner with her eyes closed, Vincent's arm around her throat and the knife blade pricking her cheek. She's mouthing a prayer, Cato trying to read her lips at the same time as he watches over Jimmy. Hands in the crowd hold up mobiles to capture the moment. Hutchens shouting.

'Drop the knife. Drop the knife. Now.'

Or was it when Jimmy scolded Vincent in their native tongue, provoking a look of deep hurt and an angry jab into the cheek of the old woman hostage? Is that when the sky began to fall in?

The pensioner's yelp of pain and a vivid spurt of blood. Farmer John taking two steps closer to Vincent and levelling his Glock: trigger finger drawing back. Jimmy's shake of the head. Another figure edging into Cato's field of vision. A uniform. Reinforcements? No. The uniform is wrong; wrong colour. Who is he and why is he so close?

At any of those moments somebody needed to take control, calm everything down and bring it to a halt. Nobody did. Cato knew exactly the moment it all went very wrong for him. It was when Jimmy Tran lunged.

Later in the report it would say that he did so in a violent and threatening manner but Cato would remember it more as a desperate attempt to try to calm the storm and the inevitable terrible consequences. He would remember Jimmy's hands facing downwards in what, retrospectively, was a placating manner. And it wasn't really a lunge because somebody had barrelled into Jimmy from behind: a centre security guard wanting to be a have-a-go hero.

Jimmy cannoning into Cato's outstretched hand and the gun going off. After the roar, a silence as Jimmy slips to the ground like a puppet with its strings cut.

It's at that moment, as his brother lies bleeding on the floor of Phoenix Shopping Centre and chaos prevails, that Vincent Tran makes his getaway: melting into the crowd like a phantom.

43

A Critical Incident team had been sent from HQ: the area was locked down and taped off, witnesses were being interviewed, CCTV footage seized, all the usual procedures. The pensioner would be fine. The blood had been spectacular but the wound was shallow and, after being stitched up she was allowed home from Fremantle Hospital. Jimmy Tran was still in emergency surgery at Royal Perth. The bullet had entered low in the neck just above the collarbone. Its exit had caused the real damage: taking part of his spinal cord with it. If he survived he would probably be a quadriplegic. Cato was in deep shock. DI Hutchens was in deep damage control. His dreams of glory had turned into another bloody fiasco and the target of the botched operation, Vincent Tran, was still out there somewhere. It emerged that he'd wrestled a young man from his trail bike as it slowed in the shopping centre car park and then disappeared through a lunch-hour traffic snarl that left the cops gridlocked.

'Dog's breakfast doesn't begin to describe it.' Hutchens appeared shrunken, defeated and ten years older. If Cato had any empathy to spare he would have felt sorry for the man. Hutchens read his mind. 'Go home, Cato. Look after yourself. There'll be an inquiry but I'll do what I can to keep a lid on things.' He placed a hand on Cato's shoulder. 'It wasn't your fault. The record will show that, don't worry.'

'Thanks.'

'And don't worry about Vincent, we'll find him.'

'Okay.'

Cato had every confidence that, in the immediate term, the DI and the HQ spin doctors would bury the shooting beneath a shitpile of hyperbole about heroic quick-thinking action, the welfare of innocent bystanders, and any other razzle-dazzle they could conjure. He had less confidence in the longer-term outcome of an internal inquiry, particularly if the hush-hush deal with the bikies unravelled. He had no confidence at all in his own ability to believe that none of it was his fault.

And he could only hope like hell that the DI was right in saying he'd find the desperate and vengeful Vincent Tran. Cato did as he was told and went home.

Late afternoon and the heat had subsided. Kids were home from school and Cato could hear the laughter, squeals and chatter coming from the park just a few doors up at the end of the street. Over the fence, Madge was barking again, fully recovered from her food-poisoning ordeal. The weariness that had descended on Cato as he left the office hadn't translated into sleep. He tried to play the piano but the keys and pedals were coated in glue. He tried to do a crossword but it mocked him. Staring dumbly into space was all he was good for. Staring dumbly into space and seeing Jimmy Tran trying to bring calm to the chaos and taking Cato's bullet in the neck for his trouble.

He'd had enough. He dialled a number.

'Is that the Council Ranger? I want to report a barking dog nuisance.'

Cato gave his details and promised that he would put it all in writing, notify the offending owner, and allow an opportunity for rectification. Cato dashed off an email, printed a copy and took it next door.

'You're a real hater aren't you?' said Felix after reading it. The look was one of revulsion. Madge stood behind, head cocked inquisitively.

Cato scanned the stickers and posters in Felix's window: against this, for that, stop the other. He prodded him in the chest. 'And you're a dickhead.'

'Touch me again and I'll have you up on an assault charge.'

Cato bunched his fist and drew it back. 'May as well be hung for a sheep as a lamb.'

Felix stepped back sharply and trod on Madge. The Jack Russell yipped. The noise dissolved the red mist before Cato's eyes. He turned around and went home again.

'You haven't heard the last of this.' Felix's voice had a quaver in it. Madge was yapping again.

'Just shut up, for goodness sake.' Cato slammed his door behind him.

Lara had heard it on the radio earlier as she was driving back from her appointment with Dr Kim. It was brief and vague: an old woman injured in a hostage situation in a southern suburbs shopping centre, a man critically injured when police opened fire, another man on the run. That man's name was Vincent Tran. Then the weather forecast said sunny and warm.

Her session with Melanie Kim had settled into an abstract but restful search for sense and meaning in her current emotional turmoil: not unlike that painting on the counsellor's wall, muted daubings and occasional splashes. At least it felt restful at the time. Kim instilled calm and structure on Lara's mad world for that one hour. It was still early days but already there was the glimpse of a path back to equilibrium. Apparently some layers needed to be peeled away first: think bruised onion, said Dr Kim. Lara was tempted to dismiss it as psycho-babble. As backup she'd bought more chocolate on the way home. Mildly Dark again – she was developing a taste for it. She'd drifted through the rest of the day on autopilot – chocolate, TV, snooze, but throughout it all there was only one thing on her mind. Why were the Trans back in play? She phoned Hutchens and found him still at work even though it was just gone six. Must be a real crisis, she thought.

'You got time to talk, boss?'

A pause: a mental clicking from one gear into another. 'Sure, Lara, what can I do for you?'

'I heard the news. Just wondering what happened today, what's going on with the Trans?'

Another gear change, down. 'You've got enough on your plate; you need to relax and take time out. Focus on getting yourself better again.'

She ignored him. 'Tell me what's going on.'

'Leave it, Lara.'

'The Trans have always been my case; you know that. I just need to know. Please.'

Something about the way she said it must have convinced him, maybe it was because she asked nicely. They'd had a new lead on Vincent for the nail-gun killing of Papadakis and followed it up. The operation to bring him in went skewiff and Jimmy Tran got shot by Cato. Lara had the impression there was a lot more to the tale but that's all she was going to get for now.

'How's Cato?'

'A bit like you: under the weather. Lying low at home.'

'Poor bastard.'

'Yeah, there's a lot of it going around at the moment.'

'Need me back in to help out?'

'No.'

'I'm going troppo watching crap telly. I need a distraction.'

A slow breath in. 'Well, when you put it like that I suppose we could do with more help manning the phones.'

'Give me half an hour.' Lara closed her mobile and went and brushed the chocolate off her teeth.

Cato felt as if the fibro walls of his home were closing in on him and no matter how high he played his music, Madge's yaps penetrated and scraped at every nerve ending. He knew it was an over-reaction. He knew this was most likely a symptom of stress. He needed to get out. Cato picked up his car keys and mobile and left.

Down the beach end of the street there was an amber halo over the Sealanes fish factory as the sun released them for another day. His old Volvo struggled to start but after a few coughs it growled into action. A curtain twitched in Felix's window. Cato gave it the finger. He found himself following a familiar route north, hugging the coast at Leighton and Cottesloe, the black ocean rolling in under an indigo sky. On up West Coast Highway with the tacky tower blocks of Scarborough in the distance: a reminder to those who would wish the Gold Coast upon Perth. Yes, he knew now where he was headed: maybe he'd always known.

44

In all of the double-dealing, the lies and deceits, the mistakes, the spilled blood – one thing remained clear. If Cato did nothing else, the least he could do was bring Shellie's daughter back to her one last time. The sun was long gone when Cato pulled into the car park nearest to the spot where he'd last stood: the dumpsite for Gordy Wellard's other murder victim, Caroline Penny. Star Swamp.

The place was deserted. No other cars. No people. Lights were on in houses but, at just gone seven-thirty, this suburban street felt like an abandoned Hollywood backlot, a ghost town.

Cato stepped out of the car and peered into the dark shadows of the bushland. He took a torch from the boot and looked once again up and down the street. Early evening and quiet as the grave. Was it just such a time that Wellard had brought Caroline Penny here? Cato tried to imagine himself into Wellard's way of seeing the world. It wasn't easy, there was no way he was as twisted as that evil fucker. But he could try.

He went back to the boot once more. There was a roll of black bin liners from times gone past when he took an interest in his domestic affairs. He tore one off, flicked it open with a snap of air, and began packing whatever he could find into it. Jake's deflated soccer ball and the boots which were now too small for him: a towel, musty and mouldy from a long-ago beach trip: his perished snorkelling fins: the car jack and tyre lever plus assorted tools. An umbrella. There wasn't much else. He looked around him. A low wall with some loose bricks where a car had scraped it in passing. He kicked a few free and put them into the bin liner too. Now it was splitting from the sharp edges so he snapped off a couple more bags and put the original one and contents inside those for reinforcement. It still wasn't anywhere near as heavy as a body but at least it was a weighty and awkward encumbrance. So, if he had a mind to, where would he bury it?

Lara was on phone duty and it suited her just fine. The dobbings had spiked after the evening news, with reported sightings of Vincent Tran all over the metro area and as far south as Albany and as far north as Kununurra. That narrowed it down to half a continent. The photograph and physical description had been taken as just a loose guide by most callers: Vincent was variously reported as being 'among a group of other Middle Eastern men hanging around outside Kewdale Mosque and looking suspicious' or 'loitering at Thornlie railway station with a group of other Aboriginal youths'. Lara listened patiently as a woman with an English accent recalled the man sitting next to her on the bus home to Mount Hawthorn.

'He were moving his hands around in his pocket. Not in a nice way like, you know what I mean?'

'Can you describe him?'

'Aye, he were a bloody filthy old bugger.'

Lara fed through the least bizarre sightings: the ones where the subject was at least male, Asian, and the right age range.

As the phone traffic slowed, she filled her time by logging in to the official history of the Trans. She'd already been through this when she and Colin Graham were lining them up for the murder of Santo Rosetti. The leaky boat from Vietnam in the early 80s; the Malaysian detention centre; the petty crime and teenage street gang in Balga in the late 90s; the ascent to leadership and the criminal big time during the noughties. Big brother Jimmy took up most of the file space: he was the leader, he was the one who'd made all the moves with Vincent tagging along behind as a faithful lieutenant and occasional enforcer. That must have been when Vinnie had developed a taste for it: his sadism evolving from a business necessity into an intrinsic pleasure.

Both Jimmy and Vincent had the usual drugs, assault, affray and weapons charges that gangsters collect on their way up the food chain. For both brothers these charges had dropped off in the last few years as they got smarter and others did the shit work for them. The most recent charge that stuck was an assault just over two years ago. Somebody had looked at Vincent the wrong way at a Sunday afternoon session in a Cottesloe pub and had ended up blinded in one eye and needing surgery to reconstruct the shattered cheekbone and torn flesh. Vincent had served nine months for that.

Lara thought about Vincent and the violence he was clearly capable of, yet how his presence barely registered in the shadow of big brother Jimmy. There was no brooding menace, no simmering cauldron of rage; Vincent just wasn't there. Jimmy's shadow: it was a good place to hide. The phone rang again.

'You after that Chinese bloke on the telly?'

'Vietnamese, yes. Something to report, sir?'

'Yeah, I'm watching him now. He's just parked up beside Star Swamp and he's obviously up to no good.'

Cato slung the bin bag over his shoulder and set off through the dark bushland like one of Snow White's more sinister dwarves: the eighth one, Creepy. With the torch in his free hand, he headed for where he thought Caroline Penny's dumpsite was. When he was here last time, in broad daylight, he'd estimated it was about thirty metres from the car parking bays to the grave. There was a fork in the path just two metres ahead. Cato cursed the fact that on that previous visit he'd neglected to trace the route from the car bays to the grave more diligently. He panned the torch beam, searching for a familiar feature in the dense bush. A breeze rustled the gum trees, creaks and other strange noises emanated from the darkness. Lost already. What the hell was he doing here anyway, what was all this meant to prove?

Cato turned back to face the direction he'd come from and tried to get a reverse fix on where he needed to go. When he'd last stood at the dumpsite and looked towards the car bays he'd been aware of something in his left field of vision. Then he remembered: a mobile phone tower on a hill behind the houses. He could see it now. Readjusting his bearings, it was clear that he should take the right fork in the path. He took it, the lumpy contents of the bin bag clunking and clinking and digging into his back. Cato Kwong – the Method Detective. This was bullshit: he'd be better off using a water-diviner and ouija board. The load wasn't that heavy but he was sick of the constant poking from the sharp protuberances so he put it down for a moment. He estimated he was now between fifteen and twenty metres in from the car bays and at least ten away from Caroline Penny's grave.

Standing still once again, surrounded by the dark bush and the whisperings and rustlings of the breeze, something tugged at the edges of his memory. Something he'd read in the files and background notes. Cato flicked the torch off in the hope that the meditative darkness might help him concentrate. He cricked his neck and eased his shoulders as the blackness settled around him. Cato braced himself to reassume his burden and it came back into focus: the missing memory. Then he heard a footscrape and the ratchet of a shotgun and saw the blinding light.

'Good question,' said Cato when the TRG man had given him back his ID and asked him what the fuck he was doing there.

'So answer it.'

Cato was facedown with his right nostril pressed into the sandy soil, a knee in his back, his wrists cuffed behind him, and a Glock in his ear. 'Call DI Hutchens at Fremantle.'

'We did, he told us to ask you what the fuck you're doing here and to not let you go until you tell us.'

'It's a long story.'

'We've got all night and you're not going anywhere.'

So Cato told him.

'Yeah, the DI said you were fucking weird.'

'Can I go now?'

'Sure.' The TRG man summoned a colleague. 'Help Santa put the presents back in his sack and escort him to his sleigh.'

45

Friday, February 19th.

Lara had signed off from her phone-manning duties by about ten-thirty the previous night and headed home with a guilty giggle after she'd heard what happened to Cato. Well he was Asian, within Vincent Tran's age range give or take ten years, and he was acting suspiciously. Poor bugger, he really did have a bad day. All in all, the non-taxing phone duties and the jokes at Cato's expense seemed to have done more for her wellbeing than half-a-dozen therapy sessions and a shipload of chocolate. A good night's sleep had helped too. That was the story so far today anyway.

She'd agreed to go into the office again for another round of low intensity phone-manning and file-shuffling. She was actually looking forward to it and wondered whether she'd ever get back to being a proper cop or whether she should just quit and get a job in an office or a call centre. Today, neither prospect worried her.

Vincent Tran remained on the loose and, according to the Crimestoppers hotline, he was here, there, and everywhere. Lara scanned the log of reports. Mistaken identity, grudge calls, time wasted: from Mirrabooka to Mandurah and Swanbourne to Swan Hill, all points north, south, east and west of the metro area had produced nothing. DI Hutchens crossed her line of vision.

'Any progress, boss?'

'Nah. You up for another day of this?'

'Sure. I'll keep you posted if I'm heading for a meltdown.'

'That'd be good. Got enough spot fires to put out already.'

'Perils of leadership.' Lara scanned the office partitions and the array of heads poking just above them. 'No sign of Cato?'

'Santa Kwong's got an appointment with the Inquisition today, the Tran shooting.'

'Lucky boy. Where do you want me today, boss?'

'Phones have quietened down, maybe trawl the files yet again, see if anything gels.' Hutchens continued on his way, voice trailing over his shoulder. 'Any chance of a coffee?'

'No,' she said, without rancour.

Hutchens grunted and closed his door behind him.

'Did you issue a warning before you discharged your weapon?'

'I believe we did, yes.'

'Did *you* issue a warning before *you* discharged *your* weapon?' The Inspector from Internals reminded Cato of the woman from H&R Block who did his tax every year. She seemed similarly single-minded.

'I believe *we* did, yes.'

And so it went on like that for another twenty minutes. Thrust, parry, thrust, parry.

'So in your professional judgement, both your life and the lives of your colleagues and members of the public were in immediate danger and you acted according to your training and within the prescribed guidelines?'

'Pretty much.'

'Is that a yes?'

'Yes. Ma'am.'

The Accountant finished typing on her laptop. She pressed print and something rolled out of a nearby machine. 'Read this and sign at the bottom. Three copies.' Cato did as he was told. 'One for me, one for you, one for your boss. That's all for now. You'll be hearing from us again.'

'Look forward to it.' Cato cleared his throat. 'So am I suspended or what?'

'Why would you be? You don't appear to have done anything wrong, until and unless our investigations show otherwise. In the meantime your decision to work as normal or take stress leave or counselling is a matter for you and your supervisor to work out.'

'Right. Thank you.'

'Pleasure.' She stuck out a firm hand for shaking. 'Good luck.' And then she left, whistling 'Jingle Bells'.

Cato sauntered back into the detectives' section and heard it again floating out over the partitions: a chorus of whistling from his colleagues. 'Jingle Bells.'

'Ho, ho, ho,' he replied, mustering a smile.

On his desk, a stack of yellow post-it notes from his colleagues letting him know what they wanted for Christmas. He swept them into a bin, sat down and logged on. Should he take stress leave? It would be good timing with Jake coming over later today. He could have some quality time with his son and make a very long weekend of it. Cato glanced around the office. Banter and humour could be therapeutic at times like this. At others it could tip you over the edge. Those who hadn't been whistling 'Jingle Bells' were casting furtive looks to see how close he was to post-traumatic crack-up. Some were no doubt taking bets: Cato first, or Lara? He caught Lara Sumich looking back at him.

'Coffee?' she said.

Was it a trap? 'Sure, thanks.'

He wanted to follow up on the revelatory nugget he'd uncovered last night, just before he found himself face down with a TRG boot on his neck. Still, it wasn't every day that Lara Sumich offered to make you a coffee. He joined her in the kitchen. The last time they'd shared this kind of enclosed space was in Hopetoun town hall when he'd embarrassingly got the notion that just because she'd had sex with him she might actually like him and want to spend some time with him. Huh.

'Milk and sugar?' she said.

'Milk and none, thanks.' Lara spooned some instant into a mug and added water. His coffee snobbery was being sorely tested of late. 'You're back,' he said.

'Yes.' Lara sloshed some milk in and handed him the mug.

'Is that a good idea?'

Lara's face darkened. 'That's my business.'

'Okay.' Cato warily sniffed the coffee. 'No sign of Vincent yet then?'

'No. Our most promising lead turned out to be you.'

'Yeah I know, we all look alike.' He drank some; not quite as disgusting as he expected.

'How was the Inquisition?'

Cato shrugged. 'Pussycats. I get the impression it's already been decided.'

'There's a lot of that going around lately.'

'That's fine as long as looking after us suits their purposes. It doesn't always work that way.'

Lara sipped her tea and said nothing.

'Thanks for the cuppa,' said Cato. 'Keep me posted if you find Vincent.' He rinsed his cup out in the sink and left it to drain as instructed by the angry note on the cupboard door. He placed a hand on Lara's shoulder and felt her flinch. 'I'm sorry about how it all ended up with Colin.'

'Yeah,' she said flatly and rinsed her cup out too.

Cato found what he was looking for with a few clicks. It had come to him as he stood in the dark at Star Swamp bracing himself to pick up the dead weight of the bin bag and continue his walk through the bush. The files confirmed it. Caroline Penny had been a mere slip of a thing, weighing in at not much more than forty-five kilos. Bree, by contrast, was up nearer sixty-five. Was it a simple weight equation? Caroline was lighter and so could be carried further. Plus she was the second victim, so Wellard probably wanted to take her deeper into the bush and further off the path to minimise the chances of discovery. Except he'd been unlucky and a woman and her inquisitive dog had stumbled across Caroline's remains anyway.

If Bree was the first and the heaviest did that suggest a shorter journey along the bush path, both because she was harder to carry and because Wellard was less experienced at identifying optimum dumpsites? Cato's load had only been twenty kilos max and he'd felt the need for a break about fifteen metres along the path. From where Cato stopped to where Caroline was buried was about another fifteen metres – and the accessible area off the path into the bush before it got too dense was around two metres either side. That was a total area of perhaps sixty square metres. It was a simple, indeed overly simplistic, theory but it was more than anything else they had. And it helped narrow down the search site considerably. All he had to do now was persuade DI Hutchens that it was a really great idea.

'Go home, Cato. You're under a lot of stress.'

'We're only talking about sixty square metres.'

'We're only talking out of our arses. Go home.'

'One GPR team could cover it in an hour or two.'

'Do you know how much it costs for two blokes and a hoover?'

'Sir, I ...'

'Cato.' A warning growl. 'Go home. That's an order.'

It was nearly lunchtime. Jake would be dropped at his house around 6 p.m. The decision on whether or not to take a longer weekend with his son had just been made for him. Cato grabbed his things and left.

From the back of the crammed meeting room Lara surveyed the glum, frustrated faces of the team behind the Vincent Tran manhunt. Up front, perched on the edge of a desk, DI Hutchens was the glummest and most frustrated of them all.

'We've just had a report that he's doing figure-of-eights down at Cockburn Ice Rink as we speak. Anybody want to check it out?' There were a few bitter chuckles in reply. 'Family, friends, known associates, we've knocked on all their doors more than once, some are under constant watch but so far not a peep. We've run down those on his mobile call list: again nothing. We've also tried GSM phone tracking but he's savvy enough to only use it for a few seconds at a time then turns it off and keeps moving. He's probably got a few spare unregistered prepaids anyway. So, any suggestions?'

A hand was raised. 'Take hostages?' It was Debbie Hassan, the surviving guard from Dieudonne's hospital rampage.

Funnily enough nobody laughed; that's how desperate things were.

'Like who?' said Hutchens. 'This bloke's a loner. The only one he cares about is big brother Jimmy and we've already got him.'

Another hand. 'How about: come in now or we turn off Jimmy's life support?'

Hutchens creased his brow. 'How about we cut the funnies and get on with the job?' That was the cue for the meeting to break up. Hutchens caught Lara's eye and summoned her over. 'Anything in the files?'

Lara shook her head. 'As you say, he's a loner. Everybody we're looking at is really Jimmy's circle and Vincent tagged along.'

'Definitely no crew of his own, then?'

'No.' A thought occurred to Lara, a stone left unturned. 'The only time he was away from Jimmy in the last couple of years was when he was in prison. We could see if he made any lasting acquaintances there that we don't know about.'

Hutchens nodded, unconvinced. 'Get onto Corrections for a list of his cellmates over the years then run a crosscheck with his recent mobile phone records.' The DI ran a hand through his grey fringe. 'If we haven't got any progress by the end of the day I might revisit that life support idea.'

46

'Eat in or out?'

'Can we have Missy Moos?'

'Go on then, twist my arm.'

The gourmet burger joint on the corner was standing-room only so they placed their orders and wandered over to the beach to catch the last of the sunset. Cato suggested a swim and Jake readily agreed. They chucked off shirts, kicked off thongs and dived in as the sun flashed its farewell on the horizon. Tonight Jake seemed jittery and on edge: eager to please, needy, slightly manic. Kids. Parenting. Life. So precious yet so often taken for granted. That afternoon he'd phoned Karina Ford.

'The attack on the kids wasn't a drug debt. It was some bikies, Apaches, scoring a point against their rivals. Nothing personal. It'll be hard to prove but I'll try and see somebody charged for it.'

'Any names?'

'No.'

'Don't worry,' said Karina. 'I know people. We'll ask around.'

'These guys aren't to be messed with, Karina. Leave it to us.'

'Thanks anyway, mate. Hey, Cryssie's up and about again. Little Brandon's pleased to have her back.'

'That's great. Look after yourself, Karina.'

'Oh, I will. Don't worry.'

Cato allowed himself to be ducked by Jake. It seemed that after so many years of neglecting his son for the sake of the job, Cato's wish to try to connect was badly timed. Cato's problem was that he'd never got to know Jake well enough in the earlier years to be able to read the signs now for what his son did and didn't need from him. Sometimes they felt like brothers, sometimes they were strangers, and Cato was still struggling to recognise what may or may not be the odd father-and-son moment. Maybe he should stop analysing everything and just get on with it. They ducked each other, splashed, and raced. Jake did backflips off Cato's shoulders. They burnt energy and laughed and by the time they wandered, dripping, back into Missy Moos to pick up their orders, the sharp edges of Jake's mood had softened.

Cato unwrapped the burgers at the back patio table and grabbed a Coke and a Coopers out of the fridge while Jake rinsed off the sand under the cold outdoor shower. Then they both attacked their food.

'Whatcha been doing the last week?' said Jake through a mouthful of fried mince and salad.

'I shot somebody.'

Jake stopped chewing. 'Serious?'

'Yeah.'

'Did they die?'

'No. But they're in pretty bad shape. Probably won't walk again.'

'Shit.'

'Hmmm.'

'Why did you shoot them? Were they gunna shoot you?'

'No, it was an accident.'

'Shit.'

'Does your mum let you say that at home?'

'Only if it's important and in the right context; I'm not allowed to use it gratuitously.'

That was the thing about Fremantle kids: a smart answer for every bloody thing. 'Fair enough,' said Cato.

They chewed on in silence for a few minutes, taking occasional sips from their drinks as the evening closed in, the mozzies whined, and the Friday night South Terrace traffic rumbled.

'How did it feel, shooting him?' Jake looked over the top of his bulging burger with wide eyes both fearing and relishing the answer.

Cato thought about it for a short while. 'Shit,' he said.

Lara's email beeped just as she was packing to leave the office. There were still people buzzing around the place following up increasingly bizarre leads on Vincent Tran as the phone traffic dwindled to the truly sad bastards. Anything of interest would be passed over to DS Meldrum, who was in charge of the night shift, and DI Hutchens was on call for any worthwhile developments.

She could have ignored the email until Monday morning but it might just be the one she was waiting for, from Corrections, with any possible leads on Vincent Tran's old cellmates. It was. They'd sent through an Excel spreadsheet with dates, last recorded contact details, and notes as to whether they were still incarcerated, released, or 'other'. A quick scan of 'other' suggested a depressing number were dead; usually from drug overdoses or drug or alcohol-related illnesses. She was about to forward the email to Meldrum for an overnight follow-up on those still alive when she noticed a familiar name amongst the list of 'other'.

The good thing about Missy Moos, apart from the burgers, was the washing-up factor. Zero. Comfortably overfed and drowsy, Cato and Jake sat on the couch and watched a DVD: *Hoodwinked*, a postmodern animated take on *Little Red Riding Hood*.

Jake giggled at the banjo-playing, hippy, hillbilly goat and burrowed his head into Cato's shoulder. 'Reminds me of Simon.'

Cato was drifting, half-asleep. 'Simon?'

'Mum's boyfriend.'

'Oh yeah, right.' Cato felt his third Coopers glide down his throat and numb his senses. 'He still teaching you guitar?'

'Yeah, sort of.'

'Sort of?'

'He's a bit busy at the moment. Lots of gigs.'

'Right. Cool.'

'Yeah.' Jake yawned. 'What we doing tomorrow?'

'Oh, I reckon a swim, and brekkie, and take it from there. Any ideas?'

There was no reply. Jake was asleep. Cato carried him to his room and put him to bed. The boy was heavy and Cato's injury whinged at the effort. He toyed with the idea of hitting the sack too but Madge was yapping next door and he didn't fancy trying to sleep with that going on. He returned to the lounge, put on a CD of the Pigram Brothers, lay on the couch and resumed his beer.

So the honeymoon period with Simon the new boyfriend was pretty much over as far as Jake was concerned. The guy wasn't so cool and interesting any more. A bit busy. Aren't we all? Cato tried to repress the schadenfreude but he couldn't help himself. Things were no longer quite so rosy in Mum's household, hence Jake's earlier manic demeanour. Cato lifted his beer in mock salute. 'Cheers and up yours, Simon.' He belched, drained the bottle and fell asleep on the couch.

'Are you the people after that Asian man on the TV?'

Here we go. DC Chris Thornton adjusted his headphones; they were making his ears sweat. He tweaked the mouthpiece, opened a new notes screen on his monitor, and clicked his biro in case the computers crashed again. He took down her name, address and phone number. 'Yes, madam, how can I help you?'

'What a lovely phone manner, I haven't been called madam in years.'

His mum reckoned he had a lovely phone manner too. Told him he would go places with it. He'd love to be going places tonight. Friday night. You were meant to be out with your mates on the piss. No. He gets phone duty like he's some schmuck selling something from a call centre in Delhi. When he was fresh out of the Academy he'd been warned you get all the shit work: the drunks, the domestics. Bring it on. Nobody had warned him about Safer Streets and Nanna Duty though.

'Have you something to report, madam?'

There was a breathless kind of pigeon coo noise at the other end of the phone. 'I'm pretty sure I've just seen him, I literally bumped into him when I was getting off the 532 bus.'

WTF? 'Where was that, then?' he said, keeping his voice as bright and interested as possible.

'Well he was walking down Douro Road in South Fremantle and obviously not looking where he was going. Didn't even apologise.'

'Right, and did you notice what direction he was headed in?'

'Yes of course, I followed him.'

Cool, I'm talking to Miss Marple. 'So where did he go?'

'I followed him down onto South Terrace as far as that noisy pub and then he turned right into that street.'

'Which pub and which street is that, madam?'

'The pub is the South Beach Hotel but I forget the name of the street. Silly me. But that'll be on a map won't it?'

'Okay, so you didn't follow him any further?'

'Oh no, the street was too empty and dark and my cover would have been blown.'

'Good decision, madam. Can you describe him, say what he was wearing?'

She told him and he made a few cursory notes on the computer screen before using his biro to doodle the word 'nutter' in big *Crusty Demons*-style letters while she wittered on. When she'd finished he said thank you madam and pinged the file note through to Detective Sergeant Jabba the Hutt.

Lara sat on her balcony and crunched an apple. She thought about that name on the Corrections list: the now deceased cellmate of Vincent Tran who'd shared close quarters with him during his stint for the Cottesloe assault. At the time both had been on remand in Hakea, awaiting sentencing. The cellmate was only familiar as a name to Lara but she knew Cato would find it particularly interesting that Vincent Tran had, for nearly three months, enjoyed the company of Gordon Francis Wellard. He was the one who'd led her colleagues on some wild-goose chase in bushland further south: the same bushland where they found the nail-gunned pig. Coincidence? Not any more.

Lara checked the clock: nearly nine-thirty. Was it urgent enough to bother Cato at home or was it something that could wait until Monday morning? Cato could make that decision but she would at least give him the information. Lara scrolled through her mobile and pressed call. No answer, straight to messagebank.

Hi Cato. It's Lara. Sorry to be calling you so late at home but something came up you might want to know about. Can you give me a call? Cheers.

Detective Sergeant Meldrum had just binned his Hungry Jack's wrappers when his email beeped with a new list of call summaries. Of the six, four were not actionable because they were either too vague or several hours too late – *I saw a bloke riding a quad bike through the bush in Yanchep yesterday arvo. No I don't know what he looked like 'cause he had a helmet on but he was going way too fast and gave me the finger when I told him to be more careful* – the remaining two were worth a flick to a mobile patrol for checking just to keep his arse covered. The first, a possible sighting up in Maylands in a block of units flagged as having Tran connections. Imagine having those nasty bastards as landlords. That looked promising and was probably worth bringing the DI back in for. The second was local, an old lady in Fremantle who'd literally just bumped into Tran down at South Beach. Yeah right. He gave Hutchens a call about the Maylands prospect.

Cato woke up to the furious yapping of Madge. He felt fuzzy, thick-headed and his neck didn't want to work. Vengeance coursed through his veins; Madge was not long for this world. There was another sound: a creak. Maybe it was Jake going to the toilet. This was an old house with a life of its own and he'd grown used to the noises it made over the years. Still, he did have precious cargo on board: it wouldn't hurt to go and check. He stood up from the couch, stretched and ironed out the kinks in his back.

He picked up the Coopers stubby for depositing in the recycling bin in the kitchen, flicked off the lounge room light and headed down the hall. Jake's bedroom door was closed. Cato was sure he'd left it ajar but then most of the windows in the house were open and a breeze could have swung the door shut. He gently turned the handle but as he did so the stubby slipped from his grasp and he ducked to try to catch it before it hit the floor and woke up Jake.

That's probably what saved him.

There was a thwap sound and something thudded into the wall behind. The light from the hallway showed Jake in bed, wide-eyed, an arm around his throat. The arm belonged to Vincent Tran. In his free hand, Tran held a nail gun. He stopped pointing it at Cato and placed it against Jake's temple, about a centimetre away from his right eye.

47

DI Hutchens had moved quickly to dispatch a TRG team up to the Maylands address along with two carloads of detectives and any spare patrols in support. He was snapping on a Kevlar to head there himself when Meldrum remembered the arse-covering aspect of his job and mentioned the other report in case they should action that too.

'Show it to me,' snapped Hutchens, in a hurry to get away.

Meldrum brought it up on the screen and Hutchens bent down for a squint. 'Waste of time, boss?'

'Shit.'

'Boss?'

'That road beside the pub where she said he walked up?'

'Yeah?'

'That's where Cato lives. Remember him? The one who shot Vincent Tran's brother?'

'Vincent.'

Cato crouched down to eye-level. He tried to present as calm and non-threatening. His throat was dry, his heart was pounding.

'I forgot your name, sorry,' said Vincent.

'Philip, Phil, or most of my workmates call me Cato.'

'I like that. Like the kung-fu guy in *The Green Hornet*, right?'

'He's Kato with a K, mine's a C.'

'Whatever. Reminds you that you're one of us anyway.' He tapped the nail gun lightly against Jake's eye socket. 'What's his name?'

'Jake.' Cato resisted the temptation to dive over there and kill Vincent. He couldn't do that until the time was right. The balance of probabilities just now was against him, against Jake.

'Jake.' Vincent turned his face to the boy. 'Do you know what your dad did yesterday, Jake?' A widening of the boy's eyes. 'He shot my big brother. He didn't kill him but I still don't know how he is.' He turned back to Cato. 'How is he, Cato with a C? He gunna live?'

'He'll live but he'll probably need some help getting around. He'll need you.'

Vincent sang a line from the song 'He Ain't Heavy, He's My Brother'. His voice was remarkably clear and tuneful. 'In some ways you probably did me a favour.'

'How come?'

'Jimmy's a bit of a control freak. Always had to be centre of attention. Always had to have everything, first. Even my friends, he had to own them too.'

'So if I did you a favour, what are you doing here? What's this all about?'

'Love, hate, love, hate. That's brothers for you, eh? Jimmy looked after me on the boat, you see. He looked after me in the camp in Malaysia – kept the dirty old men at bay. He took it up the arse to protect me. How's that for staunch? He's looked after me ever since. Family.' He nodded, enough said.

'What do you want from me, Vincent?'

His eyes filled. 'I don't know. I'm screwed either way. But somebody has to pay.' His arm tightened around Jake's neck, his finger tensed on the nail-gun trigger. Jake squeezed his eyes shut.

Cato launched himself across the room, hearing another thwap and Jake's agonised squeal. He was on Vincent and clawing blindly to try to get the nail gun off him. They struggled on the bed then rolled onto the floor, gouging, punching, scraping, butting, tearing. At some point a knee or an elbow went hard and deep into Cato's knife wound and he thought he might die from the fire engulfing him. Then Vincent was on top, pinning Cato's arms with his legs and raining punches into his face. Cato knew he was losing.

The punches ceased and Cato breathed again. Then he realised it was only because Vincent was scrabbling for the dropped nail gun. Cato struggled but he was weakened, he couldn't unpin his arms. Vincent wiped a smear of blood from his face and ratcheted the gun. He pressed the muzzle against Cato's nostril.

'Drop it.' Lara Sumich stood in the doorway, silhouetted by the hall light, her gun levelled at Vincent. 'Now.'

Vincent was clearly weighing up his options: a life inside, a crippled brother, suicide by cop. Cato felt the muzzle pushing harder against his nose. He smelled the metal, the plastic and paint, a hint of oil: pictured a nail travelling up through his face and into his brain. Jake was outside his field of vision. Was he still alive?

Lara's trigger finger curled tighter. 'Do it.'

Madge yapped at phantoms. A breeze crept through the window.

Vincent nodded to himself like he'd just made up his mind.

48

Hutchens, Meldrum, and the TRG turned up about five minutes too late. They found Cato kneeling on the floor of his bedroom cradling his son, tears streaming down his face. They found Lara Sumich bestride Vincent Tran, the latter facedown and deadly still. They found lots of blood.

'Christ,' said Hutchens.

Two ambulances arrived a further five minutes later. Even though the hospital was just down the road it had been another busy Friday night. It turned out they only needed the one. Jake was taken away and Cato went with him. The boy would require several stitches in his cheek where the misdirected nail had sliced across the fleshy surface after the gun had been knocked from Vincent's hand. Vincent himself was, apart from the results of the vicious hand-to-hand with Cato, relatively unscathed. His decision had been to surrender to Lara and go quietly. Either something about the look in her eye told him she meant business – or something about a life locked up had its appeal. Maybe it was the chance to step out of his big brother's shadow and to be his own man. He was cuffed, stood up, and taken away by the ninjas. Lara re-holstered her Glock.

'What are you doing here?' said Hutchens.

'Good question.'

'So answer it.'

'Women's intuition?'

'No such thing.'

She weighed that one up and decided it didn't deserve a response. 'Okay, how about diligent police work? I had some information for Cato. Thought it might be urgent. I was twiddling my thumbs and going mad at home. Needed to get out.'

'That's better,' said Hutchens.

In some small part, Lara still credited women's intuition. Call it what you will, she'd had a strong sense of unease or urgency that she should deliver the message personally.

'So what was the information?' said Hutchens.

Lara told him about the prison links between Vincent Tran and Gordon Francis Wellard.

'Fuck me,' he said, impressed and thoughtful.

'How did you know where he lived?'

It wasn't yet midnight but they decided to strike while the iron was hot, as they say. Vincent Tran himself wasn't kicking up any fuss and was content to proceed. An air of calm resignation seemed to have settled over him. That could be good news or bad, Lara wasn't sure yet. Tran's injuries had been checked and patched up where necessary. He wore a paper suit, his clothes confiscated for forensic testing. While on the run he'd had a number three buzz cut to try to alter his appearance. He ran his hand through like he was still getting used to it. The recording equipment was on, Vincent had declined a lawyer, Hutchens led and Lara was along for the ride.

'Vincent? You with us?' Hutchens tapped on the tabletop to get his attention. Vincent's eyes refocused and he returned from wherever he'd been. 'How'd you find Detective Kwong?'

Vincent smiled. 'I followed him home from the police station. Clever, huh?'

'You mean we've been looking all over the metro area for you for the last forty-eight hours and you're sitting outside the front door of the cop shop?'

'Over the road, yeah. The multi-storey, we've got a long-term parking bay reserved on level two. Overlooks you guys.'

Hutchens shook his head in disgust. They dotted the i's and crossed the t's on how and why Vincent went after Cato, and then got down to what Hutchens called brass tacks.

'The nail gun. Was it you that killed Christos Papadakis?'

'Yep.'

Hutchens got him to repeat it more formally for the record. 'Why?'

A shrug. 'Because I could.'

Lara noticed Hutchens' fists clench and unclench. They went through the details of how and when.

'So Mickey Nguyen didn't do it?'

'No, Mickey was set up for it. He'd become unreliable.'

'In what way?'

'He lacked hundred percent loyalty.'

'So whose idea was it to kill Mickey, yours or Jimmy's?'

'Mine.' The answer came too quickly.

'How did you do it?'

'Poured a bottle of vodka down his throat: voluntarily at first, then with help from me to finish it off. He passed out. I put the old man in the boot of the car, sat Mickey in the front, and torched it. The bushfire coming through must've helped confuse things.'

'Must've,' agreed Hutchens grimly.

More finessing of details for the record. Lara glanced at the clock on the wall behind Vincent: it was heading for one in the morning yet nobody seemed sleepy. Tran wanted to lay all his cards on the table and offer himself up. She knew why. The aim was to keep big brother Jimmy out of the frame: confined to a wheelchair for the rest of his natural, he had enough on his plate.

'So why this nasty little fetish for nail-gunning people?' said Hutchens.

A rustle of the paper suit as Vincent leaned forward. 'I saw it in a film. Looked cool.'

'Lovely. And Jimmy was up for letting you do all that creepy stuff? Doesn't seem like very smart business practice to me.'

'Jimmy didn't know anything about it.'

'Do you expect me to believe that?'

'Yes.' It came out as a challenge: take what I'm offering and lay off him.

'So there's nothing deep and meaningful about the nail gun? No childhood traumas you're working through?'

'No, it's a tool, plain and simple.'

'What about the pig?'

Vincent rolled his eyes. 'Fair cop. I confess. I also killed the pig.'

'Why?'

'It gave me a funny look.' So did Hutchens. Tran explained. 'Pigs are a good substitute for humans when testing stuff like that. They use them to train forensics people.'

'How do you know this shit?'

'The internet.'

'Where did you get the pig from?'

'Market.' Another funny look from Hutchens. 'A farmer, out Wickepin way.'

'Why did you bury him down at Beeliar?'

'The farmer or the pig?'

Hutchens looked alarmed. 'You tell me.'

Vincent was enjoying himself. 'The pig was a her. She was a bit old so we couldn't have cooked her up, too tough, and it would have been a bugger pulling all those nails out.'

Hutchens leaned forward. Lara noticed pearls of sweat around his temples and the look of a man who's just felt a tug on a long-dead line.

'Yeah, but why Beeliar?'

49

Saturday, February 20th.

When Cato woke he couldn't move. The sun blazed through the window onto his pillow. He'd forgotten to close the curtains. He tried twisting his head to look at the bedside alarm clock but his neck was locked. He used an arm to lever himself over and his whole body complained. It was still only just past six. He'd had about four hours sleep.

Cato couldn't go home: his house was a crime scene and Duncan Goldflam and his crew wouldn't be releasing it for a while yet. Jake had been stitched, dosed up with as many painkillers as his little body would allow, and sent home with his mum. He may or may not be scarred for life, time would tell. Words couldn't describe the look Jane had given Cato and he wouldn't be surprised if it developed into a Family Court matter. A room had been booked for him down at The Esplanade hotel. The receptionist had taken a look at his bruised and battered face and his bloodstained clothes and summoned security. Things ran smoother once he'd flashed his police ID and quoted the reservation number he'd been texted.

Cato pulled the sheet over his head and slowly and painfully turned away from the sun. He needed more sleep. His mobile went. Caller ID: Hutchens.

'You awake?'

'No.'

'Good. How you feeling?'

'Shit.'

'Shame. Got some interesting news for you. Up for a coffee?'

'Is it important?'

'Wouldn't disturb you if it wasn't, mate.'

'Where are you?'

'Down at Reception. See you in five?'

'Beeliar?'

'That's what he reckons.' Hutchens took a sip of his flat white and licked his lips appreciatively.

Even though it was Saturday morning, the DI was dressed formally for another working day and he'd been unable to hide his frown when Cato showed up in T-shirt and shorts. Somebody had the wherewithal to arrange for an overnight bag to be left for Cato at the hotel last night. He was obliged to wear whatever had been packed for him. They'd left the hotel and strolled, or in Cato's case limped, a hundred metres up Essex Street to the X-Wray Cafe. The place still carried disturbing memories of an earlier encounter with Dieudonne but you couldn't fault the coffee. Hutchens had gone to the counter to do the ordering: Cato's battered face was likely to put people off their breakfasts.

'I don't buy it.'

'Why not?'

'I saw the look on Wellard's face when the cadaver dog started barking. Gordy wasn't expecting anything because it was a deliberate wild-goose chase as far as he was concerned.'

'Maybe he wasn't expecting anything to be found in that particular spot where he took us.'

Cato pinched the bridge of his nose and squinted against the glare of the early morning sun. 'Sorry, I'm not a hundred percent right now. Take me through it again.'

'No worries, mate.' Hutchens was unnervingly good-natured today. With Colin Graham dead and Dieudonne and Vincent Tran in custody, the DI's clear-up rate must have gone through the roof. Between them the trio had been responsible for most of the major crime in the metro area for the last month. Hutchens was a one-man Safer Streets success story. 'Vincent shared a remand cell in Hakea with our good friend Wellard. Two psycho soul mates they were: swapping tips and recipes, the best dumpsites, bargains on nail guns, effective choke holds, that kind of thing.'

Cato was getting depressed. Or rather, even more depressed.

'He reckons Wellard recommended Beeliar to him. Told him about a car access track through the back of someone's property, about a hundred metres away from the main public gate.'

Cato was taking notice now. One of the things that hadn't gelled that day was how they'd all had to troop through a turnstile to get in there and just how the hell were you meant to get a body through that? This private vehicle track was a lot nearer than the others they knew about. Now the area Wellard took them to was a lot more viable. 'Go on.'

'You're thinking about the turnstile, right?'

'Yeah?'

'I thought it was a bit funny at the time, too, but let him lead us his merry dance. As agreed, Wellard was setting the agenda that day and he always was a bit of a joker.'

'Yeah, Shellie reckons he was a laugh a minute.'

Hutchens frowned. 'Poor Shell, maybe she'll get her answer now after all these years.' He brightened again. 'Anyway Tranny reckons Wellard knew so much about that spot that the body has to be there and we've just got to get the diggers and radar in and Bob's your proverbial.'

Cato recalled his son's history lesson: Fremantle, part of the ancient Aboriginal district of Beeliar, a place of crying, a place for funerals. Maybe Wellard's game was to take them to the right place but the wrong spot? 'So Wellard didn't draw him a mud map?'

'Not as such, no.'

'Did Vincent mention Star Swamp?'

'Yeah, he said Wellard told him he'd buried another one up there.' Hutchens seemed a little hurt and disappointed. 'You're not convinced it's Beeliar, you're still hanging on to your Star Swamp theory?'

Cato shrugged and conceded some ground. 'I suppose Beeliar's the best lead we've had so far. So what are you going to do about it?'

'Monday, get a couple of GPR teams out there covering the area

330

from the drive-in track he mentioned, along to where we were on day one with Wellard.'

Cato did the sums: at least a hundred long by God knows what wide. 'That's a big area.'

'I'm also getting a survey plane to do a fly-over with one of those special whiz-bang cameras that shows up all that shit.'

Cato raised an eyebrow. 'Expensive.' He decided to push his luck. 'As you're paying anyway, while they're up there maybe they could swing round and take a few snaps over Star Swamp as well?'

Hutchens twisted his mouth and nodded. 'What price justice, Cato mate?' Cato couldn't argue with that. 'Speaking of which.' Hutchens chucked an envelope on the table between them. 'Lab results on Stephen Mazza came through. You might find them interesting.' Cato did a quick scan. They were. He looked up expectantly. The DI pointed at Cato's 'Waves not Walls' T-shirt. 'You might want to change the threads first, dude.'

'And this man has admitted to it?'

'Yes.' Lara saw the old woman's eyes cloud over. Mrs Papadakis was dressed in black, again. Maybe that was all she would wear now until she died. The back room of the Northbridge restaurant was unlit but there were thin slashes of sunlight through the blinds.

'What will happen to him?' Mrs Papadakis gazed at the floor, perhaps afraid of the answer.

'He will probably spend the rest of his life in prison.'

'Probably?'

'Yes.'

The old woman nodded. 'Thank you.'

'There is nothing to thank me for.'

'I know.'

Lara wondered if she should ask what Mrs Papadakis would do now but it seemed like such an inane question. Instead she stood to leave. 'If there's anything I can do.'

'I think you've done enough. Goodbye.'

As she drove back down the freeway Lara felt the tightness

return to her chest. This was how it was now. The mechanics of the job were fine: the phone calls, the files, the meetings, even the encounters with occasional danger. She knew she was a capable officer, a very capable officer. Christ, she'd even saved Cato's life last night. No. It was the stopping and the thinking and the trying to make sense of it all later. The unrelenting misery, stupidity and waste: that was just too hard to bear. The blood, the pain, the victims, those left behind: their worlds shattered into tiny sharp fragments of shrapnel that buried themselves too deep to dig out.

Lara became aware of tears on her face. She'd slowed down to forty or fifty k and other cars on the freeway were flashing their lights, giving her the finger, honking their horns. She found a gap in the traffic and took the off-ramp at Canning Bridge, pulling into a petrol station near the Raffles Hotel. Lara took some deep breaths until her vision cleared and something like equilibrium returned. She reached for her mobile and keyed in a number.

'Dr Kim?'

'No need to be so formal, Melanie is fine. How are you, Lara?' That question again. 'Sounds like you're ready for another appointment?'

'Yes,' she steadied her voice, 'I am.'

Stephen Mazza must have been waiting for this moment to arrive. There was something about his expression and his general poise: like a yoke had been shed, or a boil lanced. He'd had another run-in with the prison bikies and their friends: his face bore fresh bruises and scrapes. Cato tenderly fingered his own wounds: they could have swapped war stories. The DNA and other test results confirmed Mazza didn't just come into incidental contact with the ISD – improvised stabbing device. The trace patterns on the toothbrush effectively showed that he was the one who shoved it through Wellard's eye and into the brain.

'So how come you knew how to do that?' said Hutchens. 'Precision brain surgery, bit specialised isn't it?'

'I shared a cell for about a year with a bad doctor. He taught me all kinds of stuff.'

'Ah,' said Hutchens. 'The university of life.'

And death, thought Cato.

Hutchens pushed on. 'Why all the bullshit? Why not just fess up? You must have known we'd get there eventually. You must have known the bikies weren't going to put their hands up for your dirty work?'

'That all suggests it was premeditated.'

Hutchens sat back, hands behind head. 'We're all ears.'

'When I found Wellard he was still alive. There was a half-chance he would survive. I only made the decision there and then to finish him.'

'What, you just happened to have the weapon with you?'

'This is Casuarina. It's the way we live.'

'Puts a whole new spin on "don't forget your toothbrush", doesn't it?' said Hutchens.

'I knew Wellard was due for a kicking. I was there, right place, right time. The opportunity presented itself. I didn't think about what would follow. I just wanted to try and get away with it for as long as possible.'

'How did you know he was due for a kicking?'

'Because I arranged it.'

'We hear otherwise. Shellie told us she arranged it with a bikie mate.'

'No. She's making it up to protect me.'

Neat, thought Cato. He gets Shellie out of the frame and the bikies off his back in one fell swoop.

Hutchens had a humour-me look about him. 'Okay, so you arranged it for Shellie?'

'Not directly. She didn't ask me. She told me about her unhappiness, her distress. I acted off my own bat.'

'Bullshit.'

Mazza shrugged. 'Do you want to hear me or not?' Hutchens waved his fingers obligingly. 'I was due out within the next year or so. I hoped to get away with it. I was wrong. Nothing premeditated. Nobody knew about it except me.'

Cato gave Hutchens a sideways look and was given nodded permission to have his two cents worth.

'If it wasn't premeditated how come you've been doing your damnedest to stay close to Wellard for at least the last year when you could have been in a cushy pre-release joint by now?'

Mazza smiled. 'Fair cop. But staying close because I wanted to do him doesn't mean I ever got the nerve or the opportunity to carry it out.'

'But you stayed patient anyway until your day came.'

'Yes.'

'Why?'

Mazza tilted his head. 'You know the answer already, I reckon.'

'We need it for the tape,' said Cato.

Mazza sighed, his eyes drifted to a spot on the blank wall. 'Briony is my daughter.'

He was right; Cato did already know that. It was the other half of the requested lab results, a match with Briony's DNA retrieved from samples from her hairbrush and toothbrush and filed away for any future body find.

'So you killed Gordon Wellard because you believed him responsible for the death and disappearance of your daughter Briony Petkovic?'

'Yes.'

'And you insist that Shellie Petkovic was unaware of your intentions and she did not specifically attempt to persuade you or anyone else to harm Wellard?'

'That's right.'

Hutchens turned to Cato. 'You coaching him or what?'

Cato felt oddly at peace. 'Just trying to get the facts straight one last time, sir.'

'You looking to get Shellie off the hook, then?' Hutchens had a half-smile in place.

They were on Rockingham Road driving past Phoenix Shopping Centre. It reminded Cato of something else he wanted to do before all this was over. 'Whether she's in it up to her neck or innocent and ignorant, the question has always been – is justice served by pursuing her?'

'Thank you, Rumpole.' Hutchens popped a mint and offered one to Cato who accepted. 'That stuff should always be left to the judges, the juries, the prosecutors' office and the pollies. It's not our call.'

'But we are in charge of compiling the prosecution brief. We have nothing to suggest conspiracy to murder or assault apart from a vague "woe is me" on Shellie's part.'

'Come on, it was more premeditated than that. What about those letters she fabricated?'

'Wasting police time, perverting the course of justice. Products of a disturbed and distressed mind: a fine or suspended sentence at most I would have thought.'

'Got it all worked out haven't you?'

'Just thinking of the paperwork and the PR, boss.'

'Now you're speaking my language.' Hutchens reclined his seat, admired the view of the southern suburbs, and let out a soft chuckle. 'Heard the latest on Safer Streets?'

Uh-oh. 'What?'

'Last night: while you were sleeping. Riot squad gets called to a party in Mount Pleasant. Usual bullshit. Hundreds of dickheads, broken bottles, trampled begonias, et cetera.'

'And?'

'Hosted by the Police Minister's son.' Hutchens barked out a laugh. 'The government is reassessing its priorities as we speak. The Stiffies have been put on the backburner.' He turned on the radio and found some old pop music. Simple Minds. 'Promised You A Miracle'.

It was going to be yet another warm day but the reception from Jane was frosty. She nodded over her shoulder.

'He's out the back, lying on the trampoline. Don't be too long and don't upset him.'

Cato smiled through his face-ache and walked over the threshold, down the passageway through the East Fremantle house he used to share with Jane and Jake. Nothing much had changed. Same polished floorboards, smell of flowers and baking and air freshener. Simon the Boyfriend was sitting on a kitchen stool reading the weekend papers and sipping coffee.

'Hi,' he said raising his mug and smiling and trying to seem like totally relaxed and unthreatened and cool. Actually, to be fair, he seemed like an okay bloke. Jake was right though, he did look like the hillbilly hippy goat from *Hoodwinked*. Cato gave him the peace sign and continued out the back. When Jake looked up from the trampoline, Cato's heart lurched. The boy's face was raw and swollen and there was a red, ugly sutured weal running diagonally across his right cheek.

'Dad?' It was a confused look. Cato was on the wrong territory.

'Mind if I join you?' Jake shifted up and they both lay on the sagging canvas, springs squeaking with the adult intrusion. Cato lifted a finger to the cheek. 'How's it feeling?'

'Sore. How about you?'

'Yeah, sore as.' Cato could see through the French windows, Jane standing beside Simon at the kitchen counter with a proprietorial arm around his neck, trying to be casual and not too interested in what was going on outside. He turned his attention back to Jake. 'Sorry about all that, mate, it must have been pretty scary.'

'It was a bit.' Jake looked away and pulled distractedly at a loose thread on his T-shirt. 'I thought you were going to die.'

Cato's chest was bursting. 'Ditto.' He searched Jake's face for a clue to the answer to his next question. 'You coming over next weekend then?'

'Why wouldn't I?'

Cato mock-frowned. 'Dunno, you might get a better offer.'

'Yeah well, I'll let you know if I do.'

'Yeah well, I might be washing my hair that night anyway.'

'Yeah, you need to.'

'S'pose you reckon you're gunna be a real chick magnet now with a scar on your cheek. Well just wait until I wash my hair.'

'Yeah, polish your walking frame while you're at it, grandad.'

And so it went. A round of petty insults that signified all was well with the world. Jane and Simon looked out, bemused, at the two puerile squabbling boys and continued sipping their coffees.

Another knock on another door and another frosty reception.

'What do you want?'

Felix wasn't prepared to open the door further than about ten centimetres. Behind him, Madge yapped and Janice hovered.

'I want to say thank you,' said Cato. He had a warm humanitarian glow about him today. Jake was going to be okay. Everything was going to be okay. Fremantle was a great place to live and society wasn't going to the dogs.

'What?'

'Thank you.'

'What for?' said Felix, looking for an ambush.

'Can I come in?'

'No.'

Cato waggled his fingers in a wave and smiled. 'Hi, Janice.'

Her face lit up. 'Open the door, pumpkin, he's not going to hurt you.'

'How do you know?' Felix muttered back over his shoulder.

'Open it,' she growled.

He did and Madge rushed out yapping and nipping around Cato's ankles. Cato found another smile and held fast. 'Just the girl I wanted to talk to.' He crouched down and tried to pat Madge but the dog bared her teeth. Cato backed off and stood to face Felix and Janice. 'Madge's yapping saved my, and my son's, life. If she hadn't woken me up things might have turned out very different.'

Felix beamed and scooped Madge up into his man-bosom. 'Madgy sweetie, you're a hero and you've made a new friend!'

Let's not get carried away, thought Cato. 'So anyway, thanks, and forget that complaint notice I put in. I'll tear it up.'

Felix manfully put out his hand for shaking and Cato obliged. Janice pecked him on the cheek. Madge snarled and bared her teeth again.

'Got a moment?'

They were in DI Hutchens' office, door closed. This was Lara's decisive step towards a new start. She braced herself.

'Yeah, what's up?' said Hutchens, half-tuning in.

Lara handed him a piece of paper. 'I need you to sign this.'

Hutchens read it. 'Major Crime want you seconded to them?'

'Yes, boss. For a year. Starting next month.'

'You'll be keen to go then, I expect.' The expression and voice were neutral but there was no disguising the bruise there.

'It's a great opportunity, boss.' Lara's eyes were shining with emotions she never expected to feel.

'Of course.' He scribbled his consent signature in the space provided. 'Bit out of the blue?'

'Yeah. Look, I really appreciate you giving me that second chance, after Hopetoun. I won't ever forget that.'

'No worries. You're a good cop, Lara. Just remember to stay on the right side of that line. All shortcuts do is get you nowhere fast.'

'Right, boss.'

'And when you get to Major Crime, choose your friends carefully.'

Colin Graham's words as they shared a beer that first day in the Sail and Anchor.

Lara left and closed the door behind her. Farmer John had delivered on his part of the bargain. Now, he was someone she really could learn a few tricks from. She scrolled through to his number and her thumb played over the keypad.

Fancy a drink?

50

Tuesday, February 23rd.

It was just before ten when they found the sneaker with the foot bones inside it. Mintie the cadaver dog had barked once and sat down to receive her reward. The photographs from the fly-over on the day before had picked up a couple of sites worth investigating and the GPR teams had been brought in early that morning. The circus was back in town, minus the jester this time. No Wellard, no sick games: this one was strictly by the book. Cato took a step closer, shading his eyes against the midmorning glare. Hutchens appraised him.

'Looks like your Santa Claus trick with the big black sack paid off.'

Hutchens was right. The science and the gadgets backed up Cato's theory. The body was at Star Swamp, within the block of earth he'd guesstimated. Wellard had stuck with familiar ground for his burial sites. Basic animal instinct. Beeliar had been a charade. It might well have been a place he'd recce'd as a possibility but he'd stuck with Star Swamp for Bree Petkovic and, later, Caroline Penny. This was Briony's last resting place and, as the day progressed and the forensic team patiently sifted, more bones were added to the sad jigsaw.

'Finders keepers,' said Cato, wondering how he should break the news to Shellie.

'Yeah,' said Hutchens. 'Losers fucking weepers.'

Cato looked at his boss. 'You know I can't help feeling that if you'd done the right thing with Gordon Wellard way back then, we might not be here today.'

'Way back when?'

According to the files there was at least one more body out there somewhere from the time before he disappeared off the database.

Was this where he also buried that much earlier nameless victim? Maybe some in Thailand too? Wellard wasn't a serial thrill killer in the classic sense, more like a serial disregarder of human life. A man who valued no one and nothing but himself. And he made no real effort to hide what he was. He didn't have to.

'You've known he was a nasty piece of work for a couple of decades now. You protected him because he and his brother gave you titbits of information about armed robberies.' Cato scuffed the dust with his heel. 'The TABs, the banks, they're all insured against loss. That's more than you can say for those who crossed Gordy Wellard's path.'

Hutchens sighed. 'I'll have to live with that.'

'Yeah, so will Shellie.'

TWO WEEKS LATER

Stephen Mazza sat stony-faced in his prison greens between two corrections officers. The funeral was at Fremantle Crematorium: discounting the police and prison officer contingent there were only two legitimate mourners.

It wasn't a religious service; Shellie had never been into that. Instead a calm and businesslike woman from the funeral directors spoke about the importance of living and loving and focusing on the good things about people and life. She spoke about seizing the moment because you never knew when it was going to get snatched away from you.

Cato was seated next to Shellie, for a brief instant their shoulders had touched and she'd jolted away like she'd been burnt. She sat rigid: folding a hankie tight in her thin hands. The pain hadn't ended when he'd told her about the discovery of the body. The autopsy on the remains had drawn an unsparing picture of the level of violence Bree had suffered at the hands of Gordon Francis Wellard and it had been Cato's job to pass on the details. For Shellie there was no closing of books or finding of peace.

Finally some music, 'Bridge Over Troubled Water', and the coffin rolled away to a last haunted look from Stephen Mazza. Shellie choked out a sob and stared at the displayed photo of her daughter in pink tutu and fairy wings, casting spells with a plastic wand.

EPILOGUE

'You've done a good job for those round-eye mates of yours, bro.'

Jimmy Tran was out of intensive care and propped up in bed. In the month or so since the shooting, Cato had been cleared by the Internals but he still felt a need to face Jimmy. The weather had finally cooled, autumn was in the air, and the notion of buying air conditioning had once again receded.

'Round eyes?' said Cato, pretending he didn't know what Jimmy was talking about.

'The dirty denim and leather boys. The Village People from Hell.'

'Oh, the Apaches.'

'If I could lift a finger I'd wag it at you. You put me in a wheelchair, Vincent in jail for life, and the infamous Tran Gang broken up. No need for a war now, the Apaches just walk in and pick up the pieces you left behind.'

He was right of course and now that Vincent was locked up, the bikies had even withdrawn their allegation against him. So, in public at least, they could still hold on to their precious outlaw code of silence. They did have one setback though. A fortnight earlier Apache Sergeant-at-Arms Bryn Irskine, AKA Eyebrow Stud, had suffered terrible burns in a freak domestic accident with a barbecue gas bottle. Karina Ford had sent Cato a happy face text the day after. Coincidence?

'I'll cop to putting you in a wheelchair but Vincent put himself where he is. The Tran Gang broken up? Your loyal underlings buggered off first chance they got. It's not about round-eyes or slants, Jimmy. It's about good guys and bad guys.'

'Polly want a cracker?' Tran sucked at a straw near his head. 'They trained you well, didn't they?'

'I still can't work out why you guys couldn't divvy up the spoils.

Boom state. Plenty for everybody. Turf wars are just so last-century, Jimmy.'

'Don't think I never tried, mate.' Tran cleared his throat. 'It's funny how your colleagues – the late Mr Graham, most of the Gangs guys, the undercovers – all found it easier to reach "accommodations" with the Apaches but they never thought to see if I was up for any deals. I'm a smart fellow, a deep thinker. I can grease the palm of a dirty cop as well as the next gangster. I guess my face didn't fit, eh?' Tran laid his head back against the pillow like all the words had tired him out. 'Sound familiar Cato-san?'

'No,' Cato lied.

'You know it was me that let Santo know he'd been blown?'

'You? How come?'

'I heard, via one of my Northbridge associates, a few days before the murder. Graham must have been behind it. Leaking left, right and centre. Either he was hoping I'd kill Santo for him or he was planting it as a motive for when he came after me later.'

'And?'

'I sat on it for a day or two then summoned Santo to meet me in the club that night. We did our ... business, as usual. Then I told him somebody had dobbed on him.'

'What did Santo say?'

'Nothing, just looked a bit crook. By then Graham must have assumed I wasn't going to do what he wanted when he wanted. His little African hit man must have been Plan B.'

'You never raised this earlier.'

'Didn't work it out until later. Got plenty of time to think lying here.'

It made sense: Graham was capable of having Santo killed but getting the Trans to do it first would have been a good move.

'Would you have killed Santo eventually?'

'Maybe, probably. First I wanted to try to use the knowledge over him. Col was obviously too impatient. Must've had a deadline.'

Cato waved a hand at the medical paraphernalia. 'Anyway I came here to say sorry for this. It wasn't intended.'

Tran studied him for a second. 'I can see that. Pity you didn't shoot straight and put me out of my misery.' He smiled sadly. 'I guess that's what they call karma.'

Cato had no reply. Seeing Jimmy Tran trapped in this limbo, once again the story of Tantalus came to mind. Greed. Blood sacrifice. And now the punishment: everything just beyond reach.

'You know they intend to finish us off don't you?' said Tran.

'How do you mean?'

'For good. They've already marked Vincent in Casuarina. He's on his own and the screws aren't going to help him.'

'Protective custody?'

'What, with the child rapists and the psychos in the Boneyard?'

'The nail-gun thing should tick a few boxes.'

'You know what I mean.'

Cato gave the matter some thought. He didn't like how the Apaches were getting it nearly all their own way, and Karina Ford would attest that they easily matched the Trans for viciousness. He came up with a suggestion. Cato as Cupid, the matchmaker. He preferred not to think too much about the possible consequences but karma moves in mysterious ways. If the prison bikies went looking for trouble, they could have it.

Vincent Tran was aware that the showers had emptied in the last thirty seconds and realised that his time must be at hand. Steam hung in the air, taps and showerheads dripped, water ran down plugholes. Condensation beaded the off-white tiles. There was the squeak of trainers on wet ceramic.

'Vinnie.'

It was the bikie they called Kenny, with a lump of metal unscrewed from the exercise bike in the gym. He was with a friend. What was his name again? Danny, yes Danny, and he had something sharp. Vincent stood naked before them. Instinctively he cupped his genitals, closed his eyes, and waited for the end.

There was a gurgling sound. When Vincent opened his eyes he saw Danny on the floor of the showers with something sticking out of his neck and a crimson geyser spouting forth. Kenny had disappeared. A short wiry African stepped out of the mist with a friendly smile and offered his hand for shaking.

'I am Dieudonne, it means "gift from God". I think we are going to be great friends.'

ACKNOWLEDGEMENTS

Many thanks to Michael Rowson, Greg Balfour, and Rex Haw of the Western Australian Police Service for showing me the delightful yellow decor of the Fremantle Detectives offices and answering my sometimes silly questions about the finer aspects of life on the thin blue line. Likewise Brian Cowie of the WA Department of Corrective Services for the tour of Casuarina Prison. Anything that is right is down to them – anything that is wrong is all my own work. Thanks also to Jim McGinty for some clarifications on certain points of law and to Dr Isaac Harvey for showing me what kind of damage you can do with a ballpoint pen. I owe a Fat Yak to early reader Dave Whish-Wilson for his timely wisdom and encouragement.

Undying gratitude as always to Georgia Richter for editorially steering me through the turbulent seas of the second novel. Also to Conor McCarthy and Naama Amram for insightful feedback along the way. To Clive Newman, Claire Miller and everyone else at Fremantle Press, thanks heaps for looking after me and making me feel at home. As ever, my wife Kath and my son Liam should be granted sainthood for putting up with those many periods of me staring blankly into space. Usually it was because I was trying to think great criminal and literary thoughts.

ABOUT THE AUTHOR

Alan Carter was born in Sunderland in the United Kingdom. He holds a degree in Communication Studies from Sunderland Polytechnic and immigrated to Australia in 1991 where he now works as a television documentary director. Alan's first novel *Prime Cut* was shortlisted for the UK Crime Writers' Association Debut Dagger Award 2010 and received a Ned Kelly in 2011 for Best First Book. *Getting Warmer* is the second novel in the Cato Kwong series. Alan lives in Fremantle with his wife Kath and son Liam.

SHORTLISTED FOR THE 2010 CRIME WRITERS' ASSOCIATION
DEBUT DAGGER AWARD

ALAN CARTER

PRIME
CUT

...assured feel for genre, classily written with mordant
wit and a fine sense of place... — Graeme Blundell

available from www.fremantlepress.com.au
and all good bookstores

First published 2013 by
FREMANTLE PRESS
25 Quarry Street, Fremantle 6160
(PO Box 158, North Fremantle 6159)
Western Australia
www.fremantlepress.com.au

Also available as an ebook.

Consultant editor Georgia Richter
Cover design Ally Crimp
Cover photograph Daniel Craig, Matsu Photography
Map Chris Crook, Country Cartographics
Printed by Everbest Printing Company, China

National Library of Australia
Cataloguing-in-Publication entry

Carter, Alan
Getting warmer / Alan Carter

ISBN 9781922089205 (pbk)

A8233.4
Crime—Western Australia—Fiction

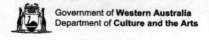

Fremantle Press is supported by the State Government through the
Department of Culture and the Arts. Publication of this title was
assisted by the Commonwealth Government through the Australia
Council, its arts funding and advisory body.